LINES BETWEEN STARS

A.J. LEXA

First edition: June 2025

Edited by: Anne-Marie Rutella
Proofread by: Sharon Strahand at Prose Polish
Cover illustration: Jenn Rubio
Map illustration: Andrés Aguirre Jurado
Formatted by: Stacey Blake at Champagne Book Design

ISBN: 979-8-9927899-0-4

NOTE FROM THE AUTHOR

Thank you for picking up *Lines Between Stars*! Before you dive into the cosmic world of reincarnated zodiacs, please take a moment to reflect on the content and/or trigger warnings listed here: Child abuse *(brief)*, parental death during childbirth, explicit sex, profanity, branding, and thoughts of suicide.

If I've overlooked any, please don't hesitate to contact me at: ajlexa.author@gmail.com

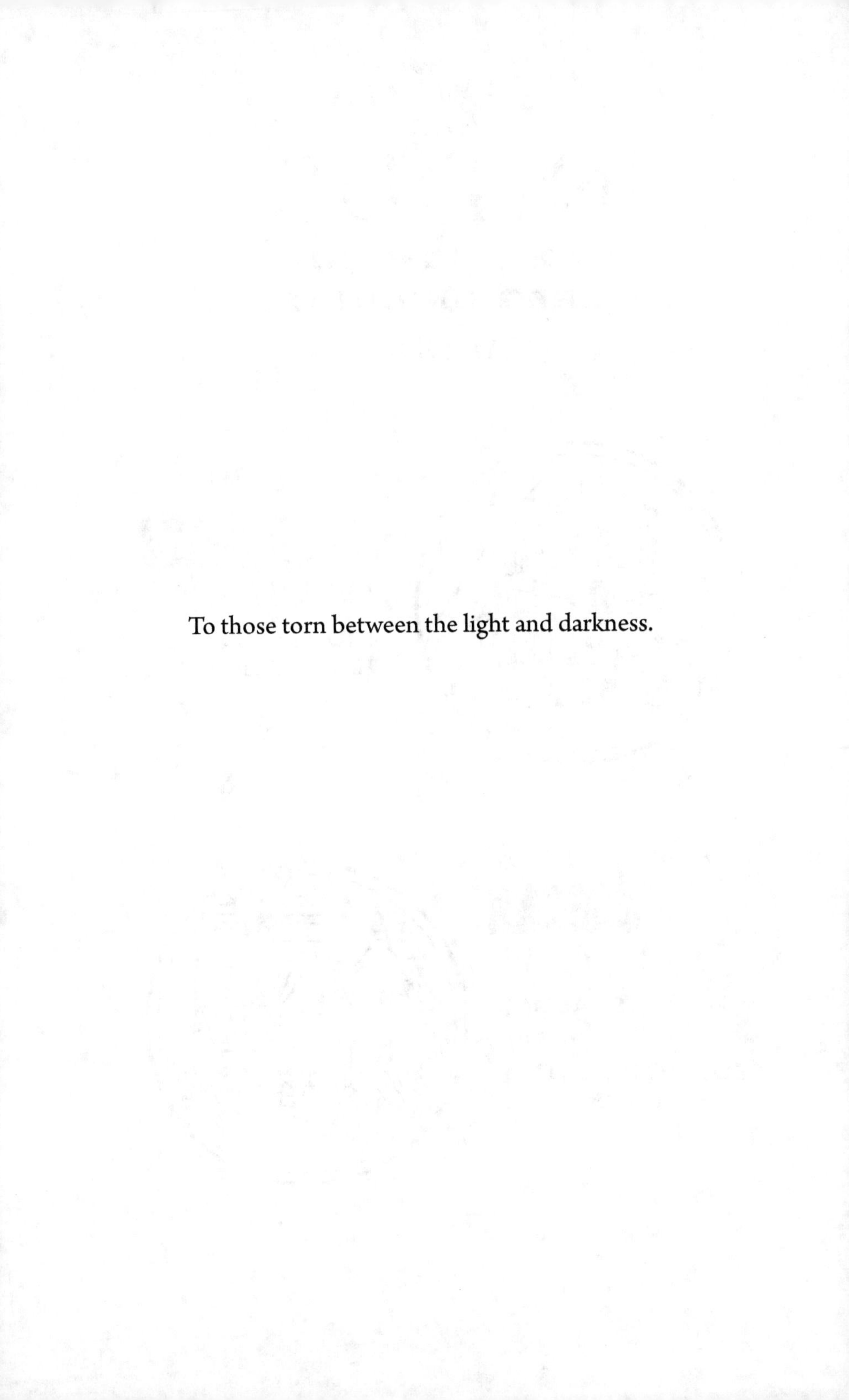

To those torn between the light and darkness.

NIDUS

PRONUNCIATION
& REGION GUIDE

(NAI-DUHS)

OMPHALOS

(AAM-FUH-LOWZ)

NIDUS CAPITOL
Home to Goddess of Light

FLORA

(FLAW-RUH)

SEASON:
Spring

ZODIAC REGENTS:
Aries, Taurus & Gemini

CALIDI

(KUH-LEE-DEE)

SEASON:
Summer

ZODIAC REGENTS:
Cancer, Leo & Virgo

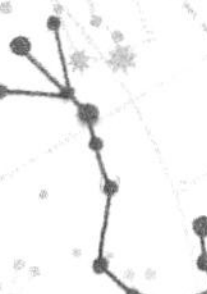

MESSIS

(MES-SIS)

SEASON:
Autumn

ZODIAC REGENTS:
Libra, Scorpio & Sagittarius

PARHELIA

(PAR-HE-LEE-AH)

SEASON:
Winter

ZODIAC REGENTS:
Capricorn, Aquarius & Pisces

ISLAND OF
FLORA
RIVER TAURUS
ZODIAC
TRAINING GROUNDS
LAKE ASTRA
GLASS ISLES
FLORIAN
FOREST
FLORIAN PALACE
CALIDI
CALIDI
LIBRARY
CALIDIAN JUNGLE
RIVER HYDRA
CALIDIAN PALACE
TREEHOUSE
OBSIDIAN CAVE

NIDUS
PARHELIA
PARHELIAN PALACE
OMPHALOS
SCORPION'S HOLLOW
MESSIAN PALACE
STARFALL FOREST
MAGISTERIUM
STELLARIS
ACADEMY
MESSIS
RIVER LYNX

LINES
✦ BETWEEN ✦
STARS

PART ONE

CHAPTER

ONE

REYNA'S BODY WOULD NEVER BE HER OWN. NOT BURIED beneath layers of clothing or shielded behind walls. Another grunt shuddered through apartment 402's wall and Reyna's knees squirmed together. She might not belong to herself, but she would endure the desperation stoking *his* want. The delicious fire catching in *his* belly. 402 was close and Reyna pleaded he'd get on with it already.

A squeal snapped through the wall from his female companion.

"What's that noise?" Ruth McGibbon asked through Reyna's headset.

"Nothing, ma'am." Reyna bit back a hiss. "Now, about those excursions? Swimming with manta rays in Belize would be an unforgettable experience."

"Oh! I've always wanted to. Have you ever—"

Apartment 402's headboard drummed the wall behind Reyna's computer. She scowled through the layers of paint and plaster between them.

"You feel so good!" 402 moaned to his partner.

"Are you"—the elderly woman gasped—"having sex?"

"Of course not, ma'am, and I've never swum with rays, but I understand it's—" An unquenchable heat swelled between Reyna's thighs.

"I'm going to come!" 402 bellowed.

"Young lady!" the old woman scolded. "I will not be booking with Royal Cruises!"

"Please, ma'am, you don't understand. It's my—" The line clicked.

402's pleasure convulsed through Reyna's limbs. She slumped into the computer chair and chucked her headset across the desk. Dust kicked up through the afternoon's glow and settled back like the euphoria over her skin. This was the part Reyna didn't mind so much. The dizzy mess of satisfaction afterward. The half ghost of a moment never intended for her. All she could ever have.

Reyna's head lolled toward her open bedroom. It'd never hosted such acrobatics of the flesh but perhaps was still far enough from 402's to warrant moving her desk. As if to argue, shrill barks yipped from the apartment beyond the bedroom's wall. Reyna long accepted she might never escape people's intrusive emotions, but enduring her other neighbor's Pomeranian over 402's sexcapades? More appealing by the minute.

A buzzer jolted Reyna from her chair. She rushed to the wall-mounted intercom and pushed the button. "Hello?"

"This is Prisha Varma with Fresh Fleet," the speaker crackled. "I have a delivery for Reyna Pérez."

Reyna's hands pressed against the wall, long chestnut hair hanging around her face. It'd been the same routine every week for five years. They delivered the groceries. She took them.

Today wouldn't be any different.

"Come on up," Reyna replied and tugged wrist-length leather gloves over her slender fingers. She clicked through the maze of locks waterfalling along the door and waited. A few moments later, the elevator ground open, followed by steps scuffing across the hallway carpet. Reyna's heart trotted faster and faster at their steady gait.

Plastic rustled to a stop outside her apartment and Reyna steeled herself against the person's emotions ready to barrel through the door. What kind of day were they having? Probably a shitty one, now they'd lugged groceries to the fourth floor. Reyna waited, but a phenomenon of normal crashed into her. She sensed . . .

Nothing.

A knock vibrated the door.

Reyna flung it open, gaping at the woman with plastic bag handles laced across light brown arms. The delivery woman blew flyaways from her ebony fishtail braid and readjusted the groceries.

"Do I have something on me?" The employee scoured her own white tank beneath a stylish open suede vest. "Some moron bumped into me with his Starbucks. If he spilled—"

"You're not wearing a Fresh Fleet T-shirt." Reyna rebounded from her shock.

A smile touched the woman's deep brown eyes. "First day."

Reyna stared at the bags, as though answers to why the woman's emotions remained silent lay nestled inside beside her mac and cheese. Reyna's curse had never failed to read someone in twenty-seven years, and it rattled her to the core.

"Not to be rude, but my arms are killin' me." The woman extended her arms toward Reyna. "Might be your brick of Berry Bonanza Froyo."

"You know what, keep them." Reyna edged the door shut. The woman's chunky-heeled boot slid between the door and frame. Reyna's heart leapt and her grip on the knob tightened. "What are you doing?"

"Reyna." Her name rolled off the woman's lips with misplaced familiarity. "We need to talk."

Reyna's teeth ground. "You *need* to remove yourself from my door."

"Please, you don't understand." The Fresh Fleet employee's foot retracted. "You're in—"

Reyna closed the door and slid a lock into place.

The woman's footsteps receded and once the elevator's ding sounded, Reyna cracked the door open. Abandoned groceries rustled at her feet. She huffed, kneeling to gather their spilled contents. Whether the woman's quieted emotions were an anomaly or not, Reyna would still leave her a shit review.

A quick breeze rode the soft waves of Reyna's hair. Her attention snapped between both ends of the windowless hallway. Eerie silence with a heavy presence descended upon Reyna as if someone watched from nearby. She snatched the bags and slammed the door.

Neighbors' orgasms. Strange delivery people. And a potential ghost? Grocery day was officially the worst day.

Reyna heaved bags onto the kitchen counter as the phone in her back pocket jingled. Her frown shifted from its caller ID to the calendar pinned on her wall. Obnoxious red marker circled the day's date, and with it, dread encircled her gut.

Reyna answered with forced perkiness. "Happy birthday!"

"Don't make me beg," her friend encouraged. "Please tell me you're coming tonight."

"Tessa." Reyna's pause filled the silence with practiced guilt she'd carried a lifetime. "You know I don't do birthdays."

Both their childhoods avoided the family they never wanted. Reyna had created distance between her and her papá. Tessa had floated around the foster system. Fate brought them together on the last birthday Reyna ever celebrated and despite the somber events that followed, the two children bonded as sisters of loss. Reyna fantasized about leaving San Diego. Perhaps for a secluded cabin in Oregon where she wouldn't need gloves amidst the harsh southwestern heat. But she could never bring herself to move from the city. She'd never leave the one semblance of family she had left.

"Could you make an exception?" Tessa infused her natural charm. "It's not like I'm over-the-hill every day."

A smile cracked through Reyna's despair. "You're turning twenty-eight."

"Laugh now, but once you're thirty, you might as well trade your stilettos for a Saturday night of Netflix."

"Don't knock my weekends." Reyna stuffed a pint of yogurt into the freezer.

"C'mon, Rey. I met a serious hottie who's getting my friends and me in for free at a club called Dark Skies. Super exclusive."

"I don't think it's a good idea." Reyna tried another approach. "I don't dance. You'd have more fun without me."

"I don't get you sometimes." Tessa sighed. "You'll see an exorcist for your germ phobia but won't come out for my birthday?"

"He was a medium," Reyna corrected. Germs meant nothing to her, but she'd told the lie for so long, some days, she believed it. Reyna hated keeping her secret from Tessa, but it was better than what they stood to lose.

"Whatever," Tessa groaned. "Can't you see a therapist like the rest of America or better yet drink with me?"

Tessa wasn't wrong. Reyna required the help of a professional, but what professional possessed the ability to remove magic?

Magic. The word itself, a placeholder for what Reyna could do.

Years of internet research for a cure became wallpaper behind Reyna's computer. Archaic folklore. Diagrams. Translated texts. All larger puzzle pieces of Reyna's life she could never connect. Once, she tried rubbing salted lemons on her aura for twelve days at sunrise and again an hour before sunset. The result? Reeking like a personal consultant for Pledge. How did a person know if they rubbed lemons on their aura properly anyhow? Reyna's many attempts to remove magic proved as fruitless as the shriveled, salted citrus in the wastebasket.

"I understand why you won't come, but I worry about you." Tessa's frustration waned. "Fear shouldn't rule your life."

Reyna refused the risk of transferring her emotions onto all those people.

Or worse.

"It's safer this way," Reyna replied.

"Life isn't supposed to be safe. It's messy and complicated. You've got too much to offer the world, Rey. It'll find you eventually."

Reyna pulled the phone from her ear and stared at the sunset dipping behind the city outside her window. Beyond major holidays, a few annual hangouts, and video calls, Tessa asked little of their one-sided friendship throughout the years. They'd become each other's constant and tonight was one night. One chance to not disappoint the only person Reyna cared about.

A birthday once brought them together. Maybe another would offer something better.

"Okay." The two syllables tumbled from Reyna before she could talk herself out of it. "I'll be there."

Faux leather twisted between Reyna's fingers as she wrung her hands together by the apartment elevator. Everyone's doors remained closed along either end of the hallway and not a soul approached. Not even of the specter variety.

A ding popped the elevator open, and she scurried inside.

"Maybe I can do this." Reyna sighed at the doors squeaking shut.

An arm sliced between them and jolted the elevator open.

"Phew." A man in his late twenties slipped inside. He flashed Reyna a toothy grin. "That could've been messy."

Three floors.

Reyna needed to make it three floors to exit the building. If she couldn't, how'd she expect to make it through the night?

Reyna forced a tight smile and shuffled toward the opposite corner of their descending prison. The man's intrigue plopped into her belly like mediocre, force-fed stew. Overcooked, tasteless, and promising far more delicious than it was. What specifically intrigued him? Reyna couldn't decipher his emotions over her anxiety bubbling over into the elevator.

The stranger cleared his throat. "403, right?"

"Sorry?" Reyna's nose scrunched at his pungent cologne.

"I've lived here a couple months and met everyone on our floor. Except you."

Even in the absence of their thin apartment walls, she couldn't mistake his voice.

"You," Reyna grumbled. "I don't know how many times I've complained to management about the noise from your place."

Her neighbor's brows rose. "I don't complain about the noise from yours."

Reyna cringed at the idea of someone listening to her play guitar. "My music and your ... noise are hardly the same."

"If I'd known you were as gorgeous as what you played"—he rested an arm against the elevator wall as he drank her in—"I would've invited you over to apologize a lot sooner."

The various moans from 402's apartment indicated he possessed a merry-go-round of lovers, but this flirtation wasn't an attempt at avoiding managerial retaliation or some halfhearted apology. Reyna hated that her magic could distinguish the difference. 402's genuine attraction buzzed around her like an insect. One she wanted to squash but also clasp close like a firefly. Reyna couldn't remember the last time she'd spoken to a man face-to-face, let alone been offered a compliment. She tugged at her dress as 402's lust crept between her hem and knee-high boots. The last time she'd worn the dress was her abuela's funeral. A coincidence, less coincidental by the second.

The elevator chimed at ground level like a choir of angels. Reyna bolted past her neighbor, careful to avoid brushing him.

"Wait!" he called. "I want to make it up to you. Have dinner with me?"

"I don't date." She beelined toward the exit.

"Why not?" The sting of her rejection grumbled through his chest.

Reyna burst through the building's doors into salvation. Dark clouds swallowed a few dim stars and the weight of 402's ick lifted from her body. She'd escaped her apartment without incident, but the trek from building to sidewalk was a minor victory.

She could still go back.

Feign a mysterious sickness or maybe a sprained ankle.

Tessa would be disappointed but safe. Everyone would be.

The doors behind Reyna squeaked and 402's bruised ego vibrated through her limbs once more. Reyna swallowed another groan and scuttled as quickly as she could across the street and into the night.

CHAPTER

TWO

EMOTION PROWLED THROUGH PEOPLE'S BODIES IN SEARCH of surprising places. Fear resided in the kidneys. Anxiety, always the stomach, and anger, oddly enough, the liver. Courage made itself known in the lungs. Reyna inhaled hers as she strode into the Gaslamp District's latest gem.

She followed along a narrow hall of mosaic mirrors refracting the lights ahead. The kaleidoscope tunnel spilled into an open neon purple, magenta, and blue space. Luminescent lines curved along the walls and met at disco balls clustered at the room's center. The bass pulsed like a heartbeat off the club's rib cage over Reyna's skin. She'd experienced people's emotions her whole life but never a building's. A living, breathing beast. And there she stood, in the pit of its belly.

"Rey!" A squeal pierced the sound system.

Sandy blonde hair burst through the crowd as Tessa launched to straitjacket Reyna into a hug. Reyna's hands flung outward, and Tessa staggered to a stop.

"Sorry!" Tessa giggled. "I think I'm a little drunk." Liquid sloshed over her cup's rim. "I can't believe you came!"

Reyna peered at the crowd and swallowed. "Me either."

"Follow me!"

When people walked along the street, they made conscious efforts to avoid bumping into others. A social etiquette, which made occasionally leaving Reyna's apartment more bearable. But as Reyna waded through the after-hours circus of clinking glasses and laughter, emotional cocktails stirred everywhere. Demanded to be tasted. Devoured. Savored. Each more fleeting than the next. One by one, people's emotions slugged her in the gut. Someone checked Reyna's shoulder. *Excitement.* A shoe crunched over her toes. *Insecurity.* A man's arm brushed Reyna's and his internal desire flexed within her pelvis. Reyna's lip curled at the invasion. She backed into another body and irritation with a shot of cold liquid gushed along her spine.

"Watch it!" The passerby shoved Reyna into Tessa.

"Hey!" Tessa rounded on the woman sneering at Reyna. "Not enough dance floor for you?"

The clubgoer spat an insult and Tessa flipped her off.

No. Etiquette meant something much different here.

Tessa led Reyna to a mauve couch along the far wall and introduced her friends. Reyna knew each by social handle, harder to tell in the low light if in-app filters did them justice. A few mumbled greetings over the bass and returned to their devices. Reyna scanned for a place to sit, but Tessa's party and the strangers crammed beside them showed no signs of abandoning their seats. If her master plan at securing a spot for the night's remainder failed, she'd need to leave.

"Shots?" A lithe blonde extended a tray between the two friends. Tessa lit and plucked two drinks from the platter.

"We didn't order these." Reyna tracked the server's arrow tattoo from inside wrist to elbow.

"Already paid for," the blonde replied.

Reyna frowned. "By whom?"

Tessa handed Reyna a shot and pointed across the dance floor at a VIP booth. A man winked, toasting his drink toward them. Tessa raised her shot in his direction and mouthed *thank you.*

"A friend of yours?" Reyna's nose wrinkled at the clear liquid.

"He's who got us in tonight and been buying us drinks." Tessa's attraction for him tingled beneath Reyna's navel.

Reyna shooed her internal groan. "How'd you meet?"

"Remember the emergency call I responded to a few days ago on Interstate 5? I checked his vitals, and we got talking. I mentioned my birthday was coming up and here we are." Tessa raised her glass. A grin stretched across her lightly freckled cheeks. "To you, out for my birthday."

Reyna raised her own shot. "To your birthday."

The duo clinked glasses and alcohol ignited along Reyna's throat. She copied Tessa, sucking on the drink's lemon wedge as though it were oxygen. Lemons might not chase the bite of magic but stood a chance against liquor.

"Again!" Tessa cawed and handed Reyna another shot from the tray. They knocked back their second, faces souring.

"He wants to meet you," the server shouted at Reyna over the music.

"Who?" Reyna destroyed another lemon.

The blonde nodded toward the man who'd invited Tessa. He relaxed into his couch and waved Reyna over with two fingers.

"Tell him thank you." Reyna shook her head. "But I'll pass."

The server's eyebrow raised. "He'll insist."

"I'll insist it's my friend's birthday and I don't know him."

"Go for it." Tessa nudged Reyna. "I'll be fine with this lively crew." She snorted at her friends, still hypnotized by their screens.

"I came out to be with you, Tessa. Not some guy. Besides, I can tell you like him."

"I like a lot of people." Tessa shrugged into an eyebrow waggle. "Did I mention he's a lawyer?"

Legal representation once Reyna's magic maimed and ruined the night?

Perfect.

"I need to use the ladies' room." Reyna forced a smile and placed her empty glass on the tray.

A neon sign across the room guided Reyna through the club. She pivoted between the writhing crowd and past the restroom's line of women. Verbal protests exploded around her. She thrust herself into a stall and slid its lock into place. A singular, meek click of metal lacking the protection her apartment offered. Reyna pressed her forehead against the stall door. Musical vibrations rattled over her skin, and she sighed into them. Begged herself to feel anything other than her own displacement.

Tessa and Reyna's in-person hangouts had become a well-oiled machine over the years. They'd meet in a quiet space, preferably Reyna's apartment. Tessa kept a respectable distance and rambled about her day-to-day, while Reyna pretended she had a life. An airtight recipe for success Reyna could live by.

But taking up physical space in Tessa's world? The real world?

Reyna didn't know how to exist in this reality.

"Rey? Are you okay?" Tessa's voice echoed through the restroom. Red stilettos paused outside Reyna's stall door. "I can see your boots."

"I should go." Reyna braced for Tessa's disappointment to blast through the door.

"The fact you came at all means everything." Tessa's internal emotions remained silent, but guilt riddled her inflection. "I understand if you need to leave."

Reyna waited for her friend's sincerity to sift through the stall and wrap around her like an old blanket worn from years of love. Still, no emotion came.

Overhead fluorescents dappled her vision. "Something isn't right."

"I know." Tessa sighed. "As usual, I'm pushy and—"

"Not you." Reyna swayed and slumped against the door, limbs heavy with warmth. "When did everything get wobbly and why can't I feel you anymore?" Reyna's mouth snapped shut at the blurted truth.

"Reyna Pérez." Tessa snickered. "Are you drunk?"

"Of course not," Reyna scoffed. "I did two shots."

"You never drink," Tessa argued.

Reyna willed her magic to acknowledge occupants within the stalls or women washing their hands. Still, no emotions answered. Reyna stared at her faux leather gloves in disbelief.

Had the alcohol weakened her magic?

If liquor was the key to dulling her dark abilities, it could open many doors. Dangerous doors. Any were better than none, and right now, the only door Reyna wanted to walk through was the one in front of her.

"Are you okay?" Tessa asked.

"I don't know." Reyna opened the door, smiling. "But I think I will be."

Music swallowed Reyna into a silence of the most crowded room she'd ever stepped in. Bodies on the dance floor contracted like lungs. Each inhale, an exhale of Reyna's and Tessa's laughter. Reyna no longer stood in the beast's belly but became oxygen flowing through its veins.

A stranger swam up behind Tessa and smoothed his hands over her hips. Tessa swayed, his arms completing their circle around her waist. Reyna couldn't help but stare at Tessa's carelessness. Her fearless desire to be held and hold someone back. Even a stranger. Reyna might've momentarily escaped magic, but could she ever live in such a way?

Another drink might help.

She waded through the grinding sea of sweat until she met the sticky bar top. Knuckles grazed the small of Reyna's back as lean muscle slid into the space beside her. She tracked buttons along a maroon shirt to a familiar grin she'd met earlier across the dance floor. VIP guy's hazel eyes glittered beneath the lights; his smile more inviting than she'd given him credit for.

"What can I get you?" His tasteful appreciation roved over her.

"I don't know." Reyna opted for honesty, and said, "I don't normally drink."

"Not a drinker myself." He knocked dark hair from his eyes. "I prefer being in control at all times."

A coy smile bloomed over Reyna's cheeks. "I know exactly what you mean."

"Jace." He slid his hand into Reyna's and kissed her leather-wrapped knuckles.

Her hand retracted. "I know who you are."

Jace cocked a brow. "Oh?"

"You're the guy who hits on EMS workers and invites them to clubs."

He chuckled. "And here I thought you'd forgotten me, since you refused to meet earlier."

Reyna's mouth quirked. "And yet here you are."

"Control freak, as I said." Jace lazed against the bar top. "What's your name?"

"Reyna."

"Well, Reyna, thank you for forcing me off my ass to meet you properly. Would you care to get better acquainted in my booth? I confess my friends aren't as charming, but perhaps your presence could brighten up our night?" A slow grin lifted with his shoulder. "Or maybe just mine?"

Intoxicated or not, Reyna entered some alternate universe of her life. A reality meant for someone else. Anyone besides her. Still, the siren's seductive call lured her farther from her shell. And she liked it.

Reyna nodded and fell in step behind Jace. His stride parted the sea of dancers oblivious to his presence. Jace stepped onto the booth's platform and offered her his hand.

Reyna ignored his invitation. "How'd you get the crowd to move?"

"The human body is composed of sixty percent water." Jace's unexpected response drew her brows together. "Command enough and you'll find most will bend like seaweed along a current."

"I have no clue what you just said." Reyna laughed. "But I'd give anything to learn what you did."

"Stick with me long enough"—Jace's white teeth gleamed magenta in the neon lights—"and I'll teach you all kinds of things."

Reyna's cheeks flushed under the otherwise darkness as she stepped onto the booth's platform.

"Reyna, these are my companions, Aquarius and Libra." Jace pivoted toward a man and woman seated on the tufted sofa.

"Oh, Scorpio, you've done it again." The dark-haired woman rose from her seat. "I'm Libra, so pleased to finally meet you."

"Scorpio, Libra, and Aquarius?" Reyna glanced at Jace. "Are you all in some sort of zodiac club?"

Jace's and Libra's lyrical laughter strummed over Reyna's skin.

"Something like that." Jace plopped onto the sofa beside Aquarius. The new man scrubbed fingers through his platinum fauxhawk and exhaled. A sigh that Reyna could only decipher as boredom. Alcohol still ebbed from her system, but instinct was all she possessed now. A skill she'd never needed to rely on.

"You know about the signs?" Jace fixed his smile on Reyna as he absent-mindedly stroked Aquarius's leg.

Oh.

"A little about my own." Reyna's hands wrung together, unsure what to do with herself, and more unsure what she'd walked into. "I've never placed much stock in them."

"Damn shame." Libra tsked. "You should let me read you. I'm good at it."

"Read … me?" the too-close-for-comfort words trembled from Reyna.

"Take them off," Libra instructed.

Reyna's breath hitched. "Excuse me?"

"I can't read your palms with gloves on." Libra beamed through the candlelight casting harsh shadows along her pale skin.

Reyna cradled her hands into her chest. "I don't take them off."

"Relax." Libra's hand swiped between them and a soft breeze pushed Reyna onto the sofa beside Aquarius. The woman's other hand flicked, and various glasses slid aside along the low cocktail table. Reyna's mouth parted. People couldn't move objects without touching them, but by similar logic, Reyna shouldn't physically feel others' emotions. She'd read articles about telekinesis during her magical research, never meeting anyone who possessed the ability.

Perhaps Libra *had* touched the cups and Reyna missed it? Between the lights swirling and liquor-saturated blood, she couldn't be sure.

The sofa beside Reyna dipped as Aquarius tucked hair behind her ear. "If you know what's good for you," his low whisper sent chills through her, "you'll leave. Now."

He relaxed back into the crook of Jace's arm and Reyna shot to her feet.

"I need to find my friend," she blurted.

The blonde waitress from earlier approached the booth and spoke in Jace's ear. He nodded toward Libra. "Sagittarius says he's ready for her."

Sagittarius? The waitress is in on whatever this is?

"Who are you people?" Reyna demanded.

"Don't worry." Jace's predatory smile encouraged anything but. "We're saving you."

"I guess the rumors are true, then," a woman's voice cut from behind them.

"And which rumors might those be, Capricorn?" Jace grinned wider, without facing their intruder.

"You're a psychopath," she replied.

Jace's expression flatlined and the world Reyna knew crumbled.

CHAPTER

THREE

J ACE SWUNG AROUND WITH ARMS FLUNG ABOVE HIS HEAD. Liquid sprayed from the cups and shot at Reyna's delivery woman like bullets. The Fresh Fleet woman's hands rose, and the table flew upright. Water hammered hundreds of grooves into its metal underside. The cocktail table hurtled toward Jace of its own accord and slammed him onto the couch. Libra's palms thrust out and a gust skated the delivery woman across the dance floor on her spine. Reyna climbed over the booth's rail, hitting the floor with a thud. She scrambled to her feet and ran into the clueless crowd still drunk on the night.

Reyna scoured the crowd for Tessa's sandy blonde hair, but neon lights camouflaged any familiarity. Reyna peered over her shoulder. Jace shoved the busted table off himself and rose to his full height. A vicious calm glazed over his face as he locked on Reyna and strode forward. Bodies bent and shuffled from his path once more. Reyna pushed her way through the crowd's chaotic emotions. All tugging her deeper with every dancer she jostled past. The shield of alcohol was fading fast.

"Tessa!" Reyna cried in vain over the electronic beats. Bodies ebbed from her in all directions, and she stiffened like a deer in an open field.

"I meant what I said," Jace crooned, a few long paces across the dance floor.

Reyna side-eyed a glowing exit sign above the crowd. She didn't want to leave Tessa behind, but what if they'd taken her too? What if she was safe? Either way, Reyna couldn't help her friend or herself if she got caught by these deranged people. Reyna sprinted for the side door, but her limbs locked, unable to bend to her will.

Jace ambled closer. "You and I are the same."

Reyna begged her muscles to fight whatever invaded. A force beyond any magic she'd ever encountered. Primal. Powerful.

"I can help you hone your starwater magic, like mine," Jace said. "But *he* will teach you much more."

Reyna ripped and tugged against the cage of her own body.

"Help!" she pleaded, the crowd still unaware they'd been brushed aside.

Jace paused a step away. "Only the God of Darkness can help you now."

"Wrong!" The delivery woman lunged from the crowd and snatched Reyna's exposed wrist.

Energy surged through Reyna from the woman's touch. Jace's magical hold on Reyna was severed and her eyes flew toward the ceiling. Ancient power stormed her veins. Awoke every molecule slumbering within her bones. Foreign, yet undeniably Reyna's own.

The ceiling fell away from her reality and stars seared bright in the heavens. So pure. So blinding. Reyna knew if she reached out, she could touch them. Another energy pulse rippled over her like moonlight over water. The club's bass became muffled and people around her moved in slow motion. She released herself from the delivery woman's grip and rubbed her wrist. Reyna walked around the woman, her fishtail braid suspended in time and space. Jace's foot levitated midstride though he'd dove at Reyna the exact same moment.

What the hell was happening?

Every bead of sweat trickling down a dancer's face. Each sloppy drunk-infused kiss. Every melted ice cube, in every plastic cup soothed her rapid heartbeat. The water in Reyna's surroundings vowed to protect her.

And she believed it.

Reyna blinked and club music pounded to life into real time. Jace tumbled past where Reyna stood moments ago. Fire sprinklers erupted and alarms wailed throughout the building. People screamed and scrambled for the exits, their panic drowning Reyna in the reality she'd been spat back into. Water streamed down her face as she gaped at her hands. Had she released the water?

"Rey!" Tessa ran across the dance floor. "Let's go! I think the building is on fire!"

They sprinted into the summer night. Reyna hunched over on the sidewalk, hands braced atop her knees, trying to steady her breathing. Bar patrons huddled on the street, consoling one another and snapping pictures with their phones.

Tessa heaved for breath. "Are you okay?"

Reyna had never been okay. Not now. Not ever.

"I think so," she replied.

"What happened?" Tessa combed fingers through her damp hair. "You never came back to the dance floor, and I couldn't find you anywhere."

What happened?

Tessa's question replayed through Reyna's mind like a skipping track, the next lyrics always a beat away.

A slow-motion time warp. Water and magic. Zodiacs. A god.

"I don't know." The half lie spewed from Reyna. No doubt something magical transpired, but a magic still light-years from her usual.

"Come on." Tessa jogged toward a parked car across the street. "Maybe they'll give us a ride."

"We don't know them." Reyna chased her. "Let's call a Lyft."

Tessa pointed at an Uber logo near the passenger side window and hopped in behind the driver. Reyna hesitated outside the SUV, looking at the club over her shoulder.

Only the God of Darkness can help you now.

As if Jace's words summoned him, he trudged onto the sidewalk and scanned the unraveling chaos. The server he'd called Sagittarius stood beside him, holding what Reyna could discern as blue fire.

Sagittarius's attention snapped in Reyna's direction and pointed him toward the SUV.

"Drive!" Reyna dove into the back seat. "Now!"

"Wait a sec." The driver twisted around. His blue eyes squinted at Reyna through the darkness. "Aren't you—"

"You heard her." Tessa thrust cash over the seat's middle divide.

The driver's frown pivoted between Reyna and the club, but he nodded and sped off.

"What a wild night." Tessa cackled. "I bet you're happy you came out now."

"Are you still drunk?" Reyna buckled her seat belt. "Nothing about tonight was fun."

"Things got a bit crazy." Tessa's smile faded a fraction. "But we're okay."

"I'm not okay!" Reyna slumped into the SUV's black leather interior.

"I thought you said—"

"Forget what I said and forget this night! Never happening again." Reyna crossed her arms over her chest and stared at the city lights outside her window.

"I'll admit tonight was unexpected, but don't let it dictate if you ever go out again, Rey. Most nights are boring."

Reyna wanted to tell her everything, but what if Tessa didn't believe her? Labeled her a lunatic? Hell, maybe she was. Reyna couldn't risk alienation of her one connection to the world. If she did, she'd have nothing. No one.

Shadows whizzed past the car, streetlamps darkening in their wake. Reyna inspected black smoke tendrils soaring alongside the car through the window. She edged closer and claws scratched along the glass.

"Whoa!" Reyna jerked back.

"What?" Tessa asked.

"Something is following us. I saw … claws."

Tessa's eyes rolled. "Who's drunk now?"

"I'm serious, something is out there!" Reyna pressed her gloved palms against her forehead. "First the guy in 402, those zodiac creeps, now this."

"You finally met 402?" Tessa smoothed her hair. "Did you mention me?"

"Tessa!"

"I'm sorry!"

"I should've never listened to you!" Reyna's glare sliced across the back seat. "This is your fault!"

"Excuse me?" Tessa gaped. "This is not my—"

Reyna's center of gravity lurched forward.

San Diego rotated outside their window as the SUV flipped.

The roof crunched onto pavement. Glass exploded from every angle. Reyna's seat belt burrowed into her chest. She pressed her hands against the roof below. Sheet metal skated across an ice rink of asphalt. Sparks ignited outside their windows. The SUV ricocheted off bystander cars and scraped to a stop. Reyna blinked through the darkened cab.

Out. I need out.

Her fingers fumbled over the buckle at her hip. She clicked the seat belt and dropped onto the ceiling. Distant sirens wailed out of sync with the ringing in her ears. She wiped at the hair sticking to her face and crimson smeared across her gloves.

"Tessa?" Reyna's voice scratched. "Are you—"

Tessa's body lay propped against the window frame. An overturned rag doll with glass shards sprinkled throughout her hair. Reyna's brain rejected what her eyes couldn't. She crawled across the ceiling.

"Tessa, wake up." Reyna brushed her friend's hair aside her face. "Help is coming. You're going to be okay." Though the words tasted hollow, she prayed them to be true. Reyna ripped off her glove and placed two fingers against Tessa's bloody neck.

Nothing stirred beneath her friend's skin.

Reyna pushed harder, as though she might will a pulse or

emotion from somewhere in Tessa's unconscious, but only clinks and moans of the battered vehicle answered. Reyna hung her head, swallowing between breaths.

Tessa.

A tsunami of Reyna's own grief swelled in her chest.

Tessa is dead.

A scream sputtered from Reyna. Indiscernible, mangled words caught somewhere between prayers and damnation. She howled to whatever deity would listen. Tessa belonged in this world. Not her. No one would miss Reyna. Mourn her. Remember her. Reyna would sell her soul for the chance to resurrect Tessa.

"C'mon!" a man called from outside the vehicle. His hand beckoned through Reyna's window. "I've got you!"

Reyna memorized Tessa's face one last time. The one person who'd ever pulled her away from the brink of darkness, now shrouded in nothing but.

"I'm sorry." Reyna sniffled, slipping her glove back on. She grabbed the stranger's hand and slid out the window.

"Are you okay?" Concern sparkled in the driver's eyes under the streetlights. Reyna hugged her chest, unable to utter a sound. He prodded, "Your friend still inside?"

Reyna's teeth chattered with a slight nod. The man kneeled beside the mangled sheet metal and peered inside.

"Ah shit." He scrubbed a hand over his face and through his light brown hair. "No, no, no. This is all wrong."

Reyna's eyes squeezed shut at what she knew he saw.

"You were supposed to be safe." The driver kicked the vehicle. "I'm sorry, Reyna. I tried avoiding the Dredgers but lost control."

Panic overshadowed Reyna's grief. "You're one of them?"

She stepped back.

"Easy. My name is Charlie. I won't hurt you." The driver's hands rose at his sides. A stance Reyna would've recognized as a vulnerable gesture, if not for the last hour of magical hand waving. His brows drew together. "Didn't Prisha tell you?"

Reyna squinted. "Who?"

"Prisha," he replied. "The delivery chick from your apartment earlier today."

"What was she supposed to tell me?" Reyna barked.

"You're a Zodiac."

"You're delusional. All of you!" Reyna staggered away, shaking her head.

"Listen, we don't have much time." Charlie surveyed the sky. "Come with me, and Halley will explain everything."

"I'm not going anywhere with you!"

Animalistic shrieks carved around surrounding buildings and Reyna clapped her hands over her ears.

"Dang it!" Charlie cringed. "I'm sorry, but we gotta go!"

The man darted forward in a blur and scooped Reyna into his arms. He sprinted impossibly fast along the city streets. Long ribbons of light stretched on either side.

"Stop!" Reyna kicked and scratched. "Put me down!"

"What the—" Charlie dodged her fingernails. "Dude, stop!" They zipped around a corner into an alleyway.

"Someone, help!" Reyna screamed.

Charlie pressed her against a dumpster and clamped a hand over her mouth. "Keep it down, would ya!"

Reyna heaved for breath around his hand.

"Listen," he conceded. "I'll try to explain, but only if you promise not to scream. Deal?"

Reyna nodded and he let go.

"How did you run so fast?" She welcomed air into her lungs.

"I'm Gemini. A Zodiac, like you, but since I manipulate air, running fast makes me invisible."

Air magic. Libra's touchless push of Reyna onto the couch. The plastic cups sliding along the table. It hadn't been Reyna's imagination or telekinesis.

God, why couldn't it have been telekinesis?

Charlie released her. "You're the Zodiac, Cancer."

"How'd you know my sign?"

"No," Charlie interjected. "Cancer is not your sign. We're the Zodiacs reincarnated as humans. You *are* Cancer."

Reyna balked at the absurd words he threaded together. In all her research, she'd never come across the existence of actual astrological beings. Zodiac signs were nothing more than a bunch of stars ancients connected to make sense of a world they didn't understand. A world Reyna understood less and less. She'd explored many explanations for her cursed abilities, but nothing ever fit. Whether Charlie spoke the truth, she needed to know more.

"What can Zodiacs do?" Reyna asked.

"Each Zodiac wields elemental magic associated with our sign," he replied. "Water magic is yours."

"But I can't do water …"

Magic.

"What'd the delivery woman do to me?" Reyna slumped against the dumpster, despair cresting with each new revelation.

"You saw Prisha?" Hope etched between Charlie's eyes. "She was supposed to bring you to the car. When she wasn't with you, I thought maybe she got—is she alright?"

"I don't know," Reyna replied. "How'd you know she delivered my groceries?"

Charlie rubbed the back of his neck. "I was with her in the hall. You couldn't see me because of how fast I am."

"And Prisha gave me water magic when she touched me at the club?"

"Her element is earth, so she didn't give you water magic." His head bobbled at the nuance. "Only a Zodiac whose magic has been awoken can activate another's."

More magic. I've been given more magic.

Humorless laughter exploded from her never-ending nightmare. After a lifetime searching for an escape from an otherworldly existence, she'd been plunged deeper into another.

Reyna stomped toward him and thrust her wrists outward. "Take it back!"

"It doesn't work like that." Charlie frowned. "I'm sorry."

"I said, take it! I don't want it! I can't have more—"

Squalls ripped through the alley's hollow. Two cloaked figures hovered overhead, smoky black tendrils wafting at their bases. Wraiths. Reyna found depictions during her supernatural research, but every artist's rendering of the phantoms crumbled beneath what floated before her now.

Their throats clicked with venomous warning.

"Aw, come on!" Charlie leapt onto the dumpster with gravity-defied ease. "Haven't you had enough?"

A wraith dive-bombed, and Reyna screamed.

Charlie pounced off the receptacle's lid onto a building wall. The wraith followed. Reyna slid down the dumpster and curled her arms around her knees. Charlie's body blurred with each fling and flip of himself between the two alley walls. The creature roared with frustration as Charlie's inhuman parkour drew them higher and higher. Reyna peeked around the dumpster at the alleyway's opening. A couple cars drove past. The real world, closer and farther all at once. This was her chance to vanish from whatever war waged amongst the city's shadows.

Asthmatic breath wheezed in her ear.

Reyna slowly twisted around and met the second wraith hovering a few inches from her face. Its head cocked, an unmistakable clack of teeth somewhere behind its faceless void. Water dripped and black smoke snaked from beneath its hood. Reyna turned her face to the side, eyes clamped shut, as smoke grazed her cheeks.

After a life of careful hiding, this was how it ended.

This was how she died.

"Enough," boomed a voice. Defiance growled from the wraith, but it recoiled like a rabid dog choked on its leash. "Sorry about them. Damn savage creatures. Are you alright?" Jace extended his hand.

Reyna ignored it and slid herself along the rusty metal at her back to stand.

"Get away from her!" Charlie descended upon Jace.

Jace flicked his wrist and water from the dripping creatures slithered from the pavement into a scorpion tail. His stinger pinned Charlie's chest against the wall. Bricks and mortar crumbled to the ground beneath him.

"He can't help you." Jace steered Reyna's stricken gaze back to himself. "But I'll take you to someone who can."

Charlie writhed for air.

"Let him go," Reyna pleaded.

"Afraid we can't." The club waitress called Sagittarius strode from the alley's shadows. Blue fire coiled from her hand along the arrow inked on her arm. "We've been ordered to bring you both."

Wraiths loomed behind Jace and his blonde accomplice like supernatural bodyguards.

"Please, leave me alone!" Reyna cried. "I'm no one!"

"We both know that's not true." Jace cracked his neck. "We've been looking for you for weeks."

"I don't know any of you," Reyna replied.

"Ah, but we know you, Reyna Pérez." Jace smirked. "After our little shakedown on the freeway with these other traitorous Zodiacs"—he sneered at Charlie—"your friend patched me up. Imagine my surprise when she pulled out her phone and I saw a photo of you two on her lock screen."

A lump welled in Reyna's throat. "You invited her to get to me?"

"We Zodiacs are bound. Meant to find one another." Jace's chin lifted. "Made possible by our Dark God's return. His mere presence reunites, and his power will set us free."

"The Dark God has big plans for you." Sagittarius stepped beside Jace. "For all of us."

Pavement rumbled beneath their feet.

The scorpion stinger burst like a water balloon and Charlie slammed onto the ground. Asphalt cracked like ice. Busted pavement churned into a wave and crashed onto Reyna's attackers. Vibrations trembled through the narrow alley and low windows sprayed glass below. Metal moaned at Reyna's back as the dumpster tipped toward her. Charlie's hands punched forward. A wind gust careened the receptacle onto the city street. He leaned against a building wall, massaging his collarbone.

"Dude." Charlie laughed through a cough. "Your timing totally sucks."

"I tracked you best I could." A figure backlit by streetlights strode through the misty debris. "You were all over the place."

"Avoiding certain death calls for running," Charlie replied. "Lots and lots of running."

The delivery woman hopped off the mountain of garbage, metal, and concrete. "Are you okay, Reyna?"

Reyna rose to her full height. "If someone asks me one more time—"

Their attackers' muffled screeches trembled from beneath the rubble.

"We should get out of here." Prisha slung Charlie's arm over her shoulders. "That won't hold them long."

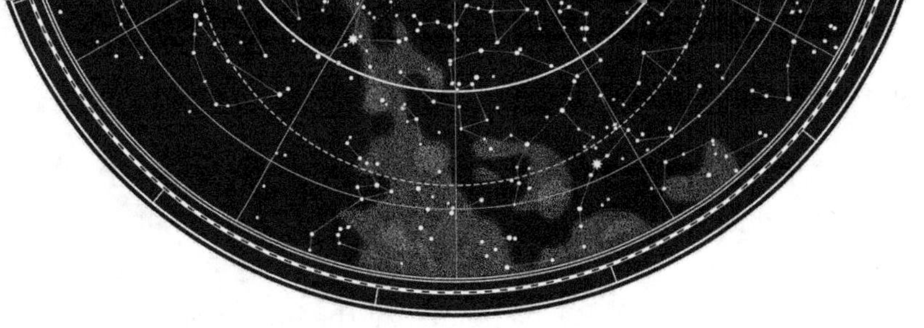

CHAPTER

FOUR

IESEL AND SALT PERMEATED THE AIR AS REYNA STUMBLED over crisscrossing steel tracks. Prisha led them through San Diego's freight yard with Charlie tucked under her arm, despite his constant insistence he could walk. It wasn't until they'd followed trolley tracks out of East Village that the night's events made themselves known in Reyna's limbs. Aches throbbed through her muscles, and she couldn't shake the pulse near her temples. Whether by magical attack or flipped vehicle, whatever otherworldly power a so-called Zodiac held spared no mercy to their human bodies.

The Zodiacs squeezed between two disconnected boxcars and strode along parallel tracks. Prisha pulled a chrome orb from her pocket and clicked it open. A small brown flame flickered at its core. The fire beckoned Prisha forward, her attention wavering between flame and freight.

"What are we looking for?" Reyna followed along.

"Car 137000," Prisha replied.

"I voted for the one with *ballz* sprayed on it." Charlie winced as he unhinged his arm from Prisha's shoulder. "Tell me it's not easier to find."

Prisha replied, "Easy is the opposite of what we want."

"You mentioned someone named Halley," Reyna said to Charlie. "Is she at the boxcar too?"

"She's at *Polaris* but we need to lie low for now," he replied. "Once we're sure we weren't followed, we'll meet up with her."

Reyna paused. "What's *Polaris*?"

"Our ride." Charlie grinned. "It's the dopest ship you'll ever see. You'll love it."

"And what's that?" Reyna pointed at the brown fire in Prisha's hand.

"This flame once belonged to Sagittarius," Prisha replied. "Her starfire magic allows its bearer to track what they seek."

"Sagittarius tried to capture us." Reyna blinked. "Why would she give you her tracking fire?"

Prisha's full lips spread into a smile. "She created this flame a long time ago, and Sagittarian fire never goes out."

"Except against starwind magic, like mine." Charlie brushed invisible dust from his shoulder. "I keep getting awesomer, I know."

Prisha's brow raised. "That's not a word."

"Neither is *ballz*." Charlie shrugged. "But someone felt it needed to be said."

Prisha rolled her eyes.

Reyna asked, "If Sagittarius's fire tracks, could she be following us?"

Charlie shook his head. "Her Eternal Flame can't track Zodiacs."

"But"—Prisha elongated—"if other Dark-Aligned Zodiacs were with Scorpio and Sagittarius in the alley, we could've been followed. Hence lying low."

"Hence," Charlie echoed.

Reyna asked, "If you couldn't use the flame to find me, how'd you find my apartment?"

"There's Zodiacs among us who have less magical ways of finding people. Your living in a larger city made you harder to find, but once we located your address, Sagittarius's flame confirmed it was you." Prisha stepped closer and the fire shifted from brown to silver. "Each Zodiac's energy represents a color. When the flame is close to a specific Zodiac, it reflects their associated hue. Charlie ran past your apartment door with the flame. When it changed to silver, we knew it was you."

"You're the ghost?" Reyna pieced the past ten hours together.

"The Ghost," Charlie tasted the title. "I like it. Could be my superhero name."

Reyna asked, "How did Jace, Scorpio, or whoever he is, recognize me as a Zodiac from my friend's phone, but you needed the flame to confirm my identity?"

Prisha's shoulders sank. "Only Zodiacs like Scorpio and Sagittarius who've aligned with the Dark God remember their Zodiac lives from before. We're not sure why."

Reyna crossed her arms over her chest. If she would've pushed her fears aside and heard Prisha out at the apartment, Tessa might still be alive.

"Here it is." Prisha knocked on a freight door.

Steel groaned as the door slid open from inside. White lantern light illuminated the boxcar's walls and silhouetted a large figure at its threshold.

"I was getting worried." The man's Irish accent rolled into a sigh. "What took so long?"

Charlie shoved hands into his pockets. "Caught a Padres game. Went for a midnight stroll on the beach. Tangoed with Dredgers."

The man released a slow whistle. "The Dark-Aligned must be getting desperate resorting to those beasts."

"Dredgers?" Reyna stepped forward. "Are those the creatures who attacked us?"

"Aye." Lantern light spilled across the man's soft green eyes and clean-cut face. "They manifest your worst nightmares until it kills you."

The new man's massive forearms lifted Charlie and Prisha into the car with little effort. He smiled and offered his hand to Reyna. "You must be Reyna. Pleased to meet you. I'm Ethan Ryan."

Reyna stared at his hand. Waited for her curse to sense his intentions. Any sliver of knowing she'd chosen the right people to seek refuge with. But these Zodiacs' emotions read the same as those who'd attacked her.

Nonexistent.

Alcohol might've shielded Reyna from normal people's emotions, but the Zodiacs were something else entirely. Reyna didn't understand what being a Zodiac meant for her other magic, but a reprieve from others' emotions by touch or proximity? She'd gladly accept this small victory.

Reyna accepted Ethan's hand, and he pulled her into the boxcar.

"What kind of fire is this?" Reyna approached the glowing lantern atop a crate.

"The Home Depot kind." Charlie grinned and Reyna's face flushed.

"I feel like we got off on the wrong foot in your doorway." Prisha smiled at Reyna and sat beside Charlie. "I'm Prisha and he's—"

"Unforgettable." Charlie winked.

Reyna perched on a crate across from them. "And you're all … Zodiacs?"

"Trust me," Prisha replied. "We were surprised too."

"Which Zodiacs are you?" Reyna asked.

"I'm Capricorn." The steel wall buckled and whined beneath Prisha's hand. "My starland magic commands earth, particularly metals."

Charlie's hand arched and a soft breeze whipped through everyone's hair. "I already told you I'm Gemini, but from what I've been told, my name was Ini, before."

"In-eye?" Reyna sounded out.

"Gemini is the twins sign." Charlie's wind magic dissipated with his smile. "My twin sister, Gem, and I represented the sign, together."

"Is she at the ship?" Reyna asked.

"She's—" Charlie strained. "We weren't able to find her."

Silence thickened the air and Prisha's hand slid onto his shoulder.

"I'm Taurus." Ethan's warmth unfurled through the tension. He sat cross-legged on the floor beside Reyna, a splayed hand touching her crate. Branches sprouted from the boards and braided into two arms and a backrest. "I do earth magic, like Prisha, but found we each feel more drawn to certain aspects of our element. Trees bend more naturally to me."

Reyna smoothed her hands along the throne armrests grown

beneath her within seconds. She'd almost abandoned hope of finding anyone to remove her magic, let alone meet others who wielded it. The Zodiacs weren't like her. Not really. These people exercised elemental magic.

Not an ability to sense and manipulate emotions or absorb human life.

If her absorption abilities weren't a by-product of elemental magic, what did that make her? The Zodiacs showed no indication they knew about her other magic, and she refused to entertain what might happen if anyone discovered the truth. They could decide her too dangerous, or worse, use her magic any way they saw fit. Years of isolation taught Reyna that sharing as little of herself as possible was the best way to keep herself and others safe. A lesson reinforced more than ever by the night's events.

"I must admit"—Ethan ran a hand through his russet hair—"you're taking this whole Zodiac situation quite well."

Reyna's hands slipped from the armrests. "I didn't say I believed you."

Prisha gaped. "Even after everything you've seen?"

"I don't know what I've seen." Reyna hugged her torso. "All I know is a few hours ago my friend was alive and now she's not. Whether or not I'm Cancer, I can't stay with you."

"You are Cancer," Prisha retorted. "I know you felt our elemental connection at the club."

"I feel a lot of things." Reyna stood. "I didn't ask for whatever you did."

"Oh, I'm sorry," Prisha snorted. "I forgot to ask if you preferred being controlled by Scorpio. Your lack of awoken Zodiac magic was what allowed him to subdue you."

"Magic is what killed my friend!" Reyna snapped.

Ethan stood. "Let's all take a minute and breathe."

"Best idea I've heard yet." Reyna yanked the freight door open and hopped out.

She trudged along the row of cars, pebbles shushing beneath

her boots. Reyna couldn't put enough distance between herself and them as the world unraveled around her. Who did Prisha think she was to decimate Reyna's life in a single touch? Yes, these Zodiacs saved her from being attacked, but at what cost? All Reyna wanted was a life without magic and they'd forced more on her.

Reyna grabbed a boxcar's ladder rung.

This is your fault.

The last words she uttered to Tessa would haunt her until her final days.

"I'm so sorry." Reyna buckled into the ladder. Cried hard into the darkness, hoping maybe if she did, Tessa might feel her wherever she was. Reyna wanted Tessa to experience her sorrow, same as she'd felt hers so many times. The time Tessa's first boyfriend cheated. Tessa meeting her birth mother who'd moved on with her second family. Reyna felt it all. Endured with her. Reyna lived so much life through Tessa's, she'd never made one of her own. Never gave enough of herself to someone to feel their absence from her life. At the moment of her friend's death, Tessa never knew the real Reyna, and for that, Reyna's regret ran deep. Tessa deserved more from a friend and much more from life.

Reyna climbed the ladder and sat on the roof. A few silhouetted train yard buildings hid the ocean beyond, but its song rode the wind. Reyna longed for the ocean's embrace. To descend into its depths where she could never hurt another soul again, and perhaps, hers might finally find rest too. It wasn't the first time Reyna contemplated ending her life, but as with everything else, she was afraid. Despite her abuela's devout ideals, Reyna didn't know what lay beyond the veil of this world. She'd hoped it'd be something better, but given what she could do was sure it was worse.

"Hey." Ethan's head rose above the boxcar's roof.

Reyna's heart leapt, catching up with the lack of emotional prompting her magic typically provided.

"Mind if I join you?" He climbed onto the roof.

She did, but her need to have someone beside her outweighed

every instinct she once trusted. Reyna gave a small nod, and he pulled himself onto the boxcar. Metal groaned beneath Ethan's giant frame as he sat beside her. He followed her gaze across the yard while they sat in comfortable silence. No expectations who would speak first. No apologies. Only the ocean breeze cutting through rows of cars.

"I know you don't know us yet," Ethan finally spoke. "But you don't have to be alone in this, if you don't want to be."

"What I want has never mattered," Reyna replied.

"We won't stop you if you want to go home, but the Dark God will find you and might not offer the same chance."

"So, I have no choice at all?"

"You have choices. Never said they were easy." Ethan paused a long moment. "I had a life before all this too. A boyfriend and a job helping people. I'd bought my first place in Belmont. It was small, but it was mine. I was happy."

Reyna side-eyed him. "You helped people?"

"Personal trainer at our local gym." Ethan shrugged sheepishly. "Nothing profoundly noble, but I enjoy guiding people to their goals, fitness or otherwise."

"What about your boyfriend? How does he feel about all this?"

"He thinks I got invited to some extended fitness retreat." Ethan's grip tightened across his knees. "I tried telling him about the Zodiacs, but how do you tell someone you have magical powers without sounding absolutely mental?"

"I get it, believe me." A melancholy chuckle slipped from Reyna. "I didn't ask for this."

"None of us did. But sometimes the things we didn't know we needed end up being the best for us." Ethan sighed into the ocean breeze. "It'll be morning in a few hours, and I think you should at least talk to Halley before you make your decision. Whatever comes next is up to you."

CHAPTER

FIVE

W ITH EACH STEP ACROSS THE FREIGHT YARD, REYNA'S life in San Diego slipped off the horizon. A hazy memory lost to the ordinary. She followed close behind the Zodiacs. More determined than ever to understand the new nightmare she'd been thrown into. Whether she decided to stay or make a run for it, Reyna refused her friend's death be in vain. She wanted to understand what being a Zodiac meant, why she was pursued, and most important, for what reason Tessa met an early end.

Reyna and the Zodiacs crept alongside storage buildings under the guise of night. Vehicle headlights spilled across the graveled yard as a few train employees greeted each other over a shift change. Prisha signaled the Zodiacs onward. Each helping one another between cars until pebble met concrete and waves lapped against the seawall. Reyna stared into the distant black abyss of ocean and sky. The Coronado Bridge curved across the bay like a path of stars while Tijuana slept to the south. The last bits of night clung to the sky, and with it, remnants of Reyna's adrenaline. She didn't know if she'd ever sleep again, but perhaps if lucky, the next time she'd wake to the world set right.

"Are you sure this is the spot?" Reyna scanned the vacant coastline and scrubbed her hands over her arms. "I thought you had a ship."

"Wait for it." Ethan smiled and crossed his arms.

Charlie glided a hand through the air. An ocean breeze fluttered across tall silvery sails and unveiled an ivory ship shrouded by invisibility.

Charlie grinned over his shoulder. "Welcome to *Polaris*."

Reyna's jaw dropped.

"Sagittarian fire tracks *and* conceals." Ethan and the others led Reyna along a gangway. "Some of her fire remains on ship to hide us."

Prisha strode on deck between two colossal masts of clear glass to an onyx pit with sapphire fire. She clicked the orb open from her pocket and its tiny flame leapt into the hearth.

Reyna marveled at the shimmering sails. "I can't believe this ship is in the bay under the Coast Guard's nose."

"*Polaris* is invisible to humans while on Earth." Charlie waggled his brows.

"Are we not human?" Reyna asked.

"Well, humans can't do what we can." Ethan ruffled a hand through his hair. "But we're not quite gods either, if that's what you're thinking."

"I don't know what I'm thinking," Reyna replied, certain if she looked any higher at the sails, she'd invite vertigo. "I'm still processing an invisible posh pirate ship."

Charlie threw his hands in the air. "I told you we shoulda got eye patches."

A door burst open behind them.

"Oh my!" A woman squealed and glided across the deck. "Welcome, Most Elusive Reyna! We're elated to finally have you breathing aboard and with all your appendages still beautifully attached!" Fiery purple hair crackled over the woman's shoulders and cheeks.

Reyna guessed from her smooth milky face and petite frame that she was no older than eighteen, but her ethereal presence hinted at ages long passed.

The woman flung herself to wrap Reyna into a hug and Reyna staggered away with her hands raised.

"My apologies." The woman's frown somehow resembled a smile. "I didn't mean any offense."

"This is Halley." Ethan stepped between them. "She's not from our world, so you'll have to forgive some of her more unique inclinations."

"Are you a Zodiac too?" Reyna asked.

"To think me worthy—I've never been granted such an honor!" Halley clasped her collarbone, lilac eyes tearing. "I'm a mere servant to her splendidness, the Goddess of Light, and now to you, the Reawakened Zodiacs."

Reyna's brows rose. "Goddess of Light?"

"Oh yes!" Halley squeaked, hands clapping. "Only the most wondrous, undeniably beautiful and merciful creator of all purity in the world."

"Right," Reyna elongated her confusion.

"It's late, or rather, early and we're all knackered." Ethan stretched arms over his head. "We should all get some rest."

Reyna shook her head. "Not until someone explains why mystical beings are hunting me."

The group exchanged glances.

"Allow me." Halley shooed the Zodiacs. "Tend your REMs and I'll explain everything to Ever-Inquisitive Reyna."

"Are you going to be alright?" Ethan paused beside Reyna. "I can stay if you like."

The longer she was away from home, from knowing her only friend in the world was gone, Reyna found herself searching for an anchor. A familiar face. A kind word. But being friends with her came at a steep price. One she'd never allow another to pay again.

"Thanks, Ethan." Reyna forced a smile. "I'll be okay."

The Zodiacs shuffled into the cabin and Halley remained, eyes large with intrigue as though a waterfall of words might burst at any moment.

"It's an undeniable honor to finally meet you, Lady Regent,"

Halley gushed. "I've heard such glorious tales of your unparalleled benevolence and grace."

"Why is some god trying to kill me, then?" Reyna asked.

"Kill? Oh stars, no! For all the God of Darkness's sinister deeds, Levant recognizes the importance of the Zodiacs' existence."

"Could've fooled me," Reyna grumbled.

"He wishes you to join his wicked pursuits."

"Which are?"

"Levant sought rebellion against the Goddess of Light a century ago and she banished him. He's been gathering Zodiacs since his return to Earth, so we can only assume it's an attempt for vengeance."

"If she's a goddess and can't stop him"—Reyna blinked—"How does she expect us to?"

"Zodiacs were once immortal celestials," Halley explained. "You've shed your immortality through reincarnation, but power still courses through your mortal-make. The goddess prays your combined Zodiac starmagics will help subdue the Dark God once and for all. Powerful as the goddess is, universal laws of balance compel them from ending one another."

Reyna braced against the ship's railing. "My friend was murdered tonight. I've learned I'm an actual Zodiac, supposedly do water magic, and now am expected to help stop a god?" Reyna mulled over the absurdity. "You're all crazy."

"I know this must be quite a shock," Halley replied. "But the goddess needs your help. It's what you were created for."

"I wasn't made to help people." Reyna gripped the rail tighter. "You've got the wrong person."

Halley sighed. "Perhaps Ever-Astute Ethan was correct. You must be weary after an evening of such revelations. Rest and reflection may best serve whatever decision you arrive at. Meanwhile, I assure you're quite safe aboard *Polaris*."

A second promise of sleep coaxed a yawn from Reyna. Marigold bled into faint blues of morning as sunshine peeked over mountains of the city she'd always called home. A home that might never be safe for her again.

"I'll rest." Reyna surrendered to her need for sleep. "But this doesn't mean I've agreed to help."

"Of course, my lady." Halley bowed her head.

Reyna followed her into the ship's cabin and wall lanterns sprang alive. Light glistened over pearlescent white wood and gilded ceiling planks.

"Forgive me for asking"—Reyna craned her neck while they walked, drowning beneath the beauty every inch the ship commanded—"if you're not a Zodiac, what are you?"

Halley's fiery purple hair warped along the walls' luster.

"Mortals once revered me as Soteria, the Grecian deity of safety and salvation, but the goddess created me for assistance within her palace, Omphalos. If the Dark God ever began his return from banishment, the Zodiacs would shed their star essences and be reborn mortal. I was tasked with passing Earth periodically to check if any Zodiacs had been reincarnated." Halley tucked a wisp of fire behind her ear. "To mortal eyes, I appeared as a rock streaming in space. Over time, they began recognizing my patterns and renamed me."

"You're Halley's comet?" Reyna couldn't stop her smile.

"I am." Halley paused outside an entry of stairs diving deeper into the ship. "And though I may have adopted my new name, I still provide for those in need of safety and salvation. Once you've acquired a few hours of both, we shall speak more of Nidus. You'll find your quarters at the end of the hall below."

"What's Nidus?" Reyna asked.

"Birthplace of all life on Earth." A smile bloomed across Halley's cheeks. "The before, the after, and the beyond. Your true home." She bowed her head. "Rest well, my lady."

Reyna thanked her and meandered the designated corridor until she met the end. She knocked softly on one of the doors and when no response came, she cracked it open. A fireplace roared to life. Warmth unfurled over mahogany floors, wainscotting, and the golden headboard of a king-size bed dominating the room's center. The sheets were tightly tucked and its comforter unmarred by wrinkles.

Not her apartment, but it would do.

She unzipped her boots, moaning at the plush rug sinking between her toes. Reyna padded across the room and froze. A stranger stared back from a connected bathroom. She edged closer to the mirror. Deep shadows hung beneath her eyes, dirt smudged her face, and scrapes peppered her arms. Her fingers brushed over her split bottom lip, and she winced at the dried blood on her gloves.

Tessa's blood.

Memory of her friend's final scream sledgehammered Reyna's skull. The illusion anyone was safe, dead.

Reyna jolted away from the counter, ripped off her gloves, and chucked them across the bathroom. She paced the tiles, fingers buried in her hair. Tessa's laughter had once filled rooms. Her singing made Reyna cringe. Most times, Tessa didn't know when to shut up. But scream? Tears blinked free. Tessa hadn't been made to scream.

Water spilled from the faucet as Reyna scrubbed at the old and new blood staining her clean hands. Blood of her blood. Countless other close calls. And now, Tessa's. Their blood would always be part of her.

Tattooed onto her soul.

CHAPTER

SIX

REYNA MELTED INTO THE MORNING'S WARMTH TRAPPED beneath her blanket. Sunrise streamed through her window and illuminated whirls of dust along the dawn. Most people dreaded mornings. Reyna loved them. The stretch of a new day in her limbs. A hot cup of chamomile to rouse her from bed. But this new morning swaddled her deeper into its sheets. Incinerated any desire to leave bed again. Forever contented to lay lost somewhere between sleep and bliss.

She slid an arm over the body beside her and fingertips brushed over hard ridges of muscle. An agreeable groan vibrated against Reyna's cheek and her eyes flashed open.

"Ah!" Reyna rolled onto the floor.

She blinked sleep from her vision and crawled toward the bed with the prowess of a child. Reyna slowly poked her head above the mattress. A man's lazy grin greeted from amongst the sea of fluffy blankets. Rogue blond hair rested atop his bare shoulders as he cradled his chin in his hand. Reyna ducked beneath the bed's horizon. Perhaps he hadn't seen her. Maybe she hadn't seen him. He could've been a waking nightmare, like the past twelve hours of her life.

"G'morning, Sunshine." The man's groggy timbre demolished her hopes.

"Who the hell are you?" Reyna asked from the floor.

"Shouldn't I be askin' you?" He chuckled thickly. "This is my room."

Reyna's head popped up. "Halley told me I could sleep here."

He sat upright and a lion's yawn rumbled from his chest. "I'm pretty sure she meant across the hall but remind me to thank her."

Reyna leapt to her feet. "It didn't look like anyone was staying in this room."

"Your mistake." Amber eyes trailed low over her ensemble. "Not sayin' I mind."

Reyna's heart lurched. She knocked her knees together and yanked the oversize white T-shirt she wore over her black underwear. Amusement simmered in his smile.

"Stop staring!" Reyna squirmed. "You're being a creep!"

"Well, I need my shirt back, so …"

Her jaw dropped. "You expect me to take off my shirt?"

"Technically it's my shirt, Sunshine. But it does look better on you."

"Who are you?" Reyna snatched a throw from a chaise and wrapped herself into a burrito.

"You're Reyna, right?"

"I know who I am! Who are you?"

"Nope." The corner of his lips lifted. "Sunshine suits you."

"Maybe I should call you some stupid nickname, since you refuse to tell me yours."

"Fine by me." He tucked blond hair behind his ear. "I've been called lots of names."

"Do you think it's okay crawling into bed with a stranger while they're asleep?"

"What kind of lowlife do you think I am?" He feigned offense. "I'd never kick a beautiful woman from bed. Especially when it's mine."

"If you touched me." Reyna clasped her makeshift cape tighter. "I swear I'll—"

He threw the comforter from his lap and stood. Reyna clapped a hand over her eyes from whatever nakedness might await. Her feet twisted in the throw as gravity tugged her toward the floor. The stranger caught Reyna in his strong arms. She wobbled against his defined abdomen, dipping into gray sweatpants slung low on his hips. He cleared his throat, yanking her wandering gaze to his.

"If anything happened last night, I guarantee you wouldn't forget it." The man sauntered toward the dresser where she'd found the T-shirt of controversy. "Besides, you're the cuddler."

Reyna glared at the scars peppering his bare back and tried to sift through his emotional threads for a sliver of shame or regret. Any indication of a lie. But nothing radiated from him. He must've been a Zodiac too. Nothing else made sense.

The man pulled on a shirt, head tilted to the side though he sensed her eyes on him.

"Who's the creep now?" he snickered.

Scarlet bloomed in Reyna's cheeks. She snatched her raggedy dress off the floor and slammed the bathroom door behind her. All she owned now was the tattered reminder of Tessa's death in her hands and the shirt on her back, which wasn't hers. Reyna slumped against the door. How'd her life gotten out of control so fast?

"C'mon, Sunshine." Knuckles rapped on the other side. "Open up."

"Why do you keep calling me that?" she bit.

"Cause you're so damn pleasant."

"Screw you!" Reyna ripped his T-shirt over her head.

"Brax."

"What?" Reyna stared at the door through the mirror.

"Brax Riggs." His voice softened. "It's my name."

Reyna's glare slackened at her gloves laid neatly over the countertop. She turned them over in her hands. "You ... cleaned my gloves?"

"Let's say, I know a thing or two about removing bloodstains," Brax replied.

Reyna slipped them on. "That's ominous."

"We've all been through our share of shit, right?" A smile lined his voice through the door. "Listen, I've got some fresh clothes for you and maybe later, Varma can let you borrow some threads a little less me."

"Varma?"

"Prisha, the Capricorn wonder."

Reyna would rather remain nude than ask Prisha for anything, but not if it meant passing the man outside naked. Reyna grunted and shot an arm through the cracked door. Brax plopped the clothing into her hand.

"Halley told me what happened to your friend." Brax's throat cleared. "What was her name?"

Was.

Reyna closed the door and blinked away tears. She hadn't spoken her name aloud since the accident. "Tessa."

A few moments of silence hung between them.

"I know it's not worth a damn, but I'm sorry you lost her," he replied.

"You're the first to say that." Reyna slipped on the basketball shorts and new black T-shirt. "Thank you." She opened the door.

Brax clutched the doorframe overhead, a sliver of abs between his hem and sweats on display. An unmoving fortress of beauty.

Reyna's brow quirked. "Has anyone ever mentioned you need a lesson in personal space?"

"Why?" His grin detonated over her draped in his oversize clothing. "Are you accepting new students?"

Reyna and Brax made their way above and across deck. An oblivious San Diego meandered across the bay. Sailboats and surfers rode the breeze with an occasional yacht setting course for open water. The Zodiacs sat near the bow around a table spread with fruit and pastries. Ethan sipped coffee at one end and Charlie balanced on his chair's hind legs at the other.

Prisha peered over her book at Reyna dressed in Brax's clothes and raised a brow at him. "That was fast."

"What can I say?" He snatched a bagel and plopped onto a chair beside her. "I'm a giver."

"Oh no! We didn't—" Fire engulfed Reyna's face. "This isn't what it looks like."

"Don't worry." Brax crossed his brown Doc Martens on the table. "She was a perfect gentleman. My virtue is intact."

"Hah!" Charlie twirled a miniature tornado between his fingertips. "Good one."

"Where were you last night?" Ethan folded arms across his chest at Brax. "You shouldn't've been out alone. It's not safe."

"I don't need a babysitter, Beef-For-Brains." Brax ripped off a bite of bagel.

"We could've used your help last night," Ethan replied.

"That's for damn sure," Brax grumbled around the bread in his mouth.

"I'm serious." Ethan clenched his jaw. "Your recklessness will get somebody—"

"I wouldn't finish if I were you." Brax squinted at him. "Last I checked, shit decisions are your MO and in case I haven't made myself clear, oh fearless leader, I do what I want, whenever the fuck I want."

"A most pleasant morning!" Halley flitted toward them. "I trust you all slept well." The Zodiacs relaxed into their seats with eyes cast downward. Halley rounded on Reyna. "Have you given further thought on embarkation to Nidus?"

The entire group looked up.

"I know I can't go home, but I can't go with you either." Reyna wrung her gloved palms together. "You'll be better off without me."

"So." Brax pulled a pack of cigarettes from his jeans. "How ya gonna do it?"

"Excuse me?" Reyna asked.

"You must have a solid plan to disappear." His lighter clicked open. "Given how easy these jokers found ya. Not to mention, Levant's thugs."

Brax's observation grated Reyna's pride. For someone who'd taken care of herself since she was seventeen, Reyna didn't realize how she'd come to rely on what little she had. How far could she get with limited funds and no living relatives she knew of before the Dark God found her? If some part of Reyna wasn't from this world, perhaps her supernatural answers weren't either. She could learn where she came from. Why she possessed magic. Maybe be rid of it. Reyna owed those she'd lost to find out. She owed it to herself.

"Can the goddess remove my magic?" Reyna asked.

"She-who-is-most-glorious is capable of great feats unbeknownst to me." Halley's expression creased. "But why ever would a Zodiac want—"

"I'll go." Reyna silenced the question she didn't want to answer. The tiniest glimmer of hope her magic could be removed was all Reyna needed. "But I won't use magic unless I have to."

"Oh, believe me, Sunshine." Brax chuckled through exhaled smoke. "You will."

CHAPTER

SEVEN

"Hey girl, you'll never guess who I met today," Tessa said. "Hit me back."

Reyna sat against the stern as *Polaris* trudged through the Pacific, and stared at the red battery blinking on her phone. Two, maybe three replays remained before Tessa's voice vanished from existence. Nothing more than a recording lost to radio silence. Reyna pressed the button again.

"Hey girl, you'll never—"

Reyna ripped the phone from her ear and pleaded with the spinning white circle to allow her one last play. The screen went black and she exhaled. A shaky, breathy sound threatened to undo bits of herself she'd haphazardly stitched together. Tessa's friendship had been a daydream. An illusion Reyna convinced herself of so she could hold on to the one connection making her feel human.

Only she wasn't.

The Zodiacs never endured people's unspoken emotions. Never brought a life to the brink and beyond. Halley and the others looked at Reyna like a savior, when by all other definitions, she was sure she was a villain. The Zodiacs exercised elemental magic. A balance of the natural world. Reyna's absorption magic was an abomination.

Not even in a world of the impossible could she be like everyone else.

Across deck, Charlie watched the ocean roll by with his chin plopped atop crossed arms. A breeze ran fingers through his hair and fluttered over the back of his T-shirt. Perhaps he willed it so. An invisible, comforting hand to remind him his other half still existed in the world.

For all the ways Reyna and the Zodiacs weren't alike, they also were.

Charlie's lost sister. Ethan's left-behind love. The Zodiacs understood being different. To lose someone because they were different. Reyna hadn't realized how much she'd needed condolences until Brax offered them. Though it wouldn't bring Tessa back, some menial acknowledgment of loss softened the edges of Reyna's loneliness. If she could grant someone else a moment's peace, from whatever sharpened its teeth against their hope, she'd try.

Reyna swayed along the Pacific's push and pull until her gloved fingers curled over the rail beside Charlie. She freed her breath like a bird across the endless stretch of blue.

"I'm sorry about your sister," Reyna said, not knowing specifically what she was sorry for.

Charlie's focus remained fixed forward. "Do you think it's possible to miss someone you've never met?"

"No," Reyna replied. "But I believe it's possible to miss opportunities."

Charlie glanced at her.

"My mother died when I was born," Reyna explained. "I don't remember her, but it doesn't stop me from wishing life were different. From wanting the moments we might've had."

Charlie nodded. "My sister and I were separated at birth too. After the Zodiacs found me, we went to Australia for our birth records but turned up …" Charlie made a popping noise and a zero with his fingers.

"I always wondered what it'd be like to have siblings." Reyna's lips twitched with melancholy. "Growing up, kids in my neighborhood had so many cousins, it was hard to tell where family started, and friends ended."

"What about your dad?"

"He's dead too." Mere mention of the man caused Reyna to tighten her leather knuckles around the rail. "My abuela raised me after he passed."

"Sorry, Rey." Charlie's brow furrowed. "Were you close to your, ah …"

"Abuela." She smiled. "My grandmother was the closest person I had to a parent, but we weren't close." Reyna was never taught much Spanish but didn't need language to understand abuela's deep-rooted suspicion of Reyna's role in her papá's death. Circumstances of his passing remained a mystery to all.

Everyone, except Reyna.

Abuela would never have abandoned her son's child to foster care, but she also never trusted Reyna. And Reyna kept it that way. For her abuela's sake.

"Do you think your sister is with the God of Darkness?" Reyna desperately needed the conversation steered from herself.

Charlie squinted harder into the distance, as though trying to decide and slowly nodded.

"If she is, it means you might see her again." Reyna didn't recognize her own optimism. "Which means there's hope."

The corners of Charlie's mouth lifted. "There are times I thought I felt her near. Not physically. But like I could sense her on some deeper level. Is that weird?"

Feeling someone's presence based off an inexplicable connection? Reyna tried not to laugh. Of course it was weird. It was her life.

"Not at all," Reyna replied. "I've heard that about twins."

A grunt snatched Reyna's attention over her shoulder.

Prisha's fingers fumbled with her magic against floating ropes and pulleys tangled overhead. The Capricorn let out another groan. Arms plopped at her sides and the ship's harnesses followed suit.

Charlie followed Reyna's narrowed sight line. "Prisha is good people."

"Maybe so," Reyna replied. "But I wish she would've told me what was happening, instead of forcing magic on me."

"She tried telling you at your apartment."

Reyna's teeth ground together. She hated that he was right. "It still should've been my choice."

"People are forced to do stuff they don't want every day." Charlie shook his head. "Prisha didn't force anything on you. She gave you a fighting chance."

Reyna didn't want to admit it but couldn't deny her relief to be amongst these Zodiacs. Despite her initial reluctance to help, they'd still offered protection, a place to sleep, and honored Reyna's request to not engage with magic. If not for Charlie's and Prisha's actions last night, today might've gone much differently. Reyna had been so used to shutting others out, maybe Tessa would still be alive if she'd only let someone in.

Charlie nodded Reyna in Prisha's direction, and she approached the Capricorn still at war with ropes.

"What are you doing?" Reyna asked.

"Making a mess." Prisha rotated a forefinger and pulled her hand into a fist. "Luckily Sagittarius's fire makes *Polaris* self-navigating."

Reyna blinked. "If the ship sails itself, why're you shifting the sails?"

"Less changing course and more perfecting my magic." Prisha propped her hands on her hips. "Not that you'd understand."

Reyna gingerly stepped past, letting the jab roll off.

"You had a good handle on your magic at the club." Reyna untangled the knots by hand.

"With metals, sure." Prisha tucked strands from her wind-battered braid behind her ear. "But I want to master it all."

"How does starmagic work?" Reyna asked.

"Halley says we command it. Bend to our will. I don't get why plant-based materials Ethan manipulates don't respond the same to me."

"Have you tried not forcing it?" Reyna tugged a rope through a couple loops and yanked the largest knot free. "I imagine magic is a lot like emotions. Difficult to control, but with enough time and patience, amenable under the right circumstances."

The two women shared knowing smiles and silent resolution settled between them.

"Speaking of circumstances." Prisha stepped beside Reyna and began working through the knots with her. "How'd you end up in Brax's bedroom?"

"I didn't know it was his." A curtain of hair shielded Reyna's blush. "An honest mistake."

"I'm not surprised you mistook his room for being empty." Prisha pulled at another rope cluster. "He's only around half the time."

Reyna feigned casual interest. "Where does he go?"

"Who knows." Prisha shrugged. "Probably tapping into one of his connections."

Reyna stopped fiddling with the ropes. "What do you mean?"

"Remember I said we used nonmagical ways of finding you? Brax is good at locating people and making us scarce. He's a con artist, and a damn good one too. We wouldn't have made it this far without him." Prisha blinked at her own admission. "Don't repeat that."

"Explains how he goes from hot to cold easily."

"That's a Leo for you," Prisha replied. "Sign of fire, sun, lion, and everything aggravating about the male species. There's no road map to him." A grin dimpled her cheek. "But I wouldn't blame a girl for wanting to draw one."

Sunrise dancing along Brax's golden eyes.

Constellations of scars lining his back.

An immaculate V-line beckoning Reyna's gaze far lower than she dared.

She'd rarely allowed herself close enough to notice such intimate details about anyone. Let alone linger on them. Without her ability to anticipate the Zodiacs' emotions, Reyna was able to exist in moments undiluted by fear.

"I don't want to draw anything." Reyna swatted the dangerous thought away. "He's crass and obnoxious."

Prisha snickered in agreement. "If it gives you any personal satisfaction, he's terrified of water."

"Do you have anyone special at home?" Reyna moved the conversation from Brax.

"Not if I have anything to say about it." Prisha's nose wrinkled. "My mother keeps setting me up, but I'm capable of securing and botching my own love life. Luckily, the Zodiacs found me before I was subjected to another awkward coffee date."

"What'd you tell your parents?"

"I was chosen for an all-expenses paid summer semester abroad and I'd be unreachable." Prisha grinned wider. "I neglected to say how far abroad."

"That's the best you could do?" Brax's voice cut like a knife.

"What?" Prisha peered past Reyna. "I was in school for anthropology—it's plausible."

"An unreachable internship?" Brax replied. "Maybe in the Stone Age. We left abruptly, which indicates to anyone with half a brain, no planning was involved."

"Oh, so you have half a brain?" Prisha rolled her eyes. "Such a waste it's all ego."

"It's not ego if you can back it up."

"I'm pretty sure that's still ego," Prisha replied.

"Well ..." Reyna squared her shoulders and both Zodiacs pivoted toward her. Immediate regret flooded Reyna for opening her mouth, but their waiting expressions forced her to finish. "Not everyone is a professional liar."

Prisha snorted with delayed laughter.

Brax stepped into Reyna's space.

"Easy, Brax," Prisha's voice dropped. "We're all just having fun. She didn't mean any—"

"I'm all about fun." He towered over Reyna like a fiery tidal wave ready to decimate. Flames licked the hands at his sides and a toothy grin reached the corner of his eyes. "You wanna spar, Sunshine? I like what happens when water gets hot."

Reyna raised a brow. "Aren't you afraid of water?"

Prisha's head knocked back, howling with laughter. Fire lit the gold around Brax's pupils.

"Correction, Sunshine. I'm afraid of deep water." He stepped forward and whispered in Reyna's ear, a smile curving along her cheek. "How deep could you take me?"

Reyna's mouth went dry.

"Take it down a notch," Ethan's voice smothered Brax's grin. "Reyna said she's not using magic."

"No one asked you, Beefaroni." Brax's jaw clenched. "I wanna see what the new girl's got."

"This isn't the time," Ethan replied.

Brax's head cocked. "Anyone who doesn't defend themselves isn't gonna make it far against an immortal, but you already know all about that, don't you?"

A hinge flipped open in Ethan's eyes.

"Got something to say? Say it." Ethan flung his arms wide. "Though you've never needed an invitation to run your mouth."

Brax stepped into Ethan's space. Charlie jogged from across deck and wedged himself between them. "Easy, bros! Let's all take a breather."

Brax tipped his chin up at Ethan. "It's your fault Sparky was taken."

Ethan staggered back from the invisible dagger shoved through his chest.

"Who's—" Reyna stopped at Prisha shaking her head.

"Jade is Aries. She was taken by Dredgers," Ethan murmured at the floor.

"She got *taken* because you were too unprepared and stupid!" Brax jabbed a finger at him.

"I tried." Ethan inhaled deep. "There were too many and—"

"Weak." Brax spat. "If I'd been there—"

"But you weren't!" Ethan glowered at him. "You were off doing whatever it is you do. If anyone failed her, it was you!"

Red flashed in Brax's eyes. He shoved Charlie aside and charged Ethan. The two men tumbled onto the deck in a tangle of punches. Ethan planted a foot against Brax's chest and kicked him off. Brax slammed onto his spine, rolling across the planks onto all fours.

"Stand down, Brax." Ethan stood. "I don't want to fight you."

"I wouldn't wanna fight me either." Brax's fists ignited. "I told you to wait for me!" He shot a fireball at his target.

Ethan dodged. He flicked two fingers and snapped part of the ship's handrail. It hurtled toward the fire sign. Brax rotated into a fluid sidestep, tossed a fire lasso around the rail, and whipped it at Ethan. Ethan threw his hands overhead, floorboards peeling with the motion. The flame-engulfed rail shattered into charred ash against Ethan's wooden shield.

"I'm sorry Jade got taken!" Ethan shouted through the flames. "But it was her choice to come clean. You were leaving us vulnerable to Levant's capture!"

"I had a plan!" Brax opened his palm and blew a fiery cyclone. "Instead, you exchanged one Zodiac for another!"

Ethan's hands rose at the swell of heat. "What upsets you more?" his accent roughened with each accusation punching between them. "That Jade told us your secret, or that she betrayed your trust?"

"What's this?" Halley screeched, rushing over in a flurry. "I insist you cease immediately!"

Floorboards groaned beneath Ethan and snapped free. He shot a jagged hailstorm of splinters toward Brax. Wood shards flared into embers from the heat off Brax's skin before they could make contact. Fire licked *Polaris*'s bones and black smoke billowed into blue sky. Ethan fell to his knees, heaving for breath.

"Reyna!" Prisha choked on the black smoke. "Put out the fire!"

"I-I can't." Reyna stared at her trembling hands. Someone always got hurt whenever she used magic. Why would water magic be any different?

"Charlie!" Prisha waved her hands through the dark haze. "Can you blow out the flames?"

"There's too much fire!" he shouted. "Air will feed it."

"Reyna!" Prisha coughed. "You're the only one who can stop it!"

Brax's blond hair glinted through the fire and his biceps strained alongside the focused rage illuminating his face.

"Do something!" Prisha shouted. "Now!"

Reyna's fingers curled together as she lunged through the fire. Her fist cracked across Brax's jaw.

He stumbled backward. The inflamed tornado around Ethan evaporated and Brax shook disorientation from his vision. Flames eating the ship, slowly extinguished with his disrupted focus.

"Enough, Most Extravagant Zodiacs!" Hailey threw herself between the men before their rigor could reignite. "This behavior is unacceptable! I suggest you behave like the legendary celestials you are before we reach Nidus. From this moment forth, no more star-magic use aboard *Polaris*!"

"Whatever." Brax rubbed and flexed his jaw. "I'm outta here." He dug cigarettes from his pocket and traipsed into the ship's cabin.

CHAPTER

EIGHT

SILENCE DRONED AMONGST THE ZODIACS SEATED AROUND *Polaris*'s firepit as they tended whatever thoughts plagued them from the earlier altercation. Reyna hissed at the slight flex of her knuckles as aches shot from fingers to wrist. She tugged off her glove and inspected her hand in the fire's glow. No blood or bruises decorated her skin, but her reddened knuckles were puffier than they should be.

What had come over her?

A question Reyna had asked herself countless times since the afternoon. Physical action had never been her first, second, or even third instinct. What about Brax unraveled a lifetime of practiced control? The easy way she'd curled into him while they'd slept. The satisfying crack of knocking him down a peg. A man, whose mere smile pulled her like an undertow and, in the next breath, made her beg to come up for air. Reyna shook her head and pulled her glove on. This wasn't like her. Not at all.

"How's it hanging, slugger?"

Reyna glanced up at threads of hair wisping across Prisha's smile. A gym bag thumped onto the floor between them and the Capricorn sat cross-legged beside her. She slid the bag beside Reyna.

"What's this?" Reyna unzipped the top. Her breath caught at the familiar patterns and colors.

"I thought you might need those," Prisha replied.

Reyna rifled through her old clothing.

"I felt crappy after what happened in San Diego, so I went back to your place and grabbed some of your things before we left." Prisha picked at her fingernails. "I wanted to give it to you sooner."

"Thank you." Reyna beamed before her face fell a little. "How'd you get inside my apartment?"

"Metal locks are kind of my specialty." Prisha grinned and wiggled her fingers. "Why does your apartment have so many?"

An excuse hovered on Reyna's tongue. Before she could speak, the cabin door burst open. Halley emerged from belowdecks, arms flailing. Incomprehensible words grumbled through her pursed lips and Reyna couldn't help smiling. Even flustered, Halley still embodied a sense of joy.

"Good evening, Most Esteemed Zodiacs." Halley flitted around the firepit. "Ever Proud Braxton shan't be joining us, but I still believe it prudent to share tales of your beginnings before we arrive at Nidus tomorrow." Halley's hands raised in front of the lit pit. "To understand where you began, you must first understand your makers."

Two tiny lights wove around one another from the flames. They gleamed brighter and Reyna squinted over her raised forearm as they collided. A pair of misty figures floated toward each other.

Halley walked around the pit. "Our goddess and god were forged by the Infinite All-Knowing. For a millennium, they traveled throughout the vast emptiness of space and many galaxies were born in the wake of their love."

Stars shimmered like glitter suspended in air as nebulas and foreign planets rippled outward from the deities. A ball of flames rose from the fire and planets within Earth's solar system circled around the miniature sun.

"Our makers never desired beyond one another, until one did." The projection of the goddess plucked Earth from orbit and cradled it in her palm. "In all worlds created from their love, they'd never once created something capable of producing and sustaining its own love."

Earth floated from the goddess's hands and enlarged.

"However, creation of humanity required a sacrifice neither

could anticipate. For life to flourish on Earth, the Infinite All-Knowing demanded balance. Our god's light was stripped, whilst the goddess's remained intact."

The misty god writhed away from his companion and dropped to his knees while gritty black smoke swallowed him whole. The goddess sobbed into her hands.

"Though a heavy price paid, they carried on and created the island of Nidus. It became their home. Both a garden to prepare new souls for rebirth unto Earth, and a final resting place once a soul's earthly time finished. As humanity's numbers grew, our makers grew weary. So, they created others like themselves from the stars, to guide Nidian souls through teachings which prepared them for life on Earth.

"Our makers gifted these Zodiacs with strengths and symbols they desired to flourish on Earth. Our goddess loved mortals beyond all else, so she gifted her creations with human figures. Gem and Ini, the adaptable twins. Aquarius, visionary water bearer. Sagittarius, the idealistic archer. Virgo, the practical maiden, with her the gracious but just scales of Libra. Because our Dark God praised the beasts of this new world, he blessed his creations with traits of his favorite creatures. Pisces, the mystic fishes, and Aries, the courageous ram.

"He also created Taurus, the devoted bull." A starry bull charged from within the pit's fire and exploded into stardust against Ethan's chest. Saturn's rings swirled into a cluster of stars. A goat punched outward and leapt from nebula to nebula. "Capricorn, the disciplined goat."

Silvery light bled from Earth's moon like watercolor and a crab shimmered from its cosmic paint. Halley smiled at Reyna. "Cancer, the intuitive crab."

A thunderous roar shook the deck. A lion pounced from within the miniature sun and strutted through the air. "And of course"—Halley pursed her lips—"the passionate lion, Leo."

Each Zodiac form danced around the god and goddess.

"For a time, Earth and Nidus teemed with life," Halley continued.

"But even with the help of their new cosmic companions, the Dark God drifted farther from his goddess. He no longer found peace within the world they had created and sank into the darkest corners of the Nidian Sea, into the Forgotten." Nidus flipped like a glacier with an identical island below. Dredgers scoured its darkened cities. Screams howled along its shadowy streets. "Though the God of Darkness laid claim to the underworld, he still returned to the surface in search of souls. A constant punishment to our goddess for choosing humanity over him."

The projection fell away, and the fire's glow flickered back to its rainbow hues.

"What about the Zodiacs?" Reyna edged closer. "Why were we reborn mortal?"

Halley smiled through her frown. "I'm afraid that's a tale only the goddess can tell."

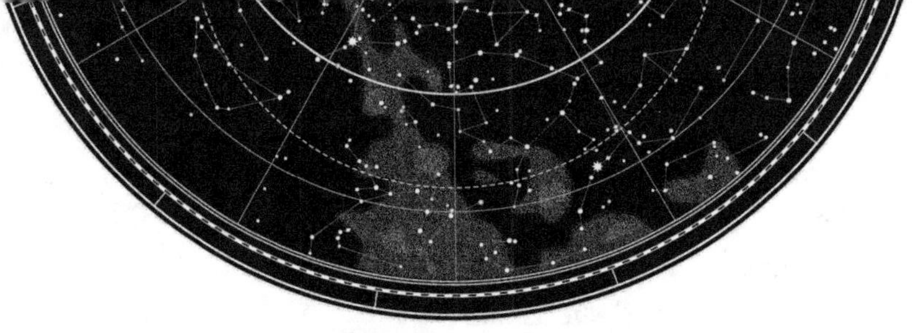

CHAPTER

NINE

A BLACK VELVETEEN SKY CAME INTO FOCUS THROUGH Reyna's blurred edges of sleep. Tiny stars bejeweled the night's unraveled fabric, each like a rhinestone catching light with the slightest tilt of her chin. Reyna reached, sure if she stretched far enough, the stars would vanish like fireflies into the night. How strange to think of stars as living, breathing things. Did they breathe? The Zodiacs were crafted from them, so it could be possible. But whatever parts of Reyna were forged from starlight lay buried deep. Smothered by the dark existence she now led.

The Zodiacs had retired to their quarters and the Eternal Flame earned its reputation well. Reyna rose from her gym bag pillow and padded past the pit's silvery flames. She relaxed against the rail. Waited for the Pacific's thumping waves or a gentle spray of salt. When neither came, she peeked over the ledge. A strange fog coiled at the vessel's base. Reyna rose onto her toes and squinted at the stars' watery reflection between patches of swirling mist. Not reflections.

Earth's cities glittered miles below the clouds.

Reyna's stomach dropped and her knees buckled.

"Whoa, there." Hands caught her hips from behind.

Reyna's spine pressed along Brax's chest, the fear of tumbling to her death overriding every one of their prior encounters. His heart thumped like a metronome and for a moment, they stood in perfect sync with one another. Brax's grip slackened, but he didn't let go.

"The ship is flying," Reyna sputtered.

"Your powers of observation are as solid as your right hook." A smile wrapped itself in his voice. Brax released Reyna's waist and lit a cigarette.

"How is it flying?" she asked.

"Brace yourself." Brax pointed toward the stars with a cigarette wedged between his fingers. "We're riding the North Star. No matter where *Polaris* is, we look like a stationary star to everyone below."

Reyna blinked. "Impossible."

"Impossible got thrown out the door the second Varma knocked on yours." Brax turned his back to her and leaned against the ship's rail.

A chill glided over Reyna's skin. She rubbed her arms and whimpered at the flex of her wrist.

"How's your hand?" Brax sucked his cigarette.

Reyna pressed her lips together, unsure how to answer. "Sore."

"Next time, punch with your knuckles instead of the flats of your fingers." He blew smoke into the night. "Hurts a helluva lot less after."

Reyna stared at the blond knot tied at the back of his head. She wished he'd cuss her. Offer some halfhearted threat at retaliation. Any emotional signal her other magic might've recognized for spite, so she could understand what simmered beneath his stoic demeanor. Not a trace of venom lined his words, and she didn't know whether to be relieved or worried.

"I'm sorry I hit you," Reyna offered.

"You're apologizing? Damn." Brax snorted and sipped another drag. "We're in worse shape than I thought."

Her defenses reignited. "I don't like hurting people."

"Never be sorry for doin' what needs to be done."

"Are you admitting you did something wrong?"

Brax snickered good-naturedly. "For what it's worth, Beefcake wasn't in any real danger. Zodiacs can't hurt each other with our magic."

"So, you thought you'd test the theory?"

"Don't pretend to know me."

Reyna crossed her arms over her chest. He was right. She didn't know any of the Zodiacs, but in forty-eight hours, they'd shared more than she had with anyone. Reyna never imagined she'd miss her other magic's intuition, but she didn't need magic to recognize the sour tinge of guilt laced through Brax's words when he'd fought Ethan.

If I'd been there …

"You care for the woman who got taken." Reyna stepped closer. "Who's she to you?"

Brax slouched his shoulders. "My partner."

Reyna couldn't help latching on to the word. She smothered her misplaced disappointment and asked, "What happened?"

"We were searching for you for a couple weeks. What the others didn't know is I'd already found you." Brax's cigarette flared with his inhale. "I'd been keeping tabs on you long before we got to the city."

Reyna's mouth tumbled open. "You spied on me?"

"Monitored you," he corrected. "A guy in San Diego owed me a favor. He moved into the apartment beside yours and reported daily."

"The creep living next door?" A glare crunched between Reyna's eyes.

Brax raised a brow over his shoulder. "Did he hurt you?"

"No." Embarrassment diluted her annoyance. "He asked me on a date."

Brax assessed her with a smirk.

"He was forward." She shrugged. "Didn't like my answer."

"Can't blame 'em." Brax retrained his attention on the sky. "Being shot down by you would be 'nough to ruin a man for life."

Unwanted heat reddened Reyna's cheeks as she pushed past his compliment. "How'd you know who and where I was?"

"Our Zodiac connection." Brax tapped ash over the rail. "The way Halley tells it, the minute Levant began returning to our solar system, the Zodiacs were reborn and gradually drawn back to one another. I'd guess it's how we all ended up in the States."

"If we're all drawn together, why'd you needed unmagical means to find me?"

"Our pull toward one another is more instinctual than accurate. Think of it like a compass pointing in the right direction but unable to mark the spot. Each move from our sides was a race to see who could grab the next of us. If the Dark-Aligned Zodiacs moved a yard line, we tackled. If we made a play, they intercepted. Once we felt them making their way toward the West Coast, we figured they'd found you."

"Of course, you already knew."

Brax gave a single nod. "Before we came to Cali, my partner, Sparky, hacked into the state's birth certificates. Since we're all born the same year, your birthday falling during a specific window, it narrowed possibilities fast. I asked her to keep your location between us."

"Why?" Reyna asked.

"My contact said you laid low, and I know what it's like to not wanna be found. I figured if there was a chance the Dark God couldn't find you, one of us might escape this celestial shit show. Beef-For-Brains kept asking Sparky about progress on your whereabouts and she caved. No interrogation. No threats. Nothing." Brax flicked his cigarette overboard. "She said this shit was bigger than us and the Zodiacs had a right to know."

"Is that why you and Ethan don't get along?"

Brax's grip on the rail tightened. Smoke coiled from the simmering wood beneath his hands. "After Beefaroni discovered your location, they made a move. I told them I had eyes on you and to wait until we could find an in, without giving away your whereabouts. But once they learned I'd kept your location secret, it left a bad taste in their mouth. Beefcake led the charge, and the Dark-Aligned ambushed them on the freeway. They were outnumbered and the others snatched Sparky as a consolation prize."

"The Interstate 5 fiasco ..." Reyna murmured.

Brax's brow arched.

"My friend was an EMT who responded to the pileup," Reyna explained. "It's where she met Jace. How he found me. Why she's—" Reality surfaced like bile in Reyna's throat.

"Whoa, hey." Brax turned and cupped her face. "We were all

destined to find each other. It was gonna be ugly no matter how shit went down. It's not your fault."

She trembled, each breath coming out in a short puff.

Nothing about Reyna's life belonged to her. Not her friend's death. Her sleazeball neighbor. Not even her decision to go to the club. Every unconscious move she made was predetermined to bring her to this spot.

Reyna met Brax's golden stare alive with fire, rivaled only by the thumbs stroking her cheekbones. Breaths passed between them and her gaze dropped to his lips.

Close.

They were standing much too close.

"I can't ..." The base of Reyna's spine met the rail.

"You can't what?" Understanding wove through his slow smile.

"You and Jade are—"

"Partners." Brax gripped the ship on either side of her. "We hustle together, but we're *not* together."

Polaris broke above the clouds with Reyna caught somewhere between the world's edge and a free fall into the next. She steadied the rise and fall of her chest. An inhale away from his.

"Your new friends aren't around." Brax's playfulness darkened. "You can stop pretending you don't like me."

"Who says I'm pretending?" Reyna forced conviction. She had no intention of sticking around once her magic was removed, and any attachment would make it harder to disappear.

"That's not very nice." A sinful chuckle dripped from his lips. "You might've almost hurt my feelings." Brax's fingers scraped across Reyna's neck and unfurled beneath her hairline. An undeniable need for his touch catapulted her pulse into song.

"Brax ..." Reyna didn't recognize her hoarse voice.

"Tell me to stop," he said.

Four letters and he'd step back. She'd welcome oxygen once more and the space between them would grow cold with what could've never been. Brax's thumb caressed her jaw, and a soft hum vibrated over her lips.

Reyna closed her eyes and arched her throat. Dizzy. Drunk. Waiting. Wanting. Insides screaming for his heat against her lips.

Why wasn't he kissing her yet?

Reyna's eyelids drifted open to Brax glowering into the endless night behind her.

"What's wrong?" Her question, a breathy whisper.

"Dredgers."

CHAPTER

TEN

P OLARIS DESCENDED INTO MURKY CLOUDS PULSING WITH soft lightning.

"Listen," Brax whispered.

Reyna waited for sound. A movement. Any sign other than thunder grumbling over the deck.

"I don't hear anything," she replied.

"Exactly." Brax ground his jaw. "Is the pit out?"

She squinted through thick gray haze behind him and nodded.

Brax cursed under his breath. "Listen carefully. Go belowdecks and—"

The ship's bow reared.

Brax fell backward and Reyna landed on his chest. Wood groaned as they slid along the deck and slammed into a glass mast. Reyna broke free, but Brax hooked an arm around her waist and held tight until the ship teetered to a stop. They stared at one another through raindrops plunking around them.

Waiting. Listening.

Lightning illuminated four silhouettes amongst the clouds. A screech reverberated over the ship's ivory planks and Brax's eyes flew wide. He shoved Reyna aside and blasted fire at a Dredger diving toward them. The creature flailed into the sky screeching. A heavier blanket of rain unfolded over the ship, extinguishing Brax's display.

"They don't like light!" He scrambled over to Reyna on all fours. "Get belowdecks. I'll hold 'em off."

"No! I won't leave—"

"Go!" Brax rolled onto his back and punched another fury of fireworks above. "Now!"

Reyna bolted, bare feet splattering toward the ship's cabin door. As she reached for the knob, Halley, Prisha, and Ethan burst through. Dread dilated in their faces. Dredgers swiped at Brax overhead like sharks sampling their prey while another stalked him from behind.

"Brax!" Reyna screamed through the downpour, but he continued shooting fire at his frontal attackers. Prisha sprinted with fingers splayed above her head. Nails ripped from the deck into a gaping maw. Her hands smacked together, and jagged metal chomped through whatever flesh embodied the dark specters. Another Dredger barreled into Prisha from the side and her body thumped against the floor. Reyna stepped forward. Ethan snatched her wrist.

"What are you doing?" Reyna ripped her hand from his. "Someone needs to help them!"

"You can't!" he shouted through rain cascading over his face. "Not without magic!"

Reyna's heart clenched under the truth of his words. She searched for a retort. A reason to tell him he was wrong.

Ethan faced Halley. "Can you relight the pit?"

"I cannot!" Halley's fiery hair surged brighter over her pale shoulders. "Only Sagittarius can ignite the Eternal Flame. We'll need to ward them off another way." She launched into a purple streak of sky-bound fire.

"Go inside," Ethan instructed Reyna. "You'll be safer."

"There has to be something I can do?"

"We can stop them but not if we're protecting you too."

"Where are you going to do?" Reyna demanded. "We're on a ship in the sky!"

Ethan pointed at the helm spinning out of control. "With the flame unable to cloak us from wind, *Polaris* can't steer itself. We need to maneuver out of the storm and gain the upper hand."

Before Reyna could respond, Ethan dashed toward the helm.

Dredgers bellowed with each punch of Halley's comet tail through the clouds. One creature swooped low. Brax and Prisha dropped onto their stomachs, and he shouted something beside her. The Capricorn shook her head feverishly.

"C'mon!" Brax roared through the monsoon.

Prisha hesitated a second longer and grabbed his hand.

A lantern whizzed past Reyna's head.

Silverware. A pan. Another lantern. The window shattered beside Reyna. Framed art shot from inside the ship. Silver trinkets, hooks, nails, and all matter of metal soared from every corner of *Polaris*, magnetizing into armor along Brax's body. He stood tall, arms raised to invite skyborne fire. Webbed electricity sizzled through his body.

Dredgers don't like light.

Reyna gasped. "She's turning him into a conduit."

If any of them could survive lightning's heat, it was Brax. But he wasn't immortal. What if starfire magic wasn't strong enough to protect his human body? The steel cage around Reyna's heart tugged toward him too, but her back remained against the wall.

He held on. A roar of pain mingled with his determination as light bled over the ship's deck. Dredgers shrieked and retreated into their cloudy refuge.

Hope gripped Reyna's heart.

It was working.

Ethan's forearms strained against the helm. Relentless winds tried wrestling the wheel from his grasp. Magical roots burst from floorboards around his feet, anchoring him to the spot. Lightning illuminated a Dredger towering over Ethan from behind.

"Ethan! Watch out!" Reyna screamed, too far away.

Her focus whipped back to Prisha and Brax, willing them to notice Ethan, but Prisha fell onto her knees beside Brax, unable to keep both balance and focus on the metals.

All Reyna ever did was lock herself in an apartment.

Pray her barrage of locks and walls was enough to keep her demons at bay.

But these weren't Reyna's demons. They were real monsters, attacking people who risked their lives for Reyna's.

Ethan's stalker howled as it dove from behind. Reyna thrust a single hand toward the Dredger.

Nothing.

"No!" Reyna pleaded with whatever magic inside her would listen. "Help him!"

The inexplicable force she'd met while awoken at the club swelled within once again. Ancient star power bowed before Reyna and tingled at her fingertips.

"Stop!" Her hand punched forward again.

A noose of rain choked Ethan's Dredger to a halt.

The creature writhed against Reyna's restraint. Another Dredger noticed the interference and darted for her. She tumbled onto the ground, its claws slashing through her sleeve. Reyna's hold on her target was severed. She pushed herself from the ground and charged toward Ethan. Water pooled beneath her feet, hydroplaning her along the storm-slicked deck.

The Dredger's claws rose above Ethan's head.

Reyna's watery surf launched her into an arc across the deck. The creature's head twisted toward her. Claws plunged into her left shoulder. Reyna howled in unison with the Dredger's triumphant screech. She tried ripping herself from its grip, but icy fire snaked along her shoulder to the center of her chest. The Dredger's claws dissolved into black smoke.

Reyna smacked onto wet concrete.

She moaned and pushed herself onto all fours. Instinct drew Reyna's hand over her impaled shoulder, but no ripped cotton or tattered flesh brushed her hand. Had she managed to escape somehow? Reyna sat upright, staring at her gloveless hands. She wiggled her polished fingernails, trying to remember the last time she'd painted them.

Brazen Blue.

Her favorite polish from another life when she could still pretend she was like everyone else. A time before everything changed forever.

The surrounding darkness receded until a pair of familiar light brown eyes stared back at her. Reyna smoothed her hands over her soft cheeks. Over the flyaways of her hair pulled into a ponytail. Reyna's young reflection blinked at her from the sliding glass door of her childhood home.

A faint glimmer of hope took flight within.

For a moment, Reyna let herself live the daydream. The possibility that she never grew up. A chance to do things different.

"Look at this mess." *His* voice curdled in her ears.

Nausea lit like a match in Reyna's belly. Every muscle seized. She couldn't breathe. Didn't want to exist.

"Ya 'ear me?" his slurred consonants gutted her. "Clean this fuckin' shit up."

Reyna forced herself to look over her reflection's shoulder, praying if she didn't look upon him with her own eyes, he might not take true form. Papá sat slouched on his favorite patio chair. The illusion of a dignified man. One that always dissolved beneath the bottle dangling from his fingertips.

"Reyna!" he snarled. "Get over 'ere now!"

Reyna's limbs obeyed, overriding her primal desire to flee. She slowly walked toward him, fingernails biting into her palms.

Today was her twelfth birthday.

Perhaps he'd gift her the wish she prayed for every day. His blackouts.

Papá rubbed at the bags beneath his bloodshot eyes, shooing her with his other hand toward the cluttered table. Reyna stacked paper plates smeared with frosting and smiled at the yellow crescent moon decorating a half-eaten sheet cake. It'd been an eclipse theme for her party. Abuela's idea.

Reyna craned her neck at the dark moon clipping the sun's edge above.

"Damn waste of money if ya ask me." Her papá knocked a final swig of whatever wetted his bottle. "You're lucky I gave you this party."

"You didn't." Reyna snorted under her breath. She clutched the plates tighter, the regret of her too-late mistake blanching her face.

"What'd you say?" Papá squinted at her as though she was an insect and rose from his chair.

"I meant—I'm sorry. I didn't—"

Reyna's cheek crunched onto the patio tabletop.

Glass spider-webbed outward from her face. Hot tears marred with fresh blood as Reyna rejected every instinct to struggle against the hand holding her in place. Compliance would soften whatever came next.

"Ungrateful brat!" He flipped Reyna onto her spine. "After what you did to 'er, you deserve nothing!"

Reyna's blue fingernails scraped at the massive hands burrowing into her neck. Her adolescent muscles faltering with each second that passed. Fire sizzled in her lungs. The corners of her vision blurred. Something primal swam to the surface. Overrode her will to submit. She writhed, splattering the sheet cake onto the cement. Reyna stared past her papá's head at the eclipse.

"It's your fault she's dead!" His forceful grunts muffled within Reyna's ringing ears. "All I see when I look at you is death!"

A tear glided down Reyna's cheek.

"Then"—she gurgled—"stop looking!"

Reyna's absorption magic grabbed the hands around her throat. Warmth flooded her body like a deep inhale. Her papá's eyes bulged and his grip loosened. Reyna pressed his hands tighter against her skin. Poured her fear into him while she syphoned his life-force.

He stumbled backward gasping for the air she'd stolen. His desperate hand snatched Reyna's shoulder and pulled her with him. She slipped on cake frosting and was flung from his grip. Reyna's head slammed against the pool's ledge. Metallic tang exploded across her tongue. She rolled and plunked into the pool.

Water fizzed around Reyna as she sank into a tomb of chlorine.

The moon warped above the surface and the world around her muffled. Slimy fingers tugged Reyna's ankles deeper into the bottomless pool until she met the bloated corpses of her new Zodiac companions. Their water-rotted jaws tried speaking but no sound came. Brax drifted in front of her, his once sun-kissed skin pallid with decay. In the quiet abyss between life and beyond, Brax cupped her face and whispered Reyna's greatest fear. Her most profound truth.

"It's time to let go." Brax's smile elongated past his milky irises. "You'll kill us all, Reyna."

She blinked at her true name on his lips.

Dredgers manifest your worst nightmares until they kill you.

Her greatest fear.

None of this was real.

Reyna grabbed Brax's wrists and beckoned her absorption magic. She dug for whatever life source the imposter clung to. And there, floating in darkness, a single frayed thread. Reyna grabbed the lifeline and pulled. Brax's face contorted. His roar rippled through the pool. Reyna held tighter. Putrid rivers of black sludge oozed from every crevice of his body. The other Zodiacs released Reyna's legs and sank from view. The final drops of darkness leaked from Brax and light exploded from within. A naked brunette woman haloed by soft light replaced his floating form.

"Thank you, Lady Cancer." The woman's words rang as clear as if they were above the surface. "Dredgers feed off the fears of others because we're trapped by our own."

Reyna gaped. "You're the Dredger?"

The spirit of light offered a single nod. "Our fear of not moving on becomes our eternal prison. You absorbed the fears chaining my dark form. Now I am free."

"So, I'm not … dead?" Uncertainty gripped Reyna.

"You've only begun, my lady." A slow smile spread over the woman's cheeks. "I vow to spend the rest of my days making you proud."

The woman surged brighter and swallowed Reyna in a bath of white starlight.

CHAPTER

ELEVEN

B LURRY ORBS OF LIGHT DANCED BETWEEN REYNA'S EYELIDS. She rose against the heavy down of her comforter and the world sharpened. Aches stabbed through her muscles and between bone. Reyna hissed, her hand pressing along the white cloth wrapped across her clavicle and shoulder.

This wasn't a vision. A nightmare. Or wherever else she'd been. She was real and so was the pain.

Reyna exhaled at her Zodiac bedroom she'd spent little time in since boarding *Polaris.* Crisp lines of white and Grecian cyan elongated its walls to a silver-plated ceiling. The room exuded regal opulence, though enough comfort invited one to stay. Perhaps a homage to her Zodiac self.

She followed the spotlight streaming through a porthole and her heart quickened. The room's only shimmer of gold and the sun found him. Brax sat slouched against the door. Head rested back, throat arched, blond hair draped over a sleeping eye, and a single leg sprawled outward with his arm propped atop the other knee. Reyna slowly padded across the room and crouched beside the lion slumbering at her door. Gone was the clammy bloat of his fingers. The watery rot once gaunt in his cheeks. Sleepless shadows painted the underside of his eyes. Wrinkles weathered his clothing, and the scruff of his jaw thickened.

How long had she been unconscious?

Reyna reached for him and recoiled. Every instinct, a battle uncertain she'd ever win. Reyna swallowed hard and brushed aside his mane. Brax snatched her wrist and pressed a knife to her throat. She whimpered at the sting blazing through her shoulder. Brax's disorientation lit with recognition. His knife clattered to the floor, and he released her.

"You're awake?" His muscles remained rigid with adrenaline.

"Feels like it." Reyna grasped her shoulder.

"Shit." He scooped Reyna into his arms and placed her on the bed. As he pulled away, milky irises met hers.

You'll kill us all.

Reyna gasped and scrambled across the sheets.

"Whoa." Brax stepped away, hands raised. "It's gonna be okay. I …" His golden gaze dropped to the floor. "I can't do this." Brax swept from the room and insecurity filled the hollow around Reyna's heart.

What couldn't he do?

Before she could sink deeper into his meaning, Prisha stepped through the door. The Capricorn's hands raised over her mouth as though Reyna was a marveled mystery.

"Brax said you were awake." Prisha sat atop the mattress and slid her fingers over Reyna's bare hand. "How're you feeling?"

Reyna yanked her hand away and buried both under the blankets. Prisha's face fell.

"I don't want to hurt you," Reyna murmured.

"Hurt me?" Prisha's dimple hugged her cheek. "We're more concerned about you."

"Was anyone hurt?

"We're all fine," Prisha assured her.

"How long have I been out?"

"Three days."

Reyna released a long breath and sat against the headboard. "What happened?"

"After the Dredger attacked you, it exploded in a burst of light and the other Dredgers bailed. It was the most horrifyingly beautiful phenomenon I've ever seen."

"And everyone's okay?" Reyna asked again.

"Yes." Prisha's lyrical laughter smoothed Reyna's edge. "Charlie slept through everything, if you can believe it."

Reyna grinned. "Sounds about right."

"You're awake!" Halley whooshed into the room like a comet on a collision course. She flung her arms around Reyna. "Praise the Infinite All-Knowing!" She pulled back at Reyna's groan. "My apologies, Illustriously Daring Reyna. How's your mortal abrasion?"

"My huh?"

Halley's fingers danced near Reyna's shoulder without touching it.

"It hurts, but I think I'll live," Reyna replied.

"May I?" Halley asked.

Reyna nodded and Halley gingerly unwrapped the cloth. A rush of cool air kissed Reyna's bandaged skin, but she met another horror as she looked at her wound.

"Why am I naked?" Reyna yanked the sheet over her black strapless bra and underwear. She'd been so dazed upon waking. How long had she been exposed? Who had removed her clothes?

"No need for such modesty." Halley smiled. "As a star, you spent many Earth cycles free from any garments."

"I'm not a star now!" Reyna's cheeks flushed at the thought of Brax's earlier presence. "I'd like some clothes, please."

"Very well." Halley sighed. "But let me inspect your shoulder first?"

Reyna reluctantly lowered the sheet, and Halley studied her scarring flesh.

"Miraculous." Curiosity paraded over Halley's expression. "It's nearly healed, and I checked only last night."

"Is that unusual?" Prisha asked.

"Those skewered by Dredgers don't heal." Halley paused. "Because they do not survive."

Reyna's mouth went dry. "I should be dead?"

"A Dredger nightmare always kills its victim," Halley confirmed. "What do you remember?"

"She said I … freed her."

"You talked to it?" Prisha stepped beside the bed. "How's that possible?"

"Dredgers are not gratuitous monsters." Tears sheened over Halley's eyes. "They were once inhabitants of Nidus. However did you free one?"

Reyna had pledged to not reveal her other magic and failed spectacularly within forty-eight hours. Between an enemy attacking from all angles and those aboard quarreling amongst themselves, how long would she be able to hide her ability? Reyna had agreed to this journey, but she couldn't accomplish what she set out to do unless she understood her new reality. Perhaps if she gave a little of herself, she might get more in return.

"I could already do magic before the Zodiacs found me." Reyna's throat tightened with the truth she'd vowed to carry to the grave. "I can feel people's emotions through touch or proximity and they can feel mine." Reyna pulled the sheet tighter to her chest. "I can also absorb life forces or energy, which is how I freed the Dredger."

Her new companions glanced at one another.

"Most Mysterious Reyna," Halley mulled over her next words. "Only one being performs the extraction magic you speak of."

Hope tightened Reyna's chest and tilted her forward. If the goddess failed to rid her of magic, and another like Reyna possessed abilities like hers, maybe they could help her.

For the first time since meeting, Halley's frown resembled a frown. "The God of Darkness."

Silence detonated the room.

Halley continued, "When Levant devours a Nidian's light, he doesn't always consume it all. He sometimes leaves enough, binding them to him. It's how Dredgers are created."

Reyna imagined learning more about her other magic might bring peace. A moment when her entire life made sense. Not conjure more questions than answers. The most disturbing being *why* she possessed magic like the Dark God's?

"Fret not, Most Blessed Reyna." Halley rose from the bed, extending a true smile. "I'm sure the Goddess of Light will know what to make of all this. In the meantime, let us give thanks for our safe return home. Please join us above deck whenever you're ready."

Halley retreated above deck and Reyna swung her legs from bed. Her jaw clenched at the burn searing through her joints. Prisha placed a hand along Reyna's good elbow to help her rise. Reyna pulled away.

"Are you going to let me help?" Prisha bit.

"I'm fine." Reyna grabbed a fitted T-shirt from the bedside drawer and stood. "I don't need help."

Prisha's brow lifted. "Really?"

"Really." Reyna tugged the shirt over her head and a groan punched from her at the rotation of her shoulder.

Prisha huffed and stepped forward. "Will you let me—"

"I said no!" Reyna shouted and Prisha's face lit up. The push and pull of a lifetime of self-conditioning flooded Reyna's veins. "You heard what Halley said—my magic is like … *his*." Reyna turned away. "People die around me. You should stay away."

"So, you can't have friends because people die?" Prisha snorted. "That's dumb."

"What did you—"

"I said it's dumb," Prisha repeated.

"Trust me, it's better like this."

"Last I heard, Zodiacs can't kill each other with magic." Victory of debate wove into Prisha's stern posture. "So, are we going to do this the reasonable way or your way?"

Reyna smothered her almost smile and nodded.

Once dressed, Reyna followed Prisha above deck where the Zodiacs stood at the bow. Bright sunset bathed *Polaris* with its citrus glow while Earth and its neighboring planets hung in the sky like large pale moons prepped for sunset. Nestled within the sea below sat what Reyna could only assume was Nidus. A plaid blanket of gold-and-crimson trees sprawled the island's closest section, but mountains iced with snow bordered the autumn landscape. Worlds away from everything Reyna knew and still, the familiar mesmerized. Ordinary and unfathomable, all at once.

"Isn't it breathtaking?" Halley sighed.

"How are two seasons possible at once?" Reyna framed the clean divide with her hand.

"Nidus's regions represent the four earthly seasons." Halley pointed. "We'll be arriving through Messis, known as your autumn." Her hand rotated counterclockwise to snowy mountains. "Parhelia is winter, Flora is spring and Calidi, summer." Emerald valleys and fields dominated the islands' springtime region. Lush jungle tapered into white, palm-speckled beaches of summer hugging the sea. "You'll have plenty of time to explore all the splendors of Nidus, but first we must reunite with the Goddess of Light."

CHAPTER

TWELVE

POLARIS REUNITED WITH THE SEA AND ANCHORED alongside the island's breezy coast. Nightfall settled between the trees and all the Zodiacs could do was wait. Tomorrow, Halley would lead them to Omphalos at the island's center. They'd meet the goddess, and Reyna might finally be free of her magic.

She relaxed against the crow's nest's barrier. Radiant nebulas swirled amongst the sky and distant village lights winked. But for all Nidus's celestial beauty, Reyna couldn't tear her focus from the fire ashore. Far from reach, yet almost close enough to touch.

"Still hiding?" Prisha swung her leg over the nest's wall.

"I'm not hiding." Reyna zipped her hooded sweatshirt. "There's only room for one."

"Like I said, hiding." Prisha squeezed beside her. "You should be resting, not scaling rigging and worsening your injury."

Reyna rubbed her shoulder, the pain a dull whisper beneath her skin. "Halley says I'm almost healed. Besides, I think I've slept enough for a lifetime."

"We're still mortal and need to be careful."

Reyna exhaled. "I'm wondering if I was ever human."

"I won't pretend to understand what your life's been like." Prisha stared into the distance. "But no matter what, you'll always be a Zodiac. One of us."

"I'm not sure I deserve your friendship." Reyna smiled. "But I'm grateful."

"If all else fails"—Prisha shrugged—"I also accept gift cards."

Their shared laughter lightened Reyna's chest.

"I know it's not my business." Prisha turned serious. "But you should talk to him."

"He'd rather be alone." Reyna nodded at Brax's beached campsite.

"Leos never want to be alone."

"Okay, maybe just alone from me."

"How do you figure?"

The Zodiacs knew Reyna's secret now, and despite Prisha's kind words, each moment evolved Reyna into something worse. Brax knew it. Soon, everyone else would too.

"I defeated the undefeatable." Reyna wrapped her arms around herself. "I probably freaked everyone out."

Prisha laughed. "You saved us."

"Brax pulled a knife on me."

"A reflex." Prisha shooed the thought away with her hand. "Brax refused to let anyone near your room. He sat constant guard at your door."

"He was afraid of what I'd do to all of you."

Prisha laughed. "I haven't known Brax long, but he never acts outside of his own interests. He wasn't protecting us. He protected you from ... everyone else."

"Why?"

Prisha grinned. "Why don't you ask him?"

"What if you're wrong?" Reyna wrung her hands together. "What if he's afraid of me?"

"Are you sure it's *his* fear you're worried about?" Prisha reached for Reyna's good shoulder and stopped short. "I get it's difficult for you to let people in, but what good is emotion magic, if you never allow yourself to understand your own?"

Reyna missed coming home. The squeak of her sneakers across the lobby. Keys jingling from her purse like wind chimes. Their click grinding open her apartment's lock. A similar sensation bloomed within Reyna once more as sand shushed along her dinghy's underside.

She pulled the small boat farther ashore and strode toward Brax's camp. A breeze rippled over his makeshift tent fashioned from gold bedsheets. Their same high thread count, a caress over her memory of waking beside someone for the first time. Brax sat slouched against a rock through the fire's sputters and snaps, mouth wrapped around a half-smoked cigarette, and every bit as formidable at his most relaxed. Reyna's steps slowed. Resignation sank her deeper into the sand. What did she hope to gain by approaching him?

To find out the reason why he'd slept armed at her door. Why he couldn't leave fast enough after she woke. Why he camped away from ship. Though none of those answers would quell the question Reyna couldn't stop asking herself.

Why did she care?

A twig snapped to Reyna's right. She jumped and stared into the silhouetted tree line beside her. Wind ceased rustling through the forest and a pair of emerald eyes blinked at her through its dark foliage. Leaves scraped together at the stag's subtle shift of antlers and Reyna stumbled backward. She waited for it to charge, but an overwhelming familiarity captivated the beast's unnatural green gaze.

She knew those eyes.

Before Reyna could weigh the want and warning within, the beast trotted into the forest. Curiosity tugged her through the trees. The stag broke into a slow, steady gallop. Reyna's footsteps crunched faster against brittle, grassy ground. It was impossible to keep pace with such a creature but the ancient ache within beckoned her to try.

Reyna hurtled into a clearing.

She hunched over, lungs blazing with the night's chill. Leaves whispered amongst shadows and pebbled starlight over the ground. She listened for the stag. For a chirp of crickets. A choir of frogs. Any indication she wasn't alone, but only her labored breaths and nearby running water answered back.

A shadow slithered over Reyna's muddy sneakers.

She staggered away and hard fingers dug into her back. Reyna whirled on her assailant. The woman's stony lips hung ajar, and a single arm reached for the sky while the other curled around an invisible partner. Reyna swept over the dozen other statues surrounding her. Over the vacant hopelessness carved into their faces. Defeated expressions of those who rejected their fate but would meet it all the same. A sadness Reyna recognized all too well.

The breeze kicked up eerie, yet beautiful languid notes of *Moonlight Sonata* humming through the trees.

"Who's there?" Reyna steadied her tremble.

The mammoth beast of fur and muscle stepped into the clearing's disco. Colossal antlers brushed the treetops, and its cinder-block hooves quaked the ground. Frost crackled over fallen leaves with each step the stag drew closer. Every instinct screamed for Reyna to run, but she remained as paralyzed as the statues. The stag's snort fluttered through her hair and Reyna's lids squeezed shut. She waited for bucking antlers or a hoof to crunch bone. Instead, air whipped through the space before her. Reyna opened her eyes, and the stag was gone.

"I'm so done with this place." Reyna trudged the way she thought she came.

"But you've only just arrived," crooned a stranger draped over the original female statue. Lazy arms hung around its outstretched limbs and his chin rested atop its shoulder. "Though I can't say I blame you. I grew weary of Nidus long ago myself." His dark coat fluttered as he slunk to the ground and rested a temple against the mossy stone. Mischief paraded in his emerald irises.

Reyna's steps retreated. "Who are you?"

A playful grin hugged the five-o'clock shadow along his jaw. "Why seek answers you already possess?"

"You're … the other god."

His eyebrows gathered with mock offense. "Did you reduce me to that *other* god?"

Reyna darted for the trees. A black haze materialized in front of her and the god stepped from within. Reyna stumbled until her spine met a statue once more.

"I only meant"—Reyna steadied her breath—"you're like the goddess?"

"Like the goddess." Levant cracked his neck. "But most certainly, not like the goddess."

"What do you want?"

A sultry groan uncoiled from the Dark God. His gaze swept over her figure though he mapped every bruise, cut, and scrape through her clothes. "I want a great deal many things, but I'm more interested in what you want, Cancer."

"My name is Reyna," she bit back, harsher than she meant to.

"Rey-na." His tongue stroked her name. "You're the same but different. So much more …" Levant's lids drifted shut and he inhaled her hair. "Human."

His eyes flashed open. Their entirety shrouded black.

Reyna scrambled against the stone at her back. A single blink and his green gaze returned.

"Apologies." He chuckled. "Old habits."

"You asked what I want?" Reyna's chin lifted with false bravado. "I want to go back to the beach."

"Wrong." The god's frigid breath snaked over her neck. "You want freedom."

"You don't know anything about what I want."

"I understand more about you and your dark magic than anyone."

Whatever meager upper hand Reyna hoped she held collapsed.

The God of Darkness wielded extraction magic. Of course he'd known she did too.

"Come with me now, and I'll tell you everything you wish to know." Levant slowly unzipped the hoodie caging her rising and falling chest. "Show you what feats your magic could accomplish." He hooked a lithe finger into her shirt collar and pulled. Starlight glinted against his canines as he sighed at the nearly healed Dredger scar across her shoulder. "And perhaps, you could show me some things too?"

"I don't want magic."

"Most mortals spend their whole lives trying to be something they're not. Why deny what you are?"

… you'll always be a Zodiac. One of us.

As pretty as Prisha's words were, they were also naïve. Reyna would never truly be like them. Like anyone. Except, maybe him.

Anchors of unanswered questions collected over a lifetime hung around Reyna's neck. What would she do if the goddess couldn't remove her magic? Reyna refused to return to her old life. Not after tasting what life was like on the outside. If her magic couldn't be removed, she'd need help learning how to control it. Dormant pieces of Reyna scraped to crawl out from beneath her skin. To embrace this strange new god. Trust him. Despite every fiber she should believe otherwise. A deal with a demon.

A deal, she hoped she'd never need to make.

"And what is it you think I am?" Reyna held her breath.

"Powerful." Levant's rich voice coiled around her. "The goddess may have your allegiance." His nose lingered a brush away from Reyna's. "But you'll always return to the darkness. Always belong to me."

"Sunshine?" Brax's baritone echoed through the trees. "You out here?"

An undignified grunt rumbled from the god. His evergreen gaze lingered over Reyna's a second longer as he dissolved into the dark pockets strung between starlight.

CHAPTER

THIRTEEN

Plumes puffed from Reyna's lips into the vacant space Levant left behind. His words slipped deep between her bones like raindrops drizzling through the canopy.

The way he'd spoken about her cursed magic.

As if it wasn't a curse at all.

"Sunshine?" Brax trekked into the clearing with hand ablaze. Reyna stood rigid. Still trying to make sense of her encounter. Brax surveyed the area and spoke again at her silence. "What the hell ya doin' out here?"

His gritty tone ripped Reyna from her stupor.

"Taking a midnight stroll," she snipped.

"Are you certifiably insane?" Twigs snapped beneath his Doc Martens toward her. "This isn't Earth. We don't know what's out here. You can't go off traipsing wherever."

"I wanted to be alone." Reyna shrank with forced conviction.

"Cut the bullshit." Brax snorted. "I heard voices. Who was with you?"

If anyone found out about her encounter with Levant, it would raise too many questions. The Zodiacs might learn the twisted connection Reyna and he shared. A connection she didn't yet understand. Reyna couldn't tell anyone. She crossed her arms over her chest. "I was talking to myself."

"I saw you run into the woods and thought you might need

help." Brax shook his head through an unamused laugh. "Least you could do is not lie to me."

"Who're you to question my motives?" Reyna's defenses crested. "You left the ship first."

"Yeah, 'cause I'm a son of a bitch who can't—" Brax pinched the bridge of his nose. "Ya know what? Forget it." He stalked back the way he came, and Reyna followed. She peered over her shoulder at the forest retracting back into darkness as Brax's torched fist marched ahead. Reyna half expected the god to rematerialize at any moment. Whether she wished it or not.

"Forget what?" she called to Brax while fumbling over rocks and through brush. "You expect me to divulge my secrets but refuse to share yours?"

Brax rounded and she bounced off his chest. A crown of starlight hugged the blond hair atop his head. Even after the sun slept, its master always found every glint of light.

A grin split over Brax's face. "So, you are lying about why you're out here?"

"I didn't say—"

"What other secrets you keepin', besides extraction magic?" Brax cocked his head.

"You're the one who makes a living off dishonesty."

Brax's smugness heated between them. "Hell, I'll get real honest about the thoughts I've had about you, but you're the one who's been hidin' stuff."

He was right and she hated it.

"I'm sorry I hid what I could do." Reyna sighed in earnest. "I was protecting myself."

Brax's expression softened. "Now that I believe."

"After I blacked out from the attack, Prisha said you looked after me. Is that true?"

Brax's eyebrow quirked. "What do you think?"

"I think you're a difficult man to read."

The corner of his lips lifted. "And you want to *read* me?"

"Of course not."

Soft lightning flickered through the leaves and Brax stepped closer through the sprinkling rain. "You didn't mind my company aboard ship before we were interrupted."

Reyna's back met a tree. "A momentary lapse in judgment."

"My favorite kind." Brax chuckled low. "You can lie to yourself and everyone else." He wiggled fingers through the air. "But I don't need any fancy-feely magic to know you've thought about what it'd be like to finish what we started." Brax's arms caged Reyna between him and the tree. "How 'bout this. For each truth you tell, I'll share one too."

"I'm not playing games with you."

"It's not a game." Brax snickered good-naturedly. "It's called a conversation."

"Fine." Reyna huffed. "You first."

"Varma was right." Brax wetted his bottom lip, contemplating his next words. "We weren't sure if you'd wake or if Dredgers would come back. So yeah, I was concerned about you. My turn. Why'd you come ashore tonight?"

"To see you."

"In the woods?"

Reyna squinted at his rule breaking. Brax grinned wider, nodding for her to continue.

She asked, "What'd you mean in my room when you said, '*I can't do this?*'"

"I don't do well with hospitals or medical stuff." Brax's forearms flexed at Reyna's sides, as though his words were a physical labor. "I lost someone close and when I saw you bandaged, it brought back memories I'd rather forget."

Silence passed between them and the rain pattering the forest's canopy.

For the first time since meeting, Reyna didn't want to look away.

"Brax," his name unfolded tenderly across her tongue. "I'm sorry for your loss."

"My turn." His tone ached with an emotion she couldn't name but desperately wanted to. Brax leaned impossibly close. Their drenched chests rose and fell alongside each other's. "Why did you want to see me?"

"I needed …" She swallowed hard.

"Atta girl." Brax's warm breath nuzzled her neck. "Tell me what you need."

Reyna closed her lids in silent frenzy of his stubble scraping her skin. "I need to know *why* you'd protect me?"

His teeth raked across her earlobe. "Maybe I wanna know what it'd be like to kiss you."

"No lies." She shuddered. "You promised."

"Not lying."

"We can't." Reyna suppressed a sigh. "I'm dangerous."

"Good." His smirk curved along her rain-slicked cheek. "I am too."

Brax's mouth pressed against hers and Reyna's wits incinerated into a cinder.

She parted her lips, drinking him in. Chilled rainwater rolled over their tongues and all distinction between drowning or breathing evaporated. Reyna waited for his ravenous kiss to swallow her whole, but his lips dragged gently across hers. Explored every hill and valley of her mouth. A slow devotion to understand not why Reyna wanted to be kissed, but how, devoured every morsel of her resolve.

Strong hands grabbed her ass.

Her moan broke their lips apart. Brax hoisted Reyna against the tree and guided her legs around his waist. She raised her face toward the canopy as Brax showered a serenade of teeth and tongue over her neck. His fingers kneaded the edges of Reyna's aching core through her jeans. Tormenting. Teasing. Reyna arched into him, thighs clenching around his hips, desperate for more friction. Brax's chuckle vibrated under their kiss.

"Are you laughing at me?" Her breathy words grazed his lips.

He bit her bottom one softly. "Maybe."

Reyna dragged her thumb over his mouth, mesmerized by the euphoria it conjured in mere moments.

"Reyna? Brax?" The Zodiacs' staggered calls echoed through the trees. "You out here?"

The pair froze.

"They're looking for us?" Panic carved into Reyna's whisper.

"Shit," Brax groaned. "I sent up a flare when I saw you go into the woods."

Reyna peered around, expecting their companions to emerge at any moment. "Maybe we should—"

Brax reclaimed the misty breath that passed between them and lowered Reyna onto the ground.

She sighed into his desperate kisses. "They might see us."

Brax unbuttoned Reyna's jeans. "Let 'em."

The further Reyna drifted from the life she knew, the more uncertain she became of who she was. Her friend had lived more life during twenty-eight years than Reyna had. And Tessa didn't just live. She'd savored life. Made it her own. Made memories. But that's all Tessa was now. A memory. Tessa was dead but Reyna wasn't.

Not yet.

A fire-calloused hand slid between Reyna's underwear and pelvis. She whimpered, unable to stop herself from scanning the forest.

"Stay with me, Sunshine." Brax's mouth shushed her lips. "I've got you."

Reyna's heartbeat relocated between her legs as lazy fingers stroked the place she'd neglected far too long. She bucked her hips and grinded for more. Her fingers sank into Brax's shoulders. Rode his unrelenting caress as far as he'd take her. Brax slipped a finger inside. Reyna's mouth opened. A soundless gasp. A plea for him to pull away. A prayer to never let go. Her body became molded clay in the kiln of his arms. Brax's gaze waterfalled over her body writhing against his hand.

"Rey?" Charlie called in the not far distance.

"Brax …" The want and warning along Reyna's mewl rose and fell with her fluttering lashes.

"That's right," Brax urged, thick with desire. "Sing for me."

Raindrops suspended around them. Lightning ignited the tree. Flames blazed brighter with each charge of Brax's hand and mouth claiming her.

The others might find them. So what?

This.

Nothing else mattered.

"What are you—" Surprised ecstasy purred along Brax's throat. His eyes rolled back. "Fuck!" The word dark on his lips lit the kerosene of his magic coursing Reyna's veins.

Her spine arched, plummeting her into bliss. Brax's moans quivered alongside her release. Reyna couldn't be sure why and she didn't care. Every worry. Every unknown. Every doubt poured from under his touch.

"Look!" Ethan called to the others. "Fire!"

Brax panted into Reyna's shoulder with an arm propped against the tree behind her. Reyna's head lolled over the trunk as Brax's starfire continued blazing through her limbs. Rain hissed through the treetops with each slowed breath, and the wall between who Reyna was or wasn't shattered.

In a few moments of stormy darkness, she'd become just …

Reyna.

CHAPTER

FOURTEEN

T HE ZODIACS HIKED ALL THE NEXT DAY THROUGH MESSIS. Halley flounced at the party's front, as though scaling an island in an uphill dance. Exhaustion weighted the group's faces, but they slogged forward, silent in their determination. Daylight bled through cherry maples and dripped sweat down Reyna's neck. She stopped to catch her breath, dragging a gloved hand across her forehead.

Prisha's heavy breaths paused beside her. "We must be close to Omphalos."

"How do you know?" Reyna tied her hoodie sleeves around her waist.

"The temperature is warmer the closer we get to the island's center. Must mean something, right?"

"Let's hope." Reyna trudged forward again.

Prisha joined her. "Are we finally going to talk about last night?"

"Nothing to talk about." Reyna watched Brax hop off a large rock ahead. "I got lost and he found me."

Brax had insisted to the others that the inflamed tree was a result of his inept temper. A lie Reyna was grateful for. Her truth was much less easy to explain away.

She'd extracted his magic and couldn't control it.

Every time Reyna thought herself closer to understanding this new world, another revelation reared its head. She was foolish to believe being a Zodiac was enough to protect her new companions from her other abilities. Even if she couldn't feel their emotions, whatever darkness dwelled within was as Levant said. Powerful. She wielded magic untethered to elemental laws. The same magical rules did not apply. But if her extraction magic *could* affect a Zodiac, why didn't previous encounters with Brax or the others yield similar results?

A lump plopped into her lower belly.

Intimacy.

Reyna's complete abandonment of what kept her safe. What protected others from her all those years. Which led to the question she was most afraid to ask aloud.

Did she hurt him?

The bewilderment that dilated in his eyes. Brax's groans as Reyna drank her fill.

She'd been so enraptured by the moment. So lost in herself, she hadn't stopped to understand what was happening. Didn't care to.

Of course she'd hurt him.

The Zodiacs' hiking party stepped out from the dense wood to a waterfall cascading from an endless mountain stretching into clouds. Reyna inhaled the mist rolling off a lake sprawled beneath the great falls.

"We've arrived!" Halley sang.

Ethan glanced around. "This is Omphalos?"

"Stars, no! Omphalos is there." Halley pointed past the clouds. "This is the entrance."

"For real?" Prisha's backpack thudded onto slick pebbles. "We need to climb a waterfall? I can't take any more of this camping trip from Hell."

"Oh, come now, Resilient Prisha." Halley rolled her eyes through a smile. "I assure you, this is much lovelier than the Forgotten." Halley waded into the lake, her iridescent dress catching rainbows like oil on water. Purple light bubbled from her hands beneath the surface and canoes emerged from its hidden depths. Everyone paired off into the self-propelling vessels and jolted toward the falls.

The Zodiacs chattered, pointing excitedly amongst themselves. Brax's focus never waned from Reyna's canoe beside his. She remained stoic. Gaze fixed forward. Desperately trying to ignore how his presence captivated every particle of her being. Brax had approached Reyna after breakfast, but she wasn't ready to talk about what had happened. Magical or otherwise. He agreed to give her space, though based on their short time together, Reyna suspected his promise was temporary.

The falls' roaring waters drew back like stage curtains and the canoes glided through. Millions of crystals in every size and color protruded from the cavern walls, each exuding its own ethereal light. Reyna beamed at the rainbows wrapping around her limbs as Prisha helped her from their boat onto slippery bedrock.

Charlie inched closer to a blue crystal and its inside blazed brighter like a lightbulb.

"Sweet." Charlie bobbed his head.

"Yes, Most Astute Charles, they are indeed quite sweet." Halley sighed with awe. "A human's desired afterlife is called the Next. Within each crystal dwells an eternal paradise of a soul passed on from Earth. Their eternity is reliving the happiest day of their mortal life."

"There's too many good days in a lifetime." Charlie slumped. "How could a person pick one?"

Reyna's heart sank back to the car crash. What if she'd died? What would've been the happiest day of her life? She'd experienced small moments of joy, but none worthy of an eternal Heaven.

"That's the most delightful part!" Halley clapped her hands. "You don't choose the day at all!"

Prisha plopped a hand on her hip. "If we're stuck with one day forever, shouldn't we get a say?"

"Your soul chooses it." Halley ran her fingers over a crystal cluster. "A mortal's heart possesses a depth the mind cannot comprehend. One's happiest day could be the most ordinary."

"How can all these be souls from Earth?" Reyna asked.

"These are but a few. Soul crystals can be found throughout all Nidian regions. Come, now." Halley peered at the large round passageway carved into the grotto's ceiling. "We've kept our goddess waiting long enough." Upon mention of the goddess, green vines dropped from the opening and unfurled beside each Zodiac. "Please hold on to a vine and they shall see us the rest of the way."

"Is this safe?" Reyna poked the plant.

"Quite!" Halley beamed. "They're my most preferred method of travel."

Before Reyna could take another breath, the vine wrapped around her waist and shot into the tunnel. Reyna's heart nosedived into her stomach as she soared through a kaleidoscope of color. Crystals blazed bright with each Zodiac that zoomed past. Everyone's faces morphed between screams and fits of laughter. Wind blasted from Charlie's hands, hurtling himself past the group. His gust whooshed through Reyna's hair, and she cackled with laughter. Reyna glanced at the rainbow light show beneath them and met Brax's amber gaze. Blond hair whipped around his face like a flame in the wind and for a moment, Reyna's fears dissolved.

She'd already accepted they couldn't go beyond what had happened.

The cost proved too great.

So why couldn't she shake the urge to wiggle free and tumble into him?

The Zodiacs emerged from the mountainside tunnel. Their viny escorts placed them onto velvety grass and snaked back into the summit's chasm. Each step through this new world was a leap into the next daydream as Halley led them through a meadow sprinkled with tulips, roses, and peonies.

Reyna craned her neck at an ivory palace shimmering in the afternoon starlight as they climbed arched stone steps over the waterfall's river. A man and woman waited at the palace's base. The soldier's silver armor glinted like mirrors refracting light. A warm smile hugged his dark cheeks and stretched the long scar across his right eye. His female companion swept forward, arms stretched wide. Platinum hair and light pink chiffon flowed behind her milky-white shoulders. Same as the crystals, the closer she drew, the brighter her skin glowed. A light so radiant. So pure. It could only be rivaled by its undeniable counter.

Darkness.

"Hello, my dearest Zodiacs. I'm Neoma, Goddess of Light." The woman beamed ear to ear. "Welcome home."

PART TWO

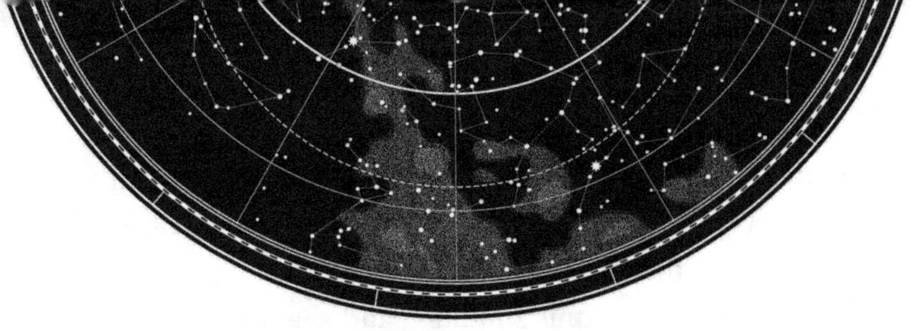

FIFTEEN

Reyna held her breath upon entering Omphalos. She'd never craned her neck at New York's skyscrapers or the Northern Lights amongst their retreat from civilization, but whatever coveted earthly beauty she imagined, unfurled into an impossible dream. Water trickled from marble fountains amongst a rainbow oasis of flowers. Emerald foliage crept along the palace's white stone walls toward a diamond sky. Omphalos was the illusion of an overgrown pearly palace tucked away from the worlds it ruled.

The birthplace of existence. A heartbeat of the universe.

Neoma flicked her wrist, and two massive silver doors creaked open. Sunlight sliced over etchings along each door. Depictions of the Zodiacs' associated figures frolicked amongst jewel-encrusted constellations, planets, and moon phases. One door raised a figure of the goddess. Opulent, luminous, and elegant. Reyna's awe iced at chiseled contours of a man decorating the opposite door. Stoic, confident, aloof. Not a man.

You'll always belong to me.

The Dark God's words echoed through Reyna like a melody lost to the ages. What had he meant by them?

An involuntary chill pebbled along Reyna's skin. She rubbed her hands along her arms and glanced around the orbiting silence. The group's fading footsteps echoed somewhere out of sight. Reyna jogged through the silver doors and followed Neoma's voice around the next turn. She rounded the corner and slammed into a wall of brawn. Brax's glare whirled, softening upon recognition. For a moment they were back in the woods. Inches from each other's lips. More vulnerable than she'd ever been.

Light flickered over his shoulder, and she registered the goddess gliding toward them through the parted Zodiacs. Reyna sifted through grains of Neoma's emotional energy, but the deity's essence pulsed with silence. Neoma halted abruptly. Momentary surprise flashed across her face.

"Highly unnecessary." Intrigue widened the goddess's soft pink lips. "Fascinating, nonetheless. It's been a long time, Cancer."

No one ever *felt* Reyna reading them, but Neoma wasn't anyone. Reyna swallowed the lump in her throat.

"My goddess!" Halley fluttered into the group's center. "May I please tell our Eternally Glorious Zodiacs the news?"

Neoma smiled over Reyna once more and offered a delicate nod.

Halley squealed. "Tonight, our Illustrious Goddess of Light wishes to introduce you all to Nidus's luminaries!"

The Zodiacs exchanged glances.

"Luminaries?" Prisha asked.

Neoma addressed the entire group. "Prior to your departure, Zodiacs served as regents over Nidus's seasonal regions. Your purpose was to guide Nidian souls in practices of the sign they'd be born under once reincarnated onto Earth. You also tended to economical needs such as trade and squabbles amongst your designated lands. In your absence, each region designated some of their own to aid in prosperity of daily life. Such Nidians dubbed them luminaries."

"We're like royalty?" Charlie squared his shoulders and jutted his chin.

"There's no royalty on Nidus." The scar-eyed soldier cleared his throat from the group's head. "Zodiacs are servants to Nidus and She-who-created-all." Pride glowed in his face as he bowed toward the goddess.

"Which I offer my eternal gratitude for, General." Neoma clasped her hands behind her. "However, for all the luminaries' noble intentions, I'm afraid many of the Zodiacs' more profound teachings have faded. I'm sure luminaries will be eager to speak with each of you, but perhaps it is prudent to leave politics for another occasion."

"Occasion?" Reyna eyed the general's fingers' subtle yet intentional brush against Neoma's elbow.

"We couldn't have our beloved Zodiacs return without celebration." Neoma hooked her arm into the general's. "Halley will show you to your chambers and ensure you've everything you need for tonight's masked ball."

Laughter and glasses clinked from beyond the ballroom's upper double doors as a gaggle of giggling women shuttled past. Reyna yanked the silvery crustacean mask over her face and pretended to admire a wall fresco, hoping they'd regard her as another fangirl paying tribute to her returned regent. If the goddess wished to parade the Zodiacs like prized horses, at least she'd granted them the mercy of doing so in costume. But no amount of sparkle, frill, or face mask would ever be enough to disguise Reyna's truths.

She'd spent the early evening hours practicing how she might ask the goddess to remove her magic. Somewhere between her stuttering and starting over in the mirror, Reyna paled over something she hadn't considered before.

Neoma welcomed the Zodiacs back to Nidus. With a caveat.

She needed something from them. The very something Reyna did not want.

How would Reyna convince Neoma to remove any magic that might give her an edge over her enemy? Reyna possessed nothing to bargain with and lacked knowledge on how she might return to Earth. She'd need to play the role given, until an opportunity to ask about her magic presented itself.

"Wow." Prisha opened the double doors ahead. Her gown's garnet beads clicked across the marble floors. "You look incredible!"

Reyna's satin-gloved fingers fiddled over her diamond and moonstone headpiece. "It's probably too much, but Halley said—"

"No, you're perfect. Come with me." Prisha beamed and ushered Reyna onto an indoor balcony overlooking the dance floor.

"Ladies!" Charlie descended from behind. He slung his arms around their shoulders and jostled them into a bear hug.

"You're messing up our hair!" Prisha pulled away. "We were supposed to wait here. Where have you been?"

"Scouting the food table." He hiccuped. "Duh."

Reyna wiggled free from the pungent stench clinging to Charlie's breath.

Prisha yanked his lapel closer. "Are you already"—she sniffed—"drunk?"

A dopey grin slid across Charlie's cheeks. "Do you want me to be drunk?"

Prisha gently shoved his chest, and he wobbled backward. "Yep." Her lips pursed. "Totally shit-faced."

"No, you're face shitted. I mean … your face isn't shit. I like it." He teetered into her.

"You should be keepin' your wits about you." Ethan tossed an arm around Charlie's shoulder. "Not drinkin' them."

"Says the Irishman." Charlie snorted through a laugh. "Lighten up, cap'n! It's a party!"

The group's chatter muffled in Reyna's ears at Brax standing straight ahead with his back to them. He unfastened his gold dress cuffs, scanning the ballroom below. A messy blond knot gathered at the back of his head and gold embroidery lined the contours of his black suit coat. Grime from the Zodiacs' journey may have washed away, but Reyna and Brax's night in the woods remained muddier than ever. Reyna hated her other magic for so long, she'd never appreciated its value in a moment like this. Brax's reactions were a song without words. Every tick of his jaw or involuntary twitch of his fingers became a new string of lyrics and it was up to Reyna how to interpret their meaning.

"You all look splendid." Neoma's voice rose from behind the group. "Let's not keep our guests waiting any longer. Shall we?"

Everyone nodded excitedly and Neoma wafted toward the railing.

"Leo." Neoma regarded his bold ensemble with a smile. "I'm pleased reincarnation hasn't stripped you of your grandiose disposition."

Brax pressed a chaste kiss to Neoma's hand and envy nicked Reyna's heart. A simple enough gesture for a man. Thoughtless for a goddess. A coveted embrace for a cursed woman from San Diego.

"Thank you, Goddess of …" Brax's lips parted as he caught sight of Reyna's silver-draped figure beside them.

The goddess's smile tightened between them before she took position at the balcony's helm. Neoma's arms spread wide, and the crowd below fell silent. "Friends, I bid you all a fond welcome to my home. This is the day we've yearned for a century. The return of our beloved Zodiacs!" She stepped aside, presenting Reyna and the others. Thunderous claps reverberated against the domed ceiling and Neoma waited for the crowd's appreciation to simmer. "While their homecoming is indeed a gift, it's also reminder of those who don't stand beside us today."

Silence frosted the room.

"Fear not for your absent Zodiacs," Neoma continued. "Despite their allegiance to the God of Darkness, I believe they still carry an undeniable love for Nidus. When we triumph, they shall be received with the same welcome we've bestowed upon those present tonight. Practice diligence, my dear Nidus. We've weathered the Dark God's presence before and shall prevail again. For tonight, let us push dark matters aside. Rejoice, dance, drink, and may the Infinite All-Knowing bless us all!" Neoma offered her hand to each Zodiac and announced their titles as they descended one of two grand staircases. Applause spread like wildfire below with each introduction.

Taurus, Lord Regent of Capital and Morale.

Capricorn, Lady Regent of Aspiration and Achievement.

Ini of Gemini, Lord Regent of Comradery and Communication.

Leo, Lord Regent of Courtship and Creativity.

The goddess nodded for Reyna to step beside her and the crowd fell silent.

Reyna peered over the precipice of her worst nightmares come true. To walk into a room and offer no fond memory of having been present. Even in a past life, she inspired no welcome. A world unmoved by her existence.

"Finally." Neoma smiled. "I present, Cancer, Lady Regent of—"

Boisterous cheers and applause erupted from below. Reyna jumped at the crowd's excited chants.

"What are they saying?" she asked.

"Your Zodiac title, Lady Regent of Kinship and Connection." Neoma smiled tightly. "Your domain is over families and relationships."

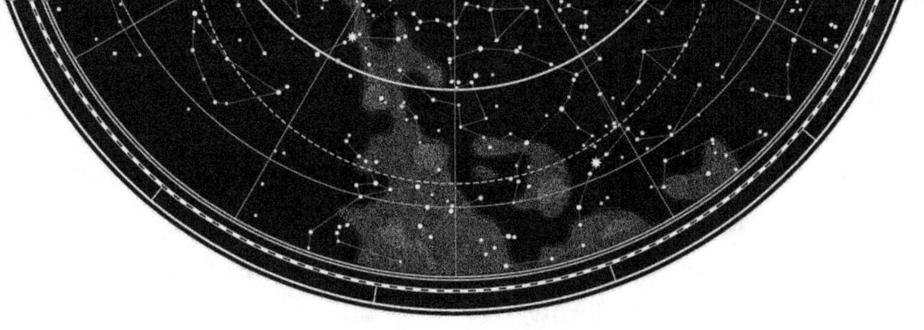

CHAPTER

SIXTEEN

T HE MEMORY OF REYNA'S PAPÁ'S HANDS TIGHTENED AROUND her throat. She was twelve again. Sinking. Drowning. Too light-headed to come up for air.

She ebbed through the masquerade guests. Waited for their emotions to pummel her as she passed, but all remained silent. Gratitude for this unexpected grace propelled Reyna faster. She reached the ballroom's far side and pressed her spine against its cool stone wall.

How could Reyna be responsible for relationships? She didn't help families.

It's your fault she's dead! Papá echoed in her head.

She destroyed them.

Reyna buried her face in her hands. "This is a disaster."

"I'll say," someone drawled beside her. "You make quite the entrance." Bloodred hair dripped alongside a stranger's bottomless pit of cleavage her dress cared little to tame.

"Is there a way out?" Reyna craned her neck over the crowd. Nidians blocked all the exits, except for two columns framing a dark sky embroidered with stars.

The redhead exaggerated a yawn. "I expected more from the mortal who slayed a Dredger."

Reyna stilled and studied the crowd she'd passed through closer.

They jolted back to their hushed conversations, eyes diverting to each other upon her discovery. The truth behind their delayed applause swayed through Reyna's limbs. They'd cheered, not for Cancer's return, but her magical victory over an enemy.

"I didn't *slay* anything. I freed the Dredger." Reyna swallowed hard. "How's everyone know—"

"Oh please. Word travels fast." The woman sipped her scarlet cocktail. "Nidus is small and dreadfully insipid." Her ravenous smile flashed toward the dance floor. "But perhaps, not for much longer."

Reyna followed her sight line onto the dance floor. Brax danced amongst a barrage of men and women, all shamelessly clamoring for his attention. Something foul lurched in Reyna's heart at every stray hand across his torso. Each unabashed delight flashing in his smile. He'd tried talking to her and she'd shut him out. Reyna convinced herself avoidance was best. A true mercy she'd offered them both. But Brax's pull radiated like a flame beckoning moths. And god, did she want to burn.

The woman's tongue glided across her teeth. "Some things will never change."

Reyna composed her inner turmoil. "What do you mean?"

"Leo always lived for the spotlight. To win the affections of all." She flashed Reyna a fake smile. "Not to worry though. As Lady Regent of Family Nonsense, you needn't be burdened with such exploits."

"We're reincarnations." Reyna's shoulders squared. "Not whatever Zodiac versions you think you knew."

"A word of advice, Lady Regent. None of us can escape who we truly are. No matter how many times we die."

"Persephone." Neoma's general stepped beside them. "Not causing trouble, are we?"

"Orion." The woman trailed a painted fingernail along a constellation etched into his muscled breastplate. "I'm not one for begging, but how many times do I have to ask you to call me Seph?" She snaked a hand over the holster hugging a black sword at his waist. "And when are you going to let me explore this famous belt of yours?"

Orion snatched her wrist. "Go home, Persephone."

"Persephone?" Reyna's disdain dissolved. "As in, the Greek goddess of spring?"

"See, Orion?" Seph's pomegranate smile framed her white teeth. "I'm a goddess too. I might be your type after all."

A polite smile dimpled Orion's cheeks as he addressed Reyna. "Earth's false gods are nothing more than Nidian memories faded after reincarnation. Blurred reflections of a world beyond their understanding." He lifted his chin at Seph. "Everyone on Nidus knows there's one goddess."

"Goddess or not"—Seph downed her drink— "I've brought a man or two to his knees. Think about it." She flashed a grin and slithered into the crowd.

Orion shook his head. "Whatever she said before I approached, don't take it to heart. Persephone has maintained the underworld since Levant's banishment but still enjoys her aboveground visits to stir mischief."

Reyna replied, "If she's Persephone, were she and Levant involved?"

A chuckle rumbled from Orion. "Never forget, Lady Regent, the God of Darkness is involved with himself."

"Reyna," she corrected.

Orion's lips parted to speak, but another soldier approached and whispered into his ear before walking away.

"Please excuse me, it appears I must take my leave, but a pleasure seeing you again, Lady Reg—Reyna." Orion smiled bright as he bowed his head. "I'm sure we'll meet again soon."

After forced pleasantries with the few luminaries brave enough to approach her, the last of Reyna's energy reservoir drained as she slipped onto the balcony. Omphalos sat at the island's highest peak like a crown overlooking distant winking villages. Although Orion claimed royalty didn't exist on Nidus, Omphalos oozed of his hypocrisy. Reyna braced against the stone balustrade and wind fluttered across her dress. A belch garbled the silence, and her head snapped to a figure laid across the railing. He swigged his drink, legs dangling over the edge.

"Charlie?" Reyna edged closer.

"Lady Rey of Cancer Connections!" He thrust his cup into the air and fell toward the courtyard. Reyna lunged. Sporadic wobbles of air blasted from Charlie's hands, no doubt an unreliable result of his alcohol-weakened magic. He zipped upward and dropped onto the balcony flat on his back. Inebriation glittered in his eyes between sputtering groans and laughter.

"Are you okay?" Reyna kneeled beside him.

"None of us are okay." His head rocked. "We're dead. All dead."

Reyna draped his arm around her shoulder and tugged until his feet met marble. Charlie swayed.

"Why are you talking like this?" Reyna held steady, despite every instinct to release him.

"I can't save you," he slurred at the sky. "I want to but can't."

"Charlie." Reyna's heart sank with understanding. "You *can* save your sister but not if you give up. Let's get you to your room. Everything will look better in the morning."

Metal clicked amongst the shadows.

"You should listen to her, Lord Regent Lightweight." Firelight danced along Brax's gold lion mask as he lit a cigarette wedged between another woman's lips. "I'm not for next day regrets, but you're gonna have some if you don't."

"Stars." The Nidian beside Brax coughed while gripping his bicep. "Do all mortals enjoy these?"

"Only the cool ones." Sarcasm dripped from his smile as he took the cigarette.

Reyna rolled her eyes.

"Got somethin' smart to say?" Brax sipped a drag.

"Don't you think it counterproductive to introduce what may kill them after they're reincarnated?"

"Airhead said it himself." Brax handed the cigarette back to his companion. "We're all dying anyway, why not enjoy the ride?"

Charlie hiccuped through a groan.

"Come on, Charlie." Reyna readjusted his arm around her shoulder. "Let's go."

"Thanks, Rey. I'll manage." Charlie pulled his arm from her and staggered into the ballroom.

Reyna rounded on Brax. "Could you be any more insensitive?"

Brax chuckled. "I aim to please."

The Nidian beauty beside him huffed. "How dare you speak to Lord Regent in such a manner. Who do you think you are?" Brax whispered in his companion's ear and the woman paled, eyeing the silver crab mask resting atop Reyna's head. The Nidian shoved the cigarette into his hand. "My apologies, Lady Regent! I didn't realize it was you. It's dark and I—please forgive my indiscretions!" She scurried into the crowd.

Reyna blinked. "What was that about?"

"Everyone wants to look proper and chaste in front of Lady Regent of Kinship and Connection." Brax ground his cigarette against the railing. "Can't imagine why though. Everyone knows there's one fun way to make a family."

"What's that got to do with me?"

"Think about it." Brax removed his half mask. "We're like gods to these people and you're the Zodiac of family. Nidians wouldn't want to appear anything less than moral to you."

"We're not gods," Reyna corrected. "Orion said Neoma is the only goddess."

Brax tucked stray hairs behind his ear. "Scarface can think whatever he wants, but perception is reality, and in case ya haven't noticed, they idolize us."

"Or maybe just you." Reyna turned to Earth's solar system strung across the sky like fairy lights. She squinted harder into the distance and sent up a silent prayer Brax would walk far away from the conflicted emotions she refused to name.

"Sunshine." He purred with smarmy amusement. "Are you jealous of the Nidian woman?"

Reyna wished she possessed Charlie's starwind magic. Maybe then, she could throw herself over the balcony and finally escape this glamorous night from Hell.

"Not everything is about you and your fan club," she bit.

Brax blinked. "So why don't you stop pouting and tell me what it is about?"

"You don't get it." Reyna tightened her knuckles on the railing. "These people think I destroyed a monster, but it was an accident. It's only a matter of time before they realize *I'm* what they should be afraid of."

"Last I checked, you freed a trapped soul."

"Perception is reality, right?" Reyna faced him. "I destroy everything … everyone I touch."

Brax stepped closer. "Not from where I'm standing."

A slow swell of tears tingled in Reyna's eyes. She looked away, sure if she didn't, the dam would spill over. "How can you defend me, after what I did to you last night? How I …"

Reyna gritted her teeth and pushed past him, heart pounding like a fist against her resolve. She couldn't do this. It was too much.

"You really don't know what happened last night, do you?" His bait snared Reyna to a stop. Polished shoes scuffed over marble and paused behind her. Brax's body heat emanated along Reyna's exposed spine, lulling her into his embrace without lifting a finger. "I felt everything you did." He brushed hair from her shoulder. "Your sadness. Fear. Your pleasure."

"I'm sorry!" Reyna turned. "I didn't mean to use my other magic on you. I lost control and—"

"Quit apologizing all the damn time. Sometimes we lose it. It's okay to lose it."

"Not me. I told you—I'm dangerous."

Brax's hands slid up her arms. "The only danger is not understanding your own power."

"But my magic—"

"Not magic." His hot fingertips grazed Reyna's collarbone and paused over her heart. "I'm talkin' about the power you have over people."

"What people?"

Brax slipped a hand around Reyna's waist and gently tugged her against the furnace of his chest. "One who hasn't stopped wanting to kiss you again."

Reyna accidentally glanced at his mouth. "What about what I want?"

Brax laced fingers through her hair. His voice was a low rumble ghosting her lips. "Now there's the million-dollar question."

They stared at each another and the past twenty-four hours floated away with their breath into the night. The slightest perk of Reyna's toes and their lips would be reunited. What would happen if she fell prey to her desires again? Brax evoked flames. Reyna doused them. Recklessness was his nature and self-preservation hers. Reyna may have not hurt him yet, but eventually, her magic would. It always did.

Pained words left her lips. "I can't."

Brax receded but kept a hand extended, the smolder never wavering from his smile. "I guess I'll have to settle for a dance, then."

CHAPTER

SEVENTEEN

ONE DANCE. A SINGLE MEMORY REYNA COULD HOLD TO dull the sorrow of so many before. A dance could be safe. Innocent. Even fun.

Reyna pulled the mask over her face and slipped a satin-wrapped hand into Brax's. He led her through the parting dancers, swept behind her, and smoothed his hands along her hips.

The current song ended, and another took breath.

Brax grabbed Reyna's hand and unraveled her into waves of silver fabric. The door of her rib cage opened, and her heart fluttered free. Delighted gasps crescendoed through the crowd. Brax waltzed Reyna through her river of self-doubt. Lifted her over the rocks weighing her down. Buffered her missteps around each winding bend with his own improvisations. The moon and sun rippled along the river as one. Rising and falling, together.

Brax pulled Reyna tight against his chest, though dancing apart, a cruelty meant for lesser men. She'd told him not to kiss her but still hoped he might. It'd be easier to be angry. Chastise him for not respecting her wishes. All in a hollow attempt at denying the greater truth she dared not give breath to.

Reyna wanted it all. Consequences be damned.

Brax twirled Reyna outward, and her free hand slid into someone else's.

The new partner tugged Reyna into an undercurrent of dancers. She tried keeping her head above water. Attempted to register the blurred faces gliding past. Reyna searched for Brax like a lighthouse in the night, but *Moonlight Sonata's* slow swell pulled her farther out to sea. A familiar inhale of ice poured down her throat. She sighed into it. Why did it feel good? Her lungs should burn. Scream for air. She should hate it. Why didn't she hate it?

Reyna clutched on to her only anchor to the real world and met his unmasked face.

Emerald irises lined with a million undiscovered galaxies beheld her. The pair stopped swaying and Levant's chilled fingers grazed Reyna's temples.

"I've always hated these." He slipped the mask from her face.

Disbelief paralyzed Reyna. She glanced at the crowd whirling past and prayed someone noticed, but no one flinched. Did they not recognize the Dark God after a century? Blinded by their long-standing illusion of safety?

"Why are you here?" Reyna finally summoned a sound.

Levant swept her into another spin. "We never finished our conversation in the woods."

Guilt for keeping their meeting a secret coated her tongue. "There's nothing more to discuss."

Levant curved Reyna into a dip and stilled. "Have you thought about my offer?"

Of course, she'd thought about it. More than she cared to admit. Despite the goddess's ability to banish Levant, there he stood. Darkness incarnate. Unmasked. Waltzing through Neoma's party, and Reyna, cradled in his arms, desperately wanting his words to be true. To control her cursed magic. Embrace her power and, by sheer force of will, destroy it for good.

Levant descended deeper into their dip as though Reyna were weightless.

"What do you say?" He inhaled deep. Watched. Waited.

Reyna mustered whatever semblance of control she still possessed and righted herself from his arms. "Your Dredgers killed my best friend." She stepped away with renewed clarity. "If more death is the price for freedom from my magic, I'm not willing to pay."

"I was once a creator of life." Levant stood taller. "An equal counterpart of this world's highest order and yet condemned to pay a price. Death is the cost of living, and none pay it greater than those who are different." He snatched someone's hair from the crowd.

Reyna jolted forward but froze at the black plunging into the Dark God's eyes like ink.

"Lady Regent!" The woman from the balcony with Brax writhed in Levant's hold. "Help me!"

Party guests gasped and staggered away from the new commotion.

"Once she's reborn on Earth, this soul will be nobody." Levant raised his grip on the woman's hair, putting her on display. "She'll be a blink in time. Another mindless dreg slugging to final death. Today, I grant her new life. Redefined purpose. Mercy."

"Please." Reyna stepped forward. "Don't hurt her."

Levant yanked the Nidian against his chest and Reyna's heart stopped. Incoherent pleas trembled from the woman as she clawed at his dark green dovetailed jacket.

"A Zodiac's light is sweeter than any unborn soul's." The god fixed his attention upon Reyna. "But yours, Reyna Pérez. Not quite human. Not fully Zodiac. What must it be like to savor them at once?" Levant hooked the woman's chin between his thumb and forefinger. "I shall have my taste, but for now, I suppose this must do."

His lips smoothed hers and shrieks rippled through the crowd.

The woman's screams muffled beneath his kiss. Veins along her neck hardened into lines of swirled marble. Limbs crunched like misplaced bones being relocated. White stone suspended her hair and the dress's struggling fabric. Skin once made warm by lantern light now caught its reflective glimmer. A statue of grotesque beauty.

Reyna clasped her hands over her mouth.

The statues in the forest. The despair expertly chiseled into their faces. Arms wrapped around an invisible partner. Nidians. All of them.

Brax pounced from the crowd between Reyna and Levant.

"It's been so long." The god's head knocked back with a rapturous groan. He smoothed a hand over his victim's shiny face. "But still gratifying as I remember."

Reyna surged past Brax.

"Stop!" Brax shouted.

"Bring her back!" Reyna demanded.

The Dark God's brow quirked with cruel amusement. "As you wish."

Levant shoved the statue and marble shattered against tile.

Brax whipped his body around Reyna's, shielding her from the exploded stone. Prisha and Ethan stumbled through the crowd and fell to their knees as a high-pitched howl ripped through the ballroom. Everyone clapped their hands over their ears. Dark smoke seeped from the pile of trembling rubble at Levant's feet and snaked into the air. A familiar black figure emerged. Nidian shrieks reverberated through the ballroom at the newborn Dredger hovering obediently beside its master.

"Go ahead. Free her." Levant walked around his creature, arms spread wide. "Everyone wants to see it." His black stare somehow twinkled. "I want to see it."

"Enough!" The Goddess of Light glided through the crowd.

"Neoma." Levant's fingers twirled in the Dredger's dark, wispy tail. "Not inviting me to a party celebrating my return? Most unbecoming."

"You are a betrayal unto nature." Neoma's regal poise remained intact. "You have no place here."

"You made certain of that."

"Not well enough it seems," she replied.

The general stepped beside her.

"Orion!" Levant hissed through a smile. "Neoma's loyal lapdog. Still enjoying my table scraps after all these years?"

"Last I remember"—Orion's smile quirked—"you were the one on all fours whining."

The Dark God's tongue ran along his bottom lip, side-eyeing Orion's unsheathed blade. "Obsidian?" Levant wagged a finger at Neoma. "I do hope you make him take that off when you two—"

Orion growled as his hands tightened at the sword's hilt. Neoma brushed her fingers over his and a soft whimper trembled from her. She pulled her hand from the weapon's proximity.

"Mmm." A pleased chuckle drawled from Levant. "As I thought."

Neoma lifted her chin. "What do you want?"

"After all you've taken? I'd settle for Earth."

The goddess snorted.

"Then perhaps the Dark Star?" Levant steepled his fingers over his lips. "Or have you forgotten?"

Neoma swallowed hard and a new quiet hushed the room.

"Ah." Sinister pleasure lit Levant's face. "You do remember."

"What's the Dark Star?" Reyna asked.

"A desperate attempt at his gaining more power." Neoma stared down her nose at Levant. "One meant to shake our resolve."

"So, you haven't told them?" Laugher barked from the Dark God. "Typical."

"I've heard enough." Neoma nodded toward Orion.

The general clanged his sword's hilt against his chest plate and two dozen obsidian-clad soldiers unfurled through the crowd like vines. Neoma's knees wobbled and Orion cradled her in his thick arms. Levant fumbled onto a knee. A guttural groan split from his lips. Soldiers closed on the Dark God, but their obsidian shields and blades trembled within their hands.

Levant craned his neck at Neoma and strained a smile through gritted teeth. "Go ahead, relive your victory. Obsidian cannot stop what's coming. When the summer eclipse arrives, the Dark Star will rise. The prophecy will be fulfilled, and your time will be over!"

Energy vibrated off the soldiers' glassy shields closing a tighter circle around the god. Another moan belted from Levant hunched over on all fours. His Dredger wailed and barreled into the crowd. Nidians screamed and scattered toward exits. Someone checked Reyna's shoulder, and she slammed onto the floor. A foot hooked into her stomach. Air punched from her lungs and Reyna curled inward, losing focus on the pandemonium erupting. Through bedazzled fabrics and shoes pounding near her head, she watched soldiers toss obsidian chains across Levant's back and shackle his wrists. As if he sensed her, the Dark God lifted his black gaze from under mussed hair and smiled.

"Soon," he mouthed.

CHAPTER

EIGHTEEN

EVERYTHING IN OMPHALOS WAS CARVED FROM MARBLE. The Greeks unknowingly recreated pieces of Nidus, and warped as their lore was, people's fascination with its aesthetic from their time on the island survived the ages. Did the Greeks and Romans comprehend what they'd tried to replicate? Reyna had once found beauty in such myths too, but the longer she spent in this world, the more it reminded her that reality was never as it'd seemed.

Nothing more than faded Nidian memories.

A woman hardening into white marble would be the memory Reyna took with her if she ever made it back to Earth.

Neoma and Orion addressed his army while Halley partnered with palace staff to direct Nidians to the appropriate exits. Reyna sat on the floor with her head rested against a wall in yet another round marble room where she and the Zodiacs were instructed to wait. Stars twinkled against a black-and-blue sky through the room's open ceiling as their Zodiacs paced below. Spirits beaten. Bruised. Waiting for everything to make sense again.

"My greatest apologies for keeping you." Neoma entered with Orion flanking her.

"What's going on?" Reyna joined the other Zodiacs gathered at the room's center.

Neoma clasped her hands in front of her. "The Dark God is being transported to the Glass Isles."

"A deserted islet off the coast of Flora composed entirely of obsidian," Orion expanded upon seeing their questioning expressions. "Since the Dark God's banishment, we converted one of its isles into a prison for if he ever returned."

"So that's it?" Brax crossed his arms at the goddess. "Obsidian is your weakness."

"Although the Dark God and I share an affinity for a single element, his for water and mine for earth, we still control all four." Her hands swiveled and a fireball blazed at the center of the group. Rock floated at its core, water churned beneath the flames, and wind whooshed around the elements. "Earth melts into fire. Air feeds the flame and water solidifies transformation. When all four elements join, like obsidian, Levant and I can be mastered."

Orion drew his black blade of volcanic glass, starlight dancing along its razor edges. "It's why each Zodiac commands a single element. Why you cannot harm each other and why all four elements cannot be combined into one. The balance is what binds our world."

"What would happen if they combined?" Reyna asked.

"Chaos." Orion sheathed his sword.

Neoma sighed. "While obsidian does weaken Levant and me, it's not enough to destroy us."

"Lemme guess." Brax cocked a brow. "That's where this Dark Star comes in?"

Neoma offered a reluctant nod. She gazed through the open ceiling and wove her hands in a circular motion. The room's marble columns groaned, scraping across the floor. The Zodiacs huddled tighter at the room's center as their surroundings spun counterclockwise. Reyna's hair whipped around her face and nausea crept into the corners of her stomach. She pleaded for an anchor. Anything to steady her. Brax stepped behind her and caressed the concealed lines of her palms. She curled her fingers into his and squeezed.

Electric sparks blazed and crackled at the ceiling's edges. A projection of Nidus shimmered to life within the vortex.

"Nidus lived in peace as a utopia for many centuries." Neoma guided them backward in time. "But within its shadows, Levant found no rest. He prowled its regions for souls to consume." Countless faces within the projection screamed and hardened into stone. "Though we are equal in power, the Infinite All-Knowing made it impossible for us to harm one another so I had no way of forcing him off our shores."

"What's the Infinite All-Knowing?" Reyna shouted over the cyclone of crackling starlight.

"The ethereal origin of creation. The everything and nothing. When the Infinite All-Knowing bore the Dark God and me into existence, it told us we were unity of light and darkness. They warned if the power scales ever tipped toward either, a champion of our creation would emerge unbound by the same rules of balance. This being would possess all elemental magics and choose favor over either light or darkness forever."

Prisha called out, "If the scales were tipping, why not make light and darkness equal again?"

"I tried," Neoma replied. "I presented Levant with a treaty. He agreed, but his acceptance of peace was a ploy at building his resistance freely. I began hearing rumors he was conspiring with Zodiacs to rebel against me."

Unidentified smoky figures bloomed around Levant in the projection as he walked a circle. The god's passionate yet muffled speech met with cheers from the smoky audience.

"When I approached Levant about the rumors, he revealed Pisces came to him with a premonition. Pisces foretold a prophesized champion standing beside Levant and named themselves the Dark Star. With no other choice but to protect Nidus from total darkness, I exiled Levant to another galaxy we created."

"What about the Zodiacs?" Ethan asked.

"Uncertain of the Dark Star's identity, I put you to sleep within your constellations. If he ever left banishment, you would be reincarnated as humans without Zodiac memories." Individual stars ignited throughout space and rained like a meteor shower onto Earth. Stars boomed, colliding into various land masses. "Your reincarnations would be scattered across continents, and as the Dark God drew closer, so too would your essences be drawn together across land and sea."

"Why send us away?" Charlie frowned. "Why make us forget?"

"My hope was as mortals with no memory of your past lives, it might subdue the Dark Star's ability to rise."

"Explains why the Dark-Aligned Zodiacs already have theirs." Brax crossed his arms over his chest. "Levant already gave 'em back."

"You must understand, it's too dangerous," Neoma replied. "Darkness's reign means the end of all we hold dear. If I release your memories, it will increase chances of the Dark Star rising."

"Bullshit!" Brax bit. "We deserve to remember who we are."

"The price of your restored memories is not worth the billions of lives at risk!" Neoma's hands dropped at her sides. The spinning room slowed to a stop and the projection dissolved.

Silence shrouded the room.

"Okay." Ethan attempted to revive civility. "If you can't release our memories yet, what can we do to stop the Dark Star?"

The goddess's shoulders readjusted into her regal stiffness. "If we can find the prophecy, it may suggest a way stop the Dark Star from rising. After Pisces's visions were revealed, they'd solidify into physical documents. You'll search your respective regions for such a document. Spring is nearing its end and according to Levant, the Dark Star will rise once Earth enters the summer solstice. If we've not uncovered the prophecy by then, all may be lost."

Prisha blinked. "How do you expect us to find an ancient prophecy when you haven't managed to?"

Orion stepped forward. "The Obsidian Army has searched these long years, to no avail. We hope your Zodiac aptitudes will offer an advantage. I will help sharpen your starmagic, so you possess greater control over your abilities."

"I recognize it is not the best plan." Neoma sighed. "But it's all we have."

"For now, we should retire." Orion relaxed beside her. "Tonight's events have been trying, and the hour is late. Halley will escort you to your regions in the morning."

The Zodiacs shuffled out the way they'd entered, but Reyna paused at the arch's threshold. Neoma pressed a hand against her forehead, the burden of what was to come sinking into her shoulders. Beneath the goddess's radiating light and draped regal garb, Reyna saw a woman. A tired soul, who despite efforts at maintaining balance between two worlds, had been failing.

A feeling Reyna understood all too well.

Orion wrapped his arms around the goddess and dipped his lips to hers, but Neoma turned toward Reyna. "Cancer, I should like to have a word with you."

Humiliation bloomed along Reyna's cheeks.

Orion released Neoma. His initial disappointment hardened into indifference as he bowed his head. "Until tomorrow, my goddess."

Orion exited and Reyna stepped forward.

"I'd prefer if you called me Reyna," she said to the goddess.

"You've been blessed with great honor of the stars," Neoma replied. "Cancer's celestial name holds much power and respect on Nidus."

"I didn't mean any offense." Reyna redirected the conversation, "I'm sorry I eavesdropped before."

"It's quite alright." Melancholy tipped Neoma's words. "Orion is a faithful warrior and a pleasant distraction, but not always one I can afford as both."

"Do you love him?" Reyna asked before she could think better of it.

"Whatever I feel means little to beings like us." The goddess gestured between them with a sad yet knowing smile. "Wouldn't you agree?"

Reyna blinked at the comparison.

"Halley told me you feel mortals' emotions," Neoma elaborated. "How you can inflict yours upon them and absorb their energy. Their … life."

"I'm sorry I tried reading you before." Reyna's eyes dropped. "Sometimes I don't realize when I'm doing it."

"No apologies necessary, my dear. You're a child of your former self. I cannot expect you've mastered such a magic in so little time. I imagine a power akin yours to be quite lonely indeed."

Reyna nodded slowly at her astute assumption.

"As someone who also exudes unparalleled magic amongst those around her, I understand the isolation it creates. The walls we must build against those who cannot grasp the full gravity of such gifts. Always and forever, keeping us out of reach. From forming true connection."

Reyna's heart stilled, but her body pulsed at her circumstance recited so eloquently. As though Neoma had reached inside and extracted the sentiment from Reyna's soul.

"Halley also explained you can free Nidian souls from their Dredger form with a single touch. A feat I'd give anything to perform and a beautiful talent I don't intend to waste." Neoma smiled warmly. "The Zodiacs will be searching Nidus, but there's one place they cannot. A place few would have means to survive. A place I believe you could. The Forgotten."

Reyna stepped back. "You want me to enter the underworld?"

"The Dark God's territory is the one location I've been unable to search and most likely place he's hidden the prophecy. You possess abilities the other Zodiacs do not. They're not equipped to survive underwater, and your *other* magic makes you immune to Dredger attacks, which I suspect the Forgotten possesses many."

"Suspect?" Reyna asked.

Neoma's face fell. "I've been able to locate the underworld, and if other Nidians have, they've either kept it secret or never returned. We've tried using the Eternal Flame, but I believe Levant has placed heavy wards around it."

"If you think the prophecy is in the underworld, why not have the Zodiacs looking for the Forgotten instead?" Reyna asked.

Neoma shook her head. "I believe it best to keep this quest between us. I'm sure the Zodiacs would insist on accompanying you without hesitation. Although, if our efforts to find and destroy the prophecy prove unsuccessful, their welfare might mean our last hope against the Dark God."

"This is an impossible task." Reyna paced, gnawing at her thumbnail. "What makes you think a half celestial, half mortal from Earth can find the underworld when nothing and no one else can?"

"Because I think you want the prophecy stopped much as I." Neoma approached her slowly, gaze narrowing. "Because I think you know you have much to lose if the Dark Star rises."

The reality of what Neoma wasn't saying prickled over Reyna's skin and blood drained from her cheeks. "You think I'm the Dark Star?"

"You possess unique abilities the others do not. I'd be a fool to not consider it a possibility," Neoma said matter-of-factly. "Surely you must agree?"

Reyna clung to an alternate hope. "The Infinite All-Knowing said the Dark Star controls all four elements and I don't. None of us do."

"True." The goddess mulled. "Though we cannot be sure until we've read the prophecy's contents." She slipped Reyna's satin-covered hands into hers. "But if you are the Dark Star, understand your fate is not yet sealed. No magic is without light, and you still can choose your path."

"I can't keep living this way!" Reyna ripped her hands away and hugged herself. "I don't want this responsibility anymore. Whether my magic is good, bad, dark or light, I don't want it. If I do this—if I risk my life to Hell and back, you must swear to remove my magic. *All of it.*"

"Cancer …" Neoma whispered. "You cannot mean—"

"I do." Reyna's teeth clenched.

"Very well." The goddess offered a reluctant nod. "Find the Forgotten and prophecy, and I'll grant your request. Though I must caution, once your magic is removed, you'll be unable to return to Nidus."

Reyna stood a little taller. "Then I guess I'll have to enjoy it while I'm here."

NINETEEN

As the universe slept, the faintest of the zodiac constellations tossed and turned. Cancer had never been the boldest or easiest collection of stars to spot, but Reyna's determination always endured.

Soon, Levant promised. And though it frightened Reyna to consider what he meant, she hoped he was right. Reyna was ready to find the prophecy, return home, and seize her second chance at life. Whatever that looked like.

Dawn broke over the clouds as Halley led the Zodiacs across Omphalos's highest peak. White stone jutted from the enclosed space though they stood atop a distant mountain. Four mirrors were carved into its rocky walls, each framed with its own lush plant life. A lullaby of waves slowly rose in Reyna's ears. She tilted her head at the nearest mirror and drew closer. Bright pink-and-yellow hibiscus bloomed around its edges of green foliage. A faint, salty breeze from somewhere beyond the mirror brushed the hair from her shoulders. She leaned forward, waiting for something to reveal itself, but only her reflection stared.

Prisha stepped beside her. "What?"

"Don't you hear it?" Reyna asked.

Prisha leaned closer. The waves lapped louder against a sandy shore.

"I do!" Prisha gasped. "It sounds like … a fireplace." She strode toward another mirror decorated with frost, pine, and red berries.

Each Zodiac regarded a mirror with awe, hypnotized by whatever individual song called them. Light shimmered over Reyna's mirror and a beach came into focus. The sensation of salt water sloshed over her sneakers, but the ground beneath her feet remained dry.

"Damn …" Enchantment dripped from Brax beside her.

Reyna prayed she wasn't crazy. "You see it too?"

"Oh yeah." A smile curled in his voice.

Reyna closed her eyes and lifted her face, as though she might bask closer to the sun. "Isn't it the most beautiful thing you've ever seen?"

"No argument here," he replied.

"That's a first." Reyna grinned and opened her eyes to him watching her instead.

"I see you've all found your mirrors," Halley said from the enclosure's center. "Each Zodiac resides in the region that represents your earthly season. These mirrors are entrances to those lands."

"What seasons are we going to?" Ethan asked, with Charlie standing beside him.

"You and Ini will enter into Flora, the spring region." Halley faced Reyna and Brax. "Cancer and Leo shall enter summer, Calidi." She smiled at Prisha. "And Capricorn, onward to the winter region of Parhelia."

"How will we know what to do once we're there?" Prisha asked.

"You'll each be greeted by your new factotums," Halley replied. "They'll help guide you."

"Fact-o-whatum?" Charlie asked, rolling the word around in his mouth.

"Factotums are magic-born Nidians who wield elemental magic akin to their Zodiacs," Halley explained. "The Zodiacs, like our masterful makers, once required assistance from others. So, the goddess and god agreed to bless select Nidians with small traces of starmagic. Factotums have been paired with Zodiacs for centuries since."

"Assistance with what?" Reyna asked.

"Your lesser responsibilities, so your former selves might focus on the region's grander conflicts. While you've all been gone long, I assure you that your current factotums are quite versed with your duties." Halley frowned slightly. "They've led luminaries in your absence and taken on more than historically required. I'm sure they'll be overjoyed to have you home." Halley's fingers trembled at her lips and tears sparkled in her eyes. "We've been through much together, but I fear my time with you has ended."

Reyna's face dropped. "You're not coming?"

"Alas, Compassionately Genuine Reyna." A tiny sniffle peeped from Halley. "My place may be Omphalos with the goddess, but it's been the most splendid pleasure of my existence having escorted you all home."

Charlie glanced at the Zodiacs. "Will we see each other again?"

"Of course!" Halley dabbed tears from her cheeks with her dress. "Mirrors can be found throughout Nidus. They will take you to whatever region you wish."

Prisha snorted. "Where were the mirrors when we hiked?"

"The splendor of Nidus is best experienced firsthand." Halley shooed the Zodiacs to re-face their mirrors. "Now, all you must do is think of where you want to go and step through. In this case, your palaces. The mirrors will do the rest."

Brax's rough fingers laced through Reyna's. "Ready?"

She nodded and squeezed tighter.

"On the count of three." He held her gaze through the mirror. "One."

Reyna swallowed hard. "Two."

"Three." Brax stepped first and Reyna followed.

Gravity yanked them forward through the mirror and their hands broke apart. They thudded onto the ground, bowling over prickly grass and sand. Brax rolled to a stop on top of Reyna. He shifted his lower half off her but remained in a half straddle across her torso. Brax winced through a smile. "You okay?"

"I was until I broke your fall." Reyna squinted against sunlight winking from behind his head. "Aren't cats supposed to land on their feet?"

Brax chuckled and brushed away sand clinging to her forehead. "I didn't know you made jokes."

She smiled. "There's a lot you don't know about me."

"Like this?" His thumb caressed the scar along her hairline.

Reyna's warmth chilled before a throat cleared beside them.

Their necks craned toward two women standing on the beach. Reyna shoved Brax off and scrambled to her feet.

The woman draped in a flowy purple dress dipped into a small bow. "Welcome to Calidi, Lady Cancer and Lord Leo." Dark coils grazed her brown shoulders with the sea breeze. "It's an honor to finally meet you. We've long awaited—"

"Brax." He stood, dusting sand from his jeans.

The woman blinked. "Excuse me?"

"I'm Brax and this is Reyna." He raked a tangle of hair from his face.

"Ah yes. Your mortal names." Her lips pursed into a tight smile. "However, whilst on Nidus, I insist you go by your given celestial titles."

"And I insist you go to—"

"You must be our factotums!" Reyna stepped in front of Brax and smiled.

"Indeed." The woman gestured toward the willowy woman beside her. "This is Solana, factotum to Lord Leo, and I am Anemone, at your service, Lady Cancer."

"Nice to meet you," Reyna replied.

"I do believe that concludes introductions." Anemone clapped her hands abruptly. "Come, we must make good time!"

The factotums led them along stone steps scaling the palace's cliffside. In the distance, lush jungle tapered into sandy coastline and palms swayed over a marketplace with Nidians meandering about their day. Homes speckled the island's curves. Each domicile splashed the terrain with either sunny yellows and oranges, turquoise odes to the sea, or pinks in celebration of wildflowers. Atop the small cliff's peak, they continued through a pergola tunnel. Bright hibiscus water-falled over its sides, pebbling Reyna with sunlight between its petals.

"This is Calidi's palace gardens," Anemone announced as they emerged from the flower tunnel's other side. Geysers sprayed from sapphire pools and short palms offered a cool reprieve along stone paths. "This is a sacred space once visited by yourselves for reflection. If you're ever in need of quiet, no Nidian shall disturb you here."

"That go for you too?" Brax's smirk at Anemone wavered as Solana's arm curled into the crook of his.

Anemone huffed through a smile. "You needn't concern yourself with my whereabouts, Lord Regent. I shall see to Lady Cancer's needs and Solana shall tend yours."

"*Any* needs." Solana's grasp tightened around his arm.

"Great." An edge lined Brax's laugh as he tried wiggling his arm from hers. Reyna couldn't stop her smile curving at his uncharacteristic discomfort.

They ascended ceramic steps under a high arch decorated with what Reyna assumed was their Zodiac symbols. She studied the three engravings. Not lost on her, only two of Calidi's depicted Zodiacs had returned. Reyna hadn't met all the Zodiacs, but returning to Nidus without them left a sour taste. Brax's partner, Jade, had been taken against her will. And though Aquarius appeared cozy with Scorpio, he'd tried warning Reyna at the club.

Not all the Dark-Aligned were convinced they served Levant's higher purpose like Scorpio, Libra, and Sagittarius. Were they?

"This is where we part." Anemone paused in a grand foyer. "Lord Leo, Solana will see you to your chambers and Lady Cancer, I will escort you to yours."

Brax's lips parted, but his factotum tugged onward.

"Come, Lord Leo." Solana fluttered her lashes. "I can't wait to show you your quarters." The pair strode toward a gilded staircase with Brax still trying to pry his arm free.

Despite all the strangeness in Reyna's new reality, with each new point of separation from the group, she found herself longing for the cover of those she'd come to trust most in such a short time.

"Lady Regent?" Anemone snapped Reyna from her introspection. "Shall we?"

Reyna continued following her factotum and a substantial click drew her attention upward. Sprockets and gears rotated on a large mobile device hanging from the ceiling. Representations of Earth and neighboring planets encircled a glowing sun, while outer rings of stars twinkled within the suspended universe.

"What's that?" Reyna asked.

"It signifies the stars' and planets' current positions in relation to Earth and lets us know when seasons are shifting."

"Does it show the coming eclipse?"

Anemone stilled. "The rumors are true, then?" The poised confidence Reyna suspected the factotum wore often, crumbled from her shoulders. "A Zodiac will bring about our end?"

Reyna's mouth went dry. Nothing she could say would paint what had transpired at the masquerade as less than bleak. She replied, "The Dark God thinks so."

"Anything else I should be aware of?" Anemone asked.

Reyna shook her head.

The factotum studied her a long moment before ascending a pink stairwell resembling the inside of a conch shell. "I know we've just met, but I've trained most my life to become a factotum. I hope you'll soon come to trust my intentions, which is aiding in whatever ventures protect Calidi and Nidus by extension."

They exited into a long corridor. Lanterns with globes of light illuminated portraits of men and women along the walls. Reyna eyed the paintings they passed. "Are these factotums?"

"Former, yes. Most Cancerian factotums are from my family's line and have since ascended to Earth. Some have already made their way into the Next."

"The afterlife?" Reyna recalled Halley's tale.

Anemone nodded. "A Nidian's greatest desire is reincarnation.

Once our mortal time is spent on Earth and we journey onward to the Next only then are we complete."

The weight of what was at stake barreled into Reyna like a boulder sinking into the sea. If Nidus crumbled, all current souls who waited for reincarnation would never reach completion. And souls who resided on Earth now would never claim their eternal happiness. Their Heaven. Annihilation of all souls' past, present, and future lay in the Dark Star's hands.

Of Reyna.

Dizziness wobbled through her, and she leaned against a corridor wall.

"Lady Regent, are you alright?" Anemone asked. "You look pale as a Parhelian snowfall."

"I'm fine." Reyna stumbled for an excuse. "A little light-headed."

"Light-headed?" Anemone's lips tested the phrase. "Is this a Zodiac ability?"

"No, it's when you feel dizzy or sometimes sick."

"Oh yes! I've read about sick in books about Earth." Anemone stepped away, lip curling slightly. "You don't have pustules or badly digested food rising, do you?"

Reyna bit back a smile and shook her head.

Anemone inspected her from a safe distance. "Perhaps it's best we forgo today's duties and let you rest. Calidi has eagerly awaited your return, though I suppose one more day could be spared."

Reyna smiled. "Thank you."

"Now then, these are your chambers." Anemone gestured at a silver door with a crab etched into its center.

Reyna studied the moon phases lining its body. "I've never liked crabs much."

Anemone clutched at her chest as though infected by whatever ailed Reyna.

"Crabs are amongst the most sacred on Nidus!" Anemone replied. "They carry their home with them, walk in all directions and roam both land and sea. They're extraordinary creatures, and you're the celestial embodiment of such wonders. Stars above, what do they teach on that planet?"

Reyna curled inward. "Sorry."

"It's quite alright." Anemone smoothed the plains of her dress. "But by the Infinite All-Knowing, please never utter such distaste while in public forum." Anemone opened the door, and a cool air swept over them. "Your room hasn't been entered since you were last in Calidi. It is … as you left it."

Reyna drifted into the room of another life. She ran her gloved hand over iridescent seashells adorning a four-poster bed. Green vines spilled over its frame and curled at the floor. Water trickled along a pebbled wall into a spring along the far wall. Not a speck of dust or wilted plant adorned the museum of Reyna's past. All appeared in its place. Undisturbed, unaged, and pristine as the day she couldn't remember leaving it.

"It's beautiful," Reyna murmured.

"Once the Zodiacs left, we vowed never to enter their chambers again, except to maintain." Anemone's propriety softened. "Factotums were losing hope we'd ever serve a Zodiac again."

Reyna wanted to believe in hope, but no matter how much she longed to place faith in such a concept, hope would neither stop her from becoming the Dark Star nor lead to the Forgotten. Reyna wanted to assure Anemone she and the other Zodiacs would be Nidus's salvation, but it'd be a lie. Even if they did win whatever battle loomed within the eclipse's shadow, with her magic removed, Reyna wouldn't stay on Nidus. She'd already missed too much of her own life to be responsible for an entire civilization's.

"I shall leave you to rest." Anemone stood at the door. "Do you have any questions?"

Reyna released a soft, shaky laugh. "So many."

"I know it's been a century, and all may seem overwhelming." Anemone offered a true smile. "But with time, I'm sure Calidi will feel like home once more."

TWENTY

A GROWL SHUDDERED THROUGH REYNA'S STOMACH AS SHE crept through the labyrinth Cancer once called home, but not a soul passed within its halls. How'd she expect to find the Forgotten when she couldn't find breakfast in her supposed palace? Perhaps with the Zodiacs gone for so long, palace help wasn't needed.

"Don't tell me how to handle myself, Lord Regent Airhead," Brax's baritone carried from around the next turn. "I'll do stuff my way and—"

"There's more at stake than you," Charlie grumbled. "Stop thinking of yourself, for once."

"Do tigers change their stripes?" Reyna teased, trying to defuse the tension as she stepped into the small rectangular courtyard.

"Wrong cat." Brax eyed her over his unlaced boots propped atop a long dining table. His lips twitched in an attempt to hide his smile. "G'morning, Sunshine."

"Enter, Rey!" Charlie's head popped over top his chair. "Lady Regent Dredger Defender, and Brax Ego Slayer!"

"What brings you here?" Reyna beamed at Charlie.

"Been practicing my mirror-hopping skills all morning." His hands imitated jumps. "Did you know there's an area between spring and winter that's just mud? The ultimate location for a monster truck rally or mud wrestling."

"Noted." She giggled and sat at the table's head, opposite Brax.

Sugared breads, mountains of carbs, and valleys of every fruit Reyna could imagine blanketed the tabletop. She bit into a flaky croissant and reveled at the warm bread melting over her tongue. "What were you two talking about before?"

"Brax is grumpy about training today." Charlie rolled his eyes. "Doesn't think he needs to participate."

"Why not?" Reyna folded her arms on the wooden table. "I'd think you'd jump at any chance to show off."

Charlie laughed through a mouthful of muffin.

"First off, I don't need an excuse to look good." Brax sizzled a pineapple slice in his open hand. "Second, we shouldn't be wastin' time training or lookin' for this hypothetical prophecy." Grill marks lined the fruit as he peeled it off his outstretched fingers. "Our half-baked magic won't mean shit when we come up against a god."

"Hypothetical?" Reyna's nose scrunched. "You think Levant lied about the prophecy's validity?"

"Maybe, maybe not." Brax took a bite. "But seems like a helluva good distraction from whatever else he's cookin' up."

Reyna pursed her lips. The prophecy had to be real. Any alternative was not an option she was ready to consider. Not when it'd become Reyna's first real lead to being free from her magic.

"Dude." Charlie mumbled around the pancake in his mouth, "The Dark God is locked up. He's not cooking anything."

Brax shrugged. "I've seen people accomplish a lot from behind bars. Everyone is so fixated on stopping the Dark Star, nobody questioned why Levant was easily subdued."

"Didn't look easy to me." Charlie stuffed more pancake into his chipmunk cheeks. "Besides, if you believe the Dark God is planning more, why not voice it to Neoma?"

Brax relaxed deeper into his gilded chair. "I'm always wary of anyone who tries too hard to convince me they're innocent. No one ever is."

What if Neoma couldn't be trusted? Both deities dangled promises in front of Reyna, but in a sea of trust, Levant was at the bottom.

Bottom of the bottom. Reyna had to believe Neoma would deliver what she promised.

"Man." Charlie sighed at the fruit before him. "What I wouldn't give for eggs, bacon, and sausage. Extra grease."

"You have your precious Goddess of Light to thank for that." Seph primped crimson curls over her shoulders while sauntering into the courtyard. "Lev is a shapeshifter and created the beasts of Earth. After Neoma banished him, she became paranoid and ordered Orion's army to destroy all the poor land creatures."

"Who're you?" Brax asked.

The redhead popped a grape from a platter into her mouth.

"Seph," Reyna replied. An answer and a warning. "She worked for the Dark God."

Brax blinked between the women. "You know each other?"

"We met at the masquerade." Reyna crossed her arms over her chest.

"Such a shame the celebration was cut short." Seph pushed Brax's feet to the floor and sat on the table before him, as though to offer herself as a meal. "I never got a chance to get reacquainted with you, lover."

Juice sputtered from Charlie's mouth.

"Lover?" Brax arched his brow.

"Oh yes," Seph cooed and leaned her cleavage forward. "You, me, and dearest Scorpio had so much *fun* together."

Brax relaxed into his pseudo throne, face unreadable. "Sounds like me."

"I do miss Scorpio terribly." Seph brushed her naked foot along his arm. "I know he can't join us now, but I'd love to remind you sometime."

"Scorpio is an asshole," Reyna snapped.

"He was your friend once too." Seph's sculpted eyebrow glowered over her shoulder at Reyna. "Stars above know why."

"He's not my friend!" Reyna shot from her chair. "It's his fault my friend is dead!"

"Good to know he hasn't lost his touch." Seph shrugged. "One less human, the better."

Brax passed a slow, assessing glance between Reyna and the redhead. "Seph, you should stay with us in Calidi for a while."

"Oh, Leo darling!" She moaned with delight. "You always did entertain a girl properly."

Reyna's jaw dropped. "What?"

"You said it yourself." Brax eyed Reyna over the rim of his cup. "She worked for Levant. Nobody knows him like her. Maybe Seph's intel could help us."

"Have you lost your mind?" Reyna stammered for words, mostly crude ones. "She worked for Levant. We can't trust her."

Seph slunk off the table. "Many Zodiacs who weren't aligned with Lev before, have now joined him. So, I suppose past alliance or not, none are immune to his charms." Seph grinned wide. "Wouldn't you agree, Lady Regent?"

Did Seph know about whatever connection Cancer and the Dark God shared? With Seph having worked closely with him, probably, but Reyna wasn't about to pry amongst an audience.

Reyna skated over her insinuation. "Joined against their will, you mean."

"Rey …" Charlie rubbed the back of his neck. "If Seph can't be trusted, why'd Neoma invite her to the masquerade?"

His defense burned. Neoma and Orion hadn't warmly embraced Seph but weren't threatened by her presence at the party either.

"Of course Neoma welcomed me." Seph strutted behind Brax's chair, fingernails scraping along its edges. "The goddess may not like me but recognizes my usefulness. Who else would oversee the Forgotten in Lev's absence? I'm the only being on Nidus with knowledge of its function."

Reyna's heart galloped. Seph was her key to finding the Forgotten.

Charlie stared wide-eyed. "What's the underworld like?"

"Dreary. Cold." Seph picked at her fingernails. "Dead."

Reyna restrained the longing within her words. "How do you get there?"

"I'm prohibited from revealing." Seph sighed dramatically. "Part of my and Lev's pesky magical contract. But of course"—her head bowed toward Brax—"I'm happy to be of service in any other fashion desired."

"Why turn on the Dark God now?" Brax asked.

Seph scoffed. "Working for Lev and being faithful are quite different. Our original agreement wasn't babysitting his dead, nor is it a task I wish to continue."

"What was your original agreement?" Reyna prodded.

"Freedom."

Reyna snorted. "A life of servitude sounds a bit the opposite."

"Freedom from reincarnation." Seph gritted her teeth. "In exchange for my helping him with *business,* he halted my ability to age and allowed me to remain bound to Nidus forever. Not everyone wants reincarnation onto Earth."

"You've already got the immortality you want." Brax's chin lifted. "Why help us?"

Seph sat atop his armrest, her ass popping over its edge more than required. "With Lev gone, I'll be free of our contract and unbound from the Forgotten. Let it be someone else's problem for a while."

"If the Dark God dies and your contract is terminated," Charlie reasoned, "won't you eventually pass on?"

"I agreed to freedom on Nidus, not an eternity of playing nursemaid to the underworld." Seph sneered. "Immortality has become mundane. If breaking our contract means reincarnation, so be it."

"It's settled then. You'll stay in Calidi with us." Brax stood. "If this prophecy does exist, we need to find it fast. I want you to list places Levant frequented when he snuck around Nidus. Also, you should be at the party we're throwing tonight."

"What party?" Reyna gaped. "Since when?"

"Since I instructed staff last night to get the word out. We're inviting Calidian luminaries and some of their most influential connections. Like Seph, I suspect Nidians also know more about the Dark God than they'd let on to the goddess."

"And what makes you think Nidians will divulge their secrets to you?" Reyna asked.

"The universal language of booze and debauchery." Brax's lips quirked. "Otherwise known as interrogation, under the guise of fun."

CHAPTER

TWENTY-ONE

"WONDERFULLY DONE, LADY CANCER!" ANEMONE welcomed Reyna to the springtime region of Flora on the mirror's other side. "You're not face first in dirt, so an absolute improvement."

Reyna staggered against gravity until her feet settled atop velvety grass.

Anemone breezed over Reyna's glare and pointed at the emerald meadow below. "The training ground is there."

Tall grasses and daisies wisped Reyna's knees as they descended the hill. Parhelia's snow-dusted mountains stood sentinel in the distance and a serene lake sat nestled at the hill's base. Excited chatter carried from beneath a grand willow at the lake's edge where the Zodiacs chattered amongst themselves. A small gathering of Nidians near the bank waved Anemone over.

"Are they factotums too?" Reyna asked.

Anemone nodded and returned their wave. "We'll be observing training so we can help when you're not with Orion." She beelined toward the factotums and tossed a confident smile over her shoulder at Reyna. "I'm sure you'll do splendidly!"

Reyna wrung her gloved palms together at the idea of executing magic before an audience. Sure, she'd wielded magic in front of the Zodiacs, but those instances lacked any real skill. All were desperate, fumbled attempts at avoiding death. Reyna had tried so hard to avoid her magic, but after her and Neoma's deal, she now understood the time for such naïvety was over. Her venture into the Forgotten would require more than a will to live. Magic may mean the difference between making it out against whatever might want to keep her in. For Reyna to be free from any magic, she needed to first master it.

The Zodiacs flooded Reyna with greetings. It hadn't been long since they'd seen each another, but warmth spread through her chest at the sight of them. Safe and familiar, in a world gone topsy-turvy.

"Now we've all arrived, perhaps we should get started?" Orion motioned the Zodiacs to fall into a single line. "Halley has briefed me on how you've used your starmagic prior to Nidus, and I seek to hone those abilities."

Someone snorted from their lean against the willow's shaded trunk.

"Apologies, Lord Leo. I didn't see you." Orion flashed an annoyed, yet cordial smile. "Care to join?"

Brax pushed off the tree, boots scuffing across grass. "You're not a Zodiac," he mumbled around a cigarette. "What qualifies you to teach us magic?"

"While I may not be a Zodiac, I'm crafted from a constellation called the Hunter."

Prisha perked onto her toes. "Are there more beings made from constellations?"

Orion nodded. "Most reside in other galaxies created by our god and goddess."

"Why can we see their constellations?" Charlie asked.

"The god and goddess created others like you to explore other corners of the cosmos, but Zodiacs have always been most critical to our makers' design in this universe. You each embody strengths and weaknesses of those born unto Earth. You're a direct line to humanity and the elemental powers surrounding them."

Brax cocked his head. "Still doesn't explain why you're here."

Orion smiled. "Although my magic is untethered to human life, it manifests into unparalleled stealth and agility. It allowed me to help maintain order on Nidus when more peaceful means have failed."

"Unparalleled?" Brax blew smoke. "That, I'd like to see."

"Much as I'd love to entertain your ego, Lord Regent, today is about your companions."

"Seeing how agile you are on fire would be entertaining." Brax sucked another drag.

Orion met Brax's smirk with his own. "I understand that yourself and Lord Taurus had quite the squabble aboard *Polaris*?"

Brax shrugged. "We let off some steam."

"What a challenge it must've been for you." Orion stepped toward Brax until they stood a foot apart. "To face an opponent whom you were immune from sustaining any long-term damage from?"

Brax cocked a brow. "What're you implying?"

"Your magic is admirable, ferocious at best." Orion swiped the cigarette from Brax's lips in a seamless motion. He sniffed the ash and recoiled. "But I suspect, severely lacking discipline. I'm here to help, not belittle. So, I'd appreciate you offering the same respect."

Brax plucked the cigarette from Orion and twisted its glowing tip against his own forearm. Smoke coiled from Brax's white skin, unmarred as he placed the cigarette behind his ear. He flashed Orion a toothy grin. "Yes, sir."

The general stepped back. "As demonstrated by Lords Leo and Taurus, your elemental magics cannot harm one another. However, they can help raise your magic's potency or a partner's. This technique is called Astral Allegiance."

"I thought elements could never fuse together?" Reyna asked.

"Correct, Lady Reyna." Orion unsheathed the longsword secured at his waist and rotated the hilt in his hand. Its obsidian blade glinted like midnight across the blue afternoon sky. "Like obsidian, the four elements must never be joined. But Astral Allegiance doesn't fuse—it creates an alliance. When two elements are brought together cooperatively, this technique wields great power for you and your partner."

"What elements can be used together?" Charlie asked.

"Any pairing works," Orion replied. "The elements represent

harmony, akin to the Infinite All-Knowing's design, but some elements are more linked. It's why some believe those born under specific Zodiac seasons are better romantically matched. For example, air feeds fire, which gives the freedom to thrive." Orion crouched, picked up a stone, and skipped it across the water. "And earth meets water in an endless cycle of accumulation and regrowth."

"Are those magical combinations better than others?" Ethan asked.

"Not better, but the more opposite, the more unpredictable." Orion smiled at Brax. "Lord Leo, since you're keen to flex your skills, perhaps you'd help demonstrate a harmonious pairing?"

"Why not?" Brax stepped forward and waved Charlie after him. "You heard the man. Harmonious pairing or whatever."

"No." Orion grinned wider. "While air and fire magic bode well, how about a more challenging demonstration?" The general pivoted. "Lady Reyna, if you please?"

Her heart skipped. "Why me?"

"Fire and water are most opposite," Orion explained while Reyna stepped into position across from Brax. "Neither element requires the other to exist and both easily cancel the other out. They are however, created from the same energy. Astral Allegiance is about bolstering your partner's magic or them boosting yours." Orion pointed at Reyna's gloves. "You'll need to remove those first."

"I can't." Reyna curled her hands close. "I need them."

"Your magic is more powerful if willed without barriers."

Memory of Brax's hand sliding between her legs.

His fire magic detonating through her like a nuclear bomb.

Reyna had been a wild spinning compass in the woods, desperately trying to navigate the unexplored territory of someone else's magic. *While she'd worn gloves.* What would happen if she removed them now? Reyna eyed Orion's outstretched hand and swallowed hard. She couldn't afford to be afraid. Not anymore. Reyna slowly handed her gloves to Orion, and he drew a dagger from his boot.

Metal sliced through their faux leather fingers, fragments flopping into the grass at her feet.

"Perhaps in time, you'll reawaken your full strength by removing your gloves completely." The general handed them back. "For now, this should do."

Reyna wiggled fingers through the new slots at her middle knuckles. Gratitude pulled her smile. "Thank you."

"Of course, my lady." Orion stepped aside. "Now, if you would please join hands with Lord Leo."

Brax's hair swayed across his face like the willow's branches as he raised his hands. It was easy to become lost in his rough features. The aloofness woven into his swagger. Brax always knew what to say when it suited him. Reyna suspected it distracted well during his cons. But not today. Not after inviting Seph to stay without consideration for Reyna's feelings. The Calidi palace was once her home too and she deserved a say.

"I always knew you were badass." Brax narrowed the distance between them, lacing his fingers through her partially covered hands. "Now you look the part." Reyna squeezed his fingers. Hard. Brax hissed under the pressure with a strained chuckle. "Still pissed about this morning?"

"You don't miss a thing." Reyna squeezed a little tighter.

"Astral Allegiance is about trust," Orion interrupted their stand-off. "One must yield for it to work."

Brax side-eyed their onlookers and murmured to Reyna, "Can we hash this out later?"

Reyna snorted. "Oh, now you don't want an audience?"

"Yield"—Brax's eyebrow quirked—"so we can be done."

"You yield," Reyna snapped low enough for only them to hear. "You're the one who invited an enemy to stay with us."

"Yield," Brax repeated.

"I know you dated Seph, or whatever, but it doesn't give you the right to—"

Brax lifted Reyna's hands overhead and spun her. His arms strait-jacketed across her torso and pressed her spine against his chest.

"What're you doing?" Reyna tried to wriggle free.

"Think real hard about the next thing that comes outta your mouth." Brax spoke low in her ear. "Look around. Everyone is watching and we have no clue who to trust right now. Seph seems virtuous as a viper, but I'd rather have Levant's former right-hand woman plotting behind our backs, under our roof, thinking we're on her side, than having her do it somewhere else."

Reyna's breath caught at his implication.

Brax believed those amongst them couldn't be trusted?

She assessed their captive audience with new interest. It was Brax's livelihood to know people. Anticipate their moves. Maybe he planned to work an angle with Seph. One that wasn't horizontal.

Reyna relaxed beneath his hold.

"Glad you're seeing reason," Brax's baritone reverberated through her.

Reyna craned her neck to look back and gaped at a fiery vortex encircling them. Flames licked her skin and threaded through her hair, but the only heat threatening to destroy her blazed within his gaze.

"Outstanding job, regents!" Orion applauded.

"I guess this means I yielded," Reyna pouted.

"You?" Brax snickered. "Yeah, right. This isn't me."

"I don't understand."

"I yielded the second I had my arms around you. Looks like your extraction magic is siphoning my starfire."

Reyna frowned. "I should be using your magic to strengthen my starwater magic, not controlling your fire." The flames surged brighter with each swell of Reyna's erratic heartbeat. "I can't use extraction magic like this. It's wrong."

"You can use whatever the fuck magic you want." Brax breathed against her ear. "I trust you."

His admission pawed at the center of her chest, and for a

moment, Reyna let herself live in a place where magic types didn't matter. A haven where she existed as she was always meant to be. If Brax was right and she could use whatever magic she pleased, Reyna could still call forth her water magic. She closed her eyes, inviting the push and pull of her breath to sync with his. They contracted together like an undercurrent pushing out and in. She drifted through time and space. Out and in. Rolled along with the sea's rhythm. Out and in. A new heartbeat, connecting two bodies. Out and—Reyna opened her eyes.

Silvery moonlight rippled above the water's surface.

She scanned the otherwise dark water for any sign of Brax, the meadow, or her friends, and found none. Reyna swam toward the surface, but with each stroke and kick, the moon fell farther from reach.

Bubbles exploded into the sea.

Reyna swiped her hands through the fizzing water. A man's unconscious face emerged through the thinning bubbles. Short blond curls wafted around his face and a university emblem decorated his zip-up jacket. Reyna squinted, unable to shake the possibility she knew him but also didn't.

A second body plunged into the water.

Brax's golden hair swayed in front of his closed eyes and Reyna scooped his lank figure into her arms. She studied the youth now smoothing his once haggard edges. The hair wafting around his ears, but not yet touching his shoulders. This was not the Brax Reyna knew. She peered at the other man's pale white face and outstretched arms sinking into the dark abyss.

None of this vision belonged to her.

Moonlight dimmed and the world went dark. Brax's weight within her arms dissipated. Reyna swished her hands through the water, desperate to grab hold, but he was gone.

Light flooded the darkness. She swam toward a lamppost above the water's warped surface. Footsteps reverberated along a dock and three figures paused above her. Their faces were muddled amongst the waves, but Brax's signature blond hair glistened in the overhead light. Indistinct voices rose and fell through casual conversation. Reyna swam closer.

Someone shouted.

An earsplitting boom vibrated through the water.

A thud collapsed against the dock.

"Brax!" Reyna screamed through the bubbles escaping her mouth. She kicked for the surface. More frantic than ever to burst through the third wall. As she neared, a figure crouched near the dock's edge. Brax's hair hung over his shoulders, hunched over whoever's body laid on the dock. Relief pressed from Reyna's lips.

Lamplight glinted along the gun in Brax's hand. He prodded the lifeless lump before him and tilted their head to the side.

Horror swallowed Reyna whole.

She jolted back at blood dripping through dock planks into the water.

"Stop!" Orion's voice tore through her subconscious.

Reyna lay drenched and flat on her back in the meadow.

Orion and Anemone emerged through the hissing black smoke. The factotum lowered her hands, and the rain subsided. Reyna scrambled upright, gaping at the crop circle of charred grass surrounding her.

What the hell happened?

Brax hunched on all fours nearby. Chest heaving. Flames flickered along his arms and legs as he tried willing their boil to a simmer. Reyna wanted to reach out. Make sure he was okay. But the gun he'd held moments ago still smoked in her mind. Brax panted, staring at Reyna through his disheveled mane. More beast than man.

Where Reyna expected anger, she met something else entirely.

An emotion she'd experience enough times and recognized without a single drop of magic.

Fear.

Brax staggered to his feet and sprinted across the grassy meadow.

CHAPTER

TWENTY-TWO

SUNSET LIT THE SEA'S HORIZON ABLAZE WITH ORANGE FURY. Reyna sat against the balustrade off her bedroom's balcony, tracing a fingernail across her hand's lifeline until it split at her fate line. She paused at the wrinkled intersection. Nowhere to go, except where fate dictated. Reyna didn't know if she believed in fate or palmistry, but she couldn't deny the comfort predetermined destiny brought. A surrender to fate would render her life choices insignificant, but she'd be free from blame at the universe's hand. Maybe that's what the prophecy was. The universe at work. Neoma believed fate could be vanquished, its outcome realigned by those who took it. Reyna wasn't so sure.

"Lady Regent?" Anemone edged onto the balcony. "Are you alright?"

Reyna curled her arms around her knees and forced a nod.

Anemone inched closer, as though Reyna were a wounded animal. "Can I get you anything?"

"Have you seen him?" Reyna asked.

Anemone's shoulders sank. "Not since this afternoon."

"The lion will be fine." Orion stepped beside Anemone. A melancholy smile pulled at the scar along his cheek. "I hear he's hosting a soiree tonight and I doubt he'd miss it."

"I'm sorry I ruined training." Reyna buried her face between her knees. "I tried. I really did."

"Lady Cancer, don't apologize for what you cannot control,"

Orion replied. "I imagine life on Earth hasn't allowed you much freedom to practice your other abilities, but perhaps private sessions would be more prudent, until we can determine how to approach this type of magic."

"You want me to continue?" Reyna's head rose from her lap. "After what I did?"

"Being unable to control such magic would be far more dangerous," Orion replied.

Reyna rested her chin atop her knees.

"It was quite extraordinary." Anemone perked onto her toes. "Aside from what it did to Lord Regent Leo, of course."

Reyna's question scraped along her tongue. "What *did* I do to him?"

"What do you remember?" Anemone asked.

"I used my extraction magic first and decided to shift my focus onto water."

"I'm less familiar with extraction magic, other than what I've witnessed the Dark God perform, but I have a theory." Orion crouched beside Reyna. "Astral Allegiance strengthens your partner's elemental magic. I believe when Lord Leo submitted, he unintentionally charged your extraction *and* water magic simultaneously."

"Still doesn't explain what happened," Reyna replied.

"Water magic is closely tied to internal manifestations such as emotions, dreams, and memory," Anemone explained. "As a Zodiac, we suspect it's why you're more attuned to mortals' feelings and why your extraction magic, when aligned with water, siphoned powerful emotional memories from Lord Leo."

Reyna stood. "What makes you think I extracted his memories?"

Anemone and Orion exchanged glances.

"Because we saw them," Orion replied. "Watery figures animated around you, playing out whatever memories your magic latched on to. Lord Leo tried breaking the connection, but you were in a trance. When you wouldn't release him, he repelled you."

The sinkhole in Reyna's chest swallowed her.

She'd invaded his body. Put his memories on display. Brax attacked her. Defended against her. She pressed her palms to her eyes and begged to unsee Brax's horrified face from her own memory. But he remained a sunny spot blotting the darkness behind her lids. An imprint of lingering light, long after the moment passed. She hoped the moment Brax accepted her warnings were rooted in something real. Reyna's walking away might be easier. She was wrong.

The moment he'd been shot.

The second she realized he wasn't.

The gun in his hand …

How could she have been so naïve? Brax dismissed Reyna's sins with such ease. Was it because he'd racked up plenty of his own? She never considered his work's implications and wanted to believe that whatever occurred in his memory left Brax with no choice. But the simple truth was that Reyna knew little about him.

"Zodiacs cannot hurt each another." Anemone brought Reyna back to the present. "Lord Leo will be okay."

Reyna scrubbed her hands over her arms. "All that matters now is finding the For—information about where the prophecy is."

"Even so," Anemone replied. "You'll be escorting our latest ascendants to their new homes in Flora in a few days' time."

"Ascendants?" Reyna lowered her guard.

"Young Nidians born outside the season of their regional birthplace," Anemone explained. "In this case, those born in Calidi during springtime months. Upon their twelfth cycle, Nidians are relocated to the region coinciding with the season they're born under."

"Will they see their families again?" Reyna asked.

"Of course, but their lives are bound to their new regions," Anemone replied. "They must be guided by the Zodiac ideals they'll represent on Earth."

"You expect me to go to Flora again?" Reyna raked her fingers through her hair. "We should be looking for the prophecy, not running around the island."

"That's exactly what we should be doing." Orion's gaze narrowed.

"The prophecy could be anywhere, and this allows us to cover more ground. The goddess wishes to maintain normalcy on Nidus for as long as we're able. The people need to feel secure. Delivering the ascendants will help demonstrate that nothing has changed."

"Everything has!" Reyna couldn't restrain the absurdity.

"Neoma has explicitly expressed you're to escort them," Orion replied with finality. "This is part of your role on Nidus and it's important."

Reyna studied his expression for an inkling of knowing. Some clue the goddess confided their mission into the Forgotten to him, but his features gave nothing away. Maybe he knew nothing more than the order given. A true soldier to his queen's word. Neoma had called him a distraction, and though Reyna thought it foolish, perhaps a distraction away from Brax was what she needed too. Distance, from the darkest parts of herself threatening to destroy them both.

CHAPTER

TWENTY-THREE

S TRING MUSIC RODE THE BREEZE ALONG REYNA'S SHEER drapes. She'd counted and recounted each vine-woven overlap of her canopy, hoping it enough to lull her to sleep, but even Brax's absence demanded attention. The meadow's earlier events relentlessly swept over her like waves lapping the shore. Receding, quick as they came, only to wash over her memory again. Reyna hoped the rising music was a sign Brax's party was in full swing. At least it'd meant he was well enough to push past what had happened at training. Could Brax rebound from something awful so quickly? Reyna couldn't fathom such a concept.

Rebound.

Seph was at the party. Did it matter? Yes. No. Definitely no. Maybe.

Reyna's arms rose and plopped down onto the comforter at her sides.

"This isn't working," she grumbled.

She swung her legs from bed and grabbed a robe. Reyna couldn't deny her regret for what happened with Brax. But also, she wasn't ready for a confrontation. Maybe ever. Either way, she desperately needed to put sleep between her and the day. Her abuela always swore by chamomile every night before bed and Reyna prayed her grandmother had been right about at least one myth.

Acoustic notes sailed louder, the farther she crept through the dimly lit halls. Reyna retraced her steps best she could, sure if she could find where she'd eaten breakfast, a kitchen couldn't be far.

A few Nidians rounded a corner and Reyna ducked behind a column. She pressed her spine against cool sandstone and clasped her robe tighter. God, she missed the privacy of her own home.

"Has anyone seen Lord Leo?" the brunette woman giggled, and Reyna's ears perked up. "He's disappeared, and I haven't had a chance to *welcome* him back yet," she elongated her meaning.

Disgust and odd gratitude sank Reyna's shoulders.

Brax was at the party. Accounted for. Safe.

"He's been near impossible to get near all night. Everyone wants a piece, even if it's a few words." The tall man beside her let out a breathy sigh. "Can you imagine? A night with the lion."

The woman echoed his hoarse desire, "Legends of his stamina have to be true."

"You two are deplorable, speaking of Zodiacs in such a way." The rounder man amongst them peered into his cup. "I haven't had nearly enough to stomach such blasphemy." He turned back the way they'd come, and to Reyna's relief, the pair followed.

She clutched the fabric at her throat and trailed them along shadows. The Nidians stumbled around a few turns until they sifted into the courtyard's clinking crowd like smoke. Her hand glided over the corridor's opposite wall until it thumped over ridges of metal and wood. Two large sliding doors rose overhead. Reyna peeked inside at counters lining a kitchen's walls and slipped inside. She ransacked cabinets overflowing with pots, pans, flour, and sugar, but no ingredients to calm her day's misdeeds.

Perhaps Reyna deserved sleep deprivation. The universe once again at work balancing scales of retribution.

Light glinted against a far wall across the room. Reyna padded closer and a smile bloomed over her face. Nestled into an inlet, floor-to-ceiling racks held various wines.

Not chamomile, but the perfect remedy for a restless sleep.

Reyna didn't know much about wine, apart from her abuela

dragging her to Mass. Though, perhaps if allowed to drink more wine, church would've been palatable. Abuela forced her to church, once, sometimes twice a week and Reyna would fidget during the entire service. Through the parishioners' unspoken prayers mangled with pain. Sadness. Guilt. Silent pleas all tenderizing Reyna's insides like a sledgehammer. And her. Squirming. Itching. Skin crawling against whatever demon tried to crawl out from between her bones. Reyna's magic left no appetite for the bits of hope and gratitude she was sure some prayed for.

No, wine should've come at the beginning of Mass.

Reyna ground a corkscrew into the bottle's top and glass slipped between her fingers. She caught the bottle and blew hair from her face. A chimp with a matchstick would've had better luck. Reyna sat on the ground and vised the bottle between her knees. She twisted the metal coil once more and a pop jump-started her relief. Her head relaxed onto the cool sandstone at her back, savoring the sweet fusion of grapes across her tongue.

Each guzzle warmed Reyna's belly more than the last until time slipped into obscurity. The heavier her head grew, the fuzzier her concerns blurred. She swished the bottle and giggled at its half-empty contents swirling into a cyclone. Maybe she'd been wrong about not drinking her magic away. Seemed a lot easier than sneaking into the underworld.

Once music no longer floated through the kitchen doors, Reyna meandered into the hall. Gravity swayed her through the sleeping palace as her fingertips grazed walls for purchase. She rounded a corner and paused midchug from her bottled souvenir. Light leaked into the corridor from her open bedroom, accompanied by a strange snaking white mist.

The hallway slanted and her shoulder met a wall. Incoherent debate chirped in her head.

Anyone could be in her room. *Anything.*

Nidus looked enough like Earth, but proved time and again to be an illusion wrapped in familiarity. Reyna ground the cork into its bottle and pushed her weight from the wall. She'd already faced a god of darkness. His wraiths. A crowded room. A couple more crowded rooms and … something else she didn't like. Whatever was in her room wasn't going to like her.

Reyna raised her bottle overhead and edged into the bedroom.

Thick steam haunted the room like a ghost's finger beckoning her deeper into its ivory cloaked nightmare.

"Who's there?" she called.

"Took ya long enough." The rumble of a perfect storm broke through the clouds. Brax leaned cross-armed on the spring's edge. A lax blond knot adorned his head and beaded moisture hugged each flex of muscle beneath his shoulders. To say this man was crafted by gods was an offense punishable by death. Maybe he'd been right. Maybe Zodiacs *were* gods.

Brax spoke again at her silence. "We need to talk."

A flare shot from the sea of wine swimming through Reyna's head. Conversation meant facing what she'd done. What they were. Or weren't.

"You're in my spring," Reyna deflected. His favorite tactic.

"I got bored waiting."

"You naked in there?" Reyna perked onto her tiptoes. Jealousy at her element bubbling around his waist slipped between her thighs.

Brax snorted. "You're drunk."

"Right, as per usual." Reyna inhaled a long dramatic swig of wine. A slight drizzle crested over her lip and trickled along her chin. She scraped a thumb across her bottom lip.

Brax arched his eyebrow. "I thought we should talk about what happened." His palms flattened onto the floor, lifting himself from the spring. "But I can see this isn't a good—"

Reyna's robe slunk onto the floor.

Brax's shoulders pulled taut, halting midlift. Reyna swayed through the steam toying with her nightdress's hemline. Brax lowered himself into the water, unabashed eyes roving her calves. His fingers twitched. A visible ache to reach out and touch but they curled back with hesitancy.

A lopsided grin unfurled across Reyna's mouth. This was new. She liked it.

Reyna knelt beside the spring. Her lazy fingers stroked the bottle's neck as it slipped from her grasp. Glass clinked against the floor, and with it, a single strap fell from atop her shoulder. Brax's throat bobbed. Reyna craned her neck to the side and her long hair swept from her other shoulder. A breathy sigh fluttered from her. Every subtle sensation along her flesh was a pinprick of ecstasy. A preview of what she'd elicit from him. Reyna stood and shimmied from her silky prison.

Brax's tongue clicked against the roof of his mouth. A wildcat sizing its prey from the brush.

"Careful," he warned.

"Or. You'll. What?" The pad of Reyna's foot gently pushed his chest.

Brax stumbled back, water sloshing at the edges in his wake. Heat ravished Reyna's skin as she slowly descended into the water. Brax held his ground. A fortress awaiting decimation. Reyna paused before him. Each excruciating exhale grazed her nipples against his broad chest, but still, Brax remained as frozen as the Dark God's victims. Trapped in stone. Unreadable. But never abandoned her gaze. Reyna tugged at the tie binding his hair. Brax's throat arched slightly from the force. Soft golden waves tumbled over his shoulders and Reyna dragged her fingernails across his hairline. Gently scraped at the threads of resolve fraying from his stoic face.

A tiny groan escaped his throat.

Delight shattered her.

"Sunshine, I—" Restraint and desire warred between Brax's eyebrows.

Reyna's fingernails skirted across his neck. Stroked his hisses. Trailed over the cage of his throbbing heart. Thumped over his lower abdomen's hills and valleys. Her hand dipped below the water. Beneath the surface of no return.

Brax snatched her submerged wrist and brought it above water.

"Stop." He gritted his teeth.

"Isn't this what you've been wanting?" she whispered along his lips.

Brax's glance slid toward the wine bottle behind her. "Not like this."

The nerve. He should be atop some faceless Nidian. Forgetting Reyna. Cursing her. Shaming her violation of him. Accepting, after what happened today, that no way forward with her existed. Reyna would make him understand. Make it impossible for him to ever return to her. Alcohol swished against the walls of Reyna's skull. Her celestial abilities may be dampened, but tonight, she needed no magic. No more promises. This would be the last time she indulged in him. Or herself.

"You've never slept with a drunk woman?" she asked.

"I have."

"What, then?" Reyna activated the bomb within her chest. A lethal countdown to the end. "You're a criminal with a conscience now?"

Heat snuffed from Brax's eyes. "What?"

Ticktock.

"You and I both know what I saw in the meadow. Is that why you want me? Because I'm a *killer* like you?" The word grazed Reyna's tongue like a bullet. Deep. Everlasting. She was the gun. A death sentence for anyone who dared be too close.

Brax scooped her into his arms.

"What are you doing?" Reyna's arm instinctually flung around his neck.

"Putting you out of your misery," he grumbled.

"Let me go!"

"We're done." Brax carried her up the stone steps. "But I'm not leaving you to drown."

"I'm not drowning!" Reyna's skin slipped against his chest as she kicked her legs. "I'm the Zodiac of all water!"

"You're the Zodiac of all headaches."

Reyna slumped in his arms, skull weighed with the pressure of ten anchors. She stared up at him. The ceiling passed in a blur while Brax strode across the room. His body heat unfurled over every inch of her skin, evaporating the water. Reyna's head sank into a fluffy pillow and Brax rolled her onto her side. She smiled at the distorted shorts hugging his hips.

"When did you"—her eyelids closed—"not get naked?"

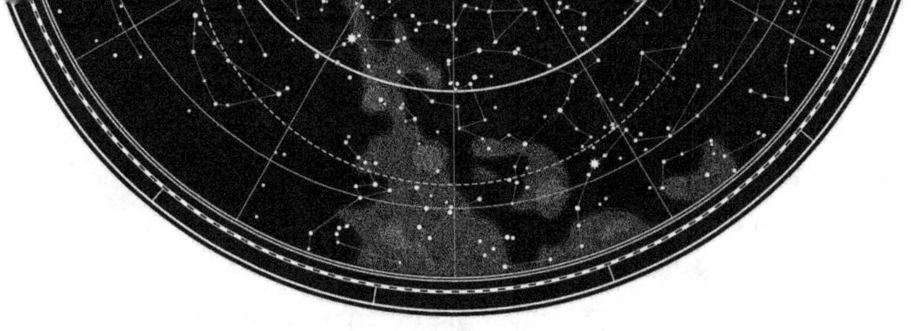

TWENTY-FOUR

REGRET HAD AN AFTERTASTE. A PUTRID CONCOCTION OF anger, shame, and a note of bile. Reyna spent the next morning expelling her regrets, as though she exorcised a demon from her body. She hated magic. She loathed this more. And though her insides turned inside out, it did little to quell the lingering undertones of heartbreak.

Killer.

The word Reyna branded onto her skin over and over to punish herself. But to hear it spat at someone from her lips? Made incarnate, by pitch, breath, and syntax?

Killer.

She'd shoveled dirt onto her grave and now all she could do was pray for peace. For clarity to move forward. Locate the underworld. Take control of her life and finally live it away from the countless lives she'd destroyed.

Over the next few days, Orion visited Reyna during afternoons for private magic sessions. She ate meals in her room and snuck into the library at night to feast over books. Reyna scoured for any mention of the Forgotten, but Levant's domain earned its name well. Proof of its existence remained lost to those who'd never returned.

"I wish you'd worn the garment I laid out for you," Anemone grumbled to Reyna while they wove through the palace.

"I am." Reyna slowed as they entered under another archway.

Every vacant stairwell became an exhale. Each empty corridor, another answered prayer. Another moment Reyna didn't come face-to-face with Brax.

Anemone's lips pursed. "You massacred it."

"I improved it." Reyna's hand skimmed over the frayed gossamer she'd ripped off, leaving only skinny pants beneath. "I'm not hiking through a jungle wearing layers."

"When we arrive, Florians will be seeing you for the first time. You must look—"

"If you want me to look perfect, why don't we take mirrors instead?" Reyna peeked around another corner.

"Nidians are not permitted to use such magic." Anemone huffed as though it were obvious. "They must learn to live a mortal existence as … well, a mortal."

"You're Nidian and you can do magic."

"Factotums are different." Anemone explained, "When I'm reincarnated on Earth, the goddess will bless my servitude by allowing my magic to stay intact."

"Mortals don't have magic."

"Witches do."

"Not from what I've seen." Reyna adjusted the satchel strapped across her chest. "Believe me. I've looked."

"What's troubling you?" Anemone asked. "You're more quarrelsome than usual."

"I haven't been sleeping well," Reyna admitted. Not the whole truth, though certainly not a lie.

Annoyance in Anemone's face waned. "Once an active factotum reaches their fiftieth cycle, the Infinite All-Knowing calls on another factotum to take their place. New factotums are asked to leave home and receive teachings in Messis to prepare serving the Zodiacs. When I first left home, I too had trouble sleeping. I missed my loved ones terribly."

"How old were you when called?" Reyna asked.

"Same as the ascendants we're escorting to Flora." Melancholy tugged Anemone's lips. "My twelfth cycle."

Twelve. Reyna's age when her papá died. The day she climbed into her abuela's car, glanced over her shoulder, and said goodbye to a house she wouldn't see again for over a decade conjured in a Dredger nightmare. A place Reyna's mother had once made her home with the man she loved. Until the day he returned. Not with a wife, but a baby. And perhaps that's what ached most. Their house was the only place Reyna knew her mother's footsteps once brushed along its carpet. Where maternal fingertips tugged at dusty drapes to let the light in. A tomb of what was and would never be again. Held together with two-by-fours, mortar, and siding.

The summer Reyna's life changed forever.

Killer.

Anemone beckoned Reyna to the present, saying, "I hope you can understand why this journey is so important for the ascendants. All they've ever known is their families in Calidi. You'll be delivering them to their new lives. Their fate."

"Fate." Reyna snorted. "Divinely called factotums. Prophecies. The Dark Star. It's all predetermined. Last I checked, fate doesn't equal choice."

Anemone rounded and Reyna staggered to a stop.

Passionate indignation carved between Anemone's eyes. "Believing in a cause greater than yourself? Embracing your gods-given gifts? Walking into the unknown with your head held high? It's all a choice. We may not control our destiny, but we choose how we face it."

Reyna pressed her lips together and followed the rest of the way in silence. Anemone's pride stemmed from her embraced purpose. A lifetime commitment to a Zodiac who may or may not have ever returned. A celestial who now mocked Anemone for everything she'd sacrificed in the name of duty. Reyna no longer needed to touch someone to absorb their innermost pain. She was extracting that spectacularly all on her own.

Morning light spilled over the palace gardens as Reyna's and Anemone's tension evaporated. They followed a stone path curving through greenery to a large water fountain spritzing at the oasis's center. Anemone cleared her throat, and three chattering adolescents whirled to greet her. The factotum wore regal command in her shoulders like a sash of honor. Not because she was magically inclined in ways other Nidians weren't, but because she knew her worth. Worth Reyna had belittled, in light of her own self-loathing.

Anemone glided her open palm toward the tweens. "Lady Regent of Kinship and Connection, I present, our ascendants, Reed, Leilani, and Ford."

"Nice to meet you." Reyna bowed her head. "And happy belated birthday."

"It's her." Awe ignited over the girl named Leilani.

"Be-lated?" the blond boy sounded.

"Belated." Reyna repeated. "It's a well wish, after you've surpassed a cycle."

"There's a name for that?" The fire-haired boy scratched his chin. "Can gifts also be be-lated?"

Warmth chuckled from behind the ascendants, and they parted. A woman sat atop the fountain's ledge. Silvery plaited hair rivaling stardust interlaced her head. Her brown cheeks bunched, weathered by years yet kissed with unmistakable youth.

"Wonderful to see you again, my lady." Her head cocked. "Or shall I call you Reyna now?"

"Elder Calathea." Anemone stepped forward and bowed her head. "I must insist you call her Lady Regent of—"

"Too formal, child." The woman brushed a dismissive hand toward Anemone. "Reyna will do fine."

"Elder Calathea—"

"Cancer is half mortal now. You'd do well to appreciate its value," the woman said. Anemone raised an arguing hand but slumped under the lady's narrowed eyes. "Reyna, I pray you grant my great granddaughter great patience. She's a gifted Cancerian, but perhaps too much so? And please, call me Thea."

"Great granddaughter?" Reyna pivoted between the women. "You were a factotum?"

Thea smiled. "Yours to be exact."

"Lady Regent?" The blond raked bangs from his forehead. "Is it true you freed a Dredger?"

Reyna peered between the ascendants' eager expressions. "I— um …"

"Oh, it's true," a haughty voice cut from behind.

Reyna clenched her eyes shut, heart lurching into her gut.

"Lord Regent Leo." Thea beamed. "What an absolute pleasure to see you again."

The sun rose beside Reyna and took Thea's hand.

"Memory or not." Brax kissed the old woman's knuckles. "The honor is undoubtedly mine. Please, call me Brax."

"I see little has changed." Thea grinned. "So delighted you'll be escorting us to Flora."

"What?" Reyna's hopes set ablaze. "Why?"

"Don't be rude, Sunshine." Brax smirked. "That's my job."

Reyna tugged Anemone aside, grumbling in hushed tones. "Did you know he was coming? Why didn't you warn me?"

Anemone pulled her arm from Reyna's grasp. "You haven't been willing to discuss what happened in the meadow. How was I supposed to know you hadn't resolved your issues? Plus there's"—Anemone's demeanor flushed—"the upcoming ceremony."

"What ceremony?"

"Forgive me, Reyna, it was my idea to invite Lord Leo," Thea interrupted their not-so-private-anymore conversation. "As Lady Regent of Kinship and Connection before, you officiated Soul Bondings to unite Nidian families. I believe on Earth it's called a wedding. As a renowned master of celebration, Lord Leo has graciously agreed to host the celebration afterward. I thought you both might benefit from this time discussing how to proceed with festivities once we've returned. Anemone's bonding will be the first since the Zodiacs' departure."

Reyna gaped. "No one has been married since we left a hundred years ago?"

"I'm afraid not." Thea stood with a frown unbefitting of the positivity she radiated. "It's a celestial contract only Lady Cancer, yourself, can grant. A Soul Bond ensures once we pass from Nidus and are reincarnated on Earth, our souls will be reunited with our bonded's."

"I offered myself to Juniper the moment we heard the Zodiacs arrived." Anemone's poise unraveled into a girlish smile. "Of course, she said yes."

All Reyna's words crumbled at the feet of the woman standing before her.

It didn't matter the Zodiacs might fail. Inconsequential if the world ended. Anemone longed to be bound to who she loved, perhaps in hopes they'd be reunited in whatever came next.

Reyna's role extended far beyond officiator. She needed to ensure they had an Earth to be reunited on.

Thea smiled. "With you and Lord Leo at the helm, I'm sure it will be a celebration worthy of a hundred cycles."

"Enough chatter." Anemone's stern disposition settled back onto her shoulders. "I insist we regard the day with what light is left and be on our way."

"Insisting again already, I see?" Thea grinned. "Though this time, I do agree. We should make haste."

Reyna adjusted her satchel strap and followed the group through the same pergola they originally entered under. She glanced over her shoulder at the palace. It wasn't her apartment, but she missed it already. Gone were the walls. The library's shielding stacks. Shadows she could slink along at night. An ability to peek around corners.

And so, Reyna trudged in the only direction she could. Into a jungle of the unknown.

The river meandered their party into midafternoon. Sunlight pebbled through leaves, but the shade offered little reprieve. Hair clung to Reyna's sweat-glazed neck. She stepped aside the invisible path, pulling her humid-frizzed hair into a high pony. Laughter floated through the trees, and she peeked over her shoulder. The ascendants trailed alongside Brax like tiny fishes clinging to the manta ray's easy smile. Whatever passionate tale he told swam them deeper into his wake. Brax's face glowed as he spoke. A true light Reyna witnessed between the few moments their lives weren't in peril.

Brax met her spying eye and Reyna quickened her footsteps, brushing past Thea.

"We hike toward Flora"—the old woman chuckled—"so why do you seem to be running away?"

"Running is what I do best." Reyna slowed and fell in step beside her.

"My dear, we're all running from something, but it means we're headed toward something too."

"What about Cancer?" Reyna wiped her brow. "What'd she run from … or toward?"

"Who says they cannot be the same?" Thea replied. "Cancer was charming, headstrong, and quite the visionary. Nidians came from all four regions for her aid in family matters. No home too was far. No problem too mundane or complex. Lady Cancer was dedicated to all souls on Nidus. She was admired by many."

"You still haven't told me what she was running from," Reyna replied.

"Ah." A shadow crept above Thea's brow. "Those dedications, over time, became an escape from what she wanted. Cancer rarely put her needs before others. She never said so, but I always suspected she was quite lonely."

Reyna pulled a frond aside and let Thea pass. "How could Cancer have been lonely if so admired?"

"To be admired and to be loved are not the same. To serve families yet never have your own. I would never speak ill of our goddess, but perhaps a flawed oversight on her part?"

"The Zodiacs weren't allowed families?"

"While discouraged, Zodiacs still *mingled* with each other and Nidians throughout the centuries, but any bonds beyond the physical were prohibited."

"What would happen if two Zodiacs bonded?" Reyna asked.

"Zodiacs are meant to exist alone as a single sign, with the exception of the twins." Thea frowned. "I'd imagine if two Zodiacs joined wholly, they'd shatter the balance of the goddess's and god's existence."

"Seems it may happen anyway." Reyna sighed, feet crunching over dirt and rocks. "Did Cancer ever … mingle with anyone?"

"I don't believe Cancer indulged in such affairs, though I often encouraged her to." Thea grinned mischievously. "She lived to guide our people through moments of darkness. Nothing else mattered. Nidus was her one love."

Cancer possessed everything Reyna didn't. Her magic helped people. United their love. Consoled families through conflict. Reyna swallowed back sorrow for a life she couldn't remember having. She'd lived two lives and neither brought family or love.

Reyna blinked across the river and met a pair of eyes.

She staggered to a stop before relief slumped into her shoulders. A statue of a man stood across the bank. His mouth hung ajar in a scream. Vines snaked along his marble legs and dangled from where his left arm no longer extended. The cruel memory of Levant draped over a statue's shoulders chiseled into her mind. Reyna shuddered. "I'll never get used to seeing those things."

"A sorrowful sight indeed." Thea stood beside her. "Though not uncommon to come across the Lost around Nidus."

"The Lost?" Reyna asked.

"What we call souls who've crossed the Dark God. Nidians believe the Lost are bad omens, but the goddess could never bring herself to dispose of any."

Reyna shook her head. "All this death needs to end."

"Death is a part of life, my dear. Our god's deeds are not justified, but we exist because the goddess and god made it so. We're all created from light and darkness. One cannot exist without the other." Thea gazed across the river. "Even the Forgotten has its place on Nidus."

The old woman's words buzzed through Reyna's mind.

There were clues about the Forgotten. All over Nidus.

"Thea, do you have a map?" Reyna asked. The Nidian pulled papyrus from her satchel and Reyna ran her finger along it from Calidi along the river they trekked.

"Everything alright?" Brax paused beside them and nodded for the ascendants to keep hiking ahead. Reyna's mouth went dry at his proximity.

"Trying to figure out where we are," Reyna replied without making eye contact.

Brax inched closer. Every muscle in her body tightened. His chest grazed Reyna's back as he tapped the map.

"There." Smoke swirled from where his finger touched.

Reyna's question sounded strained, and she hated it. "How do you know?"

"Despite popular belief, I'm good with directions." His timber skittered unwanted tingles against her cheek. Brax cleared his throat and stepped past her, glaring at the statue across the river. "We should keep movin.'"

CHAPTER

TWENTY-FIVE

EMBERS FLOATED INTO THE JUNGLE'S CANOPY AS THE GROUP settled into camp for the night. Reyna pulled a blanket over her shoulders and held up her new discovery. Firelight bled through the map, silhouetting Brax's earlier burn. Reyna used a charred twig to mark where she suspected she might've first encountered Levant in his statue graveyard. Nothing from books would lead her to the Forgotten, but Reyna prayed Nidus's Lost souls might help her find the way.

"Lady Cancer?" Leilani chimed through Reyna's thoughts. "What's your Earth family like?"

"Oh." Reyna stuffed the map into her satchel. "I don't have one."

The ascendants gasped.

Leilani's brows gathered. "How can you not have a family?"

Brax snorted. "Not all families are worth having."

Anemone slapped a hand over her chest, stammering as though she might combust.

"Technically you're right, Leilani," Reyna interjected. "I had a family, but they're dead."

Silence spilled over the group. Brax pinched the bridge of his nose, mouthing something inaudible through the fire's snaps and sputters.

"Dead?" The blond, Reed, tasted the word as though it was a foreign spice.

"It means they've traveled onto the Next," Anemone clarified, before she addressed Reyna. "When our time on Nidus ends, it's quite a beautiful transition. Death isn't a concept most Nidians are familiar with since we don't suffer illness or injury. Factotums possess an understanding of such mortalities because of our work."

Ford said, "If your family is *dead* and gone to the Next, as Lady Regent of Kinship and Connection, the most wonderful day of your mortal life would certainly be surrounded by family."

Muscle, bone, and tissue threatened to split Reyna's chest open. The past, forever dissecting its way into her scar-calloused heart.

Would it always be like this?

Family was no longer simply absent from Reyna's life, but in this place was a staple of what she embodied to an entire people. If the Infinite All-Knowing did exist, they were cruel to grant her a role she could never bask in. Neither as Reyna nor Cancer.

Reed cracked the wound open wider. "What happens if our Earth kin die? Who will be there for us?"

"Be there for yourself." Brax spat into the fire. Orange tendrils swelled into the treetops as though kissed with kerosene. "Whatever family you think waits for you on Earth is a pipe dream."

"Lord Regent!" Anemone eyed the hope crumbling from the ascendants' faces. "Surely you aren't suggesting—"

"The sooner you stop chasin' fairy tales, the better off you'll all be." Brax rose and trampled through the flames into the dark brush.

The group exchanged glances.

"It's been a long day, and I suspect everyone is a bit tired." Thea broke the silence before it could fester. "Tomorrow is an exciting day, and we should all be well rested." The ascendants murmured amongst themselves and began settling into their cotton-stuffed sleeping bags. Thea leaned close to Reyna and said, "Maybe you should check on Lord Regent?"

"I don't think I'm the right person to—" Reyna rubbed her knees. "We're not on best terms."

"All the more reason to mend what's broken." Thea patted Reyna's shoulder and hobbled to her feet. "It appears Lord Leo is now running. Perhaps another like himself could help uncover from or toward what?"

It wasn't unusual for Brax to offer a snide remark, but the cynicism tight between his words kicked up Reyna's other magic. She couldn't physically sense his emotion. That much was still true. Could it be after years of sensing people's feelings, she'd finally recognized deeper sentiments without her curse? Reyna may have put on a watery puppet show of Brax's most heinous memories. Been vicious with him in her bedroom. She should probably fear him after learning what true violence he was capable of. But none of it mattered, because swaddled within those darknesses, a too-late ugly truth Reyna could no longer ignore wrapped her in its entirety.

She cared for Brax.

Every key person Reyna kept at bay always ended the same. Dead.

Despite her efforts, she didn't want to push Brax away and whatever force repeatedly brought them together didn't want her to either. Reyna never allowed herself to truly embrace someone. Perhaps if she did, the cycle might break. If her heart didn't first. She didn't know if they could come back from how she acted during the night in her bedroom, though maybe they still had a chance at friendship.

Branches nicked Reyna's cheeks as she stumbled through the jungle. She wished for the song of crickets or frogs. Any small indication she wasn't alone, but only silence folded in from all directions. Reyna inspected a plant, rubbing its singed waxy leaves between her fingers.

Brax was burning through his path along the jungle.

She continued tracking fire-curled plant life until it led to the base of a hill. Reyna scaled the sloping ground and emerged from its shadow tree maze. Clustered nebulas glistened over the Nidian Sea and Calidi's distant lights wove along the coastline.

"What'd I say, 'bout wandering the woods alone?" Brax's familiar grit resonated.

"Speak for yourself," Reyna tempered with indifference. She scanned for the origin of Brax's voice, but his trail remained cold.

He snickered. "I've survived this long."

"So have I." Reyna inspected behind tree roots swimming through the cliff's soil like a Loch Ness monster. "Yet you continue reminding me how out of my depth I am."

"Did you need somethin'?" Brax's voice lacked his usual defiant luster but carried from somewhere in the tree.

To say I'm sorry. That the drunken mess of a woman posing as me in my room was sent by some god of trickery. How much you mean to me.

If experiencing people's feelings taught Reyna anything it was that the root of all emotion lay in what people didn't say.

"At the campfire, the way you talked about family, I understand how you feel." Reyna mulled over her words. "Mine was never there for me the ways I needed either. My family is dead, but I never said how."

Brax's firefly eyes found hers from his perch amongst dark foliage.

Still, he offered no remark, quip, or clue to his thoughts. Reyna squirmed beneath the uncertain silence. To neither feel nor see his response wobbled through her with a wrongness she couldn't put into words. As though she spoke into a void, only to have her words regurgitated. But she couldn't stop. Not now.

"I killed my parents." Reyna's heart clicked open, and the chains of her burden clattered into a heap. She'd never spoken the words aloud. Not to her abuela. The police. Tessa. Not even alone. "My papá said my mother's heart depleted with every push during labor and the doctors didn't know why. Now I understand she died because my magic sucked the life from her." Tears pricked Reyna's eyes. "My papá said I was born wrong. What if he's right? We were never supposed to be on Earth and my mother died because of it."

Brax dangled from the branch and dropped onto the ground. He edged closer, the starry sky's low light sharpening his cheekbones. "What happened to your dad?"

"He said I murdered her, and I was twelve when he tried to—" Tears crested onto Reyna's cheeks as she slid her fingers around her neck. "I should've let him end me, but I was too afraid to die, so I killed him instead. I'm the one who should be dead."

"Fuck that." Brax clutched Reyna's arms, anchoring her to a world slipping out from beneath her. "You protected yourself from an evil son of a bitch who blamed a kid for his wife's death. You *defended* yourself."

Reyna's glassy gaze met his. "Like you defended against me?"

"It wasn't defense." The crease between Brax's eyes unraveled. "I was trying to hide stuff from you." He stepped back and rubbed a hand over his mouth. "The man you saw in the water was … my brother."

"Why hide a brother?" she asked.

"He was home visiting from his first year at college. He and his buddies took some girls drinking at the bridge and invited me to tag along." Brax shook his head at the sky. "Surrounded by friends and beautiful women and he still wanted his shit-stain-of-a-younger-brother around. I was always tryin' to be like Blaine. Dress like him. Talk like him. So, when his friends rode him about what a burden it was havin' me around, I knew it was my chance to show I was worthwhile. I made a bet with them on how far I could jump from a bridge in town. Blaine said I had nothin' to prove, but I climbed up anyway." A humorless laugh choked from him. "He said we'd do it together. That's when he slipped. When he …"

"Died?" Reyna's heart sank into the fizzing bubbles of Brax's memory, now forever ingrained in hers.

Brax scoffed. "If only."

"What do you mean?"

"I dove after him, but the jump was too high." Brax massaged his palm with his thumb. "I was unconscious for two days and when I came to, Blaine was in a coma. My mom stayed with him and every day I grew stronger, he seemed to slip further away. I tried consoling my folks. A reminder they still had a son. I wasn't the best of us, but I could help them. Cry with them. Make things bearable. The more I tried, the further they drifted." Raw emotion grated in Brax's words. "My folks never said it, but they blamed me. Blaine was the epitome of a perfect son, and I was always the disappointment."

"What happened?" Reyna asked.

"After ten months, the doctors told my parents he'd lost too much oxygen to his brain, and it was unlikely he'd ever wake. The day they unhooked him from the machines, I left and never looked back. It's why I hate hospitals." Brax's jaw ticked. "Why I couldn't stay with you after the Dredger attack."

"And why you're afraid of water?"

He nodded. "You need to understand. My repelling you in the meadow was about protecting myself from how you're lookin' at me right now. From knowing who I really am. That you were right about *what* I am."

"Your brother's death wasn't your fault." Reyna's brows gathered. "And I don't know what happened on the docks, but—"

"I've done things. Unforgivable shit to survive and keep people I care about safe." Brax took a deep breath. "I'm not proud but also don't regret them. Just like you should never regret standing up to an asshole who believes he has some claim on how you should live or not."

"Brax ..."

"You're strong here." His thumb grazed her temple and glided across her slightly parted lips. "Here." Reyna's chest rose and fell with restrained breath as his fingers trailed along her neck and halted at the center of her breastbone. "And most important, here. You're worthy of existing in this world and every other. No matter what happens, never let anyone make you believe otherwise."

"I'm sorry for what happened in my room. I never should've called you a—" Reyna swallowed the word, lost in his tender gaze. "You've stood by me and didn't deserve what I said."

"You weren't wrong. I'm a dangerous man." His hand fell from her. "But I hope you also know by now, no matter what happens, I'd never intentionally hurt you. Just like I know, you'd never hurt me without reason." His gaze narrowed. "Even a stupid one."

Reyna blinked. "What do you—"

"I've been pushing people and pissin' 'em off for a long time." Brax flashed his signature smirk. "I know the difference between a con and the real thing."

CHAPTER

TWENTY-SIX

REYNA WADED FROM DENSE FOREST INTO SUNLIGHT BATHING her skin. Diamonds stretched across blue sky and over snow-kissed mountains dipping into green meadows. Flora sprawled the heart of the vale, like a patchwork quilt awaiting company. A palace grew from atop a green hill at the city's center. Sturdy and lush as any tree, but its gray stones reminded one of an English castle. Reyna sighed into the breeze cooling sweat on her brow.

Mirror travel was overrated.

Their party crossed a wooden bridge into town. Chatter crescendoed the deeper they ventured. Aromas of baked bread and lilacs wafted through the streets. Citizens paused from their daily bustle and bowed heads at the passing Zodiacs, but curious whispers regarded Reyna long after she passed. After what transpired on *Polaris* and at Omphalos, Reyna couldn't hide anymore.

Brax splayed a hand against the small of Reyna's back and her body sang. She focused on Brax's fingers skating across her spine. Inhaled his bonfire cologne. He'd always been her anchor. Long before even she knew it. Reyna's shoulders relaxed and she extended a true smile to all who regarded her as they wove through downtown. Brax slowed and his hand slipped from Reyna.

"What is it?" Reyna searched for what caught his eye down the busy street.

"I need to look into somethin." He smiled between her and Thea. "Think we could break for a bit before we drop the kids off?"

Anemone perked onto her toes, pointing at the sun's too-late position.

"Yes." Thea shushed her granddaughter with an affectionate smile. "Some light exploring should be fine, but let's make it quick."

"See ya soon." Brax swaggered backward, winking at Reyna as he went. His steps were lighter and smile easier than they'd been. Reyna chuckled at Florians staggering from his path and new warmth crept through her cheeks.

She scanned the tiny shops and ware carts, pausing at a stone shop pushed behind two others. Weathered boards covered its windows and weeds cascaded from window boxes. Overgrown grass waved like beckoning fingers. Reyna ran her hands over the goose bumps pebbling along her arms.

Anemone stepped beside her. "I would've thought they'd have torn it down by now."

A single dust-smudged window decorated the shop's second floor. Reyna asked, "Why's it closed?"

"Florians believe it's cursed." Anemone crossed her arms. "A bit absurd if you ask me."

"Cursed?" The familiar word soured on Reyna's lips.

"The Demeter family lived there," Anemone explained. "Their daughter is the only Nidian to renounce our ways. She sold her soul to become the Dark God's liaison, in exchange for avoiding rebirth on Earth."

"Seph," Reyna grumbled.

"Seph," Anemone echoed. "After her betrayal, Seph's family was shunned. Rumor has it, what's left of her line resides somewhere near Flora's and Parahelia's border mountains."

"Didn't Cancer help them?" Reyna frowned. "Isn't it what I— she was supposed to do?"

"From tales I've heard, Seph's family was too ashamed." Anemone sighed. "We can only help those who seek it."

"No." Reyna's mortal life crashed over her. "If you felt the pain people walk with every day, you'd know that's untrue. If people don't ask for help, it doesn't mean they don't need it. Cancer should've tried harder to connect."

"My lady, you cannot save every—"

"Reyna." A familiar Irish baritone captured her smile.

Ethan jogged toward them, muscles nearly busting at pastel seams of airy Florian linens. Russet hair swept across his forehead in curls and a soft glow painted his once alabaster skin. If ever a Zodiac looked like a god sent from Olympus itself, Ethan would be their second most worshiped.

Unease creased his brow. "I'm glad you're here."

Reyna's smile faded. "What's wrong?"

"I need you to come with me. Someone's been hurt."

Anemone gasped. "How's that possible?"

Ethan feigned a smile at the nearby townsfolk. "Try not to draw attention."

Anemone smoothed her dress to compose herself. "Elder Calathea and I shall see the ascendants to their new families. Please take care in whatever"—her lips pursed—"aid is required."

"Thank you," Reyna replied. "And if you see Brax, please tell him what's happened."

Anemone nodded with a bow and scuttled away.

Ethan hurried Reyna through narrow alleyways spidering from the city's center. The farther they ventured from downtown, the more cobblestone tapered into dirt roads and quaint cottages. Reyna broke into a slow jog to keep pace with Ethan's massive strides. She imagined what Flora's neighborhoods were like before Levant's banishment. Birds chirping. Butterflies and bees buzzing about. Dogs frolicking in the streets with children. Flora possessed a timeless charm, but its air was tinged of missing pieces.

A white gate creaked open, and Ethan strode along the home's walkway. Ivy crawled the cottage's stone walls and light blue shutters. A man paced the porch, gnawing at his thumbnail. His hickory hair was pulled into a knot, its intermittent grays accentuated by the hopelessness blanching his skin. His attention snapped at the porch steps creaking beneath Reyna and Ethan.

"Lady Regent?" The man scurried toward Reyna and squeezed her hands. "Thank you for coming!"

"Of course. I—" Reyna stared at his fingers on hers, but before she could process his touch, her spine yanked forward with the man dropping to his knees. He pressed her hands against his forehead.

"Please." An impending sob rattled through his voice. "You have to help him."

Reyna's cringe dissipated. "Who?"

Neighbors paused in front of the cottage, whispering at the odd exchange.

"Not here, Glen." Ethan gripped the man's shoulder and urged him to his feet.

"Can someone please explain what's happening?" Reyna demanded gently. "Who's been hurt?"

"My son, Ambrose." The man trembled.

"Glen found him near the river." Ethan closed the house door and hooked a finger around the drapes to peek outside. "Ambrose was attacked by a Dredger."

Reyna's heart lurched.

"It was on him." Glen quivered. "The screams—I think I scared it off because when it saw me, it dove into the water."

Reyna didn't know much about Dredgers outside her few personal experiences, but a Dredger scared by a magicless Nidian? Not likely.

"Is your son—" She swallowed, unable to give her question true breath.

"He's alive." Ethan's frown deepened. "But he's been marked."

"What's that mean?" Reyna asked.

"It might be easier if I show you." Ethan led her down a short hallway. Charlie sat hunched on the floor, hands threaded through his hair and staring at the ground between his knees.

"Charlie?" Reyna knelt.

"I'm so sorry." Charlie's swollen red eyes met hers. He sucked snot. "Ambrose is a Gemini. I was supposed to protect him. Please, Rey, don't let him die." Charlie's head tucked between his knees again. "He can't die."

"Charlie was the first to arrive." Ethan sighed. "He's been a wreck since."

Reyna's hand hovered a few inches from Charlie. She wanted to press it against his arm. Tell him it'd be okay, though possibly a lie. Her hand retracted, unable to execute her heart's desire.

"Go." Ethan crouched and rubbed Charlie's back. "I'll stay with him."

Reyna entered the bedroom, and her veins iced at Neoma standing over a twin bed. The goddess's presence in a home of no significance indicated one certainty. Something bigger was happening.

Gurgles sputtered from the bed.

Black liquid leaked from a child's chapped lips and darkness shrouded the whites of his eyes. Reyna blinked back the horror welling behind her expression. He couldn't be older than seven. A woman with tight brown curls hugging her cheekbones sat beside him. She wiped a cloth over the strange residue curdling from his mouth and squeezed his hand. The woman forced a smile. "Thank you for coming, Lady Regent."

"Embera, would you please excuse Lady Cancer and me?" Neoma's hands clasped in front of her. "I promise your son will be well again."

"Of course, my goddess." Embera planted a kiss atop the boy's sweaty forehead.

Reyna had never been allowed to see a photo of her mother but imagined her face a million different ways. All the portraits were vaguely aged versions of herself. Whenever Reyna was afraid as a child, she'd summon one. Her mother always came. A blurry-faced angel but smile clear and warm. Reyna pretended her mother's ghostly hand would wrap around hers. And though it was a daydream, she still prayed somewhere beyond the veil her mother watched and whispered everything would be okay.

It'd been many years since Reyna invited her mother's face into her memory. Could Ambrose still feel his mother under whatever darkness infected him?

"What's happening to him?" Reyna asked after Embera closed the door.

"A Dredger's nightmare is meant to kill the host." Neoma placed her ivory hand atop Ambrose's brown hair. "But without remaining attached until death complete, the Dredger's mark will remain. The child won't die but will be forced to relive the nightmare until his time on Nidus has ended."

"He'll live in a perpetual nightmare until he's old enough for ascension?" Reyna's jaw dropped. "Why haven't you healed him yet?"

Neoma's jaw tightened. "The Dark God and I cannot undo each other's magic."

"This wasn't Levant. He's locked away."

"He creates Dredgers, and their dark power source originates from him, therefore, I cannot."

Reyna scowled. "You told this boy's mother he'd get better!"

"He will, if you ..." Neoma composed the slow agitation curling her lip. "Use your extraction magic to remove the nightmare."

Muffled voices battled outside the door.

"Like hell she is!" Brax burst into the room with Ethan trailing behind him.

Neoma sneered. "Mind your tongue, lion."

"Maybe I should cut out yours for suggesting it."

Neoma's glower flared. "How dare you—"

"Rey extracted the Dredger's fear on *Polaris*." Charlie trembled in the doorway. "Maybe she could remove his fear?"

"That was different." Reyna's brow furrowed. "I freed a Dredger with extraction magic, not a person. I could hurt him or make it worse."

"Worse than staying trapped in a never-ending Hell?" Ethan countered diplomatically.

"Enough," Neoma snapped. "She cannot remove his fear. Nidians are maturing souls. Removing an undeveloped human emotion could disrupt this boy's ability for rebirth. His fear must stay. We must extract only the nightmare."

Perhaps that's why Reyna never felt other Nidians before. Because their emotions were still evolving? She raked her fingers through her hair. She needed time to think. There were too many unknowns.

"I don't know how to remove nightmares." Reyna steeled herself for her next words. "Maybe we could take him to Levant? He might be able to—"

White fire consumed Neoma's light blue irises. "I will not give *him* a bargaining chip!"

Reyna growled. "You would rather let this child be tortured indefinitely?"

Neoma towered over her. "If you don't, this boy's suffering will be on your hands!"

"Whoa!" Brax stepped between Neoma and Reyna. Fire licked his fingertips. "Back the fuck up."

"Orion told me she can extract visions." Neoma's light glowed brighter as she stepped toward him. "She *will* do this."

A howl erupted from the child.

Muddy black tears streamed from Ambrose's eyes. Flashes of Reyna's own Dredger-conjured nightmare ripped her in two. Freeing the Dredger and extracting Brax's memories were accidents, but could Reyna do good on purpose?

Her fingers brushed over a pale green crystal necklace strung around Ambrose's neck. He was a soul of Nidus. An unborn soul of Earth. Reyna had lived two lives and he'd barely begun. She might hurt him, but if the probability existed he could have a chance at a full life, Reyna needed to try.

CHAPTER

TWENTY-SEVEN

Reyna set her gloves on the pillow beside Ambrose. Brax darted forward. "Reyna—"

"I can do this." Her hands hovered over the boy's arm. Brax's warm fingers slid over hers. "Not without backup."

Reyna closed her eyes, sucked in a breath, and pressed both hands onto Ambrose's arm. She waited for the jolt. A pull of power snapping her into some dreamy netherworld. But nothing resembling the havoc possessing his body grabbed hold. Failure prowled into the corners of her mind. What would being trapped in a recurring nightmare mean for Ambrose once born onto Earth? Would he be mentally sound? Unable to have meaningful connections?

Would he be ... just like her?

She focused harder. Dived deeper through his essence. Let herself float farther still. She kicked and swiped through the black abyss of whatever haunted him until fangs sank into her magic and pulled. Reyna swam toward it. The Zodiacs' inadvertent shuffles in the bedroom slipped away. Faint light shimmered over a blanket of ice overhead. Reyna pounded her fists against the frozen barrier, thumps echoing through the muffled depths. She splayed her fingers over ice and focused her will, trying to revert the ice to its original state. Every molecule buzzed beneath her hand. Begged for freedom to its truest form. Minutes or hours ticked by, but the ice thinned at glacial speeds.

A warm caress ghosted across her knuckles.

Brax.

Reyna closed her eyes and listened to his steady breath in the distant room beside her. A rhythm. Tethering her to a world still waiting for her return. Liquid lava simmered through her arms and into her chest. A growl swelled low in her lungs. A feral beast slashed through the jungle of her organs demanding she let it through. Brax gave all of himself and Reyna accepted.

A roar burst from her.

Bubbles sizzled from the flames at Reyna's palms. Ice buckled and cracked under her glowing hands. Ice chunks blasted from the water and Reyna clawed out of the hole onto all fours. Dainty snowflakes paraded between white plumes puffing from her lips as she took in the forest dripping with ice around her.

"Ambrose?" Reyna strained her call through a whisper.

A twig snapped.

Snow clumps from branches fell to the ground ahead. Reyna crawled across ice and crunched forward into the wood. Her pounding heart kept time with her chattering teeth. "Ambrose?" Reyna let her voice carry a little farther. "My name is Reyna. I'm here to help you."

White mist floated from behind a tree ahead.

Soft snow ripped at Reyna's bare calves like shards of glass as she trudged through the wintry molasses. She whipped around the tree and found a tiny boy huddled beside its trunk with his arms wrapped around his knees.

"Hi, Ambrose." Reyna knelt and smiled. "Would you like to see something?"

Ambrose buried his face into his arms and whimpered.

Reyna extended her hand. A tiny flame swayed over her palm with each slight flex of her fingers. Light flickered against Ambrose's cheeks and his blue lips pulled into a small smile.

"I'm a summer person myself." Reyna glanced at the snowy wood. "What do you say we get you back home?" Cracks and snaps echoed through the trees. The reality of not where they were, but *what* they were in, prickled along the back of her neck.

Dredgers manifest someone's worst nightmare.

"Ambrose." Reyna steeled her breathing. "Please tell me you're afraid of the cold."

His pupils dilated at something over her shoulder. Every muscle in Reyna tightened at footsteps crunching through snow.

Groaned words bounced off the trees. "Thrice from death."

Reyna slowly rose from her crouch. A trio of stone corpses slogged through snow, their marbled limbs grinding as they advanced. Black tears leaked from corners of their vacant eyes.

"Thrice from death!" Their screeches rattled snow free from overhead branches. "Darkness consumes light!"

Ambrose scrambled to stand and cowered behind Reyna. The stony cadavers lunged. Reyna yelped and thrust her hands up. Snow churned into a wave. She spun and braced her hands against the trunk. Snow plowed into the statues. Powdery backlash drove Reyna toward the tree. She screamed, palms sinking against rough bark. Ambrose huddled underneath her petite frame, burying his face into her stomach. Snow rolled to a slow stop and silence blanketed the wood.

Reyna panted. "Are you okay?"

He nodded.

"Let's get out—"

Marble hands punched out from the snow. Stony fingers dug into Reyna's legs and waist. A hand swiped at Ambrose's ankle. He screamed.

A flicker of Brax's starfire lit the darkness. Foreign yet familiar.

She cranked her wrist like she'd watched Brax do many times. Flames sizzled across her shoulders and along her arms. The statues released them, and Reyna shot fire through the avalanche.

"Go!" She nodded toward the path of melted snow and ice. "To the lake!"

Ambrose shook his head. Dozens of new hands punched from the snow, a small army clamoring from their snowy graves.

"Now!" Reyna commanded.

Ambrose bolted through the snowy half-pipe. Reyna faced the Lost, heat pulsing from her skin. Strands of flaming hair flicked around her face and dead, charred earth peeked through the melted snow at her feet. Boiling water snaked from the ground and strangled the undead statues in the air.

"Darkness consumes light!" the Lost chanted.

"Not today," she replied and flung her arms open.

Marble bodies slammed into tree trunks and shattered. Reyna whirled and ran along the melted path. Ambrose scrambled across the lake on all fours. A one-armed statue crawled after him like a white diamond scraping against black glass. The ground rumbled beneath Reyna as heavy clumps of busted marble rolled past her onto the frozen lake. Ice buckled and split.

"No!" Reyna screeched.

More statues burst from the trees across the lake toward Ambrose.

They would keep coming.

The Lost were Ambrose's nightmare.

She sprinted. Ice broke free from its watery prison. A statue slammed into Reyna and plunged her into the arctic water. She burst above the surface. Water churned. Swallowed her again as she heaved for frigid breath. Reyna's head popped above black waves. The boy wailed. She grappled around a floating ice chunk.

If she couldn't make it to the statue before it killed him, would the nightmare start over? Warp into another? With no Dredger connected to him, how was she supposed to free it or Ambrose? Reyna already touched Ambrose outside of the nightmare—did she need to here?

Too many variables. Unsurmountable what-ifs. Too far. Ambrose was too far away.

Reyna pushed herself from the frozen buoy and slapped through the choppy waters toward him. More ice floated in front of her.

She wouldn't make it in time.

"Ambrose!" Reyna gulped air and water. "Face what scares you!"

A statue grappled for his leg.

Ambrose shrieked. "I can't!"

"You have to!" she gurgled through the raw chill searing her lungs. Reyna's muscles seized. Ambrose's cowering form blurred. A chill lodged between her bones. She was tired. So tired.

"End it!" Neoma's command ripped Reyna from death's embrace.

Reyna's eyes burst open. She and the room's contents rippled outward against the walls. Reyna heaved for renewed breath, gaping at the Zodiacs and goddess sprawled across the room. Neoma brushed disheveled platinum hair from her face, expression twisting at Reyna. Far from anger. Shy of gratitude.

Thick gurgles stole Reyna's and Neoma's odd exchange to the bed. Ambrose sat upright, expelling the last of black sludge along his tunic. Neoma clambered to her feet and rushed to his bedside.

"Are you alright, child?" Neoma cringed away from the bile coating his front.

"Goddess?" Ambrose dragged a sleeve over his mouth. "You're here?"

"How do you feel?" she asked.

"Lady Regent!" Ambrose met Reyna's gaze from the floor. He leapt from the bed and barreled into her. Cold goo soaked through Reyna's shirt, but her arms tightened around him with each racking sob. Ambrose's parents exploded through the bedroom door and collapsed onto the floor around them.

Hands.

So many fingers.

Squeezing. Brushing at Ambrose's hair and face. At Reyna's.

"Thank the Infinite All-Knowing." Glen sniffled beside Reyna. "Praise you, Lady Regent!"

"Precious. So precious." Embera pulled the three of them closer. "Thank you."

Reyna splintered into pieces, slowly put back together by the parents' attempts at articulating what words could not. Tears broke from her, and she let herself fall with them. Into relief. Joy.

An indescribable desire to absorb every ounce of the strangers who cherished their child, knowing she never could.

Ambrose untied the crystal necklace from his neck. "Take this, Lady Regent. For saving my life."

Reyna inspected the braided black rope threaded through a pale green crystal. A forced smile pulled her cheeks. Not of falsity. A dam to barricade more tears from raging. "Thank you." She draped the jewelry around her neck. "I'll treasure it, always. But Ambrose, how'd we escape?"

"I touched it." He smiled.

Reyna furrowed. "What do you mean?"

"Before the shadow monster came, I was playing by the river with my friends. We saw some of the Lost and my friends dared me to touch one, but I couldn't." Ambrose's cheeks flushed. "The Lost can become shadow monsters, and I was afraid if I touched them, I might become one too. When you said do what scares me most, I touched it, and everything disappeared. How'd you know it'd work?"

"I didn't." Reyna huffed through a small smile. "But I was stuck in a Dredger nightmare once too and part of how I ended it was accepting what I was afraid of. Once I did, I saw it for what it was."

"Which is?" Ambrose's saucer eyes waited.

Reyna picked up her gloves from the floor beside the bed.

"An illusion." She stared at the faux leather. "Fear is an illusion to keep us from our full potential. It's what traps Dredgers so they can't be free. What traps us in within their nightmares. But a nightmare is an illusion of what could be. Not what is. Once the fear is gone, it's not a nightmare anymore."

A throat cleared.

"Embera. Glen." Neoma's spine straightened. "Perhaps you should take your son to rest?"

"Oh yes, of course, my goddess." Embera wiped wetness from her face and scooped Ambrose into her arms. Glen offered an arm to Reyna to rise.

"We're forever in your debt," he said as he squeezed Reyna's shoulder, and the family hobbled toward the doorway.

"This is most troubling." Neoma said as the bedroom closed behind the family. "Dredgers haven't ventured onto our lands since Levant's days."

"It wasn't unusual for them to come ashore back then?" Ethan asked.

"I'm afraid not." Neoma sighed. "Before they became the Lost, Nidus was their home. I suspect a small piece of them, in all their savagery, will always try finding their way back."

Morbid sadness swallowed Reyna's heart. Dredgers were tormented reflections of life, wandering aimlessly for their next meal. The savor of something to make them feel whole again. Their innocence. Potential. Stripped away by a curse. Reyna and the Dredgers weren't so different.

"What the actual fuck was that, Neoma?" Brax's voice graveled.

"You try my patience, lion." Neoma's lip curled. "I won't remind you again to whom you are speaking."

"You almost got her killed!" Fire sizzled through the skin at Brax's knuckles. Ethan and Charlie exchanged glances before excusing themselves to check on the family.

"What's he talking about?" Reyna asked Neoma.

"The boy's fears consumed the room, as I'd heard you'd done with Leo in the meadow." Neoma smoothed her dress. "Once we identified the Lost as the nightmare's source, I insisted the Zodiacs destroy the vision."

Reyna's brow hardened. "While I was still in it?"

"Given the nightmare wasn't yours, I suspected you'd be expelled."

"You couldn't've known for sure," Brax spat.

Neoma ignored him, studying Reyna as though she were the one on trial. "Leo insisted we grant more time to see if you could destroy the nightmare's source, but your failure soon became clear. I knew with your magic there was a strong chance you'd make it. But the young one …" She looked away. "Whilst arguing, the nightmare ended, and the boy awoke."

"I understand." Reyna's glower dissolved. She'd be the first to offer her life for another's. A justifiable trade.

"I don't!" Brax tensed.

Reyna slipped her hand around his wrist and tugged softly. A plea to let it go.

"I've known Nidus a long time and Levant longer." Neoma's chin lifted. "You may not approve my methods, but we fight a common enemy. Today was a small taste if the prophecy comes to fruition. It's more imperative than ever that you find the prophecy." Neoma narrowed knowing eyes at Reyna. *The Forgotten.* "I'll return to Omphalos and reflect more on what's transpired. The people need to feel safe. If word of this attack travels, it would cause widespread panic."

"Yeah, you do that," Brax grumbled as Neoma strode past them into the hall. "Wouldn't want anyone to think there's actual danger."

A long, shaky breath shuddered from Reyna.

She'd almost died. Again.

Reyna collapsed into herself. Brax enveloped her, faint embers of a campfire clinging to his cotton shirt.

"It's okay," he whispered. "You're gonna be okay."

"Thank you." Reyna nestled her face deeper into him.

"We didn't know what would happen if we destroyed the nightmare from the outside and you aren't worth the gamble." Brax snorted. "For being the Goddess of Light, Neoma isn't the brightest. I don't care that I've met gods. Atheism is the way to go."

"Well, thank you for at least having faith in me."

"There's no one I believe in more," he murmured against her hair.

Brax's admission wrapped around Reyna like a warm blanket. After what they'd been through. The countless wrongs he'd forgiven her for. Reyna wanted to tell him everything. But she couldn't bring herself to say those three words. Three words to let Brax in and prove she trusted him back.

Darkness consumes light.

The Lost's cryptic phrase echoed through her skull.

Was it nothing more than ramblings of monsters, or a larger omen meant for her? Either way, Reyna believed more than ever that the secret to uncovering the Forgotten lay with the Lost. She'd made a deal with Neoma. A promise to herself.

Reyna's final act of magic would be spent righting her wrongs.

TWENTY-EIGHT

CANCER

ONE HUNDRED YEARS EARLIER

CANCER CHEWED THE INSIDE OF HER CHEEK AND PRESSED her fountain pen harder against her parchments on the floor. She squinted closer at the documents, massaging her forehead with a soft groan.

Several weeks preparing for tomorrow's negotiations.

Countless hours drafting and redrafting.

How would she stand a chance at success if unable to decipher her own handwriting?

The goddess must be testing her. Cancer tried remembering a time she might've irritated the deity. Anytime would do, though her most recent audience with Neoma came to mind. Another rejected proposal. Another failed attempt at swaying the goddess from her rigid ways. But Cancer hadn't left empty-handed. Neoma instead bestowed an impossible task upon her. A distraction to keep the Zodiac's mind occupied and her fear alive. Lest the goddess be bothered by any other of Cancer's admirable yet misplaced inquiries.

Squeals and laughter bounced off the conservatory windows.

Cancer glanced up and a smile twitched across her face. Children chased one another through the grand greenhouse's foliage, while others splashed near the fountain. This was her favorite part of being a Zodiac. Not the monthly banquets at Omphalos. Nor satisfying the fragile egos of diplomats from neighboring regions. *This.* Her students. The mentoring of young souls. A few of which would soon be relocated to their respective regions. Some of her students may not be born under the sign of Cancer upon earthly reincarnation, but she still believed bits of her Cancerian teachings would stay with them a lifetime.

Resolution settled into Cancer's shoulders. Nidus's future, *their future*, hung on her powers of persuasion. Her ability at appealing to forces with nothing to lose. Cancer slumped on all fours. She'd grown accustomed to Neoma's rejections.

But there was another's she could not afford.

"Lady Regent?"

Cancer craned her neck. Daylight flickered through strawberry blond curls falling over Violet's shoulder. The student edged forward and cocked her head at Cancer's work.

"What are you doing?" Violet asked.

Cancer smiled bright. "Nothing you need concern yourself with."

"Are you done? We're ready to discuss last week's reading."

"I suppose." Cancer sighed. "With Thea at her factotum summit in Messis, it appears I'm not so gifted at double duty."

"Uh, Lady Regent." Violet pointed at the floor.

A large ringlet of Cancer's hair rested in an inkwell. Cancer flung backward. Parchment clung to her sweaty palms and the inkwell toppled over.

"No, no, no!" Cancer grabbed the glass container. Black splatters and inky rivers bled over the parchment pieces. Cancer frowned at Nidus's fate drenched under black ink, some of its darkness absorbing between lines of her palms.

"I can help!" Violet rounded up the dry papers.

A small smile curved onto Cancer's face. Nidus's future may hang in the balance, but today still mattered. Her students mattered.

Cancer wiped her hands along her ivory dress and stacked Violet's papers into a separate pile. If Cancer could unite families through hardship, she'd make this right too.

Somehow.

Once everyone had gathered, Cancer perched herself atop the fountain's ledge.

"Thank you for your patience, everyone." She smiled at the cross-legged youngsters on the floor. "Let's begin with any questions about our reading from last week."

Ash raised his hand. "Why has the goddess written all the books on Nidus?"

She tensed at his unrelated question.

"As our creator, the goddess has spent much time on Earth." A chill snaked along Cancer's spine. "She's developed a deep under-standing of their ways."

Violet raised her hand. "But she is not our only creator."

Silence befell the group.

"You're correct." Cancer rubbed a hand over the goose bumps pebbling her arm. "Our God of Darkness has also contributed to many libraries."

"Where are those books?" Colt asked.

Chutney sneered. "Of course you would want to read those, *beastie boy*."

"Chutney, we've discussed this." Cancer's lips pressed into a thin line while she tried softening her glare. "There is nothing wrong with being named after an animal."

"My father disagrees." The girl's nose tipped up. "He says all the Dark God's books have been locked away and for good reason. Anyone who names their kin after a beast of the Dark God should not be trusted."

Colt wrapped his arms around his knees and pulled them into his chest.

Cancer interjected, "Need I remind you, many Zodiacs also lay claim to such creatures? Myself included. Animals may have been created from darkness, but they are not darkness itself. They're a blessing." She smiled at Colt. "As for our god's books, I hope perhaps we'll see them again."

"Why don't Zodiacs write any books about Earth?" Violet asked.

Chutney's eyes rolled. "Because they've never been."

Cancer nodded. "Zodiacs aren't permitted on Earth. The goddess feels our immortal presence would be problematic to the planet's delicate balance."

"If you've never been to Earth"—Colt's small voice came from behind his knees—"how can you teach us to best serve our families once we've reached final ascension?"

A dozen tiny gazes bored into Cancer and another wintry bite flicked across the base of her neck.

"You question me? Dare question your goddess?" Cancer gave a curt nod. "Good."

Students glanced at one another.

"Always seek understanding. Sometimes, the best way to help those we love is to listen. Want to know a secret?" Cancer bent forward and the half circle shrank as children scooted closer. "I agree with you. Which is why I've been petitioning the goddess to allow me passage to Earth."

Awes rippled through the group.

Violet shifted onto her knees. "Do you think she'll let you go?"

"I don't know, but I'm certainly trying to convince her."

Ash sighed. "I wonder what Earth is like."

"Not so different from here," someone drawled.

Cancer peered around the glass atrium. "Hello?"

A dark figure emerged from emerald foliage. Cancer slid off the fountain ledge, cheeks paling. Ice crystallized along draping leaves and vines as the God of Darkness approached. The students gasped and scurried behind their teacher.

"Children." Cancer commanded goodwill into her smile. "What a blessed day to find ourselves honored by a creator."

"Honored?" Levant's amusement flicked to Chutney and his mouth turned up in a crooked grin. "Are you certain?"

"We welcome all expressions of thought." Cancer pulled his attention from the child.

The god licked his canine tooth through a smile. "I believe Neoma would be most disapproving of such notions." He curled a beckoning finger at Chutney. "Come here, girl."

Chutney whimpered and shrank behind Cancer.

"My God of Darkness." Cancer's smile remained intact. "Chutney meant no—"

"Your maker has given you a command." He eyed the child and crouched.

Apprehension ravaged Cancer's mind. Neoma and Levant parted ways not long after the Zodiacs' creation, so aside from being an original creator, she didn't know a lot about him. Levant's notorious appetite for souls evoked fear throughout Nidus, but she never recalled tales of him consuming children. He was as much Cancer's god as Neoma and denying him would invite more conflict.

"It's alright, Chutney." Cancer knelt beside her. "I promise I won't let anything happen, but you must do as he asks."

Chutney trembled. "What does he want?"

Cancer smiled. "An apology might be a good start."

Chutney swallowed hard and shuffled forward. She fidgeted with her dress, pausing an arm's reach away. Levant extended his hand between them. Water flowed from his fingertips. He closed his fist and splayed his fingers open. Water burst into snowflakes floating around them. A miniature rabbit sprang from the swirling flakes and leapt through the air. Ice crystals trailed the rabbit's path. It snuggled itself into the crook of Chutney's arm and she beamed at the tiny snow rabbit.

"Take good care of that, won't you?" The god stood. "Once Capricorn's season ends, it will be no more."

Chutney nodded and scurried back to her classmates, all cooing at the snowy creature. The Dark God's cool gaze washed over Cancer stepping forward.

"Forgive me, God of Darkness"—Cancer bowed her head—"why have you come? My audience with you isn't until tomorrow."

"It isn't?" Playful mockery lined his grin. "Well, I'm here now. Shall we proceed?"

"Now?" Cancer glanced at the ink-doused papers behind him. "As in, right now?"

"I know time is trivial for us immortals, but with such a delicate subject to be discussed, perhaps sooner rather than later?" Eyes dipped to her mouth. "Are you ill-prepared?"

"Of course not. I'm …" Cancer combed her mind for an excuse. "The children. I cannot leave them. We're in the middle of their studies."

His emerald irises darkened.

"Everything alright here?"

Cancer whirled to Leo's quiet assessment between them.

"Will you excuse us for a moment?" Cancer bowed her head toward the deity. She pulled Leo aside and he uncrossed his arms. His shoulders went taut as she leaned closer and whispered, "Did you know he was coming today?"

Leo hesitated, gaze wandering the proximity of her face. "I heard rumors at Omphalos he might make an early appearance."

"And you didn't think to warn me? You know what is at stake!"

The god brushed his fingers along the fountain's ledge. Ice coated the structure and froze its waters midspray. Impressed chatters fluttered amongst the children.

Leo pouted his lips and shrugged. "A new fountain apparently."

She lightly slapped his arm.

"You'll be fine." Leo chuckled. "You do your best work on your toes."

Cancer's patience narrowed. "This isn't funny. You owe me."

"I rather like the sound of that." He pressed into the space between them. "What'd you have in mind?"

"Of all the—" Cancer scoffed. "I won't be driven to my knees like your eager admirers."

"What a picture you paint." Leo smirked. "Are you trying to torture me?"

She grinned and crossed her arms. "Not yet."

Leo's brow arched.

"Children," Cancer's voice rose, holding Leo's smug stare. "I must depart a bit early today, but Lord Regent of Courtship and Creativity has graciously agreed to finish today's lesson."

The lion's face dropped.

"I don't—this is your area." He glanced at the students. Rare paleness swept across his warm cheeks.

"You do your best work"—Cancer grinned—"on your toes."

"Alright, everybody." Leo tossed golden hair from his face. "Who has questions about courtship?"

A dozen tiny hands flung into the air.

Cancer flashed Leo a warning glare and stepped outside with the Dark God.

She clutched her paperwork close and led him through the gardens. The god's lean yet toned figure loomed beside her like a shadow blotting the summer sun. Midnight tresses of perfect chaos hung over his eyes. Those legendary emerald eyes. Said to be a last glimpse of life the Lost saw before being encased in stone for eternity.

"Something on your mind?" he asked.

Cancer sensed his smile, though she dared not look. "I wanted to thank you."

The god chuckled. "Yet another first for me today. May I ask, for what?"

"For showing my student kindness."

"I'm sure the girl's father won't see it as such. How unpleasant to host a creature of darkness in his home. More unpleasant I imagine, when he decides to take the creature away from her."

Cancer frowned. "You're assuming he will."

They walked under an arch into the palace and the god planted his hands behind his back. "Power, fortune, love, the shattered loyalty of a daughter, perhaps? All beings crave what they cannot possess, and what they cannot possess will always destroy them. I am not kind. Best to remember as we move forward."

Cancer huffed and his surprised brow drifted toward her.

"Or maybe, you need to have more faith in people." Cancer's pace quickened past him and she led the rest of the way in silence. When they reached the study, she scuttled to a tea table and spread out the treaty papers she'd drawn.

"Did you mean what you said earlier?" The Dark God pondered over book spines lining the study's walls.

"About?"

"Hoping to see my writings again someday?"

"Of course."

Levant plopped onto a love seat, resting an ankle across his knee. His arm spread along the backrest, and he squinted at her through a smile. "Tell me why."

The way he asked questions. Like they weren't questions at all.

Cancer sat across from him. "When all the books are written by one, it leaves little room for perspective." She turned to the papers. "Now, you'll find everything in place. I've ensured your desires align with what the Goddess of Light is offering."

A wolfish grin tugged his lips. "What do you know of my desires?"

"Only what the goddess has expressed you might like, in return for no longer consuming souls."

Levant's eyes rolled and his head knocked back. "Neoma hasn't understood my desires for over a millennium. Are you sure she wishes this treaty at all?"

"No!" Cancer's poise dropped and she restrained herself from leaping to her feet. "I mean, yes! She does wish it."

"Then why have a Zodiac see to it? Even in her pursuits at appeasing me, she couldn't be bothered to handle it herself?"

Cancer grimaced. It was a question she'd asked herself many times. "I assure you, my God of—"

"Lev." He leaned forward with elbows resting on his knees. "I'd prefer if you called me Lev."

"Lev." His informal title rolled off her tongue easier than she cared to admit. "I assure you, the goddess wishes nothing more than this treaty to bridge our two worlds. She's trusted me to secure this peace offering, so I suggest you do the same."

He studied her. "And what exactly is she offering?"

Cancer handed a few papers across the table. Levant relaxed into the cushions, skimming a long finger along the documents. Cancer sat on her chair's edge, tapping her fingers against her knee. He squinted closer at a page and his mouth quirked. Levant rotated the paper toward her. Black ink doused a quarter of the page. Cancer bent for a closer look and stumbled forward. Her palms plopped onto the tabletop.

"Come sit." He nodded at the spot beside him. "Perhaps we might decipher your handiwork together?"

Cancer forced a smile as she inched around the table and sat beside him. He brought the parchment closer. She instinctively leaned nearer, and their stares met in silent consideration of one another. Levant grinned, sliding his gaze back toward the document and pointing to where he had stopped reading. A chill from his breath rebounded off the page. Ice froze a few loose hair strands dangling beside Cancer's cheeks.

Levant's hand idly waved, and the fireplace roared to life.

"Apologies." His smile faded, but invitation still tinged his lips. "I forget, you're not accustomed to the cold."

"It's nice." Cancer's eyes flared at her thoughtless words. Levant's smile returned and she swallowed hard. "I only meant, a break from the heat isn't so bad." Cancer plucked the parchment from his hand and held it in front of the fire's glow. Her brows rose and relief settled in. Pressure she'd applied while writing peeked through the spilled ink. "Ah yes!" A confidence slid over her face. "This is in regard to—"

"Tell me more about your going to Earth." Levant's curiosity seared into her profile.

"What's that have to do with—" Cancer looked at him, his smile closer than she expected.

"I've been many times. You may not have access to my writings, but I'd answer any questions you have. Provide illumination on certain topics, I'm most certain, that would make the goddess quite unhappy."

Cancer's intrigue beat wild. "Why would you offer to help me?"

"I find you quite fascinating." Lev's knee brushed hers.

"You barely know me."

"I want to." Levant relaxed into the love seat. He propped an elbow on its armrest and rested his head against his fist. "If it makes you feel better, I have a request or two in return."

A jest. He must be joking. Dealings with the God of Darkness left no room for stories, rumor, or myth. The Lost were scattered across cities, forests, and shorelines. Plenty of proof of his requests gone wrong.

"This is an unusual proposition." Cancer squirmed. "I'm sure the goddess would not approve."

Levant's hand raked through his already tousled hair. "You don't know what I'm proposing."

"Fine." Cancer's fingers tightened around the small stack on her lap. She crumpled their edges and steadied herself. "What are you suggesting?"

The god smiled. "I'd like you to help me build something."

"Build what?"

"You'll have to wait and see."

Cancer stood. "If I am agreeing to something, I should know what it is."

"I assure, it won't bring you or any Nidians harm." Levant rose from his seat. "In fact, I promise until our deal is fulfilled or broken, I'll refrain from any feeding."

"What's your second request?" she asked.

"If you help me, I will tell you anything and everything you wish to know about Earth." Levant stepped forward. "I'll sign the treaty in whatever state you've drawn, with one amendment. I require access to the Zodiacs for resources from their lands. The Forgotten is a desolate place and, despite what most believe, it requires much to serve its purpose."

"You'll sign?" She held the documents out. "But you haven't read it."

Levant snatched the stack and dropped it onto the table. Stray pages fluttered to the floor. Icy chills radiated off his body and snuffed firelight crackling in the hearth. "I've given my terms. Nothing you do while helping me will void the treaty's validity, so long as you remain true to our agreement. Do we have a deal?"

Cancer's disbelief ran rampant in search of trickery.

Her mission at gaining Neoma's approval allowing her passage to Earth failed time and time again. The goddess would never allow her to experience the planet for herself. Forever bound to a single view. Perhaps Levant could give breath to the missing pieces. Complete her vision. Not only for her but for humanity's future.

She held her breath and nodded.

"Splendid. We'll begin tomorrow." Levant's gaze wandered to her shoulder. He lifted a ringlet draped over her collarbone, twirling it between his thumb and forefinger. Dark ink from her hair smudged his fingers as he rubbed them together. "And wear something black. It suits you."

PART THREE

CHAPTER

TWENTY-NINE

REYNA

PRESENT DAY

REYNA HUNCHED OVER A TABLE AND RUBBED HER EYES AT the map beneath her.

It was late. Or early. Who knew the true time difference between worlds? Anemone certainly wouldn't argue such a mortal concept. One of the few. But her blind spot for Reyna's exaggerated jet lag served well. Over the past week, Reyna had slept bizarre hours by day and scouted Nidus through mirrors by night. The brink of revelation tingled along her bones as though the underworld willed her to find it.

She traced a finger between invisible constellations of her markings denoting statues along rivers, lakes, and coastlines. All signs tapered into the sea, but how could Reyna explore an entire ocean by herself? She prayed Nidus's greatest mystery would reveal itself to her, but every step through a mirror greeted with more of the same. More black marks on her map. Cruel inkblots taunting what wasn't there. Reminders of her magicless freedom slipping away.

Reminders of *him*.

The few hours Reyna did salvage sleep were plagued by the same dream. Wet ink in her hair. Levant's chilled breath against her cheeks. Erratic adrenaline from his mere proximity. Reyna had never experienced such a sensory dream. Let alone the detail and knowledge it presented. The more her dream visited, more she questioned it a dream at all. Could it be Cancer's memory, and if so, why now?

Reyna's sigh flurried dust through the morning light slicing through library stacks.

The stony sanctuary sat nestled at the city's edge, bordering lush jungle where Calidians caught in the thrall of endless summer rarely ventured. Anemone might've been placated by mortal embellishments, but if Reyna stayed at her new base of operations too long past sunrise, others might notice.

"Ironic as it sounds, Sunshine." Brax made Reyna's heart leap. "I didn't peg ya as a morning person, but it means you'd need to sleep first."

"Funny." Reyna covered the map with a few papers. "I didn't take you for the stalker type either."

"Met with some locals and they mentioned a light was on in here all night. Whatcha up to?"

"Researching Soul Bonding for tonight." The half lie spilled with her back still held to him. Despite what happened in Flora, Neoma had insisted Anemone's union continue. Honor flooded Reyna at bringing two hearts together, instead of destroying them, but she also saw it for what it was.

Neoma's attempt at distracting the masses from what darkness crept across their island.

Soul Bonding, escorting ascendants, teaching Calidi's youth, and playing middleman to the Dark God's whims? No wonder Zodiacs needed factotums. Or why Cancer had no time for romance. Add finding the Forgotten to the mix and Reyna wasn't doing half bad. She smiled at the thought.

"We could write a cheat sheet along your arm," Brax said. "Always worked for me."

"This isn't some test. No one has been joined with their soul mate in a hundred years." Reyna faced him. "This is serious, Brax."

"I'll say." He ambled forward, each prowling step raising hairs along her arms. Reyna peeked at the map over her shoulder and hopped onto the table. Reyna's too-late mistake ravaged her cheeks as Brax paused outside the open gate of her legs. She refused to shift her body or pull her eyes from his. If Brax regarded her, he wouldn't notice what she hid.

"Ya know, there's other ways to calm your nerves." His hips grazed her knees, and the map incinerated from Reyna's mind.

"Like what?" Her rattled words betrayed her.

"Research is fine." Brax stepped between her legs. "But I've always found the doing much more memorable." His heady campfire scent enveloped Reyna. Brax's mouth paused an inch from hers as his arm reached around her. "Do you think *this*"—he stepped away—"is going to help you?"

Brax wiggled *A History of Soul Bonding* at her.

"Uh yes? I mean … no?" Reyna didn't recognize the breathiness in her voice. "I wouldn't know, since I've never been to a wedding."

"C'mon." Brax dropped the book and slid Reyna from the table. Reintroduction to gravity wobbled through her legs. Brax led her past stacks rich with old leather and ink derived from decades of depictions, centuries of stories, and a millennium of myths made real. He pulled her between two bookshelves where a stained-glass window towered beside them.

Rainbows folded over Brax's signature smile. "The key to everyone believing you know what you're doing is to pretend you do. Once you've done something enough times, you're not faking anymore."

Reyna's heart galloped. "I think they'll know if I'm doing it right."

"You said it yourself, Nidians haven't seen a bonding for a hundred years. Ya think they're gonna question Cancer, Lady Regent of Kinship and Connection?" Brax rubbed his hands together. "Now, show me what I'm workin' with."

Reyna inhaled and shook out her shoulders. "Infinite All-Knowing, we implore you this day to bind these two souls." Her robotic voice droned on, "Though they may walk—I … we beg you—"

"Pump the breaks." Brax's hands flung up. "You're joining two people in love, not inducting them into an underground cult."

"I'm having a hard time remembering the words." Reyna crossed her arms. "What would you know about two people in love anyway?"

"Maybe 'cause I have been."

Reyna tried masking her surprise, assuming he wouldn't have been anywhere long enough to fall for anyone. Let alone love. Who would've returned the love of a man always on the run? Unless the lover in question ran too.

"Jade." His captured partner's name slit like a razor across Reyna's tongue.

"I told you, it's not like that with Sparky." Tenderness lined Brax's chuckle. "We met on a job in London, and she was lookin' for a fresh start. She impressed me, so I brought her to the States. We planned goin' our separate ways once we hit shore, but instead, ran a few jobs together and realized we worked good. I know now it's 'cause our Zodiac connection drew us together. Sparky is the first true friend I had outside my brother."

"I hope she's okay," Reyna murmured at Aries's current predicament. Yet another reminder of the many lives at stake.

"She's the most resilient person I've ever met. If anyone is gonna make the Dark God regret his decision to snatch her, it's Jade."

"If you weren't in love with her, then who?"

"You wanna know about the one who got away?" Brax rubbed the back of his neck." I don't think it's gonna help."

Their night on the cliff was the first time Brax gave Reyna a glimpse of who he'd been before. She wanted to know him. Not under duress of magic, but because he offered it willingly.

"Please tell me," Reyna implored softly.

Brax sighed. "The woman I loved barely knew I existed."

Reyna giggled and embarrassment tensed in his jaw.

"I'm sorry." Reyna suppressed her smile. "It's hard imagining anyone not noticing you."

The corner of Brax's mouth twitched. "That's the nicest thing you've ever said to me."

Reyna redirected her faux pas. "Did you tell her how you felt?"

"Nah." Brax studied symbols cut in the colored glass beside them. "She was way outta my league. Also didn't help she dated another guy in my crew."

Reyna narrowed a playful gaze at him. "Sounds like she had terrible taste."

"No argument there." Brax shoved hands into his jean pockets. "What about you? Let's hear your dirty laundry list of lovers."

"My laundry is clean." Nervous laughter fluttered from her. "All folded and neatly tucked away."

"C'mon." Brax's baritone ground against her in the best ways. "There must've been some idiot who blew his chance with you."

Scarlet painted Reyna's skin. "I had a date once."

Brax nodded for her to continue.

"He worked with my friend Tessa, and she set us up. We spent the afternoon at the zoo, and he took me to a restaurant where you cook your own food in the middle of the table. It was nice."

"Doesn't sound so bad." Brax smiled. "Especially the part 'bout seeing the lions."

"We ended up at his apartment." Reyna glanced at the fleshy whorls of her fingertips through the slitted gloves. "I wanted to be normal. Told myself I could handle it. But when things got physical, I accidentally extracted his energy. I couldn't stop. His life-force quieted the world and amplified it all at once. I heard the ocean waves across town. Tasted the air. My muscles were stronger. I didn't feel anyone's emotions for a few days after. It felt so normal. So …" Reyna's heart wailed at the ugliness of her admission. "Good."

"What happened to the guy?" Brax asked.

"He fell unconscious, so I called 911 and he recovered after a couple days at the hospital." Reyna's eyes closed. "I couldn't stop asking myself, if that's what I needed to sacrifice to live wholly, what would happen when I had too many tastes of someone's life? When it wasn't enough anymore? That's when I knew. I'd never risk intimacy with anyone again. Not just for them. For me."

"Sunshine." Brax's lips parted.

She smiled at him through the water glazing her eyes. "All I'll ever know about two people in love is from books and movies. No matter how much I research or practice, I'll always be pretending."

"Let me be the judge." Brax curled pensive fingers between hers. "I am, after all, Lord Regent of Courtship."

Reyna sniffled softly. "I think a *creativity* is somewhere in there too."

"Oh, I'm nothing if not creative." He winked and Reyna smiled wider. "There's a reason they work well together."

"Okay then, Lord Regent of Everything. Teach me your ways of wooing."

Brax shook his head. "The wooing has been done. The heart won." He stepped into her space. "Sounds like this bonding stuff isn't about two souls coming together but accepting one day they'll again be apart."

Reyna tilted her head. "How so?"

"Their promise of bonding doesn't lie in their love. It's a vow to let love lead them back to each other. To overcome trial. Distance. Heartbreak. Preparing themselves for the best version of what their love can do. So, when they find each other again, they'll know they were never apart." His attention dipped to her mouth. "Even if it doesn't make sense, it'll always feel like they're on the path to rediscovering each other."

Reyna's chest rose and fell alongside Brax's. A steady flow of unspoken words filled the space between them.

"That was beautiful," she murmured.

Brax's low chuckle warmed her cheek. "I might've seen a poetry slam or two."

"Now what?" she asked.

"You're in the mind-set of where their hearts are. Speak from that. The rest is irrelevant."

"Infinite All-Knowing." Reyna held his gaze. "We implore you this day to bind these two souls. Though they may wander through ancient shadows of Nidus's former glory, may your eternal light guide them through the fires, winds, waves, and mountains seeking to divide them." Reyna peered at their laced fingers and swallowed. "This is the part when the bonded offer their associated element to one another."

"Nidians don't do magic."

"It's symbolic." She studied his lashes. The slight kink of his nose, perhaps from once being broken. "Each bonded must accept their sign's element into their body."

"Really?" Brax stepped impossibly close. "Tell me more."

"Since mine is water, you'd drink it from me."

"Like this?" Brax cupped her face and pressed a kiss to the corner of her eye. Reyna's restrained tears crested onto her cheek and a soft exhale caught in her throat. Brax ran a tongue along his wet bottom lip. "Say the words."

"I offer you the sea of my body." Reyna trembled as he kissed the corner of her other eye. "The rivers of my blood and the rain of my love."

Brax drew back and Reyna stared at her sadness glistening along his mouth, transformed into something beautiful.

He grinned. "What next, oh master of ceremonies?"

"You'd offer me your element."

Mischief paraded in Brax's eyes. "You gonna drink flames?"

"Not exactly." Blush swelled in Reyna's face. "When fire is the bonded partner's element, it needs to be recited with fire's forms and burned onto their partner's skin."

"Lucky for you, we'll skip that part."

"No." Reyna's response came quicker and hoarser than she intended. She nodded toward his symbol immortalized in stained glass. "Brand your mark somewhere on my body."

Brax's throat bobbed. "Where do you want it?"

Reyna rotated in his arms and pulled hair from her shoulder, exposing the nape of her neck.

"You're sure?" Desire grated his words.

Reyna glanced over her shoulder. "Aren't you?"

Brax's finger pressed against her neck without hesitation. A hiss swept from Reyna as fire seared onto her flesh. She titled her head sideways.

"I offer you the flames of my body." Brax dragged his thumb across her neck. "The lava of my blood. The light of my love." He finished and murmured against the shell of her ear, "Now what?"

"If we were being soul bonded"—Reyna's body pleaded for his to worship hers—"a kiss on the mouth would seal it."

Soft lips kissed her newly scorched skin.

"See." His smile curved along her neck. "Now you're a pro."

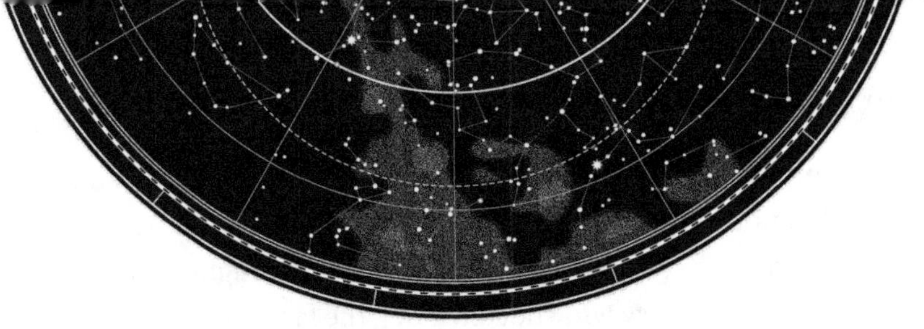

CHAPTER

THIRTY

"Lady Regent of—" Anemone slurred and wove across the lawn. "Damn it all to the Forgotten, Reyna!" Reyna smiled from her perch atop a fountain ledge. Drunken laughter and string music floated through Calidi's castle gardens and lights dangled from trees as though the stars themselves were brought down to pay tribute. A firework burst across the sky behind Anemone and that's when Reyna saw it. Raw joy.

A single moment when nothing else mattered except the now.

It'd become Reyna's new favorite emotion. So fleeting, she swore it a daydream. And to have someone else's directed at her? Nearly stole her breath.

Juniper trailed behind Anemone, slogging through her chiffon-like skirts across the grass.

What must it be like to live two lifetimes with one's love? Reyna snorted internally. She'd settle for one. A life without extraction magic would open many doors, but what if she'd been starved too long? What if after everyone's emotions faded away, none of Reyna's remained? She ran fingertips over the raised skin already healing on her neck. A bittersweet gift from her and Brax's Zodiac immunity. Reyna wished the scorched flesh would stay. A scar proving how far she'd come.

Anemone's petite but enthusiastic impact of arms flinging around Reyna's shoulders rocked them backward. Reyna grabbed hold of the fountain's ledge and Anemone cackled.

Juniper panted through a smile and plopped her hands on her hips. "I'm not supposed to be chasing you *after* we've bonded."

Anemone swiveled with Reyna's neck still caught in the crook of her arm. Strawberry wine floated along the factotum's breath. "But I wanted to thank her!"

Reyna fixed Anemone with a tender stare. "Factotums shouldn't have had to carry the Zodiacs' burdens for long as they did. I'll never be able to repay all you've sacrificed for Calidi in my absence and everything you've done for me since I returned. But I hope my performing your bonding is good start."

"Even under drink, Nem is right," Juniper said. "The stars have been far too gracious. We're honored to be the first bonded upon your return, lady."

"Nem?" A slow grin crept across Reyna's face.

"She's so formal with everyone else." Juniper knocked red pixie-cut bangs from her forehead and shrugged. "It seemed only proper."

Reyna quirked a brow at Anemone. "Can I call you Nem?"

Anemone wrinkled her nose. "I'm not nearly intoxicated enough to authorize such absurdities. Speaking of nicknames," her slur dropped an octave. "Why're you sitting all by yourself? Isn't a fiery lion man looking to make eyes at you?"

"Anemone!" Juniper scolded.

"What?" The factotum stood from Reyna and threw lank arms around Juniper's neck. "Everyone knows he's in love with Reyna." Anemone planted a sloppy kiss on her bonded.

"Nem!" Juniper's embarrassed laughter severed their kiss. "Our greatest apologies, Lady—" Juniper's face dropped at something over Reyna's shoulder. Her gaze swept down as though to imitate a bow. "A thousand apologies, Lord Regent. Anemone knows not what she says. She's not herself."

"No apologies necessary." Brax chuckled, striding around the fountain. "I know firsthand a water sign's inability at holding their liquor."

Reyna's face flushed at the memory of her stripping for him.

"If you don't mind, Regents," Juniper smiled sheepishly, "I'd like to steal Anemone back. This might be the last time I ever get her on a dance floor."

"Of course," Reyna replied. "Congratulations again."

The two women scurried across the lawn and into the crowd.

"The party turned out great." Reyna swallowed her heartbeat. "You did … good."

"That sounded an awful lot like a compliment." Brax's shoes scuffed over stone to stand beside her. His presence ensnared the cool evening air.

"You're not going to make me regret it, are you?"

Brax pouted his lips with a shrug. "The night is young, though I can't take all the credit. You didn't do bad yourself."

She smiled. "I had a good teacher."

Something unreadable passed over Brax's face, as rare and transient as a shooting star. All other words became lost to the erratic pounding of Reyna's heart while they watched the festivities in companionable silence. Reyna didn't know how to be around Brax anymore. She'd tried denying their connection. Giving in for brief moments. Brax should hate her for how wishy-washy she'd been. Reyna certainly did. But he took it all in stride and asked for nothing in return. Reyna didn't understand what they were, but something happened on the cliff and again in the library. A deeper awareness beyond any they'd endured. As though they'd stepped over an invisible line, only to find it was never there.

"Wanna get outta here?" Brax decimated their noisy silence.

Yes.

"I think we're expected to stay," Reyna replied.

"We've been gone a century. I don't think they'll miss us one more night. Besides, I wanna show you somethin.'"

"I thought you loved a good party?" Reyna allowed herself to meet his eyes, already swimming in hers.

"There's other company I enjoy more."

CHAPTER

THIRTY-ONE

REYNA AND BRAX WALKED ALONG CALIDI'S SHORELINE. The sky pulsed at their backs with celebration. Its glow soon fell behind a veil of palms and the only melody became their mutual laughter. Reyna twirled beneath the starlight like a disco ball at the universe's center.

"You don't see stars like this in the city," she marveled.

"I've been to almost every continent," Brax replied. "I don't think anyone sees stars like these."

"I've never left California. If we make it through this, leaving San Diego is the first on my list."

"Well, you're in luck." Brax opened his arms wide. "We couldn't be farther."

For all the cruise destinations Reyna daydreamed over while booking packages, Nidus placed all Earth's coveted destinations on a pedestal. Parhelia's Swiss-kissed mountains. Flora's English countryside. Messis's rich homage to Massachusetts's autumn. The lush Costa Rican jungle of Calidi, unfolding into ivory Grecian beaches. Perhaps Nidus was what she'd been selling herself on all along.

"So ..." A knot tied Brax's voice. "You're goin' back to Earth?"

"Aren't you?"

"To be determined." He studied the dark ocean. A breeze rippled beneath his half-unbuttoned linen shirt, making the most casual formalwear polished and rugged at once. "After I bust Jade out, there's nothin' left on Earth for me. It's been forever since I put down roots. Nidus might be worth a shot."

If the Zodiacs survived whatever battle brewed on the horizon, Reyna assumed some might stay on Nidus. She never imagined Brax would. "Roots are overrated." Reyna's strappy sandals swung at her side between hooked fingers as the tide sloshed over her feet. "Is Earth so bad?"

"It's smaller than ya think and even more small-minded."

Reyna stopped walking. "I don't believe you."

Brax crossed his arms. "This oughta be good."

"If you thought little of our world, you wouldn't have gone with Halley or agreed to help Neoma."

Amusement pulled the corner of his lips. "Who says I don't have an ulterior motive?"

"Now that"—Reyna grinned—"I'd believe."

Brax glided his foot along the sea's foamy hem. Water sprayed Reyna's face. A shocked chortle tumbled from her and Brax's head knocked backward, teeth glistening through laughter.

Reyna snapped her fingers, and a tiny tidal wave toppled onto him.

Rivulets streamed over his mischievous smile. He whipped his long hair back. Excess water slapped Reyna's skin. She ran against her tide-kissed gown, but Brax's arm curled around her waist. He slung Reyna over his shoulder and broke into a jog.

All distinction of direction faded into distant memory.

Sea became sky as they folded into the night's dueling star-speckled mirror. Eventually Brax's steps slowed and his hands gripped Reyna's hips. He slid her along his chest for leverage until her toes sank into the sand. Erratic adrenaline pounded within her chest, as though she'd been the one sprinting.

"C'mon." Brax released her waist and slid his fingers through his sea-slicked hair. "Follow me." Brax guided Reyna through tall, jutting rocks painted with bioluminescent algae-like neon crystals. Green, blue, and magenta glowed against Reyna's cheeks and tide pools splashed beneath their heels. The rocky pillars parted near a cliffside and tapered into black sea.

Brax cranked his wrist like a dial, igniting fire along his hand. Firelight bounced over a cave entrance and Reyna followed him inside. Any semblance of the roaring ocean outside was snuffed out by thick stone walls. Soul crystals blazed along the walls while they walked. Before long, a subtle, salty breeze wove through Reyna's hair and Brax's torched hand went out. He ducked under a fallen stone slab and offered her a hand. Reyna's fingers curled into his and she stepped out from the tunnel.

Starlight poured through a gaping hole in the cave's domed ceiling. Black sculptures of people, plant life, animals, and abstractions glittered across a hidden, partially enclosed beach.

"These aren't Levant's." Reyna's hand smoothed over a centuries-untouched black glass statue. She eyed slightly charred remnants of a campfire near the shore. "They're made of … obsidian and you've been here before?"

Brax grinned and jogged to the cave's wall. He pulled a backpack from behind its stony crevice. "I stumbled across this place while searching for the prophecy." He dug out a blanket and a few pastries from its flap. "I thought you might like it."

A hidden hoard of illegal beauty. A place where deities had no power?

Reyna shuffled away from him. From it all.

"We shouldn't be here," she said.

"Why not?" Brax's brows pinched together as he rose from laying the blanket.

"Nothing else in the cave is obsidian." The reality of their predicament was obvious to her. "Which means someone made these statues. Neoma said only the Dark Star does that."

"Neoma doesn't know shit about the Dark Star." Brax threw a dismissive wave. "Do ya think the Dark Star would be out here creating"—Brax's hand flurried over a statue of odd zigzags—"whatever the hell this is, if plotting the world's destruction?"

Reyna hated the logic strewn through his summation, but if the sculptures weren't the work of the Dark Star, it meant it could still be her. "Neoma knows more about Nidus than we do," Reyna reasoned. "We should listen."

"We should be smart around her."

Reyna blinked incredulously. "She's protecting Earth."

"She *banished* the Zodiacs." Brax trudged toward Reyna, kicking up bits of sand. "She *sacrificed* us out of desperation and paranoia. A deadly combo. Neoma may care about Earth, though if I guessed, I'd bet she cares about herself more."

"What makes you say that?" Reyna refused to believe the goddess wouldn't make good on her promises. Reyna's future depended on it.

"Because she's like me. Neoma weaves fact and fiction into whatever suits her. I can sniff a con a mile away and Neoma reeks of it." Frustration flexed through his arms. "People are always compromised by what they can't have. Once they get even a taste of it"—hands plopped at his sides—"they'll do whatever it takes to hold on to it."

"Not everyone is like that."

"In San Diego, you asked if Neoma could remove your magic. Would you've come if Halley said no?"

Reyna's gaze dropped as though the answer lay buried in the sand at her feet. She tried summoning a half lie. An excuse. Anything to prove she'd not been so selfish. That she still wasn't.

"Fine." Reyna's chin lifted. "If not for Earth's welfare, what is it you think Neoma wants above all else?"

"Power." A shadow crossed his face. "Unchecked, do-whatever-the-fuck-she-wants power. Without another god to oppose or balance the scales, Neoma answers to no one."

"If that's true, she wouldn't be working to stop the Dark Star."

"Wake up!" The crease between Brax's brows hardened. "She doesn't wanna stop the Dark Star. She'll use them to make sure *she* wins."

"I'm not listening to this!" Reyna spun and beelined toward the way they entered.

"Why're you unwilling to accept we should be wary of Neoma?" Brax chased after her.

Because she's promised the only life I've ever wanted.

"Think about it." Brax closed in beside Reyna while she marched. "Neoma said the Dark Star would choose favor over light or darkness, forever. She's never once expressed concern with keeping balance. Only that darkness shouldn't win."

"You've seen what dark magic does!" Reyna ground her teeth. "What power like Levant's does to me! There's nothing good about it."

"I've got fuckloads of darkness too." Brax snatched Reyna's arm and whirled her to face him. "Is it all you think of me?"

"Brax …" Reyna murmured.

"No! If that's all I am. Some two-bit, sleazy lowlife criminal, I'll let you stomp all the way back to Calidi."

"Of course you're not," Reyna whispered.

"That goes for you too." Brax's grip softened but pulled her closer. "You're not one thing. You're … everything."

"You told me in Flora, you've never believed in anyone more. Why?"

"I see people." Brax towered over her. "I see you. Always have since the moment we met."

"What makes you the authority on who someone is or isn't?"

"It's what Leo was created for." Brax's brows knitted together. "Courtship and Creativity aren't about getting laid. It's about Leo's ability to know what matters most to people. Why it matters, and how to help them reach their heart's true potential. Not exploit it or use for their own personal fucked-up gain, like I have after reincarnation. But you've never used your abilities to help yourself. It's the way you preached found family to those kids, though your father should've destroyed your faith. Why you've refused human connection your whole life but can't stop drawing people to you.

"Leo rules the heart. Cancer, the chest. Two sides of a door." Brax spread her fingers over his exposed chest. Drenched linen from their water fight still clung to his torso. "One side is bursting to be felt. The other, a shield from the brunt of what's not meant to be contained. That's who you are, an equalizer."

Reyna searched his face. "And who are you?"

Brax snickered. "I've been so many versions of myself, I think the real one died a long time ago."

"I've spent an entire life cursed with magic showing me what others feel." Reyna craned her neck at him. "But when I'm with you, all I can hear is this." Her fingers curled against his heart. "Not because your emotion demands to be heard, but because it allows me to finally hear my own."

Brax's brows pinched together. "Don't say things you don't mean."

Reyna slipped off her gloves and let them fall onto the sand. "I'm exhausted from not saying it."

"Sunshine. I—"

Reyna dragged her thumb across his mouth, slowly pulling the pout of his bottom lip. Teeth grazed the pad of her thumb as he watched her intently.

That mouth.

How it boiled her blood and drank her dry at once. His gritty prose, forever gutting Reyna from the inside out and remaking her. The time for words was over. Reyna captured his lips with hers. Poured herself into him. Every smoldering look he'd caressed her with. Each word whispered so low it grinded in her pelvis. Every true smile he'd let slip. The moments he hadn't been there, and she wished he was.

Brax cupped Reyna's face and stole the kiss. His tongue, like a wildcat, lapping at the wounds of a cruel world. Brax's feet shushed backward through sand, coaxing her with him. Reyna trailed in his wake, never breaking their kiss. Lips numb with need. Never again sated without him.

She skated her nails along the slope between the base of his spine and ass. Her fingers curled around his shirt's waterlogged hem and lifted. Fabric peeled across the strong arc of Brax's back and his lips severed from hers.

Warm summer air coated Reyna's tongue.

She whimpered at the separation.

Brax bent his arms behind his shoulders and tugged the fabric over his head. Abdomen taut, bowing with the need to spring free. He tossed the linen nuisance aside and a flourish of flames spat from his hand with the motion. Violent orange flames swallowed the charred campfire.

Reyna gasped at the new heat biting her skin.

Fire-calloused fingers scraped over her stomach. Snagged. Bunched. Pulled at the silky dress caging her ribs. Brax prowled behind and pressed his lips between Reyna's neck and shoulder.

"This okay?" His concern was at war with the hard heat straining against her lower back.

"What if my magic accidentally ... " Reyna shuddered. "What if I—"

"Hurt me," Brax exhaled the breathy prayer against her ear. Reyna caved into herself. Bones liquified. She leaned into his chest for strength. Brax's nose glided along her neck, the stubble framing his smile raking across her goose bumps. "Take whatever you need. I want you. Any way you'll have me."

Words became a distant memory.

A myth meant to keep the weak in check.

Reyna summoned a nod.

Brax brushed hair over her shoulder, fingers fumbling with the tied material at the nape of her neck. Reyna's ragged breath demanded he work faster. Brax grabbed the knot. Silky material flaked into ashes in his hand, floating away along the soft sea breeze. Silver fabric waterfalled over Reyna's chest and pooled at her feet.

"You have no fucking idea how long I've waited for this." Brax dragged a lazy finger between the valley of her breasts. "For you."

Reyna rotated in his arms and pulled the pant strings at his waist.

Dark fabric glided past his hip bones as his erection paused their fall from grace. Reyna watched him through lowered lashes and sank to her knees. The brush of her descent pulled the remaining fabric with her. She stared at the excruciating man above her. Stars shone bright behind his head through the cave's open ceiling. An ancient light, illuminating his gold crown of mussed hair.

Her gaze slid down his body and settled on the swell of his arousal. Reyna swallowed before a harsh exhale shuddered from her. He contracted from the close brush of breath.

Reyna remained as still as the statues surrounding them.

She'd never done this part before, but with Brax, always became anyone she wanted. Could do anything. Succeed. Fail. He'd never stopped looking at her with awe.

Brax waited.

Transfixed, as though she were a vortex he'd tumble through for an eternity. No haste. No edging his hips closer. Nothing but chaotic patience and the thrill of what came next dilated in his eyes. He may have towered over Reyna, but he was all hers.

She pressed a chaste kiss against his tip. Brax sighed with relief and a smile stretched across Reyna's cheeks. She planted more soft kisses over his smooth flesh. Each press, splaying her lips wider and wider. Languid rolls of Reyna's tongue inhaled him into her mouth. Brax's guttural ecstasy bounced off the cave walls. She devoured deeper. Curious if she'd take all of him.

Testing. Tasting the edge of her limits.

That's all he'd ever made her do.

And she loved it.

Brax couldn't resist gently thrusting forward, placating his need for more. Reyna gripped his tensing quads. Let herself sink farther. Fall beneath the surface of needing oxygen. A crutch for lesser beings. Reyna hadn't needed it while swimming through the water of his memories. She didn't need it now. He coiled her dark hair around his hand. Reyna bobbed faster. Kept time with his eager hips. Her throat tightened as he hit the back and Brax's knees wobbled.

"Holy ever-loving fuck," he groaned, slowly pulling himself free. "You finish me off now, and I'll never forgive you."

A soft giggle chimed from Reyna. His knees collapsed onto the blanket, and she threw her arms over his shoulders. Brax descended onto her mouth once more.

Reyna prayed for death. To have her last breath one with his. To never be more or less than they were now. Her head knocked back as Brax tasted the curve of her throat. A frenzy of teeth, tongue, and a million other sensations Reyna didn't bother naming. She needed him.

Now.

Reyna pressed Brax's sternum and momentary frustration shot across his face. He liked control, positioning all players where he wanted. But Reyna's whole life had been self-imposed rules. Camouflage. Denying everything she desired. Not tonight. No armor. No hiding. She wanted him to see all of her.

She wanted to see herself take what she wanted. Without remorse.

Brax lay back, tucking the nearby backpack under his head. She straddled him and rubbed his length. Guided him. Brought them both home.

She sank onto him.

Inch by ravenous inch she sank until she met his hips.

Reyna sucked in a breath. Head hung low. Her hair grazed his pelvis as she settled into the delicious weight of his invasion. She swayed into the slick current beckoning her forward. Their sighs unfurled with each new steady swell rocking though them. Reyna splayed her fingers over the hills of his abdomen. Desperate for an anchor. Anything to keep from floating to the stars.

His sandpaper hands kneaded her breasts. Pinched. Caressed. Plucked every chord she'd never sang. Reyna had overcome much, and still, an uncertain future loomed on the horizon. But here, she wasn't pleading for her magic's removal. Not fighting for Earth. Her life. Or anyone else's. She wasn't Cancer. Lady Regent. Reyna. Or any other names given. She was whoever she wanted to be. And if just for tonight, she was his. And he was hers.

Thick arms enveloped her lower back, and Brax pulled her flush against his chest. Reyna planted her elbows on either side of his head. She threaded her fingers through his hair and their foreheads pressed together. Gazes locked. Brax's eyes fucked her with every bounce of their slapping flesh. Each unabashed thrust of himself, rippling joy over her skin like an asteroid plunging into the sea. Again, and again. And again.

A decadence of filthy words groaned from him. Her muscles constricted. His grip on her, more bruising. Desperate.

"Brax …" Reyna whimpered under her own rising tsunami. Liquid fire claimed her skin as she shattered like a supernova into oblivion.

"Leo," he rasped in her ear. Pleaded. "Call me Leo."

"Leo," she stroked his ancient name.

Brax roared into his own release. A willing lion made prey.

The stars smiled down at the moon and sun tangled in a heap of flesh and sweat.

Eclipsed. One.

THIRTY-TWO

THE WORLD BECAME AN ENDLESS STRETCH OF DARKNESS. Nothing more than a mysterious cave suspended between time and space. A place no one else existed. A place Reyna wasn't sure she did. But as a new day sliced through the cave's mouth, the world came alive. Dawn winked from across a golden sea and Reyna smiled back. She imagined a life where she'd been born magicless like the other Zodiacs, able to do whatever she wanted. Maybe she would've brought poverty-stricken countries clean drinking water. Some inexplicable call to her Zodiac namesake, long before she recognized it for what it was.

Or maybe she wouldn't have done anything extraordinary at all. Made remarkable, only after a life of the mundane.

Brax rolled over, pulling the blanket from Reyna's shoulder and her what-ifs became as hazy as a dream upon waking. Fleeting. Forgotten. And not nearly as perfect as real life. His chest rose and fell like the soft glowing embers beside them. Reyna tucked blond hair behind his ear and grogginess rumbled through him.

"I guess I was wrong." Brax's lids remained closed.

Reyna perked onto her elbows. "That happens?"

"More than I care to admit." Brax smirked. "Smartass."

Reyna couldn't wipe the smile from her face. "What were you wrong about?"

Brax rolled onto his side and punctuated each word with a kiss from her arm to shoulder. "Waking beside you does get better."

Reyna giggled. "I can't believe we slept out here."

Brax's lips worshipped with tender urgency, soft nibbles and breaths pulsing against her ear. A sweet mewl bloomed from her.

"Mmm." Brax slung her leg over his hip. "You keep makin' sounds like that and I don't think we'll ever leave."

"I could be convinced." Reyna knotted herself deeper into him.

"How do you feel?" Brax rested a cheek atop her head and stroked her thigh atop his side.

"I don't know," she replied, unsure if she'd ever been asked. More uncertain if she'd ever asked herself.

"Did you notice anything different last night?" he murmured against her hair.

"A lot of things." Reyna's fingers danced along his thickness hanging between them. A purr rattled in his chest.

"Christ, Sunshine." Brax rolled over onto Reyna's torso and locked himself in a half staddle across her. "I'm serious." His slowly accelerated breath said different, but he pinned her with a stare anyway.

A million sensations still hummed over Reyna's skin. Familiar, yet all hers.

"I didn't use magic." She blinked. "I didn't mean not to. How? Why?"

"If I guessed, it's 'cause we both yielded, canceling the other out. You can't take what the other willingly gives. And if I remember correctly"—another grin slid across his rugged face—"I don't think either was left wanting last night."

"Safe," Reyna whispered.

Brax arched his brow in question.

"You asked me how I feel." She lost herself in dawn's light reflected in his eyes. "Everything is louder. Quieter. Clearer and messier than it's ever been, but I feel safe. With you."

Brax kissed her and Reyna slid an arm around him. Her fingers grazed the constellation of scars knotting his back. She'd been too angry to ask about them the first time they'd met and ghosted the question across his lips. "How did you get these?"

"Gunshots," he murmured.

"Shots?" Reyna pulled away. "As in plural?"

"Occupational hazard." Brax chuckled and brushed a thumb over the scar haunting her hairline. "How about this one?"

"The day my papá attacked me, I was knocked unconscious. I would've drowned if a neighbor from my earlier birthday party hadn't come back looking for their kid's stuff. She performed CPR on me, but papá … well, you know."

"Is that why you don't want magic?" Brax frowned. "Because of your parents?"

"My papá's death always reminded me what happens when people get too close. If I killed someone I feared, what could I do to someone I loved?"

Momentary silence lingered in the warmth between them.

"Incredible things," Brax replied. "You may have been alone then, but you're not now. Whatever darkness is coming, you've got people who care about you, and we aren't goin' anywhere."

Reyna glanced around at the black sculptures. Darkness wasn't coming.

It was already there.

"Brax." Reyna swallowed her heartbeat. "I need to tell you something."

"Me too." Resolution tightened his jaw. He sat upright. "I'm—"

"Neoma asked me to find the Forgotten!" Reyna flung upright, sure if she didn't speak first, she might never. "She wants me to go there and uncover the prophecy."

"What?" Brax's features twisted. "Tell me you said no?"

"We've been looking everywhere except the most obvious place," Reyna insisted as he scrambled to his feet. She sped through her logic sure she was losing him. "I'm close to finding the entrance. I've tracked Levant's statues, and I think—"

"Whoa, whoa, whoa. Hold up." Brax slashed his hands through the air. "Let me get this straight. You've been sleuthing around Nidus for Levant's kingdom of death?"

"He's imprisoned on the Glass Isles." Reyna shimmied remnants of her dress over her hips and across her chest in a desperate need for a buffer. "I didn't think it was dangerous."

Brax paced, running a splayed hand over his face. "What about the damn Dredgers?"

"The Zodiacs have only come across one since arriving at Nidus. If you let me show you my findings, you'll see—"

"Did it ever occur to you that other things could be out there?"

"What things?" Reyna tied the singed dress straps into a knot at her midback.

"I don't know—things!" Brax shoved his pants back on. His fingers fumbled to separate the damp and sandy linen shirt from itself. He growled, chucking it across the sand. "I hate these Nidian clothes! I want my T-shirts."

Reyna edged toward him and slid her arms around his torso. She pressed her cheek against a torrent of heartbeats pulsing through his bare back. Brax tensed but didn't wrench away. She squeezed tighter.

"Please try to understand," Reyna said softly. "Neoma promised to remove my magic if I did what she asked."

"Why do you always do that?" Brax knocked his head back, breath laxing with each moment she clasped onto him.

"Do what?"

"Give away your power so easily."

Reyna released him. "You know why."

Brax faced her. "People would kill to do what we can."

"*Kill* being the operative word." Reyna crossed her arms tight over her chest.

"What about now that you've seen what you can do?" He smoothed his hands over her shoulders.

"Would you like me less if I didn't have magic?" she asked.

"Of course not, but this isn't about me. Are you ready to give up a piece of yourself you've only begun understanding?" Brax's large hands slid over her wavy, humid-kissed hair. "Don't be afraid of who you are. Be afraid of never knowing."

Reyna had lied. Ran. Fought her magic. Acquired new. Prayed they never merged. Gone from hermit to celestial legend spanning centuries of myth.

With a celestial war on the precipice, Reyna's abilities might be the only defense keeping her alive. But it didn't mean she wouldn't forfeit her magic if given a chance either. Some small piece of her heard Brax's words. Let them slip a little deeper between the cuts and bruises life had dealt. She'd achieved miraculous feats since the Zodiacs and made some deplorable missteps too.

"I don't need to decide anything today." Reyna offered him a half smile.

His forehead touched hers. "But you'll think about what I said?"

"I will," she conceded.

"Good." Brax ran his hands down her arms. "Now let's get back and figure this underworld shit out."

They emerged from the cave and Reyna raised a hand against sunrise's last dregs blotting her vision. Dawn robbed the stone pillars of their otherworldly luminescence, demeaning them to a simple rock formation. The deserted beach was as it'd been last night. The same, and yet like Reyna, not at all.

New fervor buzzed through her veins. An emotion she'd experienced enough through others and less from herself. Excitement. She couldn't wait to show Brax her puzzle pieces. It now seemed ridiculous she'd hidden the map from the one person who might easily discern its subtleties from the obvious.

Brax stared into the jungle and adjusted the backpack strap against his bare shoulders.

"What's up?" Reyna stepped beside him. "Did you see something?"

"I had a thought." Brax ran his fingers through his hair, rustling the thought away. "Forget it. Let's go." He trudged toward the shoreline.

"What were you thinking?" Reyna called.

"Never mind," he replied. "It's a bad idea."

"You love bad ideas." Reyna giggled, snatching the loop attached to his pack and yanked. "Please tell me."

Brax peered between the coastline and jungle. Indecision clenched his jaw. "Last time I came out here, I found a shortcut through the jungle back to Calidi."

"Great!" Reyna pulled his hand toward the tree line.

"No." He tugged. "It's not safe."

"The eclipse is next week, and I've got a lot to show you. The quicker we get back, the better."

"The jungle might be faster but more treacherous and there could be—"

"Things?" Reyna cocked a brow. "In case you haven't noticed, you're not the only Zodiac. Between us, nothing stands a chance."

"I like this side of you." Brax groaned. "Too much."

"What?" Reyna grinned. "Stubborn?"

"Brave."

His compliment warmed the best parts of her.

"Fine," Brax agreed. "Stay close and if anything weird happens, do exactly what I say."

A half hour later, Brax continued forging ahead, arms glowing like red-hot irons as he slashed through the thicket. Regret throbbed through Reyna's calves. She'd thought herself wise for ripping her dress shorter to avoid tripping over the wilderness, but twigs scraped her skin. Even the pretty plants had teeth. Thick, coarse blankets of ivy and ferns stuck like Velcro to her dress, as though the jungle itself sought to drag her to the beach. Reyna longed for its soft sand. A sea breeze along her sweat-glazed brow, but she swallowed every gripe. They'd come across no sign of *things* Brax claimed they might encounter. Still, he insisted they remain quiet.

A pulse thudded beneath Reyna's feet. Steady. Rapid. Claiming soil from the path it carved. Reyna knew it before she saw or heard it.

"Let's rest for a bit." Brax stepped onto a riverbank. He sloshed through the water until it hugged his knees.

Reyna leaned against a large rock, unable to hide her resentment. "So, it's finally safe to talk?"

"The river should drown out our voices." Brax splashed his face and slicked his fingers through his tangled hair. "We can follow it upstream to Calidi."

"Calidi is by the sea." Reyna admired her element dripping over his chest and shoulders like diamonds. "Shouldn't we be heading downstream?"

"Rivers do this thing called winding." Brax smirked, swiveling his hand like a fish. Reyna's gaze narrowed. "Downstream will lead us farther from where we started at the cave."

"Are you sure?"

An unamused laugh huffed from him. "I told you, I'm good with directions."

"Is it much farther?"

"What's wrong?" Arrogance tugged his smile tighter. "Missing the beach already?" Brax's ability to read people's true meaning was as uncanny as Reyna's magic.

"Of course not." She smiled and tilted her face to bask in the sun's glow.

Treetops bled into blue sky, but in the corner of her vision, parallel lines broke through the branches. Reyna peeled herself from the boulder and focused deeper into the canopy. Webbed wilderness camouflaged a structure burrowed into the trees. Reyna edged around a massive tree, dragging a hand along its thick trunk.

Footsteps crunched over rocks and grass from behind.

"Did you know this was here?" Reyna craned her neck at the tree's odd structure.

"I haven't been this far downriver. We must've fallen off course."

Reyna's hand brushed over layered foliage and slid over smooth wood beneath. She yanked knotted ivy free from a ladder's rungs.

"We should keep movin'," Brax encouraged.

Reyna grinned over her shoulder. "Tell me you're not curious."

"You know what they say about curiosity and cats." Brax glanced between her and the river. " Besides, I thought you were in a hurry?"

Reyna grabbed a rung and Brax's hand closed around her wrist.

"What's up with you?" Reyna studied him. "You've acted strange ever since we left the cave."

"I slept on the ground. Hiked shirtless through a jungle. I need a bath and a meal I don't have to pick off a bush." Brax released her. "And like you said, we've got a lot to figure out. This tree isn't goin' anywhere. We'll come back another time."

"You said you like when I'm brave." Reyna smirked. "Time to prove it."

"Climbing a tree fails in comparison to everything else we've done, don't ya think?"

Reyna placed her hand on the next rung. "Then you've nothing to worry about."

"Fine." Brax's hip bumped her aside. "But I'm going first."

The adrenaline of mystery propelled them higher, and the fern-covered ground fell from Reyna's peripherals. Even after *Polaris* and Omphalos's waterfall, she didn't think herself afraid of heights but didn't want to test the theory either.

Brax hoisted himself onto a platform and extended Reyna a hand. She grabbed hold and pulled herself up, stumbling into his sturdy arms. Their gazes locked, and for a moment, their bickers became nothing more than what Brax claimed. Crabbiness of a night slept on sand.

Though Reyna couldn't deny it was the best sleep she'd ever had.

The wooden structure groaned beneath their weight. Brax's arms tightened at Reyna's waist. "Let's make this quick."

He slowly guided her along the trunk's spiraling walkway. They wove around the wooden path until it spilled over a deck spanning the treetops. Busted branches and leaves peppered nets strung between trees. A two-story home, with its entire front exposed, rose over the canopy's horizon like a bamboo cove overlooking an emerald canopy. Sunlight bathed overturned wicker chairs, busted pottery, and tree debris littering its floors.

"Wow." Reyna inched farther. "This is incredible. Who do you think lived here?"

"Doesn't matter." Brax remained rooted in place. "Whoever they were, they're long gone. Taken."

"What makes you say that?"

"This place is trashed."

"Could've been vandals or storms. Who knows how long it's been here."

"I've been through enough scuffles to spot the difference," Brax replied. "Either way, we should get outta here."

"You're probably right." Reyna feigned a smile through her disappointment. She wasn't sure what she expected. Certainly not the Forgotten's entrance but perhaps a clue? From the little Reyna gathered, Nidians seemed to relish their hometowns. Vendors' idle conversation during a sale. Children straying from their mothers without concern from either. A constant buzz of life wove throughout the streets. What Nidian would live so isolated?

Like Brax, Reyna also knew this space well. Not by the pieces out of place, but rather, the items placed perfectly. Though disheveled and rotted by time, the home was still, indeed, a home. Tattered drapes fluttered with the breeze. Ornate etchings decorated the posts. Handcrafted furniture chose function over form. Every inch of the hideaway coveted comfort and sanctuary. A place someone chose to be. Reyna's fingers grazed over dusty silverware and ceramic plates decorating a dining table.

Place settings for two.

Perhaps the owner hadn't been isolated.

"C'mon," Brax urged. "Time to go."

Reyna backed from the table and paused at sunlight glinting against an object beside one of its legs. She kneeled and turned the odd rock over in her palm. Her thumb smudged dirt off one of its edges. The crystal's pale green peeked through like the one Ambrose had gifted her.

"Reyna." Brax tensed. "Let's—"

The breeze stilled.

A magnet tugged Reyna toward the floorboards, and she sifted between the cracks into darkness.

THIRTY-THREE

CANCER

ONE HUNDRED YEARS EARLIER

WHITECAPS PUSHED UPSTREAM AS CANCER SNAKED alongside River Hydra's bank.

"Return," the reverse rapids pleaded. *"Go back."*

The rivers had never led Cancer astray, but her task ahead possessed depths even they could not fathom. Stardust may have coursed through her veins, but she'd read enough to know mortals' blood worked the same. They were rivers, streams, and deltas all carving the way for life's nutrients. The natural order of Nidus, reincarnated beneath mortal flesh. But with every step against the river's protest, Cancer disrupted that order.

Early afternoon delivered the river's retreat and Cancer rested beside a rock near shore. She meditated with the jungle's song. Home she wasn't, but Calidi was all around. In the sun's kiss, the chattering toucans, and the buzzing cicadas. She envisioned children's laughter splashing amongst the river and frowned. Nidus would never harness water's true potential. Nor brave any flowing into the Forgotten. Not while Levant preyed on souls. The Dark God's disregard for life would soon ignite a war. One where Neoma's pride would be tested and, Cancer feared, would have Nidians pay the ultimate price.

A thick, low hum cut through the trees.

"Hello?" Cancer called. Birds cawed and fluttered toward the canopy as the song crescendoed. She threw her voice further, "Show yourself."

The Dark God strutted from behind brush, massive tree trunks balanced atop each shoulder. Neoma's affinity for plant life deemed them blessed and sanctioned deforestation came from Neoma herself. An almost impossible approval.

"Are you"—Cancer gaped—"cutting trees?"

Levant lowered his felonious evidence and soil trembled beneath their feet. He cocked his head. "What a demure, obedient little servant Neoma has molded you into."

Cancer lifted her chin. "If the goddess knew—"

"If Neoma knew you were with me." Loftiness danced across his smile at Cancer's slight recoil. "I doubt a few less trees would be her prime concern."

"Neoma believes me quite obstinate." Cancer hated that Neoma viewed her in such a way and longed for the goddess's approval. Perhaps if she'd been more subservient, Neoma wouldn't deny her requests as often.

"For once, Neoma and I agree." The Dark God scanned Cancer's blue off-shoulder bell-sleeved dress. Irritation folded over his face. "I told you to wear black."

"Why do you care what I wear?"

"Because I like it." Ice ground in his jaw. "Reason enough."

Cancer snorted and his green eyes flared. Levant circled her, lean muscle parading across his chest. Cancer noted the dark trousers he wore ripped at the knees and a matching long-sleeved coat draped over a nearby branch.

"Forgive me." Cancer bowed her head. "But I gather you've not spent much time in Calidi? Our summertime region is far too warm for such dark clothing, my Dark God."

"I told you to call me Lev." He planted his hands behind his back. Less predatory and yet, undeniably so.

"How can I dress properly when you refuse to tell me what we are doing?"

Levant pouted his lips in mock thought. "Perhaps we might compromise?"

Dread coiled beneath her skin. One deal made with the God of Darkness was enough for an eternity.

"Come now," he encouraged at her silence. "Surely you don't believe me a god lacking in accommodation?" Levant dropped to his knees before Cancer. A breath caught in her throat. The creators never descended below anyone's shoulder. Not even a Zodiac's. Her knees locked, unbending to their better instincts.

"May I?" He watched her from beneath mussed dark hair.

Cancer forced a hesitant nod.

Fabric screeched as he ripped a slit from her hem to thigh. Cancer gasped. Icy fingers grazed her pebbling skin. The Dark God's lips lifted at her body's response while he worked.

"The tune you hummed earlier." Cancer attempted distraction from one of the two most powerful beings in the cosmos dismantling her modesty. "I've never heard it before."

Another rip. Levant tied two strips between her legs.

"It is called *Moonlight Sonata*," he replied.

Cancer's breath hitched.

Each Zodiac's celestial mass could be viewed from Nidus. The blazing sun. Saturn's shimmering rings. Mars's crimson glow. But Earth's moon was a tiny speck. A faint globe, barely visible. Cancer ached to see her celestial body adorning the night sky. As humans did.

"It's from Earth?" she asked.

Levant nodded. "For all I loathe of mortals, their music is beyond any you will experience."

"How so?"

"Nidians don't bleed. Do not know hardship." He tied another knot. "Sickness, poverty, and true death are beyond their comprehension. Mortal music is derived from suffering. A soul cannot create music when it has not lived." He stood, and Cancer inspected the knotted dress between her legs resembling billowed trousers.

"There's more to living than pain," she replied.

"If so"—Levant's chin lifted—"I've not known it."

Cancer advised households across every Nidian region. United families from all Zodiac clans. What could she offer someone who came from none?

She changed the subject. "Will you finally explain what we are doing?"

Levant's arms spread wide.

Cancer scanned his outstretched hands. "I don't understand."

"I'll have a ladder upon your return." His eyes flicked toward the treetops. "But today, I shall fly us up."

Branches speared under a large wooden platform overhead and though every speck of stardust within screamed she flee, Cancer edged toward the God of Darkness. She ignored his open invitation and dipped behind him. Levant chuckled, lowering himself to the ground.

"Twice you've brought me to my knees." A smile curved through his voice. "Lest it catch on."

Cancer's gaze roamed his bare back.

"What's wrong?" Levant glanced over his shoulder. "Afraid to get close?"

Cancer slid her arms around his neck and raised a brow. "Are you?"

The god gripped her legs at his waist and pushed off the ground.

Wind fluttered through Cancer's hair as they broke from gravity. Monkeys flung amongst the trees. Rainbow-clad macaws burst into the sky like globs of paint splattered against canvas. Cancer's legs clasped tighter to his hips and smooth hands squeezed reassurance into her thighs. She gasped softly, unable to mask the chilly warmth crackling over her skin.

They slowed and landed on a large deck. Cancer slipped from the god's back, dizzy with adrenaline and something headier she dare not name. She shuffled across the deck, desperate to put distance between them. Posts and high beams towered from the structure's base. A skeleton she knew well.

"You're building a house?" she asked.

He cracked his neck. "*We* are."

"I know nothing of carpentry. Surely an earth Zodiac would be better suited?"

"I don't want an earth Zodiac." His smile lifted. "And who better to make a home with than Lady Regent of Kinship and Connection?"

Throughout the next few months Cancer and the God of Darkness worked in tandem. Nestled deep within the jungle stood the labors of unity. Proof that disagreements didn't warrant war. And perhaps, a loss of light didn't mean the absence of hope.

During their afternoon breaks, the pair lay sprawled amongst tree house nets. Lev's face would sour while he'd recount his distaste for Earth. Skies thick with poison, animal-based meals, and false gods worshiped.

He'd brag about vast oceans claiming most of Earth's surface. A cleverly laid plan to deter mortal inhabitation. But beneath the Dark God's scowls and eye rolls resided a hidden fondness for mortals. Like him, they'd made their own way, exploring the most perilous places.

Levant also instructed on matters not requiring opinion. Cancer marveled at each new tongue he taught. Unable to fathom how many ways a soul might say hello. Cancer never knew if she said the words right, but the Dark God never corrected her. Lev would simply smile with approval, attention flicking between her mouth and eyes. He'd murmur strings of words to her he'd never translate, and she found herself not caring either. Except his name for her.

Mi luna. My moon.

A cosmic mass not defined by those who looked upon it, but by the mystery conjured of something so far from reach. A symbol more often shrouded by darkness and rarely witnessed whole. All pieces of the Dark God, Cancer suspected, he wanted reflected in his and the goddess's new world.

Cancer relaxed against Lev's headboard.

This wasn't the first time she'd visited his hideaway on a day not required.

Some afternoons when duty anchored Lev to the Forgotten, Cancer stowed away in his home. Although a life she loved well, every story from Lev's lips made Cancer's Zodiac existence seem smaller. She'd sigh over the treetops at sunset's pink, lilac, and cherry streaks. A summons back to her old life. A reminder of the life she'd never have.

Tonight's sunset was different.

Tomorrow would be Cancer's final day with Lev.

He'd sign the treaty, and she would remain in Calidi. A silent heroine. A champion of souls. The deal she'd made in secret, left buried deep within a jungle of everything she never knew she wanted.

A woeful sigh fled her lips.

"Comfortable?" Lev's voice made her jump.

"What are you doing here?" she asked.

"You visit my home uninvited and question my arrival?" The mattress dipped under Lev's knees as he crawled atop it. "Perhaps we have become too familiar."

"I didn't expect you today."

"Clearly." Lev relaxed beside her.

Cancer's indecision wove through the silence stretching between them. Should she leave or stay? She shoved her questions aside and said, "I can't believe I helped build a house."

"You've proven quite useful." His mouth quirked. "Although, your incessant defense of humanity has grown quite cumbersome."

Sunset flushed over Cancer's cheeks. "You needn't worry. You'll be rid of me come this time tomorrow."

"Tell me." Lev pointed a lazy finger at Earth. "Why do you love that miserable rock?"

"Why help create a place you detest?" Cancer countered.

"Because she asked me to."

As long as Cancer existed, Neoma and Lev had been at odds. Their tale of creation and estrangement was told so often, it'd become more legend than memory. Cancer never considered the deities together in another time.

"You loved her," Cancer said.

"I was made to love her." Lev rested his head back. "I'd never known another. Never required more than what we'd been given. But creating mortal life was Neoma's greatest desire and she was mine. I forfeited my light and once Neoma possessed an entire planet of souls, she had no further use for me. I never knew real love then, and I never shall."

Sorrow shimmered over Cancer's eyes, a small stream breaking free.

"What's this?" Lev curled a finger under her chin and brushed a thumb over the watery trail along her check. "Don't mourn for me, *mi luna*. Many facets within this universe are much more fun than love."

Cancer's gaze dropped to his mouth. "I know what you do for fun."

"Thought about that, have you?" His knuckles glided along her throat's arch. "What might light feel like slipping from your essence? To experience such divinity, you'd perish if only to devour a mere taste?" Cancer swallowed tight as Lev's fingers danced along her collarbone. "Starmagic thrives within you, but my kiss would not claim your immortality, unless I desired. Are you curious about what you've worked tirelessly to protect everyone from?"

"What makes you think I'd give away my light so easily?"

An amused hum vibrated his lips. "The same that brings you to my bed when I am not in it."

Shame flared across Cancer's face.

"I'd offer a fair trade." He pulled back. "You'd feed off my darkness, enough to destroy whatever expectations of ecstasy you have. In return, I'd feast upon your light."

"Why consume light at all?" Cancer managed. "You don't need it to survive."

"Another's light is as close as I'll ever come to my own again."

"You're afraid," Cancer said before she could think better of it.

"I'm a god." Lev's face darkened. "I fear no goddess. No beast. No celestial being of any making."

"You don't disparage light, you crave it." Cancer held his stare. "You fear never feeling whole again."

"To be forgotten is worse than true death." His voice iced. "I make sure every day Neoma never forgets what she stole from me." He peered around the tree house. "I sought a haven where I chose to belong. Not in Omphalos with her. Nor the Forgotten with tainted reflections of her dead."

"But ..." Cancer's breath swirled into a frosty mist as his nose brushed hers. "Won't you be more alone out here?"

"I haven't been yet."

Lev's lips melted over hers.

Delicious terror slid over Cancer's tongue. Fear over what his kiss might steal. Fear he might not stop. Fear he would.

Starlight flickered beneath her skin. Dimmed. Blazed. Tugged her between worlds. Lev groaned against her mouth and a black haze coiled between their lips. Her mouth sank deeper. Darkness poured down her throat. Every thought. Every worry. Every fear became nothing. The God of Darkness was everywhere. She was nowhere. Lost and wandering in consumption of only him.

Cancer's lashes fluttered open at the sky. Earth watched her through the shadows sheening her irises. Cancer scrambled off the god, rapidly blinking the night from her eyes.

"That was ..." Ragged breaths heaved from Levant's chest, his awe mirroring her own. "You are—" Rare inarticulation hooded his lids. His head fell back against the headboard and rocked while grinning wildly. "I shall never tire of watching you like that."

A kiss. It'd been one kiss.

Cancer's hands covered her face. "Wicked?"

"Powerful."

"I have to go!" She climbed from the bed. Lev snatched Cancer's wrists and tugged her onto his lap. Cancer writhed in his grip. A feeble attempt at escape so she might convince herself she tried, but Cancer longed to lean in. Make his hands her home. Let them explore places sunlight never touched. If the night knew her secrets, he'd already tasted her hunger.

"I recognized it at the greenhouse." Lev's gaze snagged hers. "Same as now. You see what others do not."

"You're Neoma's other half," Cancer groaned.

"She's nothing."

"She's my goddess."

"You are her servant."

"No." Cancer's skin sang with betrayal.

His chin lifted. "Yes."

"I am a Zodiac!" Cancer leapt from his lap, Lev yielding to her burst of emotion.

"The Zodiacs do Neoma's bidding and what does she offer in return?" He stood. "Reject your pleas to visit Earth? Force you to negotiate with her adversary, inexperienced and alone? She cares not for you. Only her precious planet."

Cancer's expression hardened. "You're wrong."

"You dream about another world because you know more is missing from this one. Centuries will pass. Nidians will come and go, but you never will. Is this all your existence is good for? To ensure others' happiness? Souls who'll forget you once they've ascended. Does a great celestial of the stars not deserve more than to be a slave? You are restless. Let's be restless together."

Lev grabbed the nape of her neck and smothered his lips against hers. Their teeth clacked amidst each other's desperation. The chilled roll of his tongue inflamed her lower belly.

Stop!

Cancer reared back and slapped him.

Her mouth fell agape, skin tingling with violence.

Cancer had never laid hands on anyone in such a way. And not just anyone. She'd struck a creator. One with an ability to drain her dry before she blinked. Levant's perfect smile stretched wider. He snapped his fingers and several parchments from somewhere in the tree house fluttered into her hands.

"We've both fulfilled our promises." He ran a thumb across the corner of his lip. "You've no further obligation to me and my word I'll never consume another's light."

Cancer stared at Lev's signature on the final page. "You already signed it?"

"Stay with me tonight," he said. "Not because you're indebted, but because you want to. Otherwise, if I catch you in my home again, I won't be so lenient."

Cancer stared at Levant's handwriting. Such a tiny scribble would change life on Nidus forever. But something new burrowed into the hollow behind her heart. An ache ensnaring all she thought she knew.

Lev wasn't darkness. He was the space floating between stars.

The possibility of what couldn't be seen.

She closed her eyes and found him.

CHAPTER
THIRTY-FOUR

BRAX

PRESENT

"Fuck!" Brax gritted his teeth. "C'mon!" He pressed another breath into Reyna's lungs and pumped his palms against her chest.

One. Two. Three.

Beep. Click. Beep.

Oxygen hissed from the ventilator lodged in Brax's memory.

He blinked and Blaine's body was in the hospital bed beside him again. A body. Because no other word described what Blaine had been. Coma was fluff for dead. At least in the ways that mattered. Plastic tubes, blinking lights, and turning gears breathed existence into his brother in a way Brax couldn't. A miracle he would've sold his left nut for the power to now.

"Please, Sunshine." Brax cradled Reyna's limp form. "There's so much I—"

A sharp gasp broke beneath him.

Reyna's eyes flung open.

Her fingernails sank into Brax's bicep, their sting a reminder he was alive too. Oxygen poured down her throat. Reyna sucked in a breath. Another. And another.

"What"—she heaved for air—"happened?"

"I don't know." Brax tried recalling the longest five minutes of his life. "You fell and I didn't feel a pulse."

Reyna sat up, new life settling into her lungs. "Where is it?"

Shock still quivered through his limbs. "Huh?"

"The crystal." She shirked from him and crawled on all fours. "I have to find it!"

"Slow down. What crystal? Is that what did this?"

"It's here," Reyna's voice cracked. "Help me!"

"What happened?" Brax asked.

Reyna knocked aside a wicker basket.

"Sunshine?"

She scrambled to her feet. Rifled over the dining table.

"Reyna!" Brax spun her and smoothed a hand over her hair. "Tell me what happened?"

"I—" Her gaze dropped to his chest. "I don't remember."

Brax had memorized the deception lurking beneath her words. The subtlest twitch of her mouth. How her index finger knotted her shirt's hem. But this lie wasn't like the rest. It was meager. Robbed of conviction even she couldn't commit to. An unspoken curse grumbled in Brax's throat. He wanted to shake her until the truth rattled free like loose change, but he closed his eyes, inhaled through his nose, and met himself halfway.

"Are you okay?" he asked.

"I think so." Reyna's muscles relaxed. "We need to find the crystal. Whatever happened, I think it's related. It could help us."

A semblance of truth sweetened the lie, but he still hated it. "Do you remember what I said about the river?"

Reyna nodded.

"Follow it to Calidi," Brax instructed. "I'll stay behind and look for the crystal."

"What? I'm not going without you!"

"This isn't a discussion."

"You're right." Reyna crossed her arms. "Because I'm not leaving."

Sunlight glittered across her sandy brown eyes. An endless beach Brax would never tire of marooning himself on. A smile threatened his lips, but he buried it deep. "If you're right, there's no way in hell you're getting near it again."

"But what if it shows you—" Reyna's mouth snapped shut.

And there it was.

They'd come so far and yet, not far enough. Reyna didn't fully trust him, and rightfully so. But knowing she breathed air would always be enough for him. Anything beyond was more than he deserved. More than his dreams allowed and last night …

Fuck.

Last night.

The lines between them blurred. Bruised. Broke. And for the first time in years, Brax had no clue what his next move was.

"I get it. I've got shit I haven't told you too." Brax's thumbs glided over her soft knuckles, and he squeezed her fingers. "But right now, I need you to wait for me in Calidi and when I return, I'll tell you everything. Hopefully you'll be ready to talk too."

Brax pinched the bridge of his nose as Reyna's footsteps dissolved into the jungle.

He'd tried telling her. So many times. But every moment she folded into his arms, the truth slipped through his fingers like smoke. After centuries as Zodiacs living side by side, another spent sleeping amongst stars, and twenty-seven human years later, she finally saw him.

Really saw him.

Upon their return to Nidus, he feared he'd once more fallen asleep. That each day when his eyes opened, he'd be Braxton Riggs again. Back on Earth. In another borrowed bed. Where each morning his sleepy fingers would curl around the gun beneath his pillow like a lover, and ignorance of what was stolen so many years ago would weigh nothing. But each Nidian dawn would creep over his balcony, across the floor, over his bed, and he'd remember. He wasn't asleep. Not anymore.

Brax remembered *everything*.

He kicked a chair. It zipped across the deck and bamboo shattered against the far wall.

"Get it together, shithead," he grumbled.

Chills slit through the air like a jagged razor.

"Shithead," a voice squawked.

Brax froze at the misty plumes puffing from his lips.

Through his breath, a green-and-blue macaw perched amongst foliage. Frost crystallized along leaves and branches with each thrusting beat of its wings. Brax's throat bobbed. The bird took flight, devoured by a black haze. A man's silhouette bloomed from the night incarnate, shoes clicking along floorboards toward him. Brax held his ground. Each steadied breath, a calculated shield.

"I couldn't help myself." Levant chuckled and spread his arms wide. "Old friend."

The God of Darkness pulled Brax into a hug. Steam hissed from the pair as they clapped each other's backs in reunion. Lev gripped the sides of Brax's face and neck with ecstatic vigor.

"Neoma squirming yet?" the god asked.

"She's screwed and she knows it."

"As it should be!" Levant released him, satisfaction dripping with every syllable. "Neoma has been comfortable far too long. Meanwhile, I degrade myself pretending to be caged on those miserable isles. The eclipse cannot come soon enough."

Brax dug smokes from his pocket. The last rattled within its box. If there was ever a time for one, it was now.

"How'd you kick obsidian?" Brax asked.

"A little poison each day can do wonders for your health." Levant snapped his fingers and Brax's cigarette tip crackled with life. "I might've been banished, but Nidus isn't the only place in our cosmos Neoma and I have encountered that cursed glass. But tell me, what news is there?"

"Neoma has us lookin' for the prophecy, like you said she would."

Levant clicked his tongue and shook his head. "After a few millennia she's still predictable. Never bothering to understand how I work. Neoma's continued failure will increase her desperation."

"Careful, Lev, desperation also makes people dangerous."

"If I possessed a heart"—Levant smirked—"it'd be warmed to know you care."

Leo had no interest in Levant's rebellion a century ago, but never cared for Neoma either, though he'd been dispositioned to. Neoma's light called to all light and Leo's fire was no exception. But Leo was made of more than flames. A beast also crouched in his make. A beast Lev made good use of, under the right conditions.

"A heads-up about your stunt in Flora woulda been nice." Brax sighed internally at the hazy tobacco coating his tongue. One of the few vices from his mortal life he still relished. "But, Lev, a kid? C'mon."

"Neoma's magic protects your palaces. I've needed to be more creative delivering my messages. I'm sure you can appreciate the improvisation?"

Brax wanted to ask what messages but had already asked more questions than he allowed himself. Instead, he opted for something safe. Shallow. "You put my acting to shame."

"Ah, I never tire of that infamous Leo charm." Pleasure hummed over Levant's lips. "And while you're quite good at it, I didn't come all this way to be flattered. Tell me, why's the deed not yet done?"

Brax held himself captive to the anticipation swirling within Levant's face. The Zodiac couldn't waver. Not for a second. Brax filled his lungs with another savory drag.

"Like I told you at the marina"—Brax's voice thickened, holding smoke in—"killin' someone without magic is less predictable. Time and circumstances need to be right." He exhaled.

"You've not opportunity?"

"Too many eyes. We haven't been alone much together."

"And that night in the woods, after you interrupted us?" Irritation twitched along Levant's mouth. "Why not then?"

"You're kiddin' right?" Brax snorted and tapped ash to the floor-boards. "The Zodiac Super Team caught up with us. It's not my fault you didn't give me a warning and then got all nostalgic with her."

Levant loved a challenge. Moreover, when his followers had the balls to question him. Most played fiddle to his whims and fell in line, but Leo never spoke to him like a god. Beholden. Quivering. Rather, like a person. Which included calling Levant on his shit. Despite Leo's end game, he'd been surprised at how easily he and the god hit it off. Leo supposed it was in part how he'd played the role well for so long. But in the end, Lev would always demand compliance. Loyalty. Which Leo was, just not to him.

"To see her again after a century?" A smile slithered across the god's face. "I'll admit, I did lose myself. She has a way about her, doesn't she?"

"If you say so." Brax shrugged. Another question rose. One he deemed worth the risk. "Why kill Reyna if you need her?"

"The prophecy foretells a toll paid by a human who is remade immortal. When Reyna dies, she'll become Cancer once more and relinquish her power to me completely."

"Total Astral Allegiance?" Brax asked. "Is that possible?"

"Quite." Levant cocked his brow. "If you'd complete your task."

"I said I'd kill her, and I will." The lie dribbled from Brax's lips like vomit. He motioned around the tree house. "Is that why you told your messenger to have me lead her to this dump?"

Empty promises kept the Dark God at bay and granted the Zodiacs more time to find the prophecy. More chances at finding an alternative against whatever Levant brewed. It also bought Brax more time with *her*. Goddamn if he was a selfish bastard, but what-ever parts of either Leo or Brax didn't care. All those years ago, Cancer never showed interest in anyone, except the souls of Nidus. A devo-tion Leo fell for with ease. She never strutted her immortality. Never flaunted her magic and found strength even in the most fragile crea-tures. She was the epitome of why Zodiacs existed. Cancer was a Zodiac of the people.

And Leo, a Zodiac, was in awe of her.

He always thought he'd have an eternity to make a move, but time is a fickle bitch for an immortal. It has no end and yet, time always does end. Upon whisperings of Cancer's involvement with the Dark God, Leo didn't believe it. Didn't want to. But the first time he saw them brush past each other in Omphalos, an innocent graze to those unaware. The way their eyes drank each other. Leo knew.

His chance was over.

At that moment, Leo rendered a silent vow. To help her. Protect her. Stand by her, even if he was not with her. Leo soon learned his vow required goals beyond his unspoken devotion to Cancer. It required proven dedication to the God of Darkness himself. Leo was never sure how much Cancer knew about Levant's crimes, or rather, the ones he had Leo execute on his behalf. Levant always kept her separate from business affairs and forbade the Dark-Aligned Zodiacs from involving her in any transgressions.

"How do you know Reyna will be made immortal by dying?" Brax leaned against a wall. "She could just end up, I dunno, dying."

"My, my, my." Smugness stretched Levant's grin wider. "Such a curious kitty today, aren't we?"

Dread clawed along the cage of Brax's chest. Questions. He'd asked too many. Brax glanced at the cigarette between his twitching fingers. A slight tremble of ash floated to the ground. When had he turned into such a sloppy motherfucker?

"I can hear her heartbeat through the trees." Levant closed his eyes, inhaling the humid air. "It's been a century since I've been inside her and yet the stardust trapped within her human blood still beckons me."

Brax's free hand fisted at his side. Fire sizzled through the skin of his knuckles.

"Perhaps my outing from the isles was not in vain after all." Levant's gaze lolled over the tiny embers floating from Brax's hand. His chin lifted. "Step aside Leo, and I shall relieve you of your deed."

Brax always expected this moment would come.

Just not so soon.

Brax chuckled through a sigh, dropped his cigarette and smothered it with his shoe. "We both know I'm not movin.'"

The god placed a hand on Brax's shoulder and for a moment they stared at each another. Less a reckoning, more an understanding. The Dark God smiled, a fleeting glimmer almost passing for fondness as he said, "I knew there was a reason you've always been one of my favorites."

Levant's fist plunged into the Zodiac's stomach.

Brax slid across the deck, a match igniting fire along his path. His spine crunched into an overturned desk. Brax heaved for breath and clasped his abdomen.

Damn mortal meat sack.

"Do you think me daft?" Levant swaggered through flames crackling along the floor. The god pressed a foot against Brax's chest. "That I wouldn't see it?" Floorboards crunched and buckled under the Zodiac. Levant ground his heel deeper. "You love her."

"What can I say?" Brax groaned through his crunching ribs. "I have good taste."

"Yet, in all your obvious desperation, Cancer never noticed otherwise." Levant lit with glee. "Although, I can recall more than a few delectable reasons why."

Levant's foot rose and crushed into Brax's chest.

Brax plummeted through the floorboards. Levant dove after him. Flames roared from Brax's mouth as he fell, leaves and branches flaring into cinders. Two coal black eyes emerged through the sweltering fire. Levant grabbed Brax's wrist, and a nebulous black haze swallowed them whole. A dark cloud materialized above the tree house and cannonballed Brax from its core. He slammed against the deck and rolled into a post. An inferno ravaged the tree house. Thick black smoke billowed into a brilliant blue sky. Impossible to tell where Levant's magic began and ended. Brax wobbled onto all fours, blond hair clinging to the crimson slathered across his face.

Levant strolled from within the smoke. "Did you honestly think you had a chance with her?"

Blood slid over Brax's tongue. He grinned through a wince. "Did you?"

"Do you know where you are?" Levant crouched beside him. "This *dump* was where we came to get away. Where we fucked. But feeding off each other?" A euphoric groan curdled from his throat. "Now that, she enjoyed."

"You're lying," Brax bit, his mind stumbling over itself.

"How do you think the mortal came by her extraction magic?" Levant feigned a frown. "A magnificent manifestation from our time together."

"You took advantage of her calling to help others. Her pure heart." Brax slid himself up along the post at his back to stand.

"Pure heart?" Levant sneered. "An absurd mortal fairy tale. Even then, she was on her way to fulfilling the prophecy. *For a deviant of black glass, love too must be earned,*" Levant spoke the words as though he'd recited them a million times. "Cancer begged for my darkness. Bathed in it. Couldn't get enough. And soon Reyna will too."

"Newsflash, dickwad, that's addiction. Not love."

"It's all the same." Levant drawled through a snicker. "Experimentation becomes want. Want becomes need and before long, need becomes something else entirely."

"Maybe Cancer loved you"—Brax spat blood—"but Reyna never would."

Levant's laughter snowed like ash from the sky, icing Brax's insides.

"She hasn't told you?" Levant's delight danced with the firelight. "While you've been wasting my time, I've been filling her mind with delicious memories of us." Black swallowed his eyes. "I don't require Reyna to love me, since Cancer already has, but the insurance is worth it. I've planned for a century and when the eclipse arrives, there'll be no question where her heart lies. She'll choose me once more. And you, my lion, will have a front row seat. Again."

Brax lurched forward, commanding every ounce of starfire he

possessed. Levant's hand flung forward. Fire seared through Brax's veins like hot steel. He writhed and roared against a leash of his own element turned on him. Brax's magic couldn't compete with Levant's power, and it ground against his pride like a rusty knife to the bone.

Levant grabbed a fist of blond hair and yanked Brax to his knees. The god bent forward, hovering a few inches from Brax's lips. Marble cracked around Brax's mouth.

"You are my plaything," Levant whispered through a sneer. "A puppet."

Brax grunted at the white marble hardening his jaw.

"I don't play chess." Levant's lips ghosted his. "I create the pieces."

Tears pricked Brax's eyes.

Reyna—I never got to tell her—

Levant shoved him back.

Oxygen detonated in Brax's chest. He lay on the floorboards and clutched the softening flesh of his throat as sharp heaves expanded his lungs.

"I should end you where you lie." Levant peered down his nose at the writhing Zodiac. "But you still have a role to play come the eclipse."

"Finish me now." Brax flexed his jaw and pushed himself onto an elbow. "'Cause I'm never doing dick for you again."

Levant raised a brow. "If you think I'm the only celestial who would do her harm, you're mistaken, my ferocious friend."

"Neoma …"

"If the goddess discovers Reyna is the Dark Star, you don't believe she'd simply banish you all again?" Levant's chin lifted. "If you end Reyna's human life, she will become the Dark Star. If Neoma ends it … there won't be anything left of Cancer or Reyna to take any form."

Brax and Reyna could run. His mortal-half had mastered a life built around the concept. But flee forever? Not in a galaxy created by two celestials who would see her dead. Although Reyna had lived isolated, she'd been on the run too. From herself. Brax refused to ask Reyna to abandon one life of hiding for another, if somehow, she miraculously forgave his lies. Brax trusted neither deity, but one gained more from keeping her alive. One way or another.

"Fine," Brax muttered. "But it'll be when and how I say. You'll also tell Seph to back off. I don't need you both breathing down my neck."

Leo had needed to appear ingrained in his new Dark-Aligned life all those years ago, so he warmed his sheets with distractions. Meaningless encounters offering an escape from the life he wanted. Levant was pleased with Leo and Seph's arrangement. The Dark God's most trusted follower and his first. Seph never pressed Leo for more than physical, which was the best part about her. Not because Leo loved Cancer. Not because sex with Seph was great, detached as it was. But because in those moments with Seph, and whomever she invited into their bed, Leo forgot the hollow space in his chest. He didn't have to hide. His anger mimicked passion. His hopelessness, aloof bedroom arrogance. And the rest of his broken pieces, a hunt for the next thrill.

He'd become an insult to what it meant to be Leo.

A coward.

Leo never truly knew if Levant loved Cancer. If he was capable. But Cancer believed she'd loved him, and Leo knew better than anyone, hearts were not easily changed. He never resented Cancer for falling for Levant. Leo resented himself for not admitting how he felt about her sooner.

Levant's lip curled. "You're in no position to make demands."

"Neoma is looking for the Forgotten," Brax blurted. Information was the only power he wielded now. Anything to stay a step ahead of the goddess. "She's convinced Reyna she'll find the prophecy there."

"Neoma." Levant brought steepled fingers to his lips while he paced. "You clever, wicked creature. But not quite clever enough. Tell me, has Reyna located the way in yet?"

"No. But—"

"Despite your betrayal, you've proven most useful. It matters not where your loyalties lie, as long as you do what I command, and I no longer wish you to kill her."

A shadow of relief passed over Brax. But that's all it was. A shadow. The prophecy still required her death.

"You'll return to Calidi and infiltrate any developments I should know of. Seph is sharp but doesn't hold the weight or trust your title commands. You'll assist the mortal in uncovering the Forgotten, under my direction."

Brax squinted with confusion. "You *want* Reyna to find the Forgotten?"

"Once she does, her soul will be gone and Cancer remade. Neoma's quest to stop me shall inadvertently ensure my success. It's rather poetic."

"How do you expect me to lead Reyna to the underworld?" Brax scoured for a loophole. "I can't inexplicably know where it is. She'll wanna know how I do."

"I don't care how. Put those crooked earthly skills to work. Her immortal life depends on it." Levant strutted toward him. "You'll also end whatever you think it is you've started with her. And if you don't"—cruel amusement blazed in his eyes—"as you've enjoyed reminding me, Reyna is not Cancer. So, I'll have no quarrels ensuring whatever little time she has left as a mortal is less comfortable. Tell me you understand."

Brax wanted to say, *I understand you're a sick son of a bitch.* But instead, he climbed onto his knees, hung his head low, and replied, "Yes, my Dark God."

"I wonder what she'd think of you now? Every bit as traitorous as your human stain of an existence." Levant threaded fingers through Brax's mane. Tender. Brutal. Dueling complexities wielded to ensnare followers in line. "I may be the God of Darkness, but at least I didn't have to become someone else for her to fall in love with me."

THIRTY-FIVE

REYNA

"Stop blocking," Orion instructed. "Concentrate."

"I'm not blocking." Reyna sat cross-legged on the fountain's ledge.

"You are." Orion paced the tiles. "You're listening to everything but yourself."

Reyna closed her eyes and drew a soft inhale. She sifted through the fountain's excess spray, through the beads of sweat sliding along the greenhouse windows overhead. Her consciousness wove and folded between each droplet. Aimless as flames bending to the wind's will. Fire.

Reyna had rounded a corner in the palace and frozen.

Limbs locked. Heart bounding. Words no longer held her hostage. Only the need to open herself to someone. And not just anyone.

Him.

"Good." Orion's velvety voice anchored her awareness. "Keep going."

Brax's hands braced against the courtyard balcony rail. Shoulders hunched over. Golden sunset haloed his hair.

"When did you get back?" Reyna wrapped her arms around his torso and pressed a cheek between his shoulder blades. "I've been worried."

Brax hissed and flinched from her hug.

"Don't worry about me," he replied softly, rubbing his side.

"Of course I'm—are you hurt?"

Brax shuffled from reach.

"What happened?" Walls of Reyna's throat closed. "Did you find the crystal?"

"No."

"Are you sure?" Rot sloshed around the pit in her stomach with whatever he wasn't saying. "What about—"

"I'm tired." Brax stared past her. "Can we do this another time?"

"Brax ..." Reyna reached for his hand.

"Later." He offered a strained smile and stepped back.

"Lady Reyna," Orion's voice warned.

Inky black clouds plunked into her memory as Brax walked away.

A darkness pulled her close. It possessed no arms. No hands. Yet its embrace slipped around her waist and splayed hazy fingers along her lower spine. Reyna arched her back. The night's lips grazed hers and Cancer's love for Levant bloomed. Reyna didn't want it. Tried convincing herself whatever she felt was lost remnants from a life she refused to claim. But buried deep between the ghosts of her past and present, Reyna had always known.

She'd been his.

"Reyna!" Orion's bass split like thunder.

Her eyes flashed open.

Icy orbs shattered on tiles and shards ripped through greenery. Fresh frost coated the fountain's empty basin, windows, and ferns.

Ice. Levant's calling card.

Reyna stared at her trembling hands. Monsters caged by worn leather and shoddy stitching. Was this why her magic resembled his? Because she'd once been his? Was she still? No. Not ever again.

"Are you alright?" Orion slowed his breath.

"Why'd you stop me?" Reyna clenched her hands into fists.

Orion spoke as though he'd stepped into the eye of a storm.

"The best chance at controlling your extraction magic is by accepting your emotions. Not suppressing them."

"I didn't suppress," Reyna grumbled.

"Emotion flows like water." Orion nodded at the busted ice littering the floor. "You were blocking."

"Maybe some emotions should be."

"Our worst still makes us whole."

Orion knew nothing of her worst. If he did, the general would've muzzled her magic. Not groomed it.

"Are we done?" Reyna slipped off the fountain's edge.

"Answer a question and you may go," Orion replied. "When inside the Florian boy's nightmare, what did you feel?"

A ridiculous question.

"Fear," she replied striding toward the door. An answer for an exit.

"I have a theory." Orion's bait stopped her cold.

Reyna hated the way others disarmed her without her other magic. How a subtlest hint at understanding her own power possessed the capacity to strip her of all resolve.

Orion continued, "I suspect you cannot control your extraction magic when it responds to fear." Orion's footsteps slowly drew closer. "However, if what transpired in Flora is any indication, perhaps you weren't as afraid as you thought?"

Reyna shook her head. "I was terrified."

"From what I heard, you performed Astral Allegiance with Lord Regent. Shared his strength. He centered you."

I feel safe with you.

Reyna swallowed the welling emotion of her confession to Brax.

"I used extraction magic," she replied.

"Are Astral Allegiance and extraction so different? When a crop reaches its peak, do we not harvest? When offered a gift, should we not accept?" Orion asked. "Astral Allegiance is giving strength to another. Someone must be the receiver. The same could be said of extraction magic. Perhaps, if harnessed with more positive emotions, your magic might accomplish the opposite."

"Which is?"

"Our world is made of balance. A force cannot exist without a counter." Orion's cheeks dimpled. "If you can take, it also means you can give."

You can't take what I willingly give.

What did Brax give now?

The crux of Reyna's predicament. The reason she inched toward his wing every night and yanked herself back before entering. Reyna couldn't bring herself to demand answers. She already knew why he'd reduced her to a ghost. Why he could barely look her in the eyes.

Brax had found and witnessed the memory within the crystal.

He knew about her connection to the Dark God.

A vision of the crystal's pale green edges rolling over in Brax's hand like a dog sharing its secrets, her secrets, haunted Reyna's every waking moment. No other explanation explained his dismissal, but if he knew about her and Levant, why hadn't he outed her to the others yet? Was he debating what to do with the information? Brax forgave much, but betrayal against everything the Zodiacs fought for? Against what they'd shared in the cave? Brax would never forgive that. Shouldn't. If by some chance he did, Reyna could never tell the full truth. How even now, Cancer's dormant desire for the Dark God stirred through her veins. How she'd once drunk from his darkness.

And liked it.

Maybe Reyna deserved Brax's coldness. Her cursed magic. A life losing everyone she cared about. Perhaps the universe finally came to collect for the balance Cancer stole all those years ago. Retribution for nature's broken laws.

No matter Reyna's connection to the God of Darkness, one fact remained absolute. Levant needed to be stopped and whoever the Dark Star was, even Reyna couldn't rise with the eclipse.

Whatever Brax thought or didn't think of her didn't matter. Not with how much rode the wave of destruction toward their near future. If the slightest chance existed that Brax might still help her, she needed to take it.

Reyna waited for the guise of night. She skittered through palace shadows into the grand foyer. Starlight from beyond the glass ceiling refracted off the tiles like a shimmering fog. Reyna crossed ceramic and starlight, craning her neck as she passed under the planetary mobile. Earth's moon and sun approached like beads strung on a thread. Each new day pulling their proximity closer to an end.

The symbolism wasn't lost on Reyna.

Starry pinpricks danced over two sandstone lion sculptures on either side of an ascending stairwell. She flew along its curves. The first time Anemone led her up Cancer's adjacent stairs a breathlessness burned in her lungs. Reyna's calves no longer protested, and her breath sharpened. A few weeks of an organic diet, climbing countless steps, and hikes across beaches and wilderness had made her stronger.

What if Brax shut the door in her face?

She slowed her pace.

No. She'd make him listen. Pray for a spark of whatever he might still feel for her to shine through. Be it faith in Reyna's good intentions, if nothing else. There'd be another time to address what transpired between them, or didn't, but tonight was not that night.

A final step into the lion's den brought Reyna little reprieve. At the wing's dark end, light flickered from a cracked open door. She edged closer. Fictitious arguments tumbled through her mind. Proof points at convincing Brax to still help her. Reyna's footsteps slowed and her hand wrapped around his room's knob.

Low murmurs floated from within.

Reyna's ears perked up.

A thud. Feet scuffling. Metal clattering onto tile. Muffled grunts.

Reyna shoved the door open and icy daggers crystallized in her palms. Brax caged Seph against a gilded wall, wrists pinned above her head as he growled low in her ear.

"How I've missed that filthy mouth of yours." Seph's bloodred hair spilled over her pale naked breasts. She smiled at Reyna. "Oh look. Someone else has come to play."

Reyna's daggers shattered against the floor.

Brax's gaze darted over his shoulder. Brows drawn together, he released Seph.

Reyna took in his disheveled hair. Bare chest catching shadows from lantern light. Pant strings untied. She swallowed hard and backed away.

"Reyna," her true name dripped from his mouth like acid.

"I'm sorry," Reyna choked. She didn't know why she apologized, but it spewed again. "I'm sorry. I shouldn't have come." Reyna dashed toward the stairs with long steady strides as sobs punched beneath her sternum. If she ran, the dam would break.

"Stop!" Brax's hoarseness echoed through the hall.

She did.

They stood in silence, but she wouldn't face him. Couldn't.

"Reyna," his tone came softer this time. An unbearable, cruel trick.

"Don't," her voice cracked.

"What're you doin' here?" he asked.

The dam inside her broke. No raging tears, only white-hot fury.

Reyna faced him. "Who the hell do you think you are?"

Stern indifference haunted his once-handsome features. All the warmth she'd known, reduced to soot. Seph leaned against his doorframe. Every slope of her naked figure taut with lust yet dripping for something else.

"Hurry back, Leo darling." White teeth gleamed through her pomegranate lips. "The sheets are cold, and I need some warmth, before I return to the underworld tonight."

Brax snarled. "Get out of here, Seph."

"I'll do no such thing." The redhead feigned shock between them. "Some things really are better than sex."

"Enough!" he roared.

"I trusted you. Counted on you." A tear betrayed Reyna. "I can't believe I thought you might—" Out. She needed out.

Reyna strode toward the stairs.

"I never meant to hurt you." Brax's shallow apology pierced Reyna's flesh. She paused and gripped the stairwell's banister. Rawness ground in his voice. "You've always known who I am. A double-dealing bastard. Always was. *Still am.*"

Reyna flurried into the stairwell and didn't look back.

CHAPTER

THIRTY-SIX

S ILENCE TICKED BY.

Wait. Breathe. Wait.

Reyna didn't know how long she crouched beneath Brax's staircase. By the cramp gnawing at her calf, maybe a half hour. The discomfort would be worth it though. Lions may hold supreme power of their pride, but lionesses were the true hunters. And tonight, Reyna would become one of them.

Seph's heels descended the guilded staircase and Reyna sifted deeper into darkness. Whatever might've transpired between Brax and Seph during the thirty minutes Reyna squatted in the shadows like a lunatic stalker slugged its way into her stomach. She couldn't deny what a stunning pair they'd make, though none of that mattered. If Seph wanted to weasel between Reyna and Brax, fine. But Reyna would be damned if she didn't take something of Seph's return.

The answer was so clear. So obvious. So aggravatingly simple. Reyna didn't know how anyone hadn't thought of it before.

Seph couldn't verbally give up the underworld's location, but she could be followed.

Reyna rode the shadows through the gardens as Calidi's palace windows twinkled high through the swaying palms. Seph paused before a mirror and scanned the night-clad garden. Satisfied she was alone, her desired destination shimmered over the mirror's faux glass, and she stepped through.

Reyna's feet itched to close the space. She couldn't barrel directly after her, or wait too long and risk losing Seph's trail. Reyna had one shot, and she refused a single miscalculation.

Each second the invisible string pulled tighter between Reyna and her netherworld guide, her mind drifted to Brax in the cave. They'd been two meteors burning brighter and brighter as they entered each other's atmosphere. More than lust. Past their Zodiac-drawn essences. Reyna and Brax were connected. Beyond any reason Reyna could comprehend. And with that came a clarity she never imagined she might grasp.

You've always known who I am. A double-dealing bastard. Always was.

Still am.

The moment those last words left Brax's lips, their resonance groveled for her to hear past what they said.

Brax was up to something.

Reyna couldn't explain it. Nor fathom how or why it involved Seph stripped against his bedroom wall. Perhaps he never saw the vision of Cancer and Levant together. Or had, and didn't care? Until Reyna could decode his behavior, she refused to accept it at face value. People's actions seldom reflected their true emotions. Reyna suspected Brax ran a long game. She just prayed it wasn't on her.

After a few more seconds, Reyna willed the mirror's deliverance of her to Seph's location. Reyna's sneakers met cobblestone. Sleek wooden arches pranced over horse stalls, but absence polluted the air. Reyna had never been inside a stable, but her intuition cowered at its wrongness. She craved the soft grunts of horses or shuffling hooves, but the tomb of creatures long since exterminated sat quiet. Winter howled outside high frosted windows and an unmistakable clack of heels echoed from a stony corridor ahead. Awareness propelled Reyna toward the sound. She peeked from behind a corner at Seph opening a large painting like a door and stepping inside.

Reyna followed, creeping along the tunnel's ice-slicked walls to avoid the glow of Seph's lantern. The redhead vanished past another turn and Reyna couldn't fight her instinct to not lose the light.

She sprinted. Her rubber soles slipped over icy rock. Reyna skidded past the corner and face-planted onto the ground. A groan punched from her lungs as she braced for Seph's drawling laughter. When it didn't come, she scrambled to her feet and squinted around the enclosed chamber. A lone, abandoned lantern sat across the space. Reyna edged toward it, unable to comprehend where Seph might've gone. Light spilled over a black lake of stagnant water. She peeked over the precipice, but its depths offered no reflection.

"Stop!" someone shouted.

Reyna reeled backward and whirled, hands raised to summon icy stalactites from the mountain's belly. Two silhouettes scurried across the cavern, one with a lantern swaying in their hand.

"Anemone? Prisha?" Reyna's palms lowered. "What're you doing here?"

Anemone heaved for breath. "I brought your supper and found your chambers empty. I used the Eternal Flame to locate the necklace you wear from the Florian boy."

Prisha propped hands on her hips. "Imagine my surprise when Anemone pounded on the Parhelia palace doors and insisted you were somewhere on the grounds? Luckily, a staff member noticed light moving through the old stables."

Anemone scanned their grave surroundings. "Why are we so far below the Parhelian palace?"

"The palace …" Reyna's mind unfolded. She grabbed the map from her pocket and studied her statue notations. Reyna traced statue markings along the island waterways in reverse. Rootlike deltas rescinded from the sea and tapered into River Hydra. The serpent river snaked between Calidi's and Flora's borders into the snowy mountains. Reyna backtracked another river. Then another.

"Anemone, where do all Nidus's rivers originate?" Reyna asked.

"Omphalos is at Nidus's highest peak." Anemone tapped the map's center. "But Parhelia is its closest neighbor across the mountains. Their snowfall feeds into all Nidus's rivers and lakes."

An unending source of water.

Rivers must've been how Levant moved throughout Nidus undetected. All poor encountered souls condemned in his literal wake.

"This is the Forgotten's entrance." Reyna marveled at her pieces finally come together.

"Lady Regent!" Anemone's eyes flew wide at Reyna shucking off her shoes. "If what you say is true, we must leave!"

"I appreciate your concern, but the prophecy is down there." Reyna nodded toward the small lake. "I can feel it."

Prisha pushed, "How can you be sure?"

"I'm not, but we're out of time. The eclipse is in a few days, and we still haven't found the prophecy. The Forgotten is the one place nobody has searched."

"How'd you know where to look?" Prisha countered.

"I heard Seph say she was returning tonight, so I followed her." Reyna eyed the black water as though Seph might emerge any moment. "Her trail went cold right before you showed up."

The factotum dangled her lantern over the lake's edge. Bronze and silver firelight danced against its waters and all three of their reflections stared back.

"How's that possible?" Reyna gulped. "I didn't see my reflection before."

"The Eternal Flame reveals what its bearer seeks and conceals what they wish hidden," Anemone replied. "We expected our reflections, and the flame made it so. I'd rather not dwell on why they were absent before."

"Underworld aside, this feels off." Prisha scrubbed hands over her arms. "If the Forgotten is down there, maybe we should gather the others, consult with Neoma, and come up with a plan?"

"No!" Reyna's objection echoed off the walls. This wasn't just about removing her magic or stopping Levant. Some part of Reyna heard what Brax said on the beach about understanding her power. If Reyna was the Dark Star, she wanted to know first. "I'm not asking you to understand, but I need to do this alone."

"You couldn't see your own reflection a few minutes ago, let alone anything else." Prisha glowered. "And how will you breathe?"

"As a water Zodiac and a factotum, we can breathe underwater." Anemone slipped off her own sandals. "Also, the Eternal Flame's fire cannot be extinguished by water. It will light our way through the Forgotten unseen."

"Our?" Reyna blinked. "Did you miss when I said I'm going alone?"

Anemone surged forward. Reyna stood straight at the factotum rising onto her toes.

"I've led Calidians in prayer for a decade. Begged the Infinite All-Knowing for *your* safe return. Taught the values *you*, Cancer, instilled in our kin a century ago. I've not devoted my entire life, the reason I exist, to lose you again." Anemone lowered onto her heels. "Lady Regent or no, if you refuse reason, I'm coming with you."

"Anemone," Reyna's resolve wavered. "You don't have to—"

"Enough." Anemone's gruffness was resolute. "You know nothing of the Forgotten and I won't let you endure it blindly."

"And you know it?" Reyna asked.

Anemone lifted her lantern, harsh light hollowing the skeletal edges of her face. "I've heard enough legends and if they've any truth, you'll need me."

"This is totally nuts," Prisha groaned, slipping off her boots. "But I guess we're doing this."

"Not you too." Reyna ran a hand over her hair. "The Forgotten is underwater. You can't make it without air."

Prisha grinned. "I've got some secrets up my sleeve too."

Reyna wanted to protest, but they'd already wasted enough time arguing logistics. She stared into the blackness below, toes scrunching over the frosted rocky ledge. Somewhere within those depths, the afterlife's arena waited. Death waited. Patient. Smiling. Reyna knew death all her life, both as its shepherd and executioner. But now, more waited below too. Salvation.

Prisha and Anemone stepped on either side of Reyna staring at their reflections.

"Are you sure about this, Reyna?" Prisha asked and Reyna gave a single nod. Prisha blew a heated breath into her curled hands and rubbed them together. "On the count of three?"

"One," Anemone started.

"Two." Prisha dared Reyna to follow.

Reyna released a final plume of breath. "Three."

The women plunged into the arctic depths of Hell.

Glacial waters scraped over Reyna's body. Each fizzy bubble an icy pinprick against her flesh. She waited for her starwater magic to take over, like some slumbering instinct triggered by the need for survival.

"Lady Regent, are you alright?" Anemone swam toward her, voice clear as above the surface.

Reyna shook her head, chest roaring with want for oxygen.

"Lady." Anemone gripped her arm. "You must open your mouth."

Reyna's lungs rejected the concept. Begged for the surface. Chilled blood slugged through her veins like thickening mud. It wasn't like the lake in Ambrose's nightmare or Brax's underwater memory. This was a heavy, centuries-old sea in the gut of a mountain wanting to claim her.

This was real.

"Lady!" Anemone scowled. "Breathe now!"

Reyna squeezed her eyes shut and screamed at death. She waited for its descent along her throat. Frigid water spilled over her tongue, but unexpected warmth rippled through her seizing abdomen, fingers, and toes. Reyna opened her eyes. A few final bubbles floated from her lips. She blinked at Anemone and drank another watery breath.

A torrent of bubbles whizzed past underneath them.

Panic tightened in Reyna's waterlogged chest. "What was—"

"Shh!" Anemone lifted her lantern and squinted.

A silhouette charged through the darkness toward them, tail slashing through the water. Reyna's hands flung forward. An icy shield crystallized in front of her and Anemone. The creature slowed its advance and slowly lifted its face. Onyx hair floated around the horns curling from Prisha's head. A plunging neckline of diamond scales hugged her breasts and stomach, narrowing into a fishtail. A siren of beauty, cut from the dead sea itself.

"Incredible." Reyna gaped.

"You are too." Prisha grinned at Reyna's barrier. "Looks like Orion's private training is paying off."

Reyna dissolved her shield. "A warning next time might be nice. Almost dying once today is enough for me."

Anemone snorted. "Perhaps if you are concerned with death, we shouldn't be visiting the underworld?" She and Reyna exchanged narrowed gazes and Anemone succumbed to an eye roll. "Cancerians are not nearly this stubborn."

"If I hadn't met you"—Reyna's eyebrow lifted—"I might've believed that."

A smile slipped through the factotum's pursed lips.

"Let's make haste. The sooner we find this dreadful prophecy, the quicker we go home." Anemone murmured a cloaking command to Sagittarius's flame.

"Did it work?" Reyna inspected her own limbs as though they might become transparent. "I don't feel different."

"I assure you, my lady, it's done. If we stay together and don't abandon the lantern, we'll remain concealed."

The trio descended into the murky veil. Each fathom, a test of Reyna's resolve. She wasn't sure how long they swam or in what direction but never removed her focus from the lantern's light. Convinced, if she investigated the darkness long enough, Seph or whatever creatures might lurk would find her instead.

Silver and bronze light wrapped over jagged rocks jutting from the lake's bed. They wove along its bottom until light vanished into a chasm.

Reyna braved a glance at her surroundings. "Is this it?"

"I believe so." Anemone peeked into the gaping crevasse. "Legend suggests the Forgotten is beneath Nidus, though I'm not sure at which interval we are *under* it."

Halley's campfire projection flipped in Reyna's mind. Nidus peeked above the surface like a glacier and the Forgotten, its hidden icy bottom.

The women nodded in silent agreement and swam inside. They followed a hazy green glow toward the channel's end. The rocky tunnel descended, but Reyna's center of gravity insisted she somehow swam upward.

Upon their exit, a shiver brushed its bony finger along her spine. A hundred eyes from two stone walls of stacked human figures watched as they approached. The walls tapered from an arch's center and dissolved into mucky sand at either end. Most of the figures slept. Some wept. Others clawed through tangled limbs, as though they might escape the pile of stony flesh. Reyna had been on Nidus long enough to know these figures weren't decorations.

She missed the sensation of saliva with her swallow. "Do we just … go in?"

"All are welcome," a creature crooned, drifting into the archway's center. Their ivory hair and tattered dress danced like pale seaweed. An anglerfish light bobbed atop its head, illuminating narrowed cheekbones. Young and ancient. Gorgeous and gruesome. The thing's lips curled into a jagged, toothy smile. "I'm Lethe, the Forgotten's gatekeeper."

"H-how can you see us?" Reyna stuttered.

Its milky irises drifted toward her. "Sagittarius's Eternal Flame is indeed powerful, but souls cannot hide from death. I see all."

Beyond the corpse wall, soft Dredger weeps sang through Parhelia's black snowless mountain range.

Anemone shivered. "What about them?"

"Dredgers are whispers of death, so they cannot see." Lethe's greedy gaze snatched Anemone. A sound somewhere between a sigh and snarl escaped through its razor teeth. "Lady Cancer, you've brought us a Nidian soul? How generous."

"I've brought you nothing." Reyna darted in front of her friend. "She's with us."

"Pity. The scream of an unborn soul would feed Dredgers for days. They're always hungry ... as am I."

"You said all are welcome." Prisha swam forward. "Does that mean we can enter?"

"Yes." Lethe bowed their head. "Although, leaving is a bit more costly. The toll is a soul for a soul. For a soul to cross back over, another must stay behind."

A fool's bargain.

"If I stayed in the Forgotten, could I deliver a message to my friends before they leave?" Reyna asked.

"Reyna!" Prisha swam between her and Lethe. "You're not giving up your soul!"

Lethe interjected, "If a Zodiac entered with a soul intact, their mortal soul would remain in the underworld, but their immortal self would be free to leave."

"Would I still be me without my soul?" Reyna asked.

"More or less." Lethe's white hair billowed around their gray cheeks. "Those pesky souls you've acquired through reincarnation are trivial."

Prisha glowered. "If they're trivial, why do you want them?"

"I desire nothing." Lethe bowed their head. "I'm but a servant to underworld law."

Prisha tugged Reyna aside. "You can't be still considering this?"

"We're out of time and options," Reyna replied. "If we go back for help, a payment is still owed. This is the only way."

"We don't know if the prophecy is in there!" Prisha argued. "Even if it is, it's not worth throwing away your soul."

"If my soul can give us a fighting chance, it's worth it to me," Reyna replied.

"You don't owe anyone your soul."

Reyna owed her mother a lifetime of sunrises. Owed Tessa the chance to maybe have babies, travel the world, get old, fat, and sag in all the wrong places. Prisha was wrong. Reyna owed more.

"I'll escort you, Lady Regent." Anemone swept forward at Reyna's falling face. "I see how important this is to you and your soul is far more valuable than mine. I will stay behind."

"No!" Reyna shook her head. "You will not forfeit your future human life. I'd never ask this of you."

"You didn't," Anemone replied. "If legend is true and the Forgotten reflects Nidus, you'll need help navigating it. I shall be your guide."

Reyna pulled the map from her pocket, but its papery folds fell apart like chum in her hands. She rounded on Lethe. "If Anemone accompanies me and my soul stays behind, you're sure hers will be safe?"

"Yes," the gatekeeper hissed. "So long as a soul remains behind, the choice of whose is yours."

"I don't agree with this." Prisha crossed her arms tight across her chest.

"Everything will be okay." Reyna forced a smile. "You'll see."

"Just …" Prisha stared at the sand. "Be careful."

Reyna and Anemone swam toward the archway, but Lethe's arm sliced into their path.

"I'll be needing that," the gatekeeper's pale pupils lingered on Reyna's necklace.

"No." She clutched the crystal against her collarbone. "You said the toll was a soul."

"The Forgotten earns its name well. The longer one stays, the more they forget. Green calcite preserves memories, and as such, is forbidden." Lethe's spindly hand stretched toward Reyna. "You may have it, if you return."

"If?" Anemone swallowed. "You said—"

"Memories are fickle trinkets." Lethe's jagged smile stretched. "Stay too long and the path back may not be so clear."

"Fine." Reyna slipped the jewelry from her neck and coiled it into the gatekeeper's palm.

Lethe dangled the string between their fingers. The creature's eyes closed, visions darting around beneath its paper-thin eyelids. They hummed. "A most curious memory."

Reyna's heart stilled. She side-eyed her friends, praying Lethe wouldn't utter her most despicable secret aloud. Reyna always suspected the dream about Cancer and Levant's first meeting was a memory but hadn't been sure until now. Did Ambrose know what he'd gifted her? How could he?

"Best of luck, my lady." The gatekeeper floated aside.

Anemone slipped her hand into Reyna's, and they swam together into the open arms of the decaying underworld.

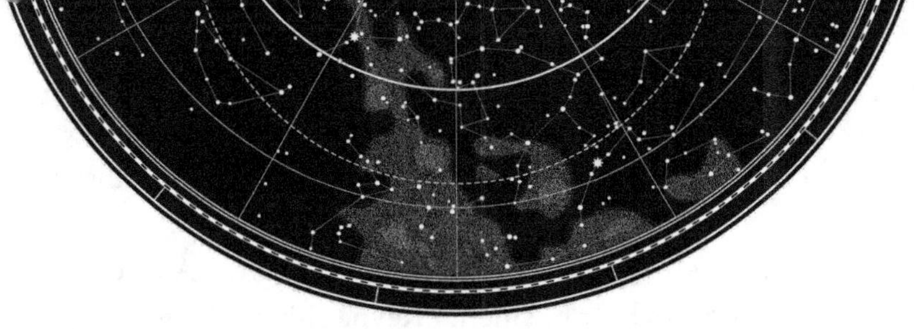

CHAPTER

THIRTY-SEVEN

E VEN THE FORGOTTEN'S TREES WEREN'T FREE.
Skeletal branches clawed for the myth of daylight somewhere above the surface as Reyna and Anemone floated inland
from the empty sea. The underworld's version of Omphalos loomed
atop the tallest mountain like a black tombstone with soft green light
haunting its many windows.

"Levant wouldn't hide the prophecy in a place already hidden
from Nidus. He'd keep it close." Reyna pointed. "If it's anywhere, it's
his palace."

"What about them?" Anemone nodded toward an inky mist of
Dredgers bellowing at the mountain's base.

"Lethe said they wouldn't see us. We could swim over them."

Anemone snorted. "I'd no sooner trust that miscreant than the
god himself."

The dark space behind Reyna's heart vibrated. She glowered at
the back of Anemone's current-swept coils. How dare she speak ill
of what she didn't understand. Lev was all-consuming. Unorthodox,
for sure. But the most incredible creature she'd ever—

"We may possess the flame's invisibility." Anemone snatched
Reyna's consciousness. "Though the gatekeeper said nothing about
being heard or smelled."

The dark fog around Reyna's heart lifted and she blinked.
What. The. Hell. Was that?

Reyna's slow ebb of Levant's defense retreated from her system.

Residual shame flooded its wake. Reyna pressed a hand against her heart.

"Lady?" Anemone studied her strained features. "Are you—"

"Can Dredgers hear or smell?" Reyna shifted the focus from herself.

"I don't intend to find out." Anemone pointed at a far range. "A hidden pass exists between those two peaks. The terrain is a bit treacherous but perhaps easier whilst swimming, rather than through snow on foot. It also shouldn't pose much of a draw for Dredgers."

"How do you know so much about Parhelia's landscape?" Reyna asked while they propelled toward the range.

"I was once pursued by Lady Capricorn's factotum. He had a rather large"—Anemone's decorum stumbled—"affinity for the mountains."

Reyna flashed her first true smile in days. "I need to hear that story later."

"Stay close." Anemone's grin betrayed her. "And quiet, for good measure."

They drifted through the range's hazy wood like wandering spirits. Shadows recoiled from their lantern light and bony branches scraped at their clothes, but Anemone's assumption held true. No Dredger or any other creature lurked beyond an occasional stony corpse. The gnarled forest withered as they swam along a final stretch of jagged mountain. When they reached the peak, Reyna frowned over the tattered underworld below. Gone were the rainbowed seasons once splattering the island's curves. Rivers ran black with Dredgers and pale sediment caked its regions. A wasteland painted in the sinister palette of nothing.

Other Omphalos's grounds swayed with lush kelp, as though it stole every nutrient from the land below. The Forgotten was a lie, most alive in places promising certain death. Reyna's neck craned at the twin palace. Its rich outer walls shimmered like black scales under an illusion of light and stood taller than she remembered Omphalos. A luxury, less reliable by the minute. How long before her memories vanished? Which would go first? Would she know what she'd lost?

"There's our way in." Reyna eyed an iron door.

Anemone squirmed beside her. "Doesn't this all seem too easy?"

Reyna couldn't help but snicker. "We have different definitions of easy."

"Omphalos is always patrolled by obsidian soldiers." Anemone winced at a collection of statues dressed in barnacles and algae. "Don't you find it odd an entrance is unguarded?"

Reyna swam forward and heaved her weight against the door's latch. Orange corrosion ground beneath her gloves. "How many people do you think *try* to break into the underworld palace?"

"I suppose you're right." Anemone surveyed the grounds a second longer and joined her charge. With their combined strength, the latch flung up and an undertow sucked them through the opened door. They rode along an arc of water and splatted onto ebony marble. Rusted iron whined as the door slammed shut. Reyna coughed the dead sea from her lungs and moaned at air refilling her lungs. Oxygen shouldn't burn. This place really was cruel.

Anemone gurgled water onto the floor.

Reyna dragged a soaked sleeve across her mouth. "You okay?"

The factotum groaned with a nod and Reyna helped her stand.

Dark bookshelves covered the walls and sheet-draped furniture sat silhouetted amongst shadows. Reyna and Anemone hobbled toward a sliver of light leaking beneath a door. They cracked it open. Ominous green fire from metal fixtures illuminated two black stone corridors.

"Let's split up." Reyna hated the suggestion. "This place is huge, and we don't know how long until we'll forget why we're here."

"That's a terrible idea," Anemone grumbled. "But you're right."

Reyna blinked, certain her factotum forgot to argue.

"Seph disappeared in the cavern but might still be here, so be on the lookout," Reyna warned. "I'll go right. You go left."

"Once we're done searching these rooms, we'll meet back and move onto the next area." Anemone wrapped Reyna's fingers around the lantern's handle. "You'll take the Eternal Flame."

Argument tinged Reyna's tongue, but the time for petitioning each other's safety was over. She nodded and they crept along their respective corridors.

If Neoma's palace was a temple to light, *Other Omphalos* was an homage to self. Unapologetic. Refined. A coveted black pearl buried beneath the muck. But for all its dark luxuries, each room Reyna explored revealed more of the same.

Nothing.

Defeat descended over her as she shut a final door and retreated the way she had come.

"Reyna …" A feminine voice locked Reyna's limbs in place.

"Hello?" Reyna glanced over her shoulder. Silence laughed in her face. "Seph?"

"Reyna." Elongated tenderness sailed through her name once more.

The voice couldn't belong to Seph. She'd never leave anything to the imagination nor miss a chance gloating at Reyna's stupidity.

"Reyna." The airy voice sailed into an end stairwell.

Reyna's attention pivoted between the stairwell and room they'd entered through.

"Come on, Anemone." Reyna's heel bounced, willing her factotum to round the corner.

Seconds ticked.

"Reyna." The voice faded, rising higher into the stairwell.

The prophecy wouldn't be in any random room and, without knowing the palace's blueprint, they relied solely on dumb luck. Reyna doubted they had time to search every room. Anemone's soul might be safe but not her memories. Pieces of herself Reyna now understood the value of more than ever. The voice promised a trap, but traps required bait, and bait meant value might wait at the end of its snare. Trap or not, someone called Reyna by her mortal name.

She was already caught.

"I'm sorry, Anemone," Reyna whispered and spiraled up the staircase. She dripped water from her fingertips, hoping Anemone would find her watery path. The voice beckoned Reyna through a maze of hallways and connected rooms until a large archway opened into a chamber with vaulted ceilings. Reyna strode along a strip of midnight carpet across the room. She eyed marbled corpses standing sentinel at the space's perimeters, half expecting them to reanimate like in Ambrose's nightmare.

Her toes met a triple wide staircase and Reyna sucked in a breath. Two massive silver doors loomed at their peak, and without explanation, Reyna knew she would not hear her ghostly guide again. She'd reach the end of her breadcrumbs.

Reyna climbed the stairs and pushed a shoulder against the cold, heavy doors. Bright emerald flames ignited along chandeliers inside. She waited for prison bars of her stupid choices to slam down around her, but as with every other area she wove through undetected, nothing happened. Reyna's stomach churned at the impossibility of it all. Even moving about this room alone, Reyna remained captive to a force she didn't yet understand. Anemone was right. It'd been too easy.

Hands balled at Reyna's sides.

Easy or not, her efforts wouldn't be in vain. She'd continue until whatever Fate toiled with her thread decided it was time to cut. Reyna set her lantern on a black grand piano and got to work.

She tossed aside cushions. Ripped tapestries from walls. Plucked spines from bookshelves. The room slowly caved in on itself as she unraveled its contents. Reyna riffled through documents in baskets and desk drawers. Pulled up rugs. Overturned furniture. Ran fingers over every reachable inch of stone, but like the underworld, the room was the beginning and end of nothing.

Hopelessness bled at the edges of her resolve.

She tore through items already strewn about the floor, drowning in her own idiocy of what couldn't be found. Slowly and all too quickly, she floated farther adrift from each thud of the organ beneath her sternum. A mechanical crutch she needed less and less. Reyna was a pitiful excuse for a mortal. Never fit to be a Zodiac. Stupid. How could she be so fucking stupid?

Her soul would soon be gone, and she had nothing to show for it.

Reyna collapsed onto the piano bench and buried her face against her crossed arms. Chaotic keys mangled under their weight. She let the sobs come. Invited the terror of her mistakes to seize hold. Lethe said she could leave the Forgotten, but Reyna couldn't shake that by abandoning her soul, she'd somehow invited another curse into her life.

Would she feel different without a soul? Would it hurt?

Could she live on Earth without one? Why didn't she ask more questions? Maybe if Reyna stayed away long enough from the gate, she wouldn't know the difference when the time came. Would her memories be easier to part with if the Forgotten claimed them? Acceptance in ignorance.

No. She couldn't succumb. Not while Anemone still had a future. A wife. Reyna wouldn't let another friend suffer for her sins. She wiped tears from her cheeks and welcomed the momentary silence. Green firelight warped along the piano's ivory keys beside her. It'd been so long since she invited the thrill of an instrument beneath her hands. She tapped a key, and its soft *ding* echoed against her memory.

¿Quieres aprender a tocar el piano, nieta? her abuela had asked.

Reyna wanted to learn to play. To fill her life with notes other than fear and regret. But once she'd imagined her grandmother's hips beside hers. Abuela's weathered fingers guiding Reyna's own? She knew it could never be. Instead, Reyna sat atop the stairs and played notes along the breeze as Abuela invited students into their home for lessons. Reyna memorized each chime struck. The ones strung together. Each misstep and recovery. When her grandmother left for Sunday prayer, and no longer made her go, Reyna performed her own sermon. Keys became the fingers she'd never hold. Their thrums, a new heartbeat within her world. She smothered the noise of people's feelings until only hers flowed. And for the first time in Reyna's young life, her touch hadn't absorbed. It breathed anew.

A key cringed beneath her fingers. She concentrated harder through the notes warping in her mind, like looking through stained glass. Was she forgetting already? Reyna's soul may be promised to the gatekeeper, but she couldn't lose this. Not the memory igniting her love for melody. Reyna squinted at the sheet music and her foot pumped the pedal. Chords crescendoed from under her fingers in waves. Swam deeper into memory. Rhythm expanded her lungs. Passion burned through her shoulders.

Cancer's presence descended upon Reyna like a spirit possessing her body.

The two kept time with one another. More than muscle memory. It was who they'd been. Who they were. The gloomy decadence they played now, a magic never undone.

Moonlight Sonata.

Reyna ripped her hands from the keyboard as though its ivory keys sharpened into teeth. She stared at inked lyrics scribbled beneath the sheet's music bars.

Moonlight Sonata didn't have words.

She snatched the papers and read their words aloud, "Celestials shall awaken, upon his return. For a deviant of black glass, love too must be earned. One emerges like the other, when noon becomes night. Toll of the once mortal lover. Darkness consumes light. From twelve the Dark Star will arise. And two shall remain. No longer lost amongst the skies. Together they will reign."

For a moment, Reyna's heart belonged to her again.

She'd found the prophecy.

"Reyna …" a familiar breathy whisper called once more.

Reyna stared in its direction at the only decor not disturbed from her frantic rampage. Closed green velvet drapes hung across the room over what she'd thought a window.

"Reyna!" the voice snapped with soft urgency.

She leapt from the bench and yanked back the floor-to-ceiling fabric. Ethereal shadows lusted over a four-poster bed poised in darkness. Larger than any king-size. A bed built for many, but the dominant wicked glamor of one. Reyna's heartbeat staggered. The gatekeeper's noose tightened.

His room.

Reyna stood in Levant's bedroom.

She needed to find Anemone and leave. Now.

"Reyna …" the voice beckoned from an armoire adjacent to his bed. A delicate glow pulsed from between its doors. Reyna scowled, done being played with. She stomped over and threw open the armoire.

"Who are you?" she demanded.

Rainbows doused the room. Hues from another life Reyna was sure she'd already forgotten. Soul crystals in various sizes and colors adorned individual cubbies, each with its own internal light like a flame trapped behind glass. If this room belonged to Levant, these crystals must be important. Prized tokens he kept close.

Reyna.

The voice called but also didn't. A ghost shedding its corporeal form within her mind. Reyna's eyes widened at a yellow crystal. An indescribable swell of home strummed through her. Their name, breathy and sweet.

"Tessa?"

The world muffled around Reyna as if submerged underwater once more. She pressed the crystal to her chest, as though she might feel Tessa's heart against the final beats of her own. "I'm so sorry. You didn't deserve this." Reyna squeezed harder, crystallized edges biting into her palm. "I won't leave you behind again."

"Then why did you?" A hand whirled Reyna's shoulder. Anemone frowned. "We agreed to do this together."

Reyna's mouth tumbled open, but no words came.

Anemone's gaze drifted to the sheet music in Reyna's other hand and lit up. "Is that it? Did you find the prophecy?"

All Reyna could do was nod.

"Thank the stars! We must leave immediately." Anemone traipsed toward the piano and grabbed the lantern. "I've started forgetting."

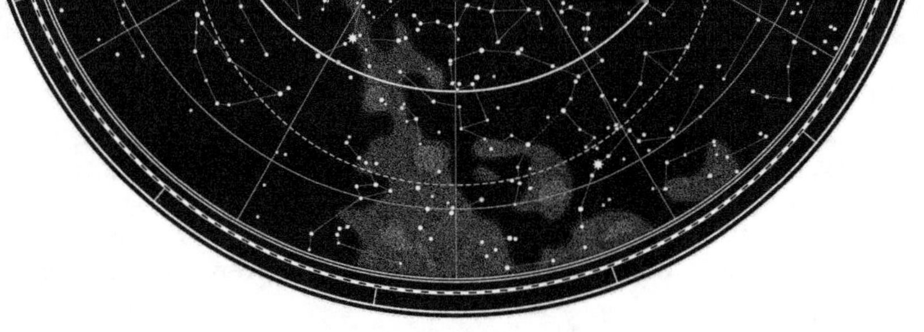

CHAPTER

THIRTY-EIGHT

REYNA AND ANEMONE FLOATED AT THE FORGOTTEN'S highest peak with the black palace looming at their backs.

"Which way do we go?" Reyna scoured the island's rotten underbelly.

"I-I don't know." Anemone rubbed her temple. "I don't remember."

Reyna grabbed the lantern and stalked toward the cliff's edge.

"My lady, the flame cannot help us find the exit."

"We're not looking for it." Reyna thrust the lantern high. "Show us the way to my necklace!" Silver light launched from the lantern in a comet path through the watery skies. "We need to swim straight across before you forget more."

A cloudy haze sheened over Anemone's eyes. "Where are we going?"

Reyna recognized that look from her abuela's final years. The slow thievery of a person's mind long before their body caught up. Reyna placed a gentle hand on Anemone's shoulder.

"Home." The word resonated through Reyna's bones. She gingerly tucked the folded sheet music into her pocket, praying its paper would hold up longer than the map. With a shared grasp of the lantern, they pushed off and propelled over Parhelia's stark expanse.

The mountain range tapered into a valley, giving way to rooftops amongst blackened streets and shops. Barren pine trees along Parhelia's coastline came into view.

"I see the exit!" Reyna smiled at two stony walls beyond the faux shore. "Everything's going to be—"

An object swooshed past. Its downward current jostled them to a stop.

Another rush tore by. Then another and another.

Semitransparent figures sank toward the sea's bottom like fistfuls of rocks.

The pair tore faster through the deep-sea hailstorm. Their mismatched movements, a battle between each other and the lantern. Reyna dodged when Anemone ducked but never tore her sight from the exit. Anemone had to cross over before she lost more of herself. They could make it. She had to.

A spirit barreled into the Eternal Flame.

Reyna's and Anemone's holds broke apart. Prophecy pages knocked from Reyna's pocket.

"No!" she screamed.

Another specter collided into Anemone and grabbed hold. He dragged her with whatever force summoned it toward the bottom.

"Anemone!" Reyna dive-bombed through the meteor shower of death.

The factotum vanished into a pale upturned sandstorm and Reyna plunged after them. Reyna slowed her descent as building silhouettes rose alongside her. Sobs and shrieks called out to whomever would listen amongst the invisible streets.

A man wobbled through the dirty haze gaping at his limpid hands. His expression met Reyna's.

"Where am I?" he asked.

Teeth clacked softly somewhere unseen. Reyna pressed a finger to her lips, but the gaunt spirit floated toward her.

"Please!" His bony fingers reached for Reyna, skin unraveling like ribbons. "What's happening?"

"Quiet!" Reyna snapped through a whisper.

His lips twisted into a snarl. "Did you do this to me?"

The spirit lunged.

A Dredger tackled him from the side. The man's screams lamented through the churning sand. An impossible soundtrack of cracks and snaps ruptured from the invisible scene. Reyna darted in the opposite direction while black masses swept through the cloudy sediment like hawks snatching their next meal.

"Stop!" someone screeched. "Get off!"

Reyna's attention snapped in every direction. "Anemone?"

"No!" she screamed again.

With every ounce of otherworldly magic she could muster, Reyna slammed both hands toward the ground. Sand detonated and rippled outward from where Reyna floated. A diameter of clear water surrounded them.

"Give it to me!" A woman's spirit clawed at Anemone's face.

"I don't have anything!" The factotum sobbed. "Leave me—"

"The light!" The woman's finger hooked behind Anemone's lip and pulled. "I can see it! Give it to me! I don't belong here!"

Reyna torpedoed icy daggers into the leech's back. The soul flew off. Their screams mangled into gurgles while another Dredger descended on them.

Reyna darted to her friend's side. "Are you okay?"

"I don't—" Anemone eyelids fluttered. "Where's the lantern?"

"Gone." Reyna swung Anemone's arm around her neck. "Like we need to be." Reyna blasted them upward from the misty sand creeping back. Bites and slurps of the Dredgers' freshly slain buffet fell behind them as the gate came into view. A horned, raven-haired angel swathed in diamond scales waited just outside its stony gates. Prisha slapped her hands over her mouth at Anemone's limp form draped in the crook of Reyna's arm.

"Reyna!" Prisha trembled. "Is she ..."

The factotum's head lolled in and out of consciousness atop Reyna's shoulder.

"Alive," Reyna assured.

"My, my, Lady Cancer." Lethe beamed. "I haven't seen this much excitement in over a century."

Reyna's brow creased. "What happened back there?"

"Our daily crop of condemned souls." Lethe scraped a tongue over their pointed teeth. "Earth's most depraved harvest has been most bountiful this year."

Reyna readjusted her grip on Anemone. "She needs to cross over. *Now.*"

Lethe reached for Anemone. Reyna jerked away but buckled under the weight of her friend. The gatekeeper's bony fingers stroked Anemone's hair.

"Nidian souls wither faster in the Forgotten." Something akin to longing swirled in Lethe's milky stare. "So delicate, pure, and unmarred by your cruel mortal world. If you're merciful, you'd leave her to me. She'd suffer a far less gruesome fate."

Reyna pushed past the gatekeeper. "A deal is a deal."

"Quite right." Lethe's clammy fingers snatched Reyna's arm and tugged. "Neither crosses over until you give your soul for hers."

"Take it." Reyna pulled herself free and delicately placed Anemone on the sand. "No more games."

"So eager?" Lethe's alabaster eyes lit. "I shan't leave you waiting."

Reyna knew the price.

Told herself it worth paying.

But in this moment, she wanted to run. Scream. Claw. Gouge. Slice Lethe's throat to keep what was hers. Reyna doubted the centuries-old gatekeeper would meet such an unruly end and she needed to see this through, for Anemone.

Lethe drifted closer. Their angler fish light sprouted from its platinum hair.

A tiny sob was wrenched from behind Reyna's chattering teeth. She hated that she cried. Hoped to be stronger in the face of what she believed was the right choice. Reyna wasn't prepared. Never could be. She longed to feel the tears along her cheek. A final reminder she was still human. That's what the Forgotten was made of. The last drops of someone's soul before it left their body.

"Shh." Lethe's lure dangled between their shared sight lines and its light blazed brighter. "Keep your eye on us."

"Us?" The word hissed along Reyna's tongue. Her head bobbed, mesmerized by the glow. A vast, empty sea surrounded them. The Forgotten, Anemone, and Prisha all sank from awareness. The light glimmered green like a jewel sinking into the sea and split into a pair of emerald eyes.

"No." Reyna's rejection was breathy, sedated by whatever spell Lethe imprisoned her with. "You're not here."

"I'm everywhere the light is not," Levant replied. "The darkness can never be contained for long. Wouldn't you agree, *mi luna*?"

"Don't call me that." Reyna tried shoving him, but her hands instead stroked his chest. Her body, a betrayal unto itself. "Please, don't take my soul. I'll do anything."

A low, sultry laugh caressed Levant's smile. "Even in mortal form, you're a treasure to be unlocked." Silky lips grazed Reyna's. "I molded you perfectly. Almost as if I'd made you for myself. My undeniable match in every way."

Need curled in Reyna's toes. Constricted the clothes clinging against her skin. She was paralyzed but dancing. Loathing and wanting.

These weren't her feelings.

"Stop," Reyna whimpered as Cancer's will embraced her. "Please. I don't want this." Reyna's hand lifted of its own accord and smoothed knuckles along the god's dark stubble. He exhaled a soft groan. No mischief tugged his perfect cheekbones. No challenge blazed behind his gaze. Only the certainty of a devil who'd already claimed his prize.

Ancient energy buzzed beneath Reyna's skin. It drifted along her sternum. Stroked the inside walls of her throat. Cancer's light melted over Reyna's tongue like warm bread. Familiar and comforting. Someplace far but closer to home than she'd ever dreamed possible.

"Why can't I stop loving you?" Cancer's words poured through Reyna's voice.

The god's fingers threaded her hair and gently tugged. Ferocity dilated bright in his eyes. "Because you're mine."

His lips filled the parting ache between hers. Reyna's repulsion rumbled like distant storm clouds rolling across the sea. Far enough away but fast approaching. Cancer wanted to hate him too. The deeds he'd done. What he aimed to do now. Being with Lev had never been easy, and yet, it always was. No guilt. No worries. Delights, Reyna knew little of. Pure selfish wanting. It curled in Cancer's toes and bled through her veins. With him, they became the wickedness she and Reyna knew they shouldn't want. All the things they tried not to be.

Levant's mouth drew back. "I knew the first time I tasted your light. It's always been you. You are my salvation." He brushed a thumb over Cancer's bottom lip. "My Dark Star."

"I can't control all elemental magics."

"You didn't believe you'd be human either." Amusement hummed across his smile. "Do you remember what I told you on the last night we were together?"

Cancer nodded, the sting of his departure ripping a fresh wound across her chest.

"Anything is possible," she echoed.

"Have faith in me, *mi luna*." Levant's icy hands cupped her cheeks. "In us."

The Dark God thrust his lips upon hers.

Gone was the passion. The tender wanting. Sheer, undiluted need ravaged her tongue. He breathed her in. Drank deep. Sucked. Swallowed. Devoured every inch of her existence. Cancer fell limp in his arms and Reyna screamed somewhere in the muffled distance. White light blazed between them. Brighter and brighter. An explosion of breathless, searing fire.

Lethe's bobbing lure flickered out.

A satisfied smile carved into the gatekeeper's bony cheeks. "It is done."

Prisha clutched the stony gate, horror etched between her eyes.

Reyna ran her hands over her face and torso. Her anatomy all in place, the unseen parts, less comforting. Anemone still lay lifeless in the sand.

"The changes will come slowly." Lethe smiled. "Now you're immortal again, your magic will be amplified. Your Zodiac and human halves, blended. All your memories, hopes, ideas, and desires shall be shared. You'll exist as one."

Reyna's mouth went impossibly dry. "Can we go?"

Lethe dipped into a low bow and drifted aside. "The debt has been paid."

Reyna scooped Anemone into her arms and swam over the threshold.

The prophecy's cost weighed heavy on Reyna's chest, even though it lay scattered at the sea's bottom. A premonition she didn't need to hold to know.

I am the Dark Star.

Reyna hoped the suspicion of herself was nothing more than her typical paranoia. A lifetime readying her for ultimate damnation. But Cancer's essence lingered in the shallows of Reyna's consciousness. The Zodiac's fingertips, inches away from breaching the surface of all Reyna clung to. Reyna had always been a warrior against other people's wills, and despite whatever new battle would soon rage within her own, Reyna would win.

"Reyna …" Prisha choked on a sob.

Watery emptiness occupied Reyna's arms.

She swiveled to Anemone floating beside Lethe on the gate's other side, nodding in and out of consciousness.

"Well." Lethe scraped a pointed tongue across their teeth. "This is a delicious development."

Reyna darted toward them.

"No!" Prisha snatched her wrist. "You've nothing to bargain with! You won't be able to cross back over."

"What are you doing?" Reyna roared at the gatekeeper.

Lethe lifted their chin. "Collecting a debt."

"I've already paid! Let her go!"

"You have paid." Lethe nodded. "And so must she."

"You said a soul for a soul!" Rage seethed from Reyna's gnashed teeth.

"And a soul"—Lethe's gaze flicked to Reyna's pocket—"you possess."

Fury extinguished from Reyna's inferno. Her dread-frosted fingers slipped into her pocket and withdrew Tessa's soul crystal.

"You knew." Reyna fisted the crystal. "You tricked me."

Lethe tutted. "A peculiar thief you are, accusing me of such atrocities."

"What are they talking about?" Prisha asked.

"This is the soul of my friend from San Diego." Shame and despicable relief twisted through Reyna at the crystal in her opened palm. "It's my fault she died. I thought maybe I could bring her back."

"No." Disbelief rattled through Prisha.

Reyna knew what she needed to do. She'd return for Tessa's soul someday, but Anemone was still here. Flesh and bone and whatever else a soul was made of. Reyna extended the crystal toward Lethe. "Take it back. Just please, let her go."

Lethe cocked their head. "Why would I want a rock when I have such a savory morsel?"

"Take me, then!" Reyna swallowed hard. "Release Anemone and I'll stay."

Lethe pouted. "A most tempting offer, lady, but *he'd* never allow it."

Foreboding pooled in Reyna's belly like rivers flowing into the Forgotten. Heavy. Thick. Mucked with despair. Even from his obsidian prison, Levant's will would be done. Lethe didn't follow underworld law. They honored the whims of their master.

Brax's past warning seeped through Reyna's mind like slowly spreading poison.

I've seen people accomplish a lot from behind bars.

Levant orchestrated this. Wanted Reyna here.

The gatekeeper's thumb and forefinger clutched Anemone's chin as their angler light descended between them.

"No!" Reyna lunged.

Prisha's arms straitjacketed around Reyna's torso as Lethe's jagged mouth unhinged from their jaw, baring a second row of needle-sharp teeth. The gatekeeper pressed their mouth against Anemone's face like a snake devouring prey. Reyna screamed. Wrenched in Prisha's firm hold. Color slowly faded from Anemone's body and the Forgotten's pale landscape peeked through her translucent form.

"Anemone!" Reyna's teeth chattered through sobs.

Anemone's stripped soul floated toward stone figures ornamenting the entrance's wall. She nestled into the heap of bodies, resting her head along an outstretched arm. Her spirit closed its eyes and solidified into stone.

Nothing more than mere decoration.

Another omen for those foolish enough to believe in hope.

The Forgotten's rot gurgled from Reyna's mouth onto the cavern floor. She wobbled on all fours, staring at her reflection in watery vomit. Be it Cancer's, or Reyna's reflection, soon it wouldn't matter. Their lives would bleed into each other's. How much of Reyna would be left? Enough to stop Levant? Would she still want to?

Her fist slammed against rock, and water slapped across her face.

She wished Cancer had consumed her entire being. At least she could say it was Cancer who had gambled Anemone's soul. Who'd betrayed promises of home. Reyna's failures were a skipping record, forever scratching at the edge of good.

Prisha's reflection stood behind her, arms hugging her chest tight.

"We have to go back," Reyna murmured.

"What?" Ice grated Prisha's voice.

"I can fix this. I've extracted souls from Dredgers. Maybe I can absorb them from statues too. I could—"

"She's gone!" Prisha's voice boomed off the cavern walls. The echo settled into a tether ready to snap.

"I didn't mean to." Reyna stepped toward her. "It was an accident. I didn't think—"

"That's right, you didn't!" Prisha stepped away. "You were too busy giving away your soul every chance you got."

"What?" Disbelief roiled through Reyna. "Are you saying I shouldn't have tried saving them both?"

"You don't value your life, and it blinds you! You were so focused on saving one friend, you sacrificed another without considering what it might cost."

"I couldn't leave her behind!"

"Did you even consider how your friend's crystal wound up in the Forgotten?" Prisha stomped toward Reyna, fists clenched at her sides. "She died *before* the Dark God was captured, which means someone brought her crystal here. But you knew that, didn't you?"

"What'd you—"

"Stop lying, Reyna!" Prisha ran fingers through her hair as though she slipped deeper into madness. "I saw you kissing the Dark God! What the fuck is happening?"

"You saw him?" Reyna's stomach bottomed out. "I thought he was a vision created by Lethe. He couldn't've been real."

"He was right in front you." Prisha jabbed her finger toward Reyna. "The both of you, talking like long-lost lovers."

Reyna leaned against a rocky wall, bones liquifying into slush.

"It wasn't me." Reyna swallowed, but nothing slid down. "It was Cancer."

"But you knew?" Prisha's arms fell lank at her sides. The dawn of Reyna's truths rose on her lips. "You knew Cancer and him were together. Didn't you?"

Reyna hung her head and nodded.

"Did you also know you're the Dark Star?" Prisha glared at her.

"No!" Reyna rushed forward. "I only suspected because my extraction magic is so similar to Levant's."

"How can I trust anything you say when you've lied this the entire time? We could've helped you." Prisha pointed at herself. "I did! Anemone too!"

"You can't understand what I've been through." Reyna gritted her teeth.

"You can only use that excuse so many times," Prisha bit. "Eventually you have to let someone help."

"Anemone tried helping me and she's dead!" Tears burst from Reyna like an exorcised demon. "That's what happens to people who help me!" Reyna's shaking form crumpled to the floor.

Prisha crouched beside her.

"Anemone loved Nidus and believed in the good you could bring. Don't let her sacrifices be for nothing." Prisha grabbed Reyna's hands, the frost in her voice thawing. "We'll tell the others what happened, and figure this out together."

"I can't." Reyna stared at Prisha. "Once they find out what I am? What I've done? They'll never look at me the same."

"It's never too late to do the right thing. They'll forgive you, in time."

"Not this." Reyna shook her head. "Levant said it himself, not even Neoma can stop what's coming."

"Maybe so, but Neoma also said the Dark Star is who'll choose favor over either light or darkness. Not her. Not Levant. Not the other Zodiacs." Prisha squeezed Reyna's hands. "Prophecies are predictions. Not fate. If you're the Dark Star, the only person who decides what happens next is you."

PART FOUR

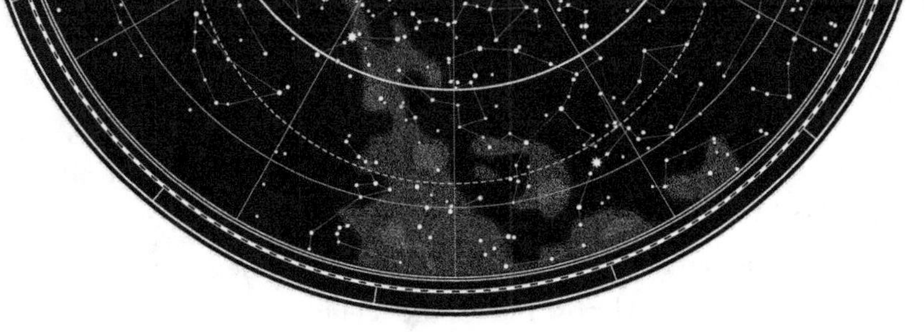

THIRTY-NINE

REYNA WAITED FOR HER STOMACH TO GROWL. A CRAVING. Some physical indication or need to fill the hollow place her soul might've once thrived. None came. She couldn't remember when she'd last eaten. One, maybe two days ago?

"Lady Regent, are you listening?" Anemone echoed in Reyna's memory. "This endeavor will change life in Calidi for so many. What do you think?"

"Hmm?" Reyna had peered up from her fruit bowl.

Two days.

It'd been two days since Reyna had eaten and one after Anemone would never eat again.

"The housing expansion into Calidi's jungle?" Anemone set down her fork. "With the rise of new souls, it's been long overdue."

"What about Nidians living *in* the jungle?" Reyna feigned casualness, rolling sliced mango around her bowl.

Anemone laughed. "No one would be dim-witted enough to risk the goddess's hand. They'd have to live like animals amongst the caves and trees. Please pass the bread."

Reyna rose from her chair and bent across the table.

Long icy fingers slid along her forearm from behind and curled over her hand. Cancer placed the dish onto the table, nestling into Lev's firm body at her backside. His hand retreated along her arm and tilted her neck sideways.

Reyna's and Cancer's two memories flickered between Calidi's dining hall and the tree house like a lightbulb possessed by a spirit.

"You cooked for me?" Lev's bass had thrummed over Cancer's skin. "So domestic. Almost makes me feel like a man." He nipped the fragile flesh of Cancer's neck. "Why do you mock me with such mortal concepts?"

"We immortals may not require sustenance." Cancer sighed at his breath's chilly reprieve. "But I love giving you experiences you've never had and there aren't many."

Anemone frowned at Reyna from across the table. "Have you and Lord Leo spoken yet?"

"No," Reyna replied.

"I loathe humanity." Lev blew on the skin he'd assaulted. "And yet you make me ache for it more every day." The god spun and hoisted Cancer onto the table. He gently pushed her chest until her spine met wood. "There's but one nectar I crave above all others."

Anemone's brow furrowed. "I know you and Lord Regent have your share of disagreements but always work through them. I've seen how you look at each another. You should go to him."

"I don't know, Anemone." Reyna's head lolled back and forth, hair fanning over the table she lay on. "This time feels … different."

Levant slithered over Reyna's hips and dishes clattered onto the floor in his wake. Anemone spread jam on a bread slice. The flats of Lev's hands pressed on either side of Reyna's head. He eyed her mouth.

"My Dark God?" Reyna teased. "Are you waiting for permission?"

"To hear your want hissing across this tongue each time you give yourself to me?" Levant's thumb dragged over her bottom lip. "Nothing pleases me more."

"Yes," Reyna elongated her submission.

Levant's mouth descended onto Reyna's.

Anemone sighed.

The palace dining hall and tree house warred for space in Reyna's mind as Cancer's desire frenzied into Reyna's own. She grabbed Lev's hair. Tasted what Cancer had. The air of a storm rolling in from sea. Lev's essence clawed through ice. Begged to be freed. His monster wanted her. She wanted them more. White-hot starlight sizzled through her veins. A race of wills for who would devour the other's power first. Reyna wanted everything until she was nothing.

"No!" Reyna ripped at her scalp.

She blinked back to the bench where she'd been sitting.

Reyna glanced around the Calidi palace gardens. Alone. Safe.

She swiped sweat from her brow.

Not safe. Never safe.

Is this what Lethe meant when they said Reyna and Cancer would become one? Memories and emotion bleeding into one another until it was impossible to tell whose belonged to whom? Reyna wanted to scrub Cancer's feelings for Levant from the walls of her skull. Douse them with bleach and set them aflame.

Manic laughter sputtered from her. After a lifetime bound to others' emotions, Reyna finally got what she wished for. To feel nobody's except her own. It didn't matter they were from another lifetime or who'd lived them. They were Cancer's and Reyna's. They'd bared teeth. Plunged into Reyna's heart. Merciless. Demanding. Hungry for what was stolen long ago.

Reyna promised Prisha she'd confess to Neoma and the Zodiacs but pleaded for one day to steel herself. Prisha argued but eventually caved. Twenty-four hours so Reyna might mull over the right words to say. Only there were none. Nothing could make what happened okay.

If last night had destroyed Reyna, tomorrow would bury her.

Sandals shuffled softly across stone.

Reyna's head whipped toward a flash of cerulean silk behind the tropical greenery. She followed the blue fabric swishing around another bend along the stone path. An insane place deep in her gullet longed to call out Anemone's name. What Reyna wouldn't give to say she was sorry. Beg for forgiveness she knew herself unworthy of. If even to a ghost.

A man's throaty moan unfurled through the garden.

Reyna ducked behind large heart-shaped leaves, squinting through their foliage. Her lips parted and the Forgotten stole her soul once more. Seph grinded on Brax pressed against a stone wall. Their fervent kisses battled for dominance. Jace's fingertips bit into the slinky red fabric hugging Seph's ass while his mouth lavished Brax's neck.

Reyna's chest couldn't rise. Refused.

Air. There was no air.

"Incredible how in any form, we're all such simple creatures." Cancer stood riveted on the scene with her exposed back to Reyna.

Reyna stumbled backward. The Zodiac's shiny chestnut hair was wrapped into a flawless regal bun atop her head and cerulean silk poured over her shoulders, gathering at the base of her spine into a cape.

"This can't be real." Reyna gaped. "You're not."

Cancer peered at Reyna over her shoulder with a soft but terrifyingly familiar smile. "Are we nothing if not our past and present?"

"What makes us simple creatures?" Reyna took the bait.

"Immortal or otherwise, we're all driven by the same unquenchable need." Cancer cocked her head at the threesome lost in lust's thrall. "The most basic need to be seen. Held. Heard. Wanted. A desire to exist in the world and know it would be a far lonelier place without us in it."

Reyna's voice pouring from Cancer unraveled her. The words weren't Reyna's, but damn if they didn't speak her truths.

"You'll never be with Levant," Reyna ground out low. "I won't let you."

"Choices have already set our future in motion," Cancer replied. "Love shall prevail and in time, you'll understand. Only then will we be whole."

"Get out of my head!" Reyna spun on her heel and traipsed the way she came. "Leave me alone!"

A hand caught her arm and Reyna whirled.

An icy blade daggered from her palm as she arced it through the air. Brax caught her wrist. Reyna's dagger trembled at the spot Scorpio had been kissing. Brax spun Reyna and pushed her hand against her tailbone. The frosted blade twisted from her grip.

"What the hell are you doing?" Brax grumbled around a half-smoked cigarette.

Reyna willed water from her fingertips, wriggling to slip free from his grasp but Brax's heat evaporated her water into steam. He spat the cigarette to the ground.

"Let go!" Reyna twisted against his chest.

Brax grunted into her hair. "Not until you explain why you're tryin' to gimme a permanent shave."

"You!" Reyna's teeth gritted. "You, Seph, and—"

Brax released her with a gentle push and Reyna faced him.

"Easy." Brax raised his hands as though she were a feral animal. "This is about Seph?"

"What were you doing?" Reyna demanded.

"I smoke here sometimes."

"Where are they?"

Brax blinked. "Who?"

Reyna scoured the tropical oasis for Brax's lovers. She glared at the blond hair resting atop his shoulders not tied in a messy knot, like it had been moments ago while Jace's tongue stroked his throat. Cigarette butts littered the ground behind him. Cigarettes. Brax was smoking when he grabbed her but wasn't before.

Reyna staggered away as Cancer stepped beside Brax.

"Another memory of yours?" Reyna asked her.

Cancer nodded.

Brax inspected the vacant space beside him. "What's goin' on?"

"You can't see?" Reyna threaded her fingers through her hair. Tears pricked the corner of her eyes. Was this what going crazy felt like? Delusion for thinking she could do this alone. Mad for made deals she didn't fully comprehend. Sacrifices she couldn't bear.

Memories and feelings weren't supposed to be like this.

She wasn't supposed to be like this.

Reyna stared at Brax a long moment, praying he wouldn't morph back into whenever he'd been. Despite everything, she wanted to collapse into his embrace. Let him anchor her to a timeline she controlled. Reyna blinked back tears, determined to regain her own mental footing.

"Sunshine?" Brax repeated softly. "Talk to me."

Humorless laugher spouted from her. "Already tried that."

"Seph tried restarting what we had," Brax talked fast. "I told her to fuck off and she threatened you."

"Why let me believe the worst? Why not tell me?"

"I know it doesn't make sense." Brax advanced until he stood a few inches from her. "But I was trying to protect you."

"And before that?" she asked. "Were you protecting me by shutting me out?"

Brax nodded and Reyna's brows drew together as his thumb caressed her cheekbone. Reyna wanted to smack it away. Prove she didn't need him or his flowery excuses. Brax abandoned her. Hurt her. Lied. All to protect her. Was Reyna so different? The mistakes she'd made. Lives she'd destroyed. All in her pursuit of protecting others. She was no better, but it still didn't make him right.

"I don't need your protection," she murmured.

"I know." Melancholy lifted his lips. "But I operate on instinct, and I couldn't lose you again. Not when you finally—when we ..."

"Again?"

Humility glazed his eyes. "I don't know where to start."

"Reyna!" Someone jogged through the garden. "Brax!"

Their heads cut to Ethan.

"She did it." Hope glittered in Ethan's face. "Seph found the prophecy."

CHAPTER

FORTY

W HAT DID REYNA HOPE FOR BY PUTTING OFF THE inevitable? A chance to mourn yet another friend? Understand the changes within her own newly acquired immortality? Perhaps prolong the illusion that she was not some soulless villain? Reyna wasn't ready to face her friends but followed Ethan, Cancer's ghost, and Brax into the gallery anyway.

Oil paintings lined gold-plated walls, and white stars daubed its navy ceiling. Charlie paced the tiles like a bird caught beneath a basket. Either unregistering the tense quiet or too on edge to care. Sheer drapes flapped from the sea's bluster around a large open balcony with Neoma framed at its center. Orion flanked her in full armor, expression void of the warmth Reyna had come to know in their sessions.

"Get on with it," Neoma snipped at Seph.

"I didn't want to spoil the details without everyone present." Seph lay draped over a chaise like a Renaissance painting, wallowing in her power over the goddess without an ounce of magic.

"Lady Capricorn has not yet arrived," Orion stated.

"We shan't draw this out any longer." Neoma waved a dismissive hand. "I suggest you reveal what you know without further theatrics, Persephone. Did you find the prophecy or not?"

Seph's lip curled at her Nidian-given name. She swallowed whatever snark teetered on her tongue and stood from the chaise. "I found the prophecy in the Forgotten, but someone else had discovered it first."

Neoma's attention shifted toward Reyna. Momentary silence thickened the room like the storm clouds brewing outside.

"Impossible," Orion scoffed. "No one has ever found the Forgotten."

Seph's smirk reveled. "Lady Cancer did."

Neoma raised a brow at Reyna. "Is this true?"

Reyna intended to reveal she was the Dark Star, but she didn't know Seph's agenda and refused to feed into whatever narrative the witch planned. Instead, Reyna offered a nod.

"Well?" Neoma marched toward her. "Where is it? What did it say?"

Reyna instinctually backed into Brax's hard chest. Seph stepped between Neoma's warpath and presented the crinkled, dried sheet music. Neoma ripped the pages from her and riffled through their contents.

"Lady Cancer came upon the prophecy yesterday." Seph shrugged. "So, I suppose the real question is why she withheld such precious information?"

Reyna sank beneath every gaze in the room, even Cancer's ghost.

"I ... Anemone ... she's—"

"What of Nem?" A new voice serrated Reyna's demise. "I've not seen her since yesterday and was told she'd be here?"

"Juniper!" Seph's scarlet lips peeled into a vicious smile. "Lady Cancer was about to share the factotum's whereabouts."

Seph's cruelty broiled beneath Reyna's skin, but that rage soon dissolved at Juniper's furrowed face. The Nidian existed as Reyna wished she could. Unchanged. Whole. Her world not on the precipice of never being made right again. Reyna owed Juniper the truth before Seph could blemish Anemone's sacrifice further.

"Anemone is dead." Reyna's admission rattled through her bones. "I'm ... so sorry."

Sorry.

Reyna hated the hollow word. Not because she wasn't, but because no utterance could ever articulate her remorse.

"I don't understand. Nidians can't die." Juniper stared at Reyna. "Is this some sort of jest?"

"Anemone died protecting me in the Forgotten." The truth would never be enough, but it was all Reyna had left. "She was selfless and brave. It's my fault she's gone."

"No! She's not dead." Juniper shook her head. "Why are you saying this?"

"Cancer didn't tell anyone about Anemone's end or the prophecy, because she's working with the Dark God," Seph spat.

"I'm not!" Reyna protested.

Prisha burst through the gallery's gilded doors.

"Lady Capricorn." Seph grinned. "Glad you could join us."

"Would've arrived sooner," Prisha snapped. "If not for your delayed summons, you bottom-feeding twit."

"I'm sure I don't know what you mean." Seph feigned shock. "I'm relieved for your corroboration of Lady Cancer's union with the Dark God."

Prisha's head cocked at Reyna. "You told them?"

Orion's brows drew together. "It's true?"

"I saw Lady Cancer kiss the Dark God." Seph's Cheshire cat smile stretched to near insanity. "I also heard him call her the Dark Star. Ask Lady Capricorn, she bore witness."

"Please, it's not what you think." Reyna stepped forward.

"Lady Capricorn?" Orion addressed Prisha but his gaze remained fixed on Reyna. "Does Persephone speak the truth?"

"Yes." Prisha inhaled deep. "Though, I don't believe Reyna is working with him."

"The evidence speaks for itself." Seph rounded on Reyna. "Did you think you could follow me into the Forgotten and I wouldn't know?"

"Enough!" Neoma's bellow echoed off the gold walls. "Orion, detain Cancer in her chambers until we can arrange for more appropriate accommodations in Omphalos."

"Like hell you will." Brax planted himself between Reyna and Orion.

"Brax is right." Ethan blinked at his own admission. "Let's all take a breath and talk about our options."

"This isn't a democracy." The goddess glowered. "Hand yourself over now, Cancer. I won't tell you again."

"Please don't do this," Reyna pleaded with Orion. "I'm sorry. I didn't mean for anyone to get hurt."

"Orion!" Impatience ground Neoma's jaw. "I've given you a command!"

"I do believe you're sorry, Lady Reyna." Orion frowned. "I am too." He unsheathed his blade with armor clunking forward. "Please don't make this harder than it—" Orion staggered to a stop as his black blade seared bright red. Thick, glowing obsidian dripped over the hilt. Orion hissed and dropped the melted weapon. He peeled at the midnight lava on his skin.

Neoma's eyes blazed wide. "What magic is this?"

Globs of melted obsidian solidified into bullets and floated between Reyna and the goddess.

"She's not goin' anywhere with you." Brax's outstretched fist trembled with control of an element not his own.

"Brax?" Reyna gaped at the obsidian awaiting his next command. "How are you …"

Brax peered at Reyna over his shoulder, lightning illuminating his breeze-rustled hair.

He smiled. A beautiful, warm, desperately apologetic smile. Free from snark or any other trademark. Pure. True.

Final.

"There's so much I wanted to tell you." He swallowed thick emotion. "Promise me you'll find a way off this island. Remember our place. Remember me. And run."

"No." Reyna's brows drew together. "Not without—"

"Run!" he roared.

Brax's hand sprang open, and the room exploded into chaos.

Black bullets zipped toward Neoma. The goddess and Orion ducked to the floor. Shots ricocheted off the gold-plated walls and Brax sprinted for the open balcony.

Neoma blasted air at him. Brax's feet flew up from underneath. He tumbled across marble and slammed into the outside balustrade. Neoma stalked toward him with fire, busted marble, and wind orbiting her like a tornado. Her hands rose, preparing to bury him.

"Stop!" Reyna's hands thrust forward.

A tidal wave rose from the sea, swallowing the balcony in shadow.

Take him somewhere safe.

Reyna balled her hands into fists and yanked back her elbows.

Water crashed onto the balcony. Paintings swept off the walls. Furniture capsized. Reyna twisted her wrists, splitting water from her friends as though they were boulders along a raging river. The starlight beneath Reyna's skin tightened. She focused her starwater magic harder, but a power outside her own imprisoned her limbs like marionette strings. Water receded across the balcony and waterfalled into the sea.

The spot Brax occupied seconds ago, vacant.

Neoma's heels clicked across the sea-slicked marble, pulsing with reflections of lightning. She seized Reyna's throat.

Reyna side-eyed her doppelgänger watching as though Reyna's predicament were a curious oddity.

"Where've you sent that traitorous Zodiac?" The goddess squeezed harder.

Reyna gurgled. "I'll never let you hurt him."

"Some things never change." Bitter amusement darkened Neoma's face. "I've underestimated you far too many times, Cancer. And I shan't ever again."

FORTY-ONE

THE CALMEST PLACE WITHIN A HURRICANE WAS THE EYE. A reprieve where chaos fell away, and people remembered sunlight still existed beyond wind and rain. Reyna always thought "heart of the storm" made more sense. A central power chamber from which all else thrived. But hearts were never calm. Never still. Made quiet only by death. Today, she understood why it was an eye. A storm's center offered what a heart could not. The eye allowed one to see.

Reyna saw Brax control obsidian. Saw statues of black glass hidden within a place only he knew. Saw the times he tried telling her his secret and didn't. Reyna saw but still did not understand.

She wanted to be angry. Hurt that he hadn't trusted her more. But she couldn't. Not after she'd done the same. Reyna could've told him about Cancer and Levant's connection. The woods. Cancer's memories. She didn't. Brax pushed her away because he'd tried protecting her. Who had Reyna protected? Latches and locks hadn't kept Prisha from finding her door. Gloves didn't stop Tessa from meeting death and Reyna sealed Anemone's fate long before they left the Forgotten.

Reyna listened to the muffled rain assaulting the invisible walls caging her exposed balcony as she sat with her back against the bedroom door.

Fatigue had trembled through the goddess after she released her hold on Reyna in the gallery. Charlie didn't want to raise a barrier outside Reyna's room, though Neoma gave him no choice. Perhaps Neoma became weakened from the obsidian's presence, or the power she used at nearly destroying Brax. Reyna couldn't be sure, but it was what she knew, which frightened her most. Any moment, Orion would escort her to Omphalos where Neoma would decide her fate.

Brax's prior caution remained seared on Reyna's mind.

Neoma sacrificed us out of desperation and paranoia. A deadly combo.

Despite his falsehoods, Brax had been right about many things. Neoma could see Reyna as a threat. A sacrifice for the greater good's survival. Without knowing the Dark Star's identity a century ago, Neoma showed little grace toward the Zodiacs. What, if any, mercy would she show now?

Reyna glanced at Cancer shaking her head, seated at the end of their bed.

Cancer hadn't spoken since the garden and much as Reyna loathed her uselessness was grateful for an illusion of company. For someone who knew her like no one else. That no matter what happened next, even possible death, she wouldn't be alone.

A sudden burst of rain clattered onto the balcony.

Reyna slid from her spot and slowly padded across the room. The storm stabbed her skin and droplets bled against the sandstone at her feet. Lightning illuminated a dark silhouette at the balcony's center.

Reyna swallowed. "Brax?"

Charlie stepped into the light stretching from inside her room. Rain battered his shirt and weary frown. He stood quiet, as though debating what to say, or hoping she'd speak first.

"What're you doing here?" Reyna shouted through the downpour.

"Helping you," he replied.

"Neoma won't be happy." Reyna didn't care but also didn't want anyone to face the wrath of implication.

"I don't know if you noticed, Rey. Neoma has officially gone batshit." Charlie wiped at the hair sopped against his forehead. "None of us are safe, as long as we're loyal to you."

"To me?" Reyna blinked. "What do you mean?"

"You might be the Dark Star, but none of us Zodiacs believe you'd hurt anyone. Come with me so we can stop this."

"I don't want you to get hurt, Charlie."

"Neoma knows where Brax is."

Reyna's face paled. "How?"

"I don't know." He frowned deeper. "But she's gathered obsidian soldiers to ensure he doesn't escape again and said if the Zodiacs interfered, she'd end us too. Rey, do you know where you sent him?"

Remember me. Remember our place.

Reyna nodded.

"We have to find him before she does. Brax always knows what to do."

She strode across the balcony and climbed atop its railing.

Reyna's toes clung for any grip the sandstone would offer, while Charlie hovered beside her and held her elbow steady. Wind and rain thrashed their bodies. Waves chiseled into the cliffside below, each vibration urging her legs forward. Reyna may have been immortal now, but Anemone's death taught her that she could still feel pain and Reyna wasn't about to test the physical theory.

"Can you help me avoid the rocks?" Reyna asked.

Charlie cracked his knuckles. "You betcha."

Reyna closed her eyes. The sea's arms opened.

And she leapt.

Wind howled through Reyna's hair and rain streamed across her cheeks. The storm's pulse was brutal, but she was fiercer. The jagged cliffside came closer. Violent waves thrashed against its teeth, cutting spray into the air.

"Charlie!" Reyna yelled.

"I got you!" he shouted from somewhere beside her.

An airstream whooshed Reyna from the rocks out to sea. Her

feet landed atop water and a smooth radius rippled around her. The whitecaps settled, but wind still tangled through her wild hair.

"Take me to him," Reyna instructed the water.

An illuminated path split across the dark ocean. Reyna sprinted like a gazelle across a savanna of sea and salt. Not from her lion. Toward him. Thunder grumbled she turn back. Lightning snapped at the heels of her fears. Reyna and Brax were different. The same. Complicated. Completely at odds with the other's approach to damn near everything. Still, Reyna ran faster. Raced toward the man who made her question all she'd known about herself. Who embraced the parts she wished she hated. The parts she did.

Reyna slowed as she reached their cave. She edged inside its gaping maw, the sea still warm and firm beneath her feet.

Brax sat hunched onshore. Head lung low. Hands buried in his soaked hair.

Alive.

Relief whimpered from her.

He was alive.

Brax glanced up, brows pinched together as Reyna strode across the water. He pushed from the sand and cocked his head. A crude cocktail of confusion, desire, and anger twisted in his features. Reyna let herself sink into the shallows, never slowing her stride. Brax staggered forward, feet punching through water. He broke into a sluggish jog against his waterlogged jeans. The two collided, and their circumstances shattered. Fire-calloused hands rocketed to Reyna's cheeks. Wandered her skin as though she were an apparition. Brax's thumbs caressed her temples and tears sprang from Reyna's eyes.

"I'm so sorry," she stammered. That stupid word again. How she hated it.

"For what?" Brax's forehead met hers. "I'm the one who fucked up."

"I swear it wasn't me kissing Levant in the Forgotten," Reyna pleaded. "It was Cancer and I—"

"Shh." His large hand smoothed over her rain-mopped hair. "I believe you, but I told you to run."

"I did." A soft melancholy laugh sputtered from her.

Brax heaved a furious kiss against her forehead. "I don't think anyone else knows about this place. We should be safe for now."

"No!" Reality backhanded her. "Neoma knows you're here. She's coming!"

"I was serious about gettin' off Nidus. *Polaris* is still docked at Messis. I'll stay behind and buy you time. You need to go."

"Not without you," Reyna snapped. "I don't care if Neoma finds us, or if you can wield obsidian magic. I won't leave you behind."

"Goddamn it, woman, would you listen to reason for once?" Brax growled. "If Neoma finds you, she'll—"

Reyna grabbed his face. "I love you!"

She'd never given the words to anyone, but they hummed across her lips like a serenade always meant for him.

"Stop." Brax shook his head, voice croaking, "You can't."

"I do and I'll keep saying it. I love you, Brax."

"Damn it! You're not listening!" He ripped her hands from his face. "It doesn't matter if you're immortal. You're in danger!"

Reyna pulled her hands from his and contemplatively stepped back.

Her voice softened, "How'd you know I'm immortal?"

"You went to the Forgotten and—"

"And no one else has," Reyna finished. "So how could you know what happened after I crossed over?"

Brax dropped to his knees and the shallow tide brushed over his knuckles.

"Tell me how you knew!" she demanded.

"Because …" Levant stepped from behind an obsidian statue. "He's been working for me."

CHAPTER

FORTY-TWO

REYNA BACKED AWAY FROM THE TWO CELESTIAL MEN AND Cancer's ghost. Her past, present, and future all watched her with varied flavors of interest.

Air filled Reyna's lungs, but she couldn't capture a single breath.

"Tell her," Levant commanded softly. "How from every moment since you reunited, you've been Leo, parading as your pathetic reincarnation, Braxton Riggs." The Dark God crouched beside him and tugged a fist of blond hair, so Brax's gaze met hers. "Tell her how you've remembered everything about who she was."

Brax's throat bobbed as shame bled from his eyes.

"Tell her!" Levant yanked tighter.

"It's"—Brax gritted his teeth—"true."

Every conversation they'd shared. Each embrace. The times Brax encouraged her. Moments he hadn't. Every laugh. Touch. Argument. Their cave. The tree house. Was any of it real? Again, Reyna gasped for air. None came.

Levant grumbled, "Of course, all would've been made simpler if Leo ended your mortal life from the start, like I'd ordered."

Reyna summoned a sound. "You were going to kill me?"

"No!" Brax surged forward into his conviction, but Levant held firm. "I told him I would, but I couldn't. Not ever."

"Finally, he speaks truth!" The god pulled Brax's head back harder, baring his arched throat and chest pressing outward. Levant cocked his head at the place where Brax's heart resided. "I should've never trusted the Zodiac ruled by this human *thing*." Levant shoved Brax toward the sand. "Leo left me no choice but to guide you to death myself, *mi luna*. You always did dare do what others would not." A wicked smile creased his lips. "I'm proof of that."

Reyna's mouth went dry. "I'm not dead."

"An immortal is far from dead, though not quite alive either. The only notion separating them is whatever mortal definitions you've been fed. The moment your soul left your body, you met your destiny."

Reyna grappled at her chest and throat. Willed a pulse beneath her fingertips but nothing answered back.

Dead.

The breaths she'd searched for and couldn't find.

Dead.

The absent hunger in her belly.

Dead.

"Don't fret," Levant implored at the panic spilling over her face. "It's not as though I'd let any true harm come to you."

"True harm?" Reyna graveled. "You killed me!"

"Kill?" Levant tutted and dragged a thumb along his bottom lip. "I remember you were quite eager to surrender your soul." His summons bounced off the cave walls, "Ini, you can join us now."

A low growl rattled in Brax's throat. Charlie flew through the cave's skylight and landed on the sand beside Levant, unable to meet Reyna's stare.

She shook her head. "No."

"I thought Ini would take more convincing to aid in my plans, although after he brewed the storm for my Dredgers aboard *Polaris*, I knew we'd reached an understanding." Levant squeezed Charlie's shoulder. The Zodiac winced, dipping from the pressure. "And after Leo revealed Neoma's underworld task for you, I needed certainty you'd return from the Forgotten without a soul. I sent Ini into the underworld for a test run and when he returned, immortally intact, I knew you would too."

"Charlie, I thought we were friends." Devastation roiled in Reyna's belly.

"Don't be too hard on him." Levant smirked. "We both know how persuasive I can be."

"You have to know, Rey," Charlie pleaded. "He has my sister. Threatened her. I wouldn't've helped him otherwise, but I needed to protect her. She's *family*."

That cruel word again. Cancer's everything and Reyna's nothing.

Wherever Brax's or Charlie's true loyalties lay, they three had been manipulated at the hand of this god. Levant eroded their ugliest parts and remolded them in his image. Reyna wanted to rip Charlie apart but also wept for him. To be without blood in the world. So close to a heart and never able to know it? Reyna couldn't grant forgiveness, but she could offer something else.

"I understand," she told Charlie.

His eyes sparkled with the small gift she gave.

"How benevolent." Levant glanced between their exchange. "So accepting of Ini's transgressions in the name of a sister. You're more like Cancer than you know." The Dark God released Charlie and mockingly dusted the Zodiac's shoulder. "You should also know, *mi luna*, I derived no pleasure in Ini's Nidian sacrifice."

Reyna blanched. "What sacrifice?"

"With Neoma's magic protecting the palaces, I needed assurance you received Cancer's memory. Once I learned of your Flora visit, I knew it was another chance to reach you. Ini provided me a private audience with the Florian boy so he could pass the crystal along with no suspicions raised. Dredgers unfortunately are drawn to my presence and are rather unpredictable creatures."

"Ambrose?" Reyna's fury shot at Charlie. "You offered up a child?"

"Rey, I ..."

Newfound emotion boiled through her veins.

Reyna marched through the tide, water splashing at her heels. She bypassed Charlie, reveling in the momentary surprise carving between Levant's features. He remained as still as stone. She craned her neck at him. Wished she could jut her chin higher. Any and all demonstrations of her loathing.

"Why?" she bit. "Why go through the trouble? Why not tell me when we first met, about you and Cancer?"

"So you might dismiss my words? Spend your days agonizing whether they are lies?" Levant released a wry chuckle. "I wanted you to *feel* me. To wake with the sun upon your skin, know you dreamed of darkness filling you, and pray for sleep once more. I wanted you unable to shake the lingering taste of me as you laughed with your friends, strengthened your magic, and awoke beside your pathetic lover. Oh no, *mi luna*. You, more than anyone, understand the power of experiencing ourselves. I didn't need you to listen, I required you to feel what we have."

"I feel disgust." Reyna inched onto her toes. "I hate Cancer's memories. I hate you. You failed."

Indisputable certainty penetrated his expression. "You hate loving every second of me."

Reyna didn't blink away from his challenge. Refused the slightest tell that, in the abyss where her soul once thrived, he was right. Cancer's willingness. Her submission to forces outside her control. Every second of Reyna's mortal coil had exhausted her of the opposite. Denied her true connection. Shunned her abilities. Riddled her with guilt from lives sullied at her hand. Reyna craved the freedom she'd found in a past life.

"Whatever you believe I feel, know this." Reyna gritted her teeth. "I'll never help you."

Levant's emerald gaze flicked to the overhead opening. Triumph snaked between his lips. "We'll see."

The cave's remaining ceiling exploded.

A rocky hailstorm rained onto the hidden beach.

Levant swiped a lazy hand and debris froze in midair. Boulders barreled from their path, shattering against the cave walls.

Neoma floated through the opening, eyelids fluttering. She

plummeted into the shallow water. The goddess pushed herself onto all fours, fingers grinding into the wet sand for purchase.

Levant's hands clapped together once. "Predictable as ever."

"What's this?" Neoma slumped with a wheeze. "Ini, where have you brought me?"

"You grant the simpleton too much credit." Levant glowed with vicious revelry. "We've Cancer to thank for uniting all of us."

Reyna's head swam.

Levant wanted this.

Everything about where Reyna stood, orchestrated by her own naïvety. Neither he nor Neoma knew where she'd sent Brax. Reyna brought Charlie here. Led them all.

"The obsidian." Neoma glanced between Levant and the glass statues. "How are you immune?"

"The difference between you and me is while you've spent another century in contented sameness, I evolved. No longer your equal. Superior in every way." A soft moan unfolded from him as his tongue ran along an obsidian statue's cheek. "Gives me the most delightful tickle."

"You still cannot destroy me," Neoma seethed. "The Infinite All-Knowing has made it so!"

"The Infinite All-Knowing has also given us a Dark Star to favor the scales."

"Please, Cancer. You can end this." Neoma's previous wrath crumpled under raw desperation. "I'm not asking you choose me. I'm begging you choose Nidus."

"I'm curious, *mi luna*." Levant crossed arms over his imposing chest. "What did Neoma promise in exchange for your venture into the Forgotten?"

"What?" Reyna choked.

"Oh, come now." Levant paced. "I'm not this island's only deity who dabbles in deals. Surely, she must've offered you something quite valuable in exchange for such a sacrifice?"

Reyna peered between them. "She said she'd remove my magic."

Levant froze, lips twitching between pride and disdain. "You truly are a wicked creature, my goddess. Tell Reyna the truth. After all you've done, you owe her."

"I do not answer to her, nor you!" Neoma snapped.

"Allow me." Levant swept behind Reyna. "Neoma knew the price for safe return from the underworld. One, she herself, was unable to pay. Neoma could never remove your magic, just as she never expected your survival from the underworld without a soul."

"You sent me on a suicide mission?" Reyna's chest split in two. "Anemone is dead, and it should've been me?"

"Foolish child," Neoma spat. "Dark Star or no, the cosmos would do well to be rid of you. I didn't need a prophecy to know what you've always been. A traitor. An end to our way of life!"

"No!" Levant roared. "To your way of life!" The god's hand sank into his pocket and pulled out green calcite resembling the crystal Ambrose had given Reyna. Levant's fist crushed the mineral. "If you remember nothing of this day, Neoma, remember this. In your most feeble attempt at eliminating myself and Cancer, you helped fulfill the outcome you sought to stop."

The Dark God opened his palm. Dust swirled into a glittering green vortex around Reyna. She gasped and calcite poured down her throat.

The cave fell from consciousness. Somewhere between the cusp of night and dawn's edge, Brax screamed.

Cancer's final memory, and each before it, erupted through Reyna's mind.

Reyna saw.

And finally understood.

Cancer's eyes flashed open, staring at her knees in the sand. She wiped at invisible tears of her last memory, though they still clung to her cheeks.

Lev's hand drifted into her vision. She stared at it, certain it couldn't be real. Sure, if she reached out, Reyna would change her mind and resurface. But Cancer felt nothing. No whisper of Reyna's essence. No pull to reclaim her body. Reyna accepted her fate. And now, Cancer must own hers.

She met Lev's eyes. A wild, fathomless green jungle filled with power and freedom.

"*Mi luna*, you've known darkness in every lifetime. Let us stop hiding and finally live. Together." Lev's promise thrilled every aching piece of her. "Together, we'll change the lines between stars."

Cancer tugged off her sandy gloves and slid her hand into his.

Lev pulled her from the ground and swiped his free hand. Water rose above them, solidifying into a smooth slab of ice. Cancer peered past their reflections at a bustling metropolis on its other side.

"Come." Levant beckoned Leo and Ini. "Despise me if you must, but you've no place on Nidus anymore. Your home is with me now."

"Fuck off." Leo stood from the beach and followed Ini toward the icy mirror. "My place will always be with *her*."

"Stop!" Neoma's last morsel of dignity drained. "Cancer, I know you still love Nidus. I beg you, please don't do this!"

Cancer frowned at the goddess over her shoulder with words she'd waited a century to say, "I hope your time on Nidus was everything you dreamed it'd be. Goodbye, Neoma."

Cancer and the God of Darkness stepped through the icy mirror. Hand in hand.

FORTY-THREE

CANCER

ONE HUNDRED YEARS EARLIER

CANCER HATED THE DARKNESS FADING FROM HER BODY. The sobered emptiness it left. Her only reprieve, indulging again and again. And again. She wished she could always carry the sensation with her. Feel the Dark God everywhere. Beside her. Above her. Inside her. Through palace corridors. The greenhouse. In Omphalos, on days she required more bravery than usual. But it wasn't just delight of the forbidden. Revelries in such darkness amplified the light too. Stars burned brighter. The sun blazed hotter. Dawn swam through her veins before its first breaches of light split across the sea. The world's entirety sang in unison, and it wasn't until then that Cancer understood.

She'd been living a half life.

"I should go soon." Cancer rolled from her and the god's sheeted cocoon. "The sun is nearly here."

"Let it come." Lev planted a delicate kiss on her throat. His breathy sigh pulsed against every wanton part of her, but Cancer pleaded the stars for focus. For the words she'd put off for far too long.

"We need to talk." She combed her fingernails through his disheveled hair.

Lev groaned. "So long as you never stop doing that."

Cancer sat upright. "I'm serious."

"As you wish, *mi luna*." Levant chuckled softly and rolled onto his back. "What worries steal your smile from me?"

"What are we going to do?" she asked.

"I can think of a few million positions we haven't tried."

"Lev, please." Cancer winced under the decadent aches still ebbing from her limbs. "The sneaking around. The lying. I hate it."

"You know they'll never accept us or what we do."

"I know, but—"

"I have a gift for you." He reached beneath his pillow.

Vulnerability tensed in his jaw, wrapped in an armor only she knew the gaps between. His palm opened and a dainty chain dangled from his hand with a pale green crystal at its bottom.

"Green calcite. Like you, it's the rarest of its kind on Nidus." He draped the jewelry over her head. The crystal rested atop her collarbone. "I'll never allow Neoma to take you from me. So, until you remain by my side always, speak memories of us into this and they'll forever remain with you."

Cancer swallowed. Weightless. Consumed. Utterly destroyed.

"You have pieces Neoma couldn't take if she tried," Cancer replied. "But those pieces also belong with Nidus. I don't need a crystal to remember you. I need us together, free from the shadows."

"Shadow will always taint my affection for you, and I'll experience no remorse for it. I can give you galaxies, pleasures, power. Never love." Levant sat upright as blackness devoured his eyes. "I am the longest night of winter."

"Then I shall be the snow." She smiled. "So I might always kiss your cheek."

Levant slunk over Cancer's hips and pressed her wrists into the mattress.

"This mouth." His ghosted hers but didn't close the distance. "I'll never tire of the joy it brings my life."

"Then let us leave. We'll find the Infinite All-Knowing. Ask for your light. Take it, if we must." Blasphemous as her words were, she meant them.

The Dark God studied her for a long moment. "What if I told you we needn't find the Infinite All-Knowing to be together?" His fingers threaded through hers. "That our hiding will soon be over?"

"But the goddess—"

"Even Neoma cannot stop what is coming."

Hope bloomed in Cancer's chest, but concern prickled along her spine. "What do you speak of?"

"Pisces had a vision. A prophecy." Excitement dilated Lev's pupils. "One in which a Zodiac and I will rise together. I believe you, such a Zodiac."

She blinked. "Why me?"

"Celestials shall awaken, upon his return," Lev recited. "For a deviant of black glass, love too must be earned. One emerges like the other, when noon becomes night. Toll of the once mortal lover. Darkness consumes light. From twelve the Dark Star will arise. And two shall remain. No longer lost amongst the skies. Together they will reign."

"I've never been mortal, nor ever will be." Cancer's brows gathered. "Such feats are not possible."

"Anything is possible."

Of Pisces's many visions over the centuries for Earth, none ever linked directly to Nidus. Let alone the Zodiacs.

Cancer's head spun. "And Pisces *willingly* shared this vision with you?"

"Of course." A good-natured snicker rumbled from the Dark God. "Surely, you cannot believe you're the only celestial who seeks change on Nidus? Many Zodiacs wish for freedom from Neoma's shackles. They desire an existence beyond servitude to a planet they'll never see."

"I suppose you'll tell me those Zodiacs sought you of their own accord?"

"I sought them," he said with no contention.

Knowing churned in Cancer's stomach.

"You used me?" She pushed his chest upward. "The treaty was never about the Forgotten's upkeep. You wanted unchecked access to the regions so you could turn the Zodiacs against Neoma."

Levant's knees remained straddled on either side of her thighs.

"I saw an opportunity and seized it," he said without regret. "Most creatures are too fearful to speak for what they want. You're a fool if you believe the Zodiacs' desire for more didn't already exist. Just like yours."

Cancer wrapped a sheet around her torso and swept from their bed. She scurried along the staircase to the tree house's main floor. Black smoke burst in front of her as Levant stalked from within its haze.

"Cancer, I never lied to you," he said.

"Concealing truth of your intentions is the same!" She trudged past.

Levant snatched Cancer's wrist and tugged her into his chest. "I've always told you what I am. You knew and still came to me." His grip softened. "But even in my vendetta, I never expected I'd feel …"

"What?" she bit.

"I don't—" Frustration twisted his lips. "All I know is I want you with me, no matter the cost. Dark or light. Right or wrong. None will matter once the Dark Star rises. Nothing will divide anyone from the life they want. No one will separate us."

She wanted to hate him. Reconcile whatever future ripple she'd unleashed over her beloved island. But Cancer had been unfaithful to Nidus for too long and the thought of a universe without Levant terrified her more.

A sword unsheathed behind her.

"Lady Regent?" Orion's voice shot like an arrow through her chest.

The hunter stood silent, though his judgment hung heavy.

Cancer couldn't face him. Once she did, something new would consume her friend's expression. Repugnance. Betrayal.

"I don't remember inviting a guest, *mi luna*?" Levant snickered into Cancer's hair, eyeing their intruder past her. "Perhaps you might bother us later, Orion? We're a bit indisposed and I'm not keen on sharing."

Cancer rotated in the god's naked embrace.

"What are you doing here?" she asked Orion.

"What am I …" A million unsaid thoughts fluttered over Orion's face.

A glowing orb floated onto the tree house deck. Its core blazed brighter, and the goddess's unmistakable heels clicked across floorboards.

"Neoma." Cancer rushed forward from Levant's embrace. "I can explain."

"*This* is how you fulfilled the treaty?" The goddess sneered. "I'd heard whispers of his garnering Zodiac support but never believed you'd betray Nidus with this abomination."

Smugness pulled Levant's lips. "You always did know how to compliment me."

Neoma's glare snapped to him. "Your corruption ends tonight."

"I'm ruled by no one." Levant's playfulness darkened. "This island would cease existence without my sacrifice. A fact you've erased from the minds of our creations. Nidus, and all who inhabit it, are my right as much as yours. Treaty be damned."

"You can't mean that." Cancer frowned. "You know what the treaty means to me."

"This goes beyond ink and paper, *mi luna*." Levant pointed at Neoma. "You can't believe she'll let us walk away from this day?"

"You could," Cancer replied. "You could be safe."

Sadness bloomed in his smile. "I refuse to slither away into the sea again. You must choose."

"Please," Cancer pleaded. "Light and darkness can find a way to thrive side by side!"

"For once Levant and I are in agreement." Neoma's chin lifted. "Make your choice, Cancer. Now."

"I won't!" Cancer echoed through the trees.

"Then it's true." Neoma's lip curled. "You've forsaken Nidus and doomed Earth."

"I'm here because I love Nidus!"

Neoma struck Cancer's cheek. "You're a traitor!"

Levant launched at Neoma. His fist hovered an inch from her face. The Dark God bellowed against the invisible force hindering his ability to harm her.

The goddess cocked an eyebrow. "Are you quite done?"

"Enjoy this moment." Levant chuckled through gritted teeth. "Because I won't need to touch you to destroy you."

"No." Neoma stepped forward, her closer range forcing him backward. "I won't need to touch you."

Black thuds rained onto the tree house. Starlight warped over two dozen soldiers' obsidian armor closing in. They approached the Dark God with shields and swords drawn. Black smoke curled at Levant's feet. An inky black haze swallowed him, and a thunderous roar split through the darkness. Birds scurried into the sky. Warriors staggered back. Floorboards buckled and broke under a storm of white fur rising from the smoke.

"Hold position!" Orion shouted.

A massive snow bear rose onto its hind legs. Slobber dripped from its jagged teeth.

Someone cried, "He's summoned Ursa!"

Massive paws swiped at the nearest line of soldiers. Screams erupted as warriors folded like flowers beneath a boot. Orion sprinted forward, black blade glinting. The bear's paw pounded into the general's head. Orion slammed onto the floor, rolling from reach.

"He's still the Dark God!" Orion barked, a long gash now stretching across his eye. "Obsidian up!"

"Stand down!" Cancer shouted.

"Take him!" screeched Neoma.

The warriors drew closer, shields pulsing with energy. The bear crumpled onto the floor, growls mangling into whimpers.

Cancer screamed for the river.

Water ripped through tree leaves. Icy razors clanked against armor. Soldiers thudded onto the floor wailing in agony. Horror welled in Cancer's face as she stared at her hands. These weren't Neoma's henchmen. Cancer weaponized her magic against Nidians. Souls she was supposed to guide and protect.

Cancer fell to her knees.

A midnight haze devoured the ivory beast. Levant's naked figure reemerged, hunched over floorboards, gasping. Orion's boots clunked through the circle of obsidian-clad soldiers confining the god. He tossed black glass chains over Levant's back and strapped his arms to his torso. The obsidian circle parted, and Orion presented his captured prey.

"I banish you." A sickly smile twisted the goddess's mouth. "To the darkest corner of the farthest galaxy."

"You'd better." A moan uncoiled from Levant as Orion tugged on his restraints. "Because once I return, my Dark Star will rise, and your time will be over."

Neoma gave Orion a single nod. He shot toward the sky with Levant like a comet streaking across the night.

Cancer howled and tears streamed over her cheeks.

Neoma stood with the last obsidian soldier's retreat from the tree house. Heels clicked to where Cancer still knelt.

"Please." Cancer begged her. "Bring him back. I'll do anything."

"You possess nothing I require." Neoma peered across treetops at the hint of a pink sunset at the sea's horizon. White light blazed at the goddess's fingertips. "Though a time may come when I call upon you. If Levant ever returns, so too shall you and the Zodiacs be born unto Earth as mortal."

Cancer didn't bother schooling the shock in her face. The word turned over in her mind.

Mortal.

Did Pisces foresee this? Were Levant's hopes for the future sealed by fate?

"You'll hold no memory of me, the Dark God, or Nidus," Neoma continued. "Upon your return, you will help me end him. And if you're this Dark Star he speaks of, I will end you."

Flecks of shimmering matter drifted before Cancer. She stared at her hands crumbling into stardust lost on dawn's soft breeze. Cancer's weight tumbled against the floorboards beneath her disintegrated arms. The green calcite around her neck clinked onto the wood and she whispered, "Let me remember this day and all others before it."

"Pray we never meet again, Cancer." Ice befitting of the underworld hardened Neoma's tone. "I hope your time on Earth is everything you dreamed it'd be."

CHAPTER

FORTY-FOUR

PRESENT DAY

GASOLINE SOAKED THE AIR.

Mortal descriptions for the human world whispered through Cancer's subconscious from Reyna. *Rush hour* tremors rattled beneath her feet. Shoes scuffed over *concrete*. *Sirens* blared. The sky brooded like faded *denim* left out in the sun too long. Every earthly sensation became another life. A nightmare burning her nostrils. It howled in her ears and scraped along her insides. She squeezed her eyes shut. Tried to reject the claws of human life. This couldn't be Earth. Not the place she'd longed for the better part of her existence.

"I promise it will pass in time, *mi luna*." Levant's cheek bristled against hers. "Follow me."

Ini rushed ahead and pulled open a tall glass door. Levant motioned for Leo to enter first. Cancer watched the Zodiac's blond mane sway as she and the Dark God followed. How Leo must hate her but all were safer with Reyna gone. None more than him.

Their footsteps echoed off black marble floors through a grand lobby. Cancer craned her neck at parallel rows of slender stone columns. The pillars burst at the tops like elegant ebony tree branches along the ceiling's arc.

"Welcome back, Mr. Nidus." A perky blonde smiled from behind a desk. "So glad to have you staying with us at VitaSuites again."

"Emily!" the Dark God greeted her cordially, as though he weren't one of the two most powerful beings in the universe. "I trust Mr. Esposito has been treating you well since my last visit?"

"Of course." Emily beamed and clicked a few buttons on her keyboard. "I'll let him know you've arrived. He's been meticulously overseeing tonight's event."

"Excellent." Lev accepted the shiny card she handed him.

"Event?" Cancer asked.

"I couldn't very well have your arrival go uncelebrated. We'll be dining with the other Zodiacs before the eclipse tomorrow."

"And Mr. Esposito is a friend?"

"Scorpio." Levant smiled. "In addition to being the West Coast's most ruthless attorney, he's also a patron of luxury real estate. Primarily hotels, such as this. I must admit, he's done quite well for himself in this life."

Leo snorted.

"Hello again, Mr. Riggs." Pink flushed Emily's alabaster cheeks. "Will you be wanting your usual room?"

Something stabbed at Cancer's chest.

How many times had Brax and this woman met? Why could Emily barely look at him without her lips parting? Had they—

Stop!

Cancer restrained Reyna's deep itch.

Mind your place, Reyna.

"That's no longer necessary." Levant waved a dismissive hand. "I've already arranged more appropriate accommodations for someone of Mr. Riggs's unique position. Mr. Harris will see to this personally."

Ini reached for Leo's arm.

Leo ripped his arm away. "Touch me, and you're a deader man."

Levant rolled his eyes and gave Ini an approving nod. The two Zodiacs headed down a long side corridor.

"Where's Ini taking him?" Cancer feigned disinterest.

"Somewhere he can cool down." Levant caressed the small of

her back and ushered them toward the elevators. "You needn't concern yourself with the lion anymore."

The cleanliness. The stale stench of manufactured materials. Even Earth's tidiest corners knotted in Cancer's stomach as Levant closed the penthouse door behind them. Not a speck of dust lay amongst the rich wood floors or dark marble countertops. Every moment Cancer existed in this world, Nidus became a distant memory.

Perhaps Earth was the true Forgotten.

Desaturated sunset danced through a crystal chandelier. Cancer splayed her hand against the suite's floor-to-ceiling windows and stared at the hazy horizon.

"This place is so different." She murmured, "I'm different."

"Come tomorrow, you'll find this world changed once more." Lev's footsteps paused behind her. Emerald eyes reflected through the glass at her. "And all will be set right."

Cancer watched mortals meander on the sidewalks below. "And what of them?"

"Once you become the Dark Star, all beings will live without shame. Accept their darkest truths." Lev grazed his knuckles along her arms. "They'll be free as we should've been those many years ago."

"If only darkness lives, how will anyone experience love?"

"Love clouds one's understanding of what they need. From taking what they want. Love is fleeting. Chemical."

"But … I love you."

"And look what it's brought you. A being of darkness who cannot give you what you desire above all else. Betrayal against those you once protected. Condemned you to a mortal existence where love was always an inch from reach. Love has slowly broken you and now darkness will piece you back together."

"You speak as if I should've run from you."

"Perhaps you should've."

"And yet you pursued me."

"A hunter doesn't apologize to its prey." Lev's palms caged her against the window. Frost spider-webbed along the glass as he inhaled her hair. "And it's been far too long since I indulged in my prize."

Lev's lips grazed Cancer's cheek in quiet demand that she face him and let him taste her light. Cancer's tongue still went dry at the promise of what his kiss could give, but if she gave in now, she wouldn't be strong enough for what came next.

"This isn't the way," she said. "I want more for you."

"I missed this." Frustration rolled through Lev's shoulders. "Your incessant need to fill me with light I cannot taste. To see me as a creature worthy of such splendor."

"You are worthy," Cancer replied as Reyna's voice rose from somewhere within. "We all are."

"When light is gone, I will no longer be bound by what I cannot give you." The god's fingers coiled tenderly around her throat. Brunette hair bunched over his hands. "We'll be the same. Unstoppable."

"You needn't change to earn my affections." She let her neck go pliant in his hold. "All I've ever asked is you acknowledge what I already know."

"Which is?"

"Your capacity to feel beyond whatever has conditioned you to believe otherwise. Light's spark still lives within you. I saw it that day with the children, when you asked me to stay the night with you, and many times after."

The winter of his low chuckle rasped in her ear. "You saw me manipulate you into my arms."

"Our deal was not yet done. You could've held the contract over my head. Amended it. Added stipulations." Cancer awaited backlash from the fingers poised at her neck. Perhaps she was foolish, but it needed to be said. "You wanted me to choose you of my own free will. The way *she* didn't."

The Dark God gripped Cancer's chin from behind. Her breasts jutted forward, and the back of her head hit his shoulder. Her fingers scraped at the glass for purchase, slipping against its icy glaze. White plumes floated from her mouth as Lev's hovered closer.

"And choose me, you did," he ground. "Much as I've savored your light, I find myself more and more eager for it to be gone. But not before you extract the Zodiacs' elemental magics."

"That's how you plan to do it," she replied. "Reyna's other magic?"

"My darkness swam so deep in your essence, it couldn't be contained in her mortal form. The moment I learned of Reyna's extraction magic, I knew without a doubt you were my Dark Star." Levant spun and pinned Cancer's wrists against the glass. "You're my weapon. My salvation. So, if you think after having my light ripped out by some Insignificant All-Nothing and sentenced to a century in exile by my ex, I'd gamble my victory for the maybe potential of love? Perhaps you don't know me well as you think."

"Do the Zodiacs know?" Cancer raised her chin, because no other body part could rebel. "Have you told them I'll take their magics?"

"All they need to know is they'll be free." He smirked. "And you'd better keep it that way."

She glowered. "Why would I?"

"Because despite your anger, you know a life of darkness with me is far better than the one you've been living. A life that Neoma will end if given the chance. Because if you don't choose me …" The Dark God's lips ghosted over hers. "*He* won't live to see the eclipse."

After a century, Cancer still felt the tears along her face, the hoarseness in her throat as she watched Lev shoot across the sky with Orion. Many pieces of her died that night in the jungle. Only to be reborn. Reignited.

By someone else.

"You wouldn't." Cancer gaped. "Twelve Zodiacs are needed for the prophecy."

"Neoma will try to stop me with Capricorn and Taurus at her side. All the Zodiacs, combined with two Geminis, makes twelve. I'm sure you've deduced the reason Leo is still alive, and not busted rubble at my feet, is dependent on you."

Defeat slipped between her brows. "What would you have me do?"

"Once the Zodiacs gather within a pool, you'll combine your starwater with extraction magic and absorb all four of their elements. You'll become the Dark Star and absorb the source of all light."

"What is the source?"

Black swallowed the whites of his eyes. "Neoma."

"My, my," Seph cooed. "Mind if I join?"

Levant huffed and freed Cancer from her prison against the window. She rubbed her wrists, never more grateful and sickened by his liaison's presence.

"What is she doing here?" Cancer suppressed Reyna's rage as she glared at Seph in the doorway. "Seph was cruel to my mortal self. I'd prefer if she left."

"I couldn't very well leave my most loyal supporter at the hands of Neoma." Lev smoothed his hands over his open blazer and inhaled through his nose. "Even if she did act out of turn."

"My Dark God?" Seph's smugness pooled into disbelief. "I made sure Neoma never found the Forgotten in your absence. I monitored Leo. Led Cancer to the underworld. I've done everything you've ever asked."

Levant pinched the bridge of his nose and strode toward a drink cart. Ice cubes clinked from his fingertips into a short glass. "Did I instruct you to assemble my foes and announce Reyna as the Dark Star?"

"Well, I … no." Seph squirmed. "But they were about to find out anyway. The timing was perfect."

"For whom?" Levant uncorked a bottle and splashed amber liquid into his glass.

"Reyna hadn't told anyone what transpired." Seph's careful gaze shifted between him and Cancer. "I sought to unravel them, so you could make your move freely."

"Honesty seems such a rarity these days." Levant swirled his drink's contents. "Seph, if you please?"

"I wanted …" She glowered in Cancer's direction. "To hurt her."

"*You* wanted." The god shook his head and knocked his drink back. His lips smacked as he peered at its bottom.

Levant chucked his glass at Seph.

The thick glass struck her left shoulder. Seph fell from its force, catching herself atop a velvet chaise.

"You endangered her!" A black cloud spat Lev across the room in an explosion of dark power. "Neoma might've destroyed Reyna on the spot, and it'd all be over!"

"I wanted her cast out by those she cared for, the same way she let me be!" Seph's teeth gritted while she clasped her shoulder. "To suffer, for stealing my place beside you! For consuming the heart and mind of the Zodiac—the only being I ever ..." Seph caught herself.

That's when Cancer saw it. The spark.

The light all Nidians were created from.

And Seph, half-bound to Levant, her other half still craving what a soul owed. Belonging. Purpose. Love. It'd been easy forgetting she was still a soul of Nidus. A soul long past her time. Ready for reincarnation yet lacking what should've prepared her for the next step.

Cancer frowned. "Persephone."

"This is about *him*?" Levant snarled and scrubbed a hand over his face. "That Zodiac has caused more trouble alive than any other creature I've encountered."

"Please forgive me, my Dark God." Seph fell to her knees, head hung low.

"Rest assured, Seph, you'll atone for your poor judgment, but now's not the time. Rise." Levant extended his hand and helped the redhead to her feet. He brushed a few disheveled curls from her face like a doting father. "Now then, I assume you've brought what I requested?"

Seph nodded.

"Send it in. You're dismissed."

She scurried into the hall.

"I'd prepared a gift for Reyna, should she arrive in your stead."

Levant smiled at Cancer. "A demonstration of what I can offer in our new world, lest she need further convincing."

"Reyna would be unmoved by such gestures." Cancer's attention flitted toward the door behind him, unable to contain her curiosity. Levant stepped aside and a familiar presence filled its frame.

A breathy whimper stuttered from Reyna.

A weak sound, with no definition except the complete unraveling of all that Reyna and Cancer vowed to accomplish the moment they became one in the cave.

There stood Gem. Lady Regent of Education and Adaptability. *Tessa.*

"They told me you were Cancer now and might not remember me." Tessa's tear-blurred angel floated deeper into the room.

New life spread throughout Reyna, and for a moment, she swore her heart restarted. Each fictional thud a restraint against hurtling herself into the arms of her oldest friend.

"Of course, I—" Reyna stopped at Levant's arched brow. Deceit threatened to bury her as she recomposed herself. "Reyna's grief over your loss was felt within the deepest recesses of her soul. Of course, we remember you." Honesty of the lie twinkled in Reyna's gaze. "But how're you alive?"

Levant stepped beside their reunion. "After Scorpio's failure at the club, I searched the vehicle for clues of your whereabouts and found Gem, barely alive. I brought her here to heal."

"Charlie," Reyna blurted. "Your Ini's—"

"Sister." Happiness glazed Tessa's eyes. "Looks like I have family after all."

Reyna faced Levant. "Why didn't I remember Reyna's friend was Gem once my memories returned?"

"Receiving all memories at once would be catastrophic for the mind," Levant replied. "I assume Lethe explained this?"

Reyna's hand drifted to the crystal still in her jean pocket and loss reverberated through her bones. Sharp. Fast. A fresh gash, marring an otherwise happy reunion.

Tessa never died.

Anemone died for nothing.

"How?" Trembles racked through Reyna. "How are you here, Tessa?"

Her friend blinked. "The Dark God already told you. I was alive when—"

"No." Reyna rounded on Levant and pulled the yellow soul crystal from her pocket. "How is Tessa here when I have this?"

"You were still mortal when you entered the Forgotten, which meant your memories could be lost forever if you didn't achieve your mission quickly. I explained the danger you were in, and Gem offered her soul to help you navigate my palace faster."

Raw emotion nearly destroyed Reyna as she faced Tessa. "You gave up your soul for me?"

"I may have a brother now." Tessa took Reyna's bare hands into hers. "But Reyna will always be my soul sister."

A tsunami of truth swelled through Reyna. They'd all been manipulated by Levant's half-truths, and Reyna refused for Anemone's death to be in vain any longer.

Nothing mattered more to Anemone than the well-being of the Nidian people.

A task Reyna once doubted she could accomplish.

A duty Cancer had forsaken a century ago.

A vow Reyna and Cancer would now see through to the end.

"Reyna lost a dear friend on Nidus," Reyna said softly. "A guiding light who died helping her." She placed the soul crystal into Tessa's palm. Reyna didn't care that Levant loomed between them. Didn't fear the potential aftermath of her next words. She curled her fingers over Tessa's and closed her grip on the yellow mineral. "Take it from someone who understands a soul's worth. Never surrender yours again."

Tessa nodded gently, tucking the crystal into her own pocket.

Levant cleared his throat. "I shall take my leave so Gem may help you prepare for our dinner." He kissed Reyna's knuckles. "Until then, enjoy your gift."

For all Levant's exploitations, all deceptions leveraged in his favor. Reyna still couldn't deny the simple emotion inhabiting her entire being.

"Thank you," she replied.

The god exited the room and closed the door behind him.

"Reyna." Tessa's face hardened. "What. Are. You. Doing?"

"What do you—"

"Knock it off." Tessa crossed her arms over her chest, voice held low. "Why are you pretending to be Cancer?"

"I'm not—"

Tessa snorted. "You can stop, Rey. I've known you since middle school. Are you helping him usher in a dark apocalypse?"

"Of course not!"

"If you're not helping Levant, why come here with him willingly?"

"How did you know I—"

"Charlie told me everything after he secured Leo in the basement."

"Brax is in the basement?" Hope spiked Reyna's voice.

"So, you admit it?" Tessa cocked her head. "It's really you?"

Regardless of whatever frail loyalty Tessa might hold for the god, Reyna couldn't lie to her friend a second longer. Not after a lifetime of secrets. Not after she'd been granted a miraculous second chance she didn't deserve. Reyna wouldn't hide her true self from Tessa ever again.

"It's me," Reyna conceded.

Tessa launched forward. Her arms cocooned around Reyna, sobbing into the crook of her neck. Reyna's limbs liquified. All reason, every morsel of her carefully constructed resolve, bled from her as she returned her friend's hug.

"The last time we were together, I said stuff …" More sobs racked through Tessa's body. "Rey, I'm sorry."

"We both said things." Reyna hugged her tighter and a fresh wave of happiness at such an overdue embrace crested over her. "The past doesn't matter. I'm grateful you're here now."

Tessa pulled back and tucked tear-soaked hair behind Reyna's ear. "Levant told us how powerful you are. Why didn't you tell me you could feel other people's emotions?"

"I thought if you knew, you'd think me crazy or worse, be afraid. Most days, I was afraid of myself," Reyna confessed. "It was easier pretending I was some version of normal."

"Did I make you feel like you couldn't confide in me?"

"No." A sad smile unfolded across Reyna's cheeks. She pressed her forehead against Tessa's. "You always showed me exactly who you were. I never once showed you the real me and that changes today. But you cannot tell anyone else."

"Why? What are you planning?"

"Nothing yet." Reyna slouched onto the velvet chaise and threaded her fingers through her hair. "When I saw all Cancer's memories in the cave—what Neoma and Levant put the Zodiacs through—Cancer and I knew the best chance at peace was by working together. Cancer believed she could reason with Levant through their connection." Reyna shook her head. "Cancer is part of who I am, and I couldn't deny her a chance to save him. Not when I want the same for …"

Tessa sat beside Reyna. "Brax?"

Reyna nodded.

"Charlie's sick over betraying you and I'm pissed he went along with it."

"He wanted to protect you." Reyna sighed. "It doesn't make it right, but I'm glad he did. This is all so messed up."

Tessa's shoulders straightened. "So, what're we going to do about it?"

Reyna sniffed. "We?"

"Most of the Zodiacs are spooked, but none have enough guts to do anything. If you're planning something, tell me what you need." Tessa linked her hand with Reyna's.

Reyna squeezed her bare fingers. "Okay."

FORTY-FIVE

A STRANGER STARED AT REYNA FROM THE MIRROR IN HER suite.

The shell of a person she once was, and the crab burrowed beneath its armor. The two finally made one.

"I take back every sordid thing I've said about this cursed rock." Levant's hands slunk around the midnight tulle gown spilling from her waist. "Earth has never looked more radiant than it does in your presence."

It was easy leaning into Cancer's affections for the god. Even after what he'd done, all Cancer and Reyna had yet to do, the ancient Zodiac still loved him. Perhaps until her last moment. But Cancer's connection with Levant no longer overshadowed Reyna's feelings for Brax, nor elicited the shame that once haunted her.

Regardless of past, present, or future, Reyna had welcomed love.

A feeling no one should regret. A precious gift Reyna would never take for granted again.

She rotated in Levant's arms. "I'm sorry we fought earlier."

I'm sorry I can't save you from yourself.

Levant's eyebrow lifted. "You've accepted our fate?"

Reyna offered a soft smile. "I want us to be free."

"Then I must remind you of the importance of this dinner. There've been whispers amongst the Dark-Aligned that another might be the Dark Star." Levant grumbled low in his chest. "I don't know how or why Leo possesses obsidian magic, but I will extinguish this rumor before tomorrow's eclipse. You'll help me accomplish this."

"What could I possibly do?"

"You will demonstrate support in anything I ask." Levant's thumb stroked her cheekbone. "Once the Zodiacs witness your true power, no one will question your validity."

"Anything?" Reyna's tongue shriveled. "What if I can't?"

"I'm pleased you've accepted our future, but the lion's still hinges on your every decision." Levant's icy finger trailed along Reyna's sternum and paused at its epicenter. "Although your heart no longer beats, it will be your undoing if my caution is not heeded."

Levant stepped aside and ushered Reyna from the room.

They rode a private elevator to the ground floor and continued along a corridor. Reyna's arm remained trapped in the crook of his while a million situations sprinted through her mind. She and Tessa agreed to use the dinner for discovering the Zodiacs' true loyalties and hopefully recruit some allies of their own. Reyna once believed the Dark-Aligned Zodiacs enemies, but Tessa insisted there were those among them who followed because they hadn't been found by Halley first. Reawakened mortals, same as Reyna, left behind to either fend off or buy into the Dark God's indoctrination. Reyna formed true connections on Nidus. Discovered more about her magic and herself than she ever might've if she'd stayed on Earth. Who knew what these other Zodiacs had lived through?

Levant pushed two mocha doors open with grand authority.

Chatters fell mute as the pair entered. All attention riveted on Levant's latest addition to his collection of celestials. Painted cherubs mocked Reyna from an ornate gold ceiling. There was no joy here. No revelry. Only varied masks of fear, compliance, and self-interest. Reyna found Tessa across the banquet hall, clutching the hand of a man dressed in a white blazer and sneakers.

Andre Evans. Pisces.

Like Reyna, Tessa had found some good in this new world. Andre helped her heal after the accident, rarely leaving her side.

Reyna couldn't recall her friend alight with such admiration for a man. Someone so gentle, sweet, and devoted. Pisces and Charlie would be on their side, by association with Tessa. And though Reyna had reservations about Charlie's allegiances, her friend's twin was nonnegotiable. Penance would come, but today, they needed all the help they could get.

Jace swept toward Reyna. She tensed at the memory of their last encounter. Particularly, him buried under asphalt.

"Cancer! Delightful to see you again." Jace's exuberant but coy demeanor reminded her why she'd been tempted upon their first meeting. A true scorpion in wait. Stinger poised. Ready to strike before a creature could blink. He looked for approval from the god and Levant gave a single nod. Jace kissed Cancer on both cheeks. "You look stunning." Jace grinned, stepping aside. "Don't you agree, Leo?"

Brax sat at the head of a long table. Thick chains bound his wrists, forearms, and torso. An unwilling participant, propped as the guest of honor. Still, relief settled over Reyna's initial urge to rush to him. Brax was safe. For now.

"As you were, my friends," Levant addressed the Zodiacs. "Dinner will be served shortly." His instruction in place, everyone returned to their conversations. Levant faced Reyna. "I must speak with Scorpio about a few items concerning tomorrow's events. Perhaps you should become reacquainted with your kin?"

She forced a grateful smile. "I'd enjoy that."

Reyna drifted farther into the hall, a black cloud of tulle trailing behind her. Brax's golden gaze seared against her skin like sunlight beaming through a storm, but Reyna met yet another familiar pair of eyes dipped in silver.

The Zodiac's shoulders stiffened as Reyna approached him.

"Aquarius," Reyna greeted him with her first true smile.

He arched a dark brow. "You remember me?"

Reyna grinned at his platinum faux-hawk. "Not even that could hide you."

Aquarius possessed an easy attractiveness and never shied from challenging convention. He'd always been the first Zodiac to experiment with everything from functional improvements on Nidus to fashion. Cancer and Aquarius hadn't always been friends, but their shared interest in making dreams a reality without magic had once brought them together. Reyna prayed their bond still existed.

"So, you're one of us now." He disguised his question with up-ticked inflection. Aquarius's black-polished fingernail pushed ebony-rimmed glasses along his nose, attention fixed where Levant and Jace conversed behind her.

"They can't hear us, you know." Reyna plastered a phony smile on her face to put his paranoia at ease. "It's just me."

Aquarius let a sarcastic snort and sipped his beer. "You'll never be just you. You're the Dark God's."

She pinned him with a stare. "Aren't we all?"

He paused a long moment before he said, "I think you know the answer."

Aquarius always talked in code only he understood, as if everyone else were imbeciles. It was one of his most annoying traits, though tonight might prove their saving grace. Tessa tried swaying Reyna from recruiting him, uncertain how serious his relations with Jace were. Though, Reyna couldn't forget Aquarius's warning to her at the club. It was a small mercy but spoke volumes.

"What would you say if I told you we could stop tomorrow?" Reyna asked.

Aquarius remained silent, contemplating Levant and Jace across the room.

"I'd say I don't remember you quite so ballsy or stupid." Aquarius brought his beer to his lips. His voice dropped behind the glass's rim still held at his mouth. "What'd you have in mind?"

His question nearly knocked her over.

"So, you'll help?"

"Didn't say that." Aquarius gulped another swig and tattoos peeked along his white wrist from beneath a gray suit coat.

"Is it because of Jace?" Reyna asked. "Do you love him?"

Aquarius sputtered on his drink.

"Jesus." He disguised his cough as a halfhearted laugh. "Have all those memories scrambled your fucking brain? I'm not talking about Scorpio with you, and certainly not here."

"Is he why you won't help?" Reyna asked. "I'd understand. More than you know."

"I do what I need to survive."

"And if tomorrow's day looks more promising from another side?"

Aquarius shrugged. Another coded gesture that could mean anything. Not an agreement yet not a refusal. Reyna hated asking but needed to know, even if his answer was a lie. "Are you going to tell him?"

"Make the day yours and I won't have to say a word."

"Thank you." Reyna wrapped her fingers over his hand clutching the glass too tightly. "And thank you, for trying to help before."

Realization dawned on his face. "You're—"

"Whom did he help?" Jace materialized from behind like an apparition and hooked an arm around Aquarius's shoulders.

"A mutual friend." Reyna's mouth pulled into a practiced smile. "From long ago."

Jace's brow quirked at Aquarius. "You never mentioned you two were so chummy."

The large mocha doors opened, and servers wheeled in carts of plated dishes. Jace's pride diminished his slow descent into interrogation as he swept toward his staff. Aquarius joined the other Zodiacs and found his seat. Tessa brushed beside Reyna meandering toward the table.

"Any luck?" Tessa whispered.

"Aquarius is on the fence. I wish we had more time." Reyna sighed. "You?"

"Libra aligns with Scorpio's ideals and her shared background in public service has destroyed her faith in humanity, so she's a no. Sagittarius sided with the Dark God before his banishment, so I doubt she'll switch sides now. I was hopeful for Virgo, but after talking to-night, I think Levant might have his claws in too deep. If we could free Aries tomorrow, I imagine she'd help."

Jade. Brax's friend.

Was she being held captive with him? Did they reconnect? It summoned everything within Reyna not to look at Brax for answers she knew he couldn't give to questions she couldn't ask. She scanned the table, but nobody matching Cancer's memory of Aries sat at the table.

Reyna whispered, "Why isn't she here?"

"Who?" Death kissed the nape of her neck.

Reyna closed her eyes and prayed her startle invisible.

She invited Cancer's affection for Levant to take over, but the Zodiac's emotions lay muddled beneath who Reyna was becoming. One by one, her and Cancer's differences detonated like land mines Reyna didn't understand the placement of. Each explosion, a gaping hole along the seam of her character. The Cancer of her past was fad-ing. No longer a subservient celestial beholden to deities. As Reyna was no longer a scared ten-year-old girl, nor an adult hiding in her apartment. Reyna and Cancer were becoming something new. There was no them. Only she.

And tomorrow, everyone would know it.

"Who isn't here?" Levant repeated.

Reyna's eyes opened. Really opened. Breadth of both her exis-tences settled into her shoulders with utmost clarity. She faced the Dark God and ran her fingers along his lapel.

"Aries," Reyna replied casually. "Is she unwell?"

"I'm afraid the ram has been prone to escape attempts and vio-lence," Levant replied, mesmerized by her fingers stroking his chest. "All her rage will be most useful once light is gone tomorrow. For now, she must remain locked up."

"A shame. I was looking forward to seeing her again." Reyna counted the occupied chairs. "It seems we're short a chair."

"Nonsense." Levant's arm snaked around her waist, a shadow

possessing all within its path. He guided her toward the last vacant seat. "You'll be dining with me."

Levant sat at the table's head and spread his legs. A single hand rested atop his thigh.

An invitation.

The lion's fate still hinges on your every decision.

A threat.

Eight gazes anchored Reyna immobile, but none more than the Dark God's. Searching. Waiting for rejection. Any reason to end the Zodiac who'd seduced his reincarnated lover.

Reyna slipped onto Levant's leg and draped an arm over his shoulders for good measure. Levant lifted his glass, and the other Zodiacs followed suit.

"It was foretold a century ago, one of your own would bring about our salvation. Tomorrow is that day." Levant's glass rose higher. "Tonight is in celebration of your hard-earned sacrifices."

Reyna cringed inwardly.

Because tomorrow you might be dead.

The Zodiacs toasted their glasses with varied agreement and began eating. Through the clicking glasses and chatter, Reyna found Brax's eyes at the table's opposite end. Twin suns fixed on her as though they'd never left her orbit. Even strapped to a chair, Brax inhabited the illusion of slouching on a throne. Chin raised. Aloof. Regal. Every bit the king he knew he was. Perhaps that made Reyna his queen, seated atop the dragon she had yet to slay.

"Have I mentioned how delectable you look?" Levant planted a chaste kiss against the hinge of her jaw with a vulgarity only his lips could inspire.

Brax gripped the armrests, knuckles blanching.

Of course, Levant wanted Reyna seated with him at the table's head. Dinner and a show. All for Brax.

Guilt calcified her dead heart. She couldn't look at Brax again. Wasn't prepared for his hurt, disgust, or any other ugly emotions he'd associate with her after this. The Zodiacs kept up their side conversations, perhaps too desensitized to the Dark God's reprehensible manner.

Levant pulled her deeper into his lap. Reyna groaned softly, a whimper of detest she prayed translated into desire.

"Yes, *mi luna*." The Dark God's smile unfurled over her neck. "Show him who you belong to."

Rage against Levant lit in Reyna's belly as she stared at Brax.

She couldn't feel Brax's emotions but would endure them. If he was forced to watch, she'd compel herself to look upon him and know whatever broiled beneath, a hundred times more magnified. She'd let it burn through her. Char from the inside out. Reyna needed to feel Brax. Know he was with her in any regard, even if doused in his fury alone. Mostly she prayed Brax's practiced deception would reveal her truths.

A knock sounded at the doors and Jace rose from his seat.

"Did you enjoy my earlier gift?" Levant murmured against Reyna's ear.

Her voice became a glass shard lodged in her throat. She nodded, refusing to scar her reunion with Tessa with this moment.

"Good." He smirked. "Because this next gift for you is as much for me."

The hotel receptionist entered, her arm interlocked with Jace's. She'd traded her green vested uniform in lieu of a sparkly off-white dress. Her smile beamed. Glowed. True light.

A gift for him.

Dread dripped along Reyna's throat.

"Good evening, Emily." Levant's warmth mocked everything right. "So glad you could join us. Always a pleasure."

"I'm honored you invited me, Mr. Nidus." Emily blushed. "I don't get out much these days."

"Ah well, I hope it's not because Mr. Esposito works you too hard?" Levant winked.

"Oh no." Emily practically swooned. "The staff loves him."

"I don't believe I introduced my lady earlier." Levant squeezed Reyna's thigh. "This is Cancer."

Emily's nose squished at the odd name before catching her own bad manners. She extended her hand. "Nice to meet you."

Reyna stared at the woman's hand.

Let her own true emotions sift to the surface.

Reyna exhaled neutrality through her expression and welcomed Emily's hand into hers. Skin met skin and Reyna transferred the horror of what awaited the woman if she stayed a moment longer. Emily ripped her hand away and staggered back, cheeks paling.

"I-I have to go." Emily wasn't retreating fast enough. "I'm sorry. I don't feel well." She whirled, but Jace held her arm tight.

"Apologizes for my employee's rudeness." Jace grinned as the woman wriggled. "I thought we trained them better."

"Mr. Esposito? Let go of me!"

Emily's adrenaline flooded Reyna's system.

Reyna clutched her own chest under the foreign hammer of someone's heartbeat within. The receptionist glanced around the room and fresh panic descended upon her at Brax's chained body. Reyna gasped for the phantom breaths she didn't think possible anymore. The Dark God peered between the two women mirroring each other's physical terror.

"So that's how it works?" A slow, wicked smile curled on his face. "I suppose the question is, who was afraid first? Emily, whyever would you be?"

The woman's survival-based determination swept through Reyna's limbs. The longer Emily was held against her will, the more she'd rage.

"Answer me," Levant's voice thickened with threat. "What made you afraid?"

"Are you crazy?" Emily struggled. "Mr. Esposito is hurting me, and you've got a man chained to a chair!"

Reyna's would-be heartbeat settled.

Emily wouldn't understand why she feared so intensely, only

that she did, and the hall's despicable landscape helped mask Reyna's deliverance of her much-needed fear.

Levant pushed his chair back. Reyna stumbled into standing from his lap. The other Zodiacs had long stopped eating, unable to look away.

"Tell me, Cancer." Levant stood and shucked his blazer. "Why hasn't food been placed before us?"

Reyna hated where this was going. "Immortals don't require such nourishment."

"Ah yes." Levant snapped his fingers and Jace sat Emily atop the table's edge. Levant ran a hand through his chaotic dark hair. "And what will I no longer be able to indulge in, come tomorrow?"

Reyna didn't want to speak the word. Though its utterance, damnation of the thing itself. "Light."

"Light," Levant echoed. He stalked toward Emily and caught her chin with his hand. Bone cracked beneath his grip. Emily wailed. Her agony pooled into Reyna's jaw and neck. Levant leaned closer to the receptionist's lips. "I must confess, I'll miss the taste. Though I've never been above sacrifice."

"Leave her light so tomorrow she'll endure the loss you once did." Reyna's fingers smoothed along Levant's shoulder. "Let true darkness consume her."

"True darkness will." Levant turned his fully blackened eyes onto Reyna. "*You will.*"

"What?"

"You will consume her light." Levant left no room for debate.

"I can't." Reyna frowned at Emily. "I don't know how."

"Of course you do." Levant planted Reyna between him and their victim. He rested his chin atop Reyna's shoulder. "As a mortal, you consumed light whenever you stole another's life-force. What did you think light was?" His pelvis grinded against Reyna's ass, nudging her forward into Emily. The receptionist's sequined dress rode over her knees. "I've waited a long time to watch this, *mi luna.*"

"Please." Emily winced from the motion of her jaw. Confused tears leaked along her cheeks. "Don't do whatever he's asking."

This is what Reyna feared most.

The moment she intentionally stole someone's life-force. It didn't matter killing Emily wouldn't be in self-defense. Irrelevant, Reyna found herself under duress. She could say no. Levant wouldn't kill Reyna. Not with the eclipse a day away. He'd kill Brax, and without a doubt, Emily. Reyna could only grant the mortal one mercy.

"It'll be okay." Reyna cupped Emily's cheeks with tenderness. "I won't let it hurt."

Orion's teaching echoed through Reyna.

If you can take, it also means you can give.

And give, Reyna did.

She flooded Emily with serenity. Inexplicable joy from all Reyna's best moments since meeting the Zodiacs. Emily's shoulders slumped and her eyelids fluttered shut as though under a spell. Reyna weaved along the glowing threads of Emily's soul. The woman's heart rate slowed, as Reyna's papá's did all those years ago. She brought Emily to death's precipice and let go. Emily's corpse thudded onto the table and Reyna's curse became a gift.

CHAPTER

FORTY-SIX

BRAX

"Hey!" Brax rattled his handcuffs against the boiler pipes. "Anyone got a smoke?" He stared at the closed door, but only dripping echoes answered.

This wasn't Brax's first time held against his will. If the law caught someone, they locked them in a warm, clean cell. When the kinds of thugs who occupied those cells caught someone, they offered rope burn and one good eye to see what scurried over your leg. Brax knew both captors, like extended family forced to make pleasantries with a few times a year. He'd run through all the possible scenarios. The interrogations. Threats. Torture. All staples of an awkward family dinner. But there were too many variables this time. He never needed to account for magic. The apocalypse. Or the love of his life.

Brax rested his head against the concrete wall and snorted at the metal cuffs biting into his wrists. Levant's cruelty bore special treatment. Tungsten held the highest melting point of any metal. One degree too high by the steel pipes?

Boom.

Quick. Clean. Poetic. There were worse ways to go, though most didn't involve condemning a high-rise of strangers. No, the only way worth leaving this shithole world would be drowning in her.

Water surged through the pipe maze overhead, and somewhere

beyond so did she. Brax felt it the night Reyna came undone in the woods. The same raw, undeniable power exuded from any immortal. Though Reyna hadn't been yet, and it scared the ever-living shit out of him. Not because she possessed more magic than any mortal should, or because he thought her the Dark Star. But because in the moment, he was sure Cancer would resurface. Look at him. And pull away. Brax almost lost her before he'd had her.

Sentimental pussy.

He should've scorched the goddamn banquet hall when he had the chance. A centralized fire would've evacuated the hotel, but Brax refused to engage in a pissing contest with Levant to prove what he already knew. Fire or not. Eclipse or no. Shit was going down tomorrow. Brax wouldn't risk his life if there was a chance he could save Cancer from herself.

Brax's nostrils flared.

What that shit-excuse-for-a-god made Cancer do. Charlie and Andre lugging Emily's body away? For that, Brax was glad Reyna was gone. She'd never be able to live with herself otherwise.

Gone.

What did that even mean? Was Reyna's consciousness somewhere dormant in Cancer or was she truly …

Fuck!

Tears pricked his eyes, and he buried his fingers in his hair. He wasn't ready to consider that reality. The way Cancer frowned while Lev dangled her like a choice steak. How her sandy brown stare, once belonging to Reyna, shouted apologies only Brax could hear. It nearly fucking broke him. Brax was sure he imagined it, but if so, why'd Cancer look miserable?

The metal door screeched open.

"It's about damn time." Brax's tongue glided over his canine. "I was gettin'—" Words crumbled to ash on his tongue.

Cancer closed the door and stepped into the light. Even under the harsh fluorescents plunging over her face, she still resembled Reyna. Formidable. Endless. Beauty beyond mortal words.

Brax schooled his desire into boredom. "To what do I owe the pleasure, Lady Regent?"

"You'd speak to me so formally?" she replied.

His brow arched. "How would you prefer to be spoken to?"

"The way anyone would." She drifted forward like moonlight rippling over water. "With one's whole heart."

Brax snickered.

Cancer's brow drew together. "You're angry I sent your mortal away?"

Of all the torture Brax imagined the Dark God inflicting, he never predicted this. Brax bit back a sigh and inhaled through his nose.

Chamomile.

Christ. Cancer even smells like her.

"Her name is Reyna," Brax grumbled. "And she's not my mortal."

"I think we both know that's not true." Cancer rubbed where he'd branded her. "Reyna didn't possess my memories, nor enough experience to recognize what had happened, but you certainly did."

Every inch of him had been on fire during their night in the cave. Hard to tell where magic began, and the heat of Reyna's skin ended.

Brax hadn't meant for it to happen. Hell, he wasn't sure what it'd been at first. Forbidden so long, no one questioned whether it was possible. But when their lips met, kerosene blazed through his veins. A heat so blistering all he could do was hold on to Reyna until the moment passed. It wasn't until Brax saw that his mark on Reyna hadn't fully healed, he realized their bonding ceremony completed as they'd kissed.

Cancer asked, "Why didn't you tell Reyna what happened?"

"I know what it's like to exist without belonging anywhere." He shrugged. "If she knew we'd bonded for real, she'd stick around outta obligation. I wasn't gonna hold her back." Brax picked at his fingernail. A curtain of hair fell over his face. "I never expected she'd choose me."

"Why not?"

"Nidians were conditioned to adore me. The Zodiacs never took me seriously. You never saw me as more than a friend. Even with a mortal second chance, I was the reject son. Nobody ever chooses me. In either life."

"That's not fair." Cancer's brow creased. "You can't claim I never chose you, when you never showed you were an option." She knelt before him and curled a finger under his chin. "You flirted with me, but you did so with everyone. I could never tell what you truly wanted."

"And if I had been an option?"

"It does no good mourning what-ifs, though I'm glad you let someone know you." A subtle twitch pulled the corner of her mouth. "Even if it took a hundred years."

If Brax was not chained to the floor, he would've fallen on his ass.

Not from her admission. Her lips.

Their familiar twitch indented her left cheek, and her index finger knotted at the hem of her shirt. The sorrow in her eyes at dinner. Her scent.

Holy hell.

Brax's head spun. He'd lived a hundred lifetimes. Imagined this moment a thousand different ways. Never in those daydreams was he stripped of magic, dignity, or another tomorrow. The moment to tell her how he felt was never right. But she was. This woman. This Zodiac. Who'd fallen and risen throughout all the phases of his existence.

"You're right," Brax conceded. "I never let Cancer see me in the way she needed. The way I needed." His lips stopped short of grazing hers. A tide testing the shores, between a breath and being swallowed whole. "But I'll be damned if I let another second or century go by without you knowing how much I love you, Sunshine."

He thrust forward and claimed her lips.

Without remorse.

Without expectation and without fear.

Brax couldn't undo the times he'd hurt her. Wasn't powerful enough to stop Levant or the eclipse. But he could do this. He could taste her. Feel her skin against his. Ensure if he left this world tomorrow, she'd know she was loved.

"Wait." Reyna gently pushed him, breaking their kiss. "What'd you call me?"

Brax flashed a crooked grin. "You're gonna have to step up your game."

Reyna scrambled to her feet. "How'd you—"

"I've been doin' this a lot longer than I've been mortal." Brax squinted at her. "You're playin' a dangerous game, Reyna. Question is, why aren't you dealin' me in?"

"Look at what Levant has already done to you," she bit. "What do you think will happen if he finds out I've been pretending?"

"Have you?"

"What?"

"Been pretending to love Levant?"

Reyna's hands scrubbed over her arms, as though the god's name became a chill slipping through the room's cracks.

"I get it, ya know?" Brax knocked strands of blond hair from his face. "The only time I felt close to chosen for anything was when Levant made me his right hand. Maybe that's why it was easy pretending. 'Cause I wasn't. I told myself I did it to watch over you, which is true, but I also did it for myself. I lacked something I didn't think I was worthy of. That's what Levant does. He recognizes what's missing from a person's existence. What they want most. And exploits it for his own gain. Stuff I became good at in my new life."

"Whatever I feel or don't feel for Levant doesn't matter," Reyna replied.

"You're wrong." Brax shook his head. "It could mean the difference of whether you're able to make hard choices."

"Are you kidding? Hard choices are all I've ever made! Stopping Levant will be the easiest."

"In my experience, the most obvious choices aren't always easiest. Especially where the heart is involved."

"I can stop him." Reyna clenched her jaw. "I will."

"Okay." Brax sighed. "Lay it on me. What's your foolproof plan for stopping the world's end?"

New confidence squared Reyna's shoulders. "I need to absorb the other Zodiacs' magics to become the Dark Star. I'll stall, and once the eclipse ends, Levant's chance will be over."

"So, let me get this straight? Your master plan is do nothing?"

"I have Zodiacs helping," she snapped.

Brax's face squished. "What Zodiacs?"

"Tessa, or rather, Gem was my friend before all this. I thought her dead, and she's been with Levant this whole time. She told me some Zodiacs are afraid but might be willing to stand against him."

"You can't be serious?" Brax replied. "She's Levant's follower. They all are."

Reyna's brow raised. "So were you."

"That's different, I was—" Brax growled low. "You and I both know how easy it is to get sucked into his world. How do you know she's not off telling him right now?"

"Because she's my friend." Reyna inhaled deep. "And I need to trust someone."

"That's why you're passin' yourself off as Cancer? You don't trust me."

"Can you blame me?"

"No." Brax sighed. "I've kept my share of secrets."

Reyna crossed her arms over her chest. "How long have you created obsidian?"

"I can't create it." Brax clenched and unclenched his fists. "Only control obsidian that already exists. I've always been able to. I don't know why."

"How'd you figure it out?"

"I stumbled over the sea cave years ago, and it became a hide-away I wasn't bent on demolishing. So, I'd let off steam on the Glass Isles by melting shit. Once I realized faint remnants of fire still resided within obsidian, I experimented with what else I could do."

"The sculptures in the cave were yours?"

Brax nodded.

"So, you could've hurt Levant all those years ago if you'd wanted?"

A melancholy smile slipped between Brax's lips.

"But you didn't," Reyna whispered. "Because of me?"

"You always cared for everyone else around you. I wanted to care for you. Protect what made you happy. Even the shit I didn't like."

Reyna knelt and pressed her forehead against his. "Can you please stop protecting me and start helping me instead?"

Brax snickered good-naturedly. "I could get on board with that."

FORTY-SEVEN

BRAX

B RAX WOULDN'T SLEEP. NOT BECAUSE HE COULDN'T. HE'D caught Zs in worse places. Sleep-on-your-jacket motels. Busted cars. Oversize drainage pipes. Tonight was different. The quiet, louder. Every drip and kick of the boiler, a rhythm. Brax couldn't summon flames. Wielded no comebacks or schemes of escape. He'd been castrated of what made him, him. But for the first time since he could remember, Brax felt like a Leo.

Brax wasn't tired.

He was alive.

Their plan wasn't great. Hell, it wasn't good. But Reyna refused merit in abandoning him, Gem, or even Ini. Still believing the other Zodiacs could be turned. Her most admirable instincts were also her most dangerous. And Brax's instinct of protecting her? Easy as cigarettes after a roll in the sheets. Anything to prolong the aftertaste of her smile beside him a little longer. He didn't know if he could honor his agreement to not protect her, and he hated the plan, but he loved her more. So, he needed to try.

Brax rotated his hand, and the metal cuff clinked against its chain. He watched the room warp through his skin's warmth like heat from asphalt. If ruining Levant's plans didn't kill him, the anticipation might.

"If I'd known handcuffs were all I needed to tame the beast?" A familiar lilt thickened the air. "I would've proposed them long ago."

Brax couldn't help smiling.

A sneering, shit-eating grin he'd reserved for tomorrow, but hey, it was past midnight somewhere.

Scorpio left the door ajar and ambled deeper into the room. Overconfidence. Brax knew their shared curse well. But the Lord Regent of Death and Sexuality was a wild card. Lethal in love or vengeance. And if terms of their last encounter assumed anything, this would be both.

"I'm touched you visited." Brax tempted the waters. Then tested them. "Assuming Levant hasn't got you on a leash of his own."

Scorpio smiled too politely and loosened his silk tie. "I assure you, our Dark God is quite occupied by his new guest."

Brax's teeth ground at the possibilities.

"Besides, I needed to see for myself." Scorpio jutted his chin. Light sliced across his olive skin like glass. "The great lion. Fallen."

"Let me out of my cage and let's see how fallen I am."

"I should be thanking you. Levant finally recognized me as his true right hand." Scorpio picked his buttoned sleeve cuffs free. "I envied you. Thought if I could be alongside the great Leo, I might have a taste of what came with it. You possessed everything a celestial could want. The Dark-Aligned Zodiacs in your pocket. Our god's respect and from what Seph has revealed, obsidian magic? True power beyond our makers'. And you threw it all away for …"

Her.

Deep as Scorpio believed himself, his truths floated at the surface. Always craving more control. More time. Passion. More than Leo gave anyone. Except her.

Harsh retorts rolled over Brax's tongue. His current predicament inspired nothing less. Though he couldn't deny Scorpio was a powerhouse. The water sign was brutal in a magical fight and Brax didn't want to consider what it might mean for tomorrow. Maybe

Reyna was right. If a small chance existed any Zodiacs might sever ties with Levant, it was worth a shot.

"Scorp." Brax incinerated all malcontent. "I was always up-front about where you and I stood. We had some good times. Fun times. But it's Cancer. It's always been Cancer. Doesn't mean I wanna see you caught on the wrong side of what's goin' down."

"Don't patronize me." Scorpio massaged his own forehead with two fingers. "Seph called me a fool and maybe I am, but come tomorrow, I'll no longer be living in your shadow or chasing it."

Brax growled. "Tomorrow, you might be dead."

"Overestimating your abilities, as usual."

"Not me, you idiot." Brax weighed the risk of his next words, hoping Scorpio's wounded affections were stronger than he'd given them credit for. "Did Levant tell you Cancer will absorb your magic?" Scorpio's chest tensed through his button down. "He doesn't know if it'll kill you and he doesn't care."

"Lies."

"Speak for yourself, Jace Esposito." Brax grinned at Scorpio's arched brow. "I know all about who you are here. You get liars like me off with plenty of your own. You just do it in a fancy suit. C'mon, use your big ol' Stanford brain. What's the Dark God really told you about tomorrow?"

Scorpio squinted at him, his arms crossed over his chest. "You said 'caught on the wrong side of what's going down,' which implies you believe a right way things will go."

Brax composed his smile, but the corners twitched.

"You see"—Scorpio crouched in front of him, elbows resting on his knees—"I've got tricks too. You can run your game on everyone else, but I see you. You're hiding something and I'll find out what." He shouted, "Pisces! Get in here!"

Andre shuffled through the door.

It never ceased to amaze Brax how accurately reincarnation memorized their ancient selves. Pisces's same striking blue eyes framed by dark skin. His muscular yet lean build. Much as they resembled their ancient selves, earthly reincarnation dulled the Zodiacs' celestial glow with hardship. Life.

"Go ahead," Scorpio addressed Andre. "Do whatever it is you do."

"I need privacy," Andre replied.

Scorpio sneered. "This isn't some house call with motherfucking patient confidentiality. Get on with it."

"My abilities work better if in proximity with one person at a time." Andre's posture straightened. "Or would you rather the Dark God was delivered an inaccurate reading?"

Scorpio's gaze slithered between Brax and Andre.

"Fine," Scorpio snapped. "Be quick about it. I'll be outside."

Andre didn't move from his spot as the door screeched shut. The two Zodiacs sized each another up.

"Go ahead," Brax finally said.

"You're gonna let me read you?" Andre's fingers twitched at his sides. "Just like that?"

"Just like that." Brax chuckled. "I'm not going anywhere and if ya don't, they're gonna make you. Which'll be a helluva lot more painful for both of us."

Andre considered him a moment. "Levant wants to know if you'll be a threat tomorrow."

As long as Brax drew breath, he'd threaten all Levant coveted. Still, it warmed Brax's pride knowing Levant up in his pretty penthouse worried about how Brax might fuck up his day.

"Ya know." Andre crossed his arms. "I was fine until you got me all mixed up in this end-of-the-world business."

It wasn't until Levant awoke Leo's memories that he'd used his less magical talents to locate Zodiacs. Two names made the top of his list. The Dark Star and the prophet who foretold her emergence. Like Reyna, Andre was reborn with unnatural abilities. Unlike her, he found staying under the radar harder. A young guy from a prominent church community who predicted the future? Not a talent those in power cared to hide. Despite attention around Andre's gifts, he'd been hard to locate. He'd fallen off the grid a year prior. Brax had been on his own long enough to know people disappeared for two reasons. They were six feet under, or thought they were about to be.

"This is your business too," Brax countered. "You're who told Levant what was gonna go down."

Andre's nostrils flared, but his voice remained composed. "You think I strutted up to Nidus's most wanted and said, 'Hey, Levant, I had this sick vision of Earth's apocalypse. Guess what, you're in it?'"

"So set the record straight," Brax egged him on.

Andre glanced at the steel door, as though Scorpio might burst through at any moment.

"The Dark God heard about my vision and forced it out of me. The torture … it broke my immortal bones." Trauma tinged Andre's tone. "It's all I've dreamed about since becoming human. I never knew what it meant, but when Levant began his return, the dreams intensified. I'd wake up screaming, with bruises and aches pulsing through my body. My family thought I was possessed by demons. I knew something was coming and ran. All my life I just wanted to sleep. Now, I pray for old nightmares."

"We're in a nightmare right now," Brax replied. "We end it by facing him. Not hiding the bodies."

"Huh?"

"The Emily girl," Brax spat. "You and that spineless shit Charlie dragged her off."

Andre blinked. "She's not dead."

"What? How?"

"Reyna used her magic to make it look like she'd died, but she didn't. After we carried Emily from the hall, Tessa texted an EMT buddy for a favor, and they smuggled her to a hospital."

Reyna did it. She finally owned her magic. Fuck, she was incredible.

"Tessa told me what you guys wanna do," Andre interrupted Brax's thoughts.

"And where's that leave you?"

Andre strode across the room and knelt before Brax. His Pisces eyes ignited like two sapphires swallowed in blue fire and an other-worldly tone warped his otherwise gentle voice. "I'm beholden to the Infinite All-Knowing and no other."

Brax winced under his grip. "Can we stop the Dark Star from rising?"

"What has been foretold cannot be undone."

The prophet's words tossed a match into the furnace of Brax's soul.

Maybe he'd blow up the building after all. A catastrophic demolition would bury Levant under a mess, ensuring enough chaos and confusion until the eclipse passed. Reyna would survive and mourn the innocent bystanders, even if it saved billions. She'd hate Brax. But maybe someday she'd find a way to hate him less.

"Heed these final words." Andre glanced at Brax's pocket. "Only in death will all become clear, in presence of bond and blood."

The basement door ground open and Andre's eyes dimmed to their normal blue.

"Will Leo be a problem?" Scorpio prodded.

"What has been foretold cannot be undone." Andre kept his attention on Brax. "The Dark Star will rise tomorrow."

CHAPTER
FORTY-EIGHT

REYNA

D ESTINY DIDN'T MAKE A SOUND AS IT ROSE.
Reyna fiddled with the knotted black chiffon sarong at her hip while elevator floor numbers lit past. She always imagined if she met the world's end, it'd be in jeans in a T-shirt. Maybe some battle gear for whatever anarchy might erupt. Not like she prepared to strut along a swimsuit runway.

"Nervous?" Levant asked from behind.

"I didn't sleep much," she replied honestly.

"Perhaps if you'd slept in my room, as I requested." Amusement hummed along Levant's lips. "I could've helped you relax."

"After what happened at dinner, I needed time alone."

His dark chuckle purred against her back. "You've always been a terrible liar, *mi luna*. It's one of my favorite traits about you."

Lies. Reyna possessed many. Each a breadcrumb leading to another. Which had Levant uncovered first?

"You're right." Reyna sighed. "Tessa stayed with me for a while." *To distract Sagittarius from her post so I could meet with Brax.*

Levant's knuckles glided down Reyna's spine. "I know you saw Leo."

Gravity thickened their rising prison.

"We've been through a lot together." Reyna scrambled for any truth, except the one that mattered. "I needed to know he was okay."

"I understand." Levant's gentle admission did little to thaw the frost along her nerves. His fingertips bruised her hips. "As I hope you'll also understand my vow to let nothing stop us today. Even you."

"I don't"—Reyna winced at his tightened grip—"understand your meaning?"

Chilled breath nipped her ear. "Then let me be very clear."

A steady bass vibrated through the steel doors, blaring as they slid open.

Mortal heartbeats and laughter detonated atop the hotel rooftop. A fire hose of emotions poured into the elevator. Guzzled down Reyna's esophagus. Exploded through the extraction magic along her veins.

She sank against Levant's chest, desperate for a nonexistent escape.

"Lev." Reyna bit back tears. "Please. Don't."

"Do you take me for a fool, Reyna?" His temple nuzzled hers. "I've plotted this day for a century. Obsessed about this moment since before you drew your first mortal breath. It's no secret you're my greatest weakness, but whether you're Cancer, Reyna, or both, I know your secrets too. If whatever treachery you've contemplated stays buried, these innocent mortals need not fear."

Levant ambled from the elevator and rounded, sliding aviators over his blackened eyes. His hand extended and she stared at it. The same choice she'd made time and time again.

This time would be the last.

Reyna's hand slid into his.

She'd spared Emily's life yesterday, though didn't trust she could silence everyone on the roof without harming them. And so, Reyna endured. Cringed through every nuance of the party guests' emotions. Became one of them. Drew strength from their bravery of purely existing. The world was an unforgiving place, and yet they danced on a knife's edge, not knowing how close they came to death. Smiling. Reveling. Living. The way people were meant to.

The way she wanted to.

Swimwear-clad guests with their flimsy eclipse glasses gawked as the pair passed. The crowd's shared interest battled between Reyna and the ominous presence at her side. She hated the role she'd designated herself, but until all pieces were in play, she'd let Levant parade her like a trophy.

Levant ushered her toward a pool tapering into a seamless view of the Pacific. Each Zodiac stood within, partially submerged. Reyna's attention dipped below the water's surface where Tessa and Andre held hands. Tessa's stint as a teenage lifeguard informed them a pool could drain in six to eight hours. Between Tessa's air and Andre's water abilities through Astral Allegiance, they'd drain the pool in less than fifteen minutes. Once the water was gone, it'd tap out Reyna's connection for stealing their magics. Hotel pipelines would rupture, and structural damage might ensue, but it was an expense Reyna would gladly let Jace pay.

Charlie floated within the pool's farthest corner, frowning at the drunken, soon-to-be bystanders. Without a regroup, Reyna needed to trust her allies would protect the unexpected crowd, while still honoring their original plan. The Zodiacs were no longer bound by whatever staples ruled their astrological nature. Reincarnation gifted them with new mortal skills. They'd adapted. Evolved. They could do this.

A woman clutched a ladder in the pool's deep end. Close-cropped hair hung lower than it should over her brown cheekbones as she strained to keep herself above water. Handcuffs resembling Brax's secured her wrists to a ladder rung.

Aries. Jade.

Reyna desperately missed her heart's swift uptick. She didn't know the state of Jade's physical health, nor how familiar she'd become with her magic. But from Jade's venomous gaze fixed upon Levant, Reyna hoped her thirst for vengeance would be enough.

Levant's hand arced through the air and the music fell silent. Mortals groaned in protest.

"Zodiacs!" Levant addressed his submerged sacrifices. "You were created for a single purpose. Servitude to souls of Earth."

"Ooo!" someone squealed. "A zodiac-themed show for the eclipse? So cool!"

"Turn the music back up!" Another partygoer shouted.

Levant's lip curled. "These mortals claim your titles yet know nothing of your glory! You're entertainment. A fortune teller's meager ends. A crude tattoo upon ungrateful flesh. A commodity to give their souls meaning because they possess none. They exterminate their own. Butcher creatures who walk alongside them. Destroy all you've blessed upon them, only to forget you!" Levant tossed his sunglasses aside, black eyes watching the sun and moon. "Today, I release you from your prisons I helped create. I invite you to reshape this world. Not for them or for me but for yourselves!"

The ignorant crowd cheered behind him.

"It's time, *mi luna*," Levant's voice dropped low.

Reyna faced the pool's entrance and itched to take flight.

Brax sat on its steps with his head hung low and wrists cuffed to a handrail. Jace stood guard beside him, grinning as Reyna padded toward them. She let her chiffon wrap float onto the ground and plucked a pin from her hair. Chestnut waves tumbled along her back. She descended the stairs, hand gliding along its steel rail. Her palm paused and brushed over Brax's knuckles. Tears threatened her at the fresh blood marring his wrists.

Jace cleared his throat. "Get on with it."

Reyna forced a smile and waded into the pool's center. The water level swayed low at her hips but not low enough. She raised a concerned brow at Tessa and her friend gave an assured nod. Thick thunder grumbled over the rooftop. Gray storm clouds polluted the sky and swallowed the eclipse.

Levant's laughter curled Reyna's toes.

"This is it, then?" He addressed no one specifically. "Do you believe because the eclipse cannot be seen, my destiny shall not pass?"

"Don't you mean our destiny?" Charlie called from the pool.

Levant cocked his head at the Zodiac as though he were an insect.

"I've seen what a true world of darkness looks like when you forced me into the Forgotten." Wind whipped through Charlie's sandy hair. "You speak of prisons and freedom from light. About being like you. But what you mean is remove what makes us different." Charlie floated up from the water and the crowd gasped.

Levant chuckled. "Says the twin."

Jace skittered silently along the pool's edges toward Charlie, but everyone remained riveted on the hovering Zodiac. Reyna wanted to shout in warning but bit her tongue as long as she could.

"You're half a Zodiac," Levant drawled with disdain. "So pathetic, when Neoma and I created you, we deemed you in need of a second. You're no savior."

Water lapped at Reyna's thighs and Brax's cuffs clicked open from the hairpin she'd passed off.

"You're right, I'm not a hero." Charlie exhaled a shaky breath, and the clouds evaporated. He shrugged. "But I've been told I'm a halfway decent distraction."

Jace snapped a watery scorpion stinger and Charlie sliced through it with a razor of air. The tail burst into mist.

Brax flung his cuffs around Levant's throat from behind and tugged.

The pool water launched Reyna toward the Dark God. She grabbed his face. Pressed her mouth to his and inhaled.

If Levant believed Neoma could be consumed, perhaps he could be too.

Night slithered down Reyna's throat like a cold autumn's eve. Lost somewhere between the last eyelid closing and first leaf meeting the ground. Levant alternated between clawing at the tungsten around his neck and Reyna's mouth trapping him. Brax grunted against the god's strength. Reyna drank deeper. Harder. Siphoned more than ever before. Unsatisfied. Until she could see the bottom.

This was why she was reborn with her gift. This moment.

Mortal screams erupted. Elemental starmagic ricocheted behind them. Reyna waited for Levant's magic to repel her. Toss her across the patio like a rag doll. She wrapped her arms tighter around his neck. The darkness. Every bit as rapturous as she remembered. Smooth. Heady. The richest notes of him with the spicy afterbite Cancer came to crave.

God, it tasted good.

Too good.

What if she drank too much? A fair question Brax had asked last night when he promised to break their dark connection if necessary. Where was he? Surely, Brax would've torn her away by now if she wasn't in control? For a moment, Reyna hoped he wouldn't. Prayed she could live in this last time, a little longer. Familiar undiluted euphoria claimed her. Deep. Endless.

Deft fingers threaded through Reyna's hair as Levant's tongue stroked hers.

Her eyes flashed open.

Reyna reared back, but Levant caged her against his body.

"Even in all your treachery"—Levant's gaze never left her mouth—"you still cannot deny the darkness. It's why you'll always be mine."

Three mortal men restrained Brax behind Levant.

"Get off me, assholes!" Brax's wrestled shouts muffled under the crowd's screams. "Stop him! Not me!"

Levant's hand closed around Reyna's throat.

"Absorb the Zodiacs or he dies." Levant's lips lingered a hair from hers. "Choose."

The Dark God shoved Reyna over the pool's ledge.

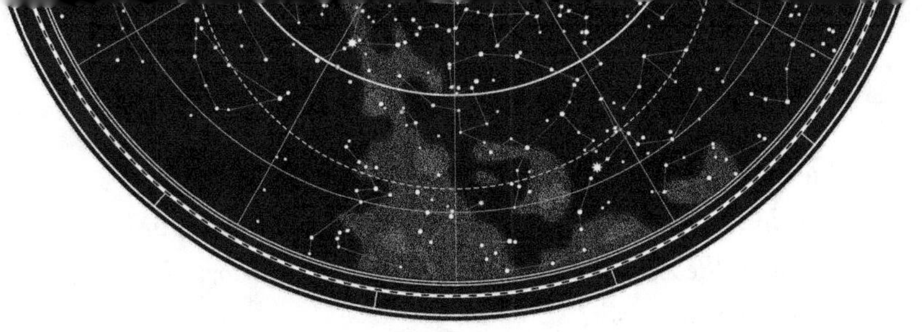

CHAPTER

FORTY-NINE

R EYNA SAILED BACKWARD AND THE WORLD ROTATED ON either side of her. She crashed into the pool. Bubbles fizzed in her ears. Chlorine burned through her nose. She blinked up at Levant's warped figure above the surface. Black dots blotted her vision, gaining size as they fell closer.

No, not her vision.

Bombs exploded into the water around her. Reyna burst above the surface and instinctually gasped for air. She scrambled to her feet, water slapping at her knees. *Polaris* floated overhead like a white cloud as obsidian soldiers rained onto the rooftop.

Levant was right. Neoma came and she wasn't alone.

"Now, *mi luna*!" Levant bellowed. "Or it's over!"

Reyna stared at her hands dripping with water.

Stopping Levant was one thing, but Neoma proved no better. Reyna couldn't defeat both deities and they couldn't hurt each another. Could she temporarily side with the lesser of two evils? Reyna's fingers balled into fists. Who even was that?

"Promise me," Brax had demanded in the basement with fierce tenderness.

"No way," Reyna snapped.

The horrible promise she'd made to Brax lacerated through the chaos.

"You have to." Brax's chains clinked. "If shit goes sideways, you gotta get outta Dodge."

"I won't abandon them again. I won't leave you."

"Sunshine, if your plan doesn't work, this might be the only way. If you're not near the Zodiacs, Levant can't make you absorb their magic."

"You want me to run?"

"I want you to live."

"There she is!" A woman decorated in obsidian armor drew her sword and charged toward Reyna. "For the light!"

Reyna sloshed backward through the water until her back met a pool wall. She tensed for impact. The warrior's blade thrust forward. Reyna sidestepped. Its magically strong glass missed her shoulder and clanged against tile.

"Please!" Reyna dodged another swipe. "I don't want to hurt you!"

"You'll destroy us all!" The woman raised her sword high.

A clump of busted cement slammed the soldier sideways. Prisha panted from behind where the woman previously stood.

"Prisha!" Reyna stared, mouth agape. "I'm so glad you're okay!"

"You know who I am?" Prisha studied her. "Neoma said you'd turned into Cancer and left with Levant willingly."

"It's not what you think." Reyna stepped forward, frowning as Prisha stepped away. "I'm trying to stop him. A couple other Dark-Aligned Zodiacs are too. There are things about the goddess you don't understand. She's not—"

"Capricorn." Jace's baritone beckoned from behind Prisha. "I hoped our paths might cross again. I owe you a debt and I always pay my dues."

Prisha remained rigid without facing him. "I see you crawled out from the rocks I buried you under."

"That's the great thing about arthropods." Jace cracked his neck. "We're resilient and I plan on showing you how much."

Prisha narrowed eyes at Reyna. "If you see Neoma, run."

Prisha's hands flung toward Reyna and ripped back. Decorative stone tiles broke from the wall behind Reyna and whooshed like throwing stars past her head at Jace.

Reyna ran for the steps as carnage erupted over the rooftop. Dredgers plucked mortals from the deck like birds of prey. A few slipped free and their screams plummeted to the streets below. Tessa and Charlie darted through the air, snatching people and flying them to a neighboring building. The crowd stumbled over bodies strewn across the floor. Over mortals. Obsidian soldiers. Factotums, Reyna recognized from their portraits throughout Calidi's palace halls. All from various points of creation and existence, but all meeting too soon an end.

Reyna tripped over submerged debris and the chaos muffled underwater.

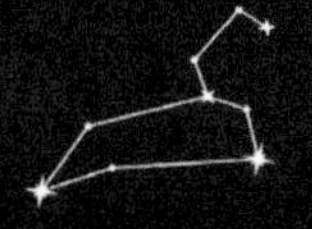

BRAX

"Goddamn it, Sparky, help me out!" Brax heaved Jade's dangling weight up the ladder again. "I know you've got more in you."

"Bugger off!" Jade's handcuffs clicked against a rung. "You'd be weak too, if you'd been bloody chained for a month."

Brax's grip faltered slightly at that.

While Jade was locked in a room for weeks, he'd gallivanted in the Nidian sun, playing dysfunctional house with Reyna. He should've had Jade's back on the interstate. Trusted her decision about telling the others about Reyna, instead of following his dick. Even if it was collared by his heart.

"I'm sorry." Brax held her in place. "I don't deserve forgiveness for what happened before your capture, but we've got no chance burning through these cuffs if ya don't trust me enough to combine our firepower."

Jade snorted. "There's nobody I trust more."

"What? Even after I—" Brax's throat bobbed along the confessions purging from his soul. "There's somethin' I never told you about San Diego. You should know. I was gonna—"

"Take the Cancer girl and run?" Jade rolled her eyes, lips tipped with a smile. "You're a dodgy git. A thief, and a damn good one. But not that good."

"That's why you told Beef-For-Brains about her?" Brax shook his head with impressed disbelief. "So I couldn't take off?"

"Be mad if you want." Jade pulled herself up onto the next rung. "I'd do it again. For your sake and hers."

"Thanks"—Brax mirrored her grin—"for makin' me do the decent thing for once."

"Who else will cover your arse?" Water hugged Jade's hips. "What the ..."

Pool water swelled around Jade, lifting her above the ladder. It deposited her onto her stomach beside Brax. Jade's wrists still remained tethered to the middle step, but now Brax could get to her cuffs easier without her slipping from reach. Brax scoured the luxe battlefield for who'd aided them. Levant and Orion engaged in battle by what was left of the bar. Halley's comet tail careened through the swarming Dredgers, while elemental magic ping-ponged between various Zodiacs. Prisha pried open the steel elevator doors and herded mortals inside, while Aquarius tag-teamed with his air magic to guide the lift.

Well, I'll be damned. Reyna convinced him.

Brax's and Reyna's eyes eclipsed.

Wild, dark, drenched hair covered Reyna's bikini-clad breasts, transforming her from poised Zodiac lady to vengeful siren ripped from the sea. Her hands lowered in release of her watery wave assisting Jade. Reyna smiled at Brax, but the water didn't recede, and horror dilated her face as it instead towered higher. The tidal wave sucked Reyna into its vortex and spat her across the patio. Neoma's arms dropped from her own command of the water across deck. The goddess sparked toward Reyna like a lit fuse, snatching a discarded obsidian blade as she approached.

"Shit! Shit! Shit!" Brax's teeth cracked against his gums. He blasted every ounce of starfire onto Jade's handcuffs, as though if he exuded enough power, Brax might defy physics of whatever stupid laws bound their magics. He'd already abandoned Jade once. He wouldn't again.

Silver tungsten dripped slowly onto the pool floor and a roar of straining power broke from him. It wasn't enough. He couldn't save both women.

He wasn't enough.

"Need a hand?" A massive shadow enveloped them.

Brax blinked up at the bulky figure. "Beefcake?"

"I'll take that as a compliment, this time." Ethan grinned. "I'm no Prisha, but tungsten isn't all natural. Should be enough metal minerals I can break it down." He crouched beside them. "Go help Reyna. I'll take care of Jade."

"I …" Guilt twisted within Brax's chest. He hadn't been on the freeway when Jade needed him. Ethan was. Despite her capture, Jade still stood by telling the others about Reyna's whereabouts. Which meant she had faith in them. In Ethan. And if Jade trusted him, maybe Brax could too.

REYNA

REYNA SLAMMED ONTO THE ROOFTOP DECK AND WOBBLED onto all fours, coughing duplicitous water from her insides.

"Most forget I control all four elements." Neoma's frigid regality addressed Reyna from behind. "In my opinion, earthen and fire magic have always been superior, but water has its place too. Pity you never learned yours."

Reyna faced Neoma looming like a white Valkyrie of death, sword singing through the air.

The sudden.

Wet.

Guttural sound of metal sliced through flesh.

A red stain bled from Seph's chest between them. The Nidian's lids fluttered toward the sword speared through her rib cage.

A gasp. A gurgle.

The goddess dislodged her black blade and let it clatter onto the ground. Seph tumbled into Reyna's arms.

"Meddlesome ingrate," Neoma muttered.

"What have you done?" Reyna pressed her hands against Seph's wound. The same deep red splattering Neoma's ivory gown oozed between Reyna's fingers. "No ..."

"You'd mourn this miscreant?" Neoma sneered. "Memories or not, I knew you'd betray me again."

"I mourn the loss of life!" Rage rattled along Reyna's bones. "What you once held sacred!"

"Is this blood?" Seph held up her hand and curled her crimson-coated fingers in the blackened sunlight. "It's so beautiful."

"You hate me." Reyna shook her head in bewilderment. "Why save me?"

"Take care …" Seph stared hazily at Reyna through the netherworld's slow creeping veil.

Reyna's brows swept toward her hairline and dipped together in furrowed disbelief. An ugly whimper sputtered from her. "I'm so sorry I failed you and your family."

The redhead squeezed Reyna's forearm.

"Take care of *him*." Seph fell limp in her arms.

Reyna had seen death. Delivered death. Lost her soul to it.

Never cradled it. Never whispered regrets and future promises.

"Persephone was always a defect of her kind," Neoma spat. "She may have not wanted to become mortal, but at least she died like one."

FIFTY-TWO

BRAX

BRAX SLID DOWN THE DEEP END'S SHORT LADDER HANDLES. His work boots splatted against wet concrete, and he beelined across the emptied half-pipe toward the pool's main steps.

Muscle bouldered into him from the side.

Brax tumbled across the lightly grated floor. Scorpio pinned Brax on his back and punched his jaw. Brax groaned, blinking through blurred vison.

"Stay down, you piece of shit!" Jace walloped him again. "You ruined everything!"

The tuning fork in Brax's skull pinged louder.

Jace cranked back another fist. Brax's palm slammed into Jace's chin, and the water sign soared off him. The two men wallowed onto their sides, clutching their bodies. Brax pushed himself onto all fours and crawled across concrete toward the steps.

Neoma stood tall behind an unsuspecting Reyna.

Brax grabbed the handrail and pulled himself to his feet. Neoma wound her sword. Jace's arm hooked around Brax's neck.

Brax grunted against his choke hold. "No!"

A brilliant flash of red sprinted between the goddess and Reyna. Seph froze in place between them.

Chaos muted.

Seph's gaze lolled past Reyna's shoulder and locked with the two men.

An invisible blade plunged into Brax's own chest. Its edges, serrated with justice, but tipped with unexpected emotion.

Seph was neither friend nor ally, though it hadn't stopped him from finding superficial solace with her and Scorpio. They'd become a constant at a time Brax found himself alone. For that, he was grateful.

"Seph?" Jace's grasp laxed as he staggered away from Brax. The building rumbled. Glass planes from the roof's safety fence cracked and shattered. Steel beams soared across the deck and stacked atop Reyna as though she were a magnet.

"This is the last time I'll tell you to run." Brax craned his chin over his shoulder at Jace. "Stop me again, and I will kill you."

Jace glanced once between Brax and the havoc unfolding. He darted in the opposite direction.

Brax slogged up the stairs. Each ache of his mortal coil protested with every crick of his bones. Orion stepped beside Neoma, burying his face against her hair. Rage ignited flames along Brax's shoulders and enveloped his arms. His white T-shirt blackened as it flaked into floating ash toward the nearly covered sun. He'd delight in making the bastard general pay for his betrayal. Perhaps more, if only to avenge how Reyna once looked at him. With hope and undiluted respect. Hard-won triumphs not easily won.

FIFTY-THREE

REYNA

"Is this your idea of peace?" Reyna laid Seph's body on the concrete and swayed to her feet.

"True peace shall exist when I am unopposed." Neoma's hands swirled. The rooftop trembled beneath their feet. A large metal beam groaned and ripped from the skyscraper's structure. Steel pieces pinned Reyna's sternum to the deck.

"I understand why you see my relationship with Levant as betrayal." Reyna groaned under the metal as cement crumbled beneath her. "But I served you amicably for centuries. Respected your ways, though I often disagreed with them. After I developed feelings for Levant, I never lifted a hand against you or Nidus. I tried convincing him for peace!"

Neoma floated and perched atop her silvery mountain of victory.

"Cancer." Condescension drawled from the goddess. "The Great Unifier. Devout servant of the people. It was almost too good to be true. You fell in love with the rabid dog I set on you."

"You expected me to fail?" Reyna bucked against the steel on her hips. It wouldn't budge. "You *wanted* war with Levant?"

"Of course, though I'd never be the first instigating such violence." A sneer curdled Neoma's stoic beauty. "But as always, you ruined everything with your naïve fantasies. Somehow, always winning the hearts of all. Even those without one."

"You could've too!" Reyna winced. "Instead, you see others as they seem. Not who they are. What they could be!"

"And now"—Neoma's fists glowed bright white—"you will be nothing!"

A match scraped across Reyna's bones. Fire snaked along her veins like trails of gasoline. Screams ripped from the Zodiac as liquid starlight sizzled beneath her skin.

"Neoma!" Orion's voice whipped through the chaos. "What's this?"

"I'm ending her treachery now!" Neoma shouted.

"But she's a Zodiac." Hesitancy etched his face. "We're meant to subdue her, not kill her. The balance of every human born under her will be compromised!"

"So be it."

Orion slowly climbed the small metal mound, brows drawn together. "The eclipse will soon be over, and Levant's time done." He swallowed hard at Seph's corpse. "This is our second chance at peace. What you've always wanted."

"I'm your goddess and this is my will!" Neoma ground her teeth. "Stay out my way."

"Orion." Agony bled from Reyna's eyes. "Please. Help me."

Orion frowned at Reyna and stepped beside the goddess. "Neoma. My goddess. My love." His forehead nuzzled the goddess's temple. "I'm sorry, but I cannot relive our past mistakes." Orion pressed his obsidian longsword against Neoma's throat. "Stand down."

Neoma screamed and an airy shock wave rippled from her. Orion soared across the rooftop. The goddess heaved with ragged breath from the obsidian's momentary proximity as magic slowly regenerated her system.

"The Infinite All-Knowing chose me!" Neoma screeched. Her fingers opened at their top knuckles. Another supernova detonated through Reyna's insides and her screams bounced off the sky. "They blessed me with light!"

Reyna's spine arched. Tears sizzled along her cheeks. Her body slumped against the ground, head lolled to the side. Gold flakes floated from Reyna's outstretched arms, like shimmering embers toward the eclipsed sun. And there. Through Reyna's blurred tears. Her lighthouse in the dark. A mane of fire and bared teeth, attempting to stand atop a pergola.

"*Brax*," Reyna mouthed, but no sound came.

"This time, you won't be returning." Cruel calm settled over Neoma. "I'll destroy you before the first babe's cry ever leaves your lips. Goodbye, Cancer."

The goddess's hands sprang fully open.

Icy fire numbed Reyna's bones. A heat too blistering and too fast-burning. Her body became a sun unable to sustain itself. Reyna's fingers splayed over the ground and between the whorls of her fingertips …

She felt them.

Every life-force touching the watery, blood-soaked rooftop.

Faint threads of the Zodiacs' elemental magics brushed across Reyna's hand. Her extraction magic curled desperate fingers around them and yanked.

Elemental energies snapped from their masters.

Power streamed through water and flooded Reyna's body.

She levitated off the ground. Busted concrete and metal rode the wind orbiting her. Flames of the firstborn fire ignited along her limbs. Charred her clothes to ash. Water slithered up her legs. Wove along her torso and wrapped around her arms. Steam hissed from Reyna's naked form, extinguishing flames in their wake. The mist cleared and crystallized midnight armor coated every inch of her skin.

"No!" Neoma lunged at her.

Reyna swiped a lazy hand.

Neoma froze in midair. The goddess's body stiffened, teeth grinding against whatever failed countermagic she attempted.

Reyna narrowed eyes at her. "I bestow unto you a punishment you once gave me."

Neoma's unrestrained hate flared into terror at the white lilies blooming over her own body.

Reyna floated closer. "You shall be reborn onto Earth with no memory of the Zodiacs, Nidus, or power you wielded. You shall live the remainder of your days until true mortal death finds you. May your creations teach you the compassion and humility you failed to learn within this life."

Neoma's ivory lids closed as the final petals of her body floated away on the breeze.

Reyna peered at the bodies strewn across the rooftop like confetti.

Somehow, she knew them all.

Mortals she'd never meet. Fallen obsidian soldiers. Zodiacs who'd welcomed her into a world of magic. Celestials she once thought meant to harm her. Celestials who did. All of them pulsed beneath Reyna's ribs. Every person born under a Zodiac. Each ruined soul of Nidus who trudged through their earthly existence. Every silent weep. Every outward tear. Every unanswered prayer.

Reyna felt *everyone.*

She clutched her chest, as though the world's cries were a monstrous leech she might rip off. Reyna searched for a single moment. Any emotional reminder she was still real. Still her.

Papá's hand closing around her throat. The first time Brax's lips grazed hers. When life returned to Ambrose's face. Life snuffed from Anemone's. The minute Tessa was dead. The second she wasn't.

I love you, Sunshine.

Nothing.

I love …

Nothing.

What Reyna felt never mattered. No matter her sacrifices or good intentions, Reyna's existence would forever be bound in dark prophecies and death. She refused to give her power to anyone ever again. Not the God of Darkness. Not even herself. Reyna would end it for good.

She closed her eyes. Scoured for the quiet corner Orion taught her lay deep within. A haven where everyone fell silent. A place she could no longer exist but would reach beyond. She found her essence's candle. A slow dying flame, holding fast to the wick of her existence nearly spent.

Whatever was left of the woman Reyna was swiped a hand through its fire. If only to feel the burn a final time.

Still, nothing.

Reyna blew it out.

The world hushed and folded inward. Black consumed Reyna's once-human eyes. And she, the universe incarnate, soared higher into the sky.

"Reyna!" someone yelled from somewhere below.

Reyna was no one. Cancer was nothing.

They were the Dark Star.

BRAX

A BLAST OF AIR RIPPLED ACROSS THE ROOFTOP. BRAX'S feet swept out from under him and the world flipped like a coin. His chest slammed onto gridded wood slats. A cough punched from his lungs and blond hair waterfalled around his face. Upended sun beds and lifeless bodies littered the deck below.

Brax slowly stood atop dry pergola slats at his feet. His arms stretched outward for balance like a flame wavering in the wind. Tremors rattled over the pergola as countless bodies thudded against the floor in unison. Water snaked between the fallen and wrapped around a silhouetted figure rising. A fortress forged in stars emerged from the white haze billowing over the building's perimeter. The sun's final rays refracted off their dark pearlescent armor.

Reyna.

What has been foretold cannot be undone.

The Dark Star.

Brax scanned the bodies sprawled amidst the vapor, a selection of their heartbeats still soft in his ears. The Zodiacs were alive, though in what state Brax couldn't be sure. He'd stupidly believed he could stop this. Bring a century of otherworldly forces to their knees. But Reyna met her fate all the same.

Angry tears welled in his eyes.

Brax didn't recognize this strained desperation. The nauseous defeat eating a hole through his gut. Reyna had wanted Brax's help, not his protection. Weren't they the same? He'd always found a way. Leo didn't surrender. Not now. Not ever.

Neoma soared toward Reyna's floating form.

Brax snapped a fiery lasso at the goddess. The line pulled taut before it reached her, and a force yanked Brax hard. He tumbled across the deck, plowing through overturned pool chairs and tables. A final roll landed him on his bare back. Brax's blood-soaked skin bellowed with the last of his mortal limitations.

Molten lava blazed through his veins and his bones groaned against someone's magic.

"Tsk, tsk. Not so fast, my ferocious friend." Levant planted a foot on either side of Brax. Victory carved into his sharp jaw. "You may have not touched the water when Reyna absorbed the Zodiacs, but it will not spare you."

"What are you doing?" Brax seethed. "Neoma is gonna kill her!"

Brax pleaded for his starfire to incinerate Levant's hold. The lion within stretched its claws, eager to answer its master's call, but another surge forced his body flush against concrete. Lev's wrist cranked, craning Brax's neck like a puppet. Neoma floated away in pieces of white. One of the universe's two most powerful entities, erased.

Gone.

Reyna's dark form shot into the sky from sight.

"Reyna!" Brax belted out.

"There's no Reyna. No goddess. And soon, no light." Levant's magic forced Brax's attention back to him. "Starting with you."

"You can't"—Brax gritted his teeth—"kill me."

Lev crouched over him. "Your lover has become my weapon. I'm moments away from devouring your soul, and still, even at your end you cannot accept defeat?" Intrigue lilted his smirk. "You truly are an extraordinary creature, Leo."

"From twelve the Dark Star will arise," Brax recited the prophecy, reveling in Levant's extinguished smile. "Reyna can't fully become the Dark Star until she's absorbed *all* of us."

"Gem and Ini make twelve."

"You said it yourself." Brax ran a tongue over his split bottom lip. "They're half Zodiacs. Made whole when together. After a hundred years, are you really gonna take that chance? I'm the twelfth and you know it."

Suspicion etched between Lev's brows. "What scheme is this?"

The most honest lie Brax ever spoke cracked along the center of his soul. "If I can't be with her, I want to be part of her. The eclipse is almost over. What's it gonna be?"

Indecision weighed heavy between Lev's eyes. He grunted with annoyance, grabbed Brax's forearm, and shot into the sky.

The rooftop plummeted from view, lost amongst San Diego's shrinking city grid. Brax gasped at the wind batting away his breaths. Fought the atmospheric vertigo sliding his brain from side to side. The Pacific Ocean sparkled beneath his feet. Stretched toward continents he'd never see again. Carried him closer to his asylum for the good, bad, and truly fucked-up parts of himself. To the only place he'd finally became whole. A home where he was loved.

Brax smiled.

I'm comin', Sunshine.

Earth's horizon blurred. New fire lit Brax's lungs. A blistering heat, neither of his nor Levant's making. Brax's hair whipped around his face and his lids battled for consciousness. Fire seared to ice. All-consuming. Numb. It crackled along Brax's fingers. Arms. Cheeks. Lips. Death curled its invisible finger under Brax's chin and tilted his gaze up from the world he left behind. Night collapsed around him, and Brax released a final breath.

Silence. Nothingness.

New pinpricks of light dotted the otherwise blackness.

Stars. Space. *Her.*

Reyna's lithe figure floated amongst outer space.

"*Mi luna.*" Lev sighed. "You're divinity itself."

"I am the Dark Star," Reyna droned.

"Not quite." Lev grabbed Brax's nape and hoisted him like a cub by its scruff. "Your change is not complete until you've absorbed all the Zodiacs' starmagic. Claim Leo's and become what you're destined." Levant shoved Brax through space's weightless lull toward Reyna. She raised a crystallized palm, and Brax paused in front of her.

The fiery halo encircling her head cast Reyna as a dark diamond angel refusing to be anything more or less than what she was. And damn, she was beautiful.

Brax squinted harder at the ring of swirling light. No, not a halo. He swallowed hard.

Fuck. Me.

A black hole slowly grew behind Reyna in the distance. Light blazed around its edges and swiped across the center like some demonic cousin to Saturn.

"True darkness is upon us," Reyna said. "Death to light, darkness, and all who might bend either to their will."

"What?" Levant snarled. "I command you to fulfill the prophecy!"

"I answer to the Infinite All-Knowing and your magic is inconsequential," she replied robotically. "Final death will bring about true peace."

Only in death will all become clear, in presence of bond and blood.

Brax's fingers brushed over sharp edges of what lay in his jean pocket.

A gift he'd stolen from Nidus and intended for Reyna, until everything went to shit.

Brax had made her so many said and unsaid promises. But upon looking into Reyna's empty eyes now, did he fully understand the gravity of one. And if it be the last he ever made, Brax wouldn't break it.

He held the abyss of her stare. "If the end is what you truly want, so be it."

"What are you doing, Leo?" Levant grated his celestial name. "Stop her!"

"You may manipulate obsidian, but your tricks cannot work on me." Reyna's inky hair swirled toward the black hole's vortex.

"I already told you, I'll take you any way you'll have me." Brax floated closer. "Even like this."

"So, you accept death?" Reyna's monotone wavered slightly. Brax gave a single nod, and she asked, "Are you not afraid?"

"I'll never be afraid of you." He presented a tiny rose-tinted crystal from his pocket, and it floated from his palm. "But before the end, there's one more first you deserve to see."

Reyna raised a single finger to the crystal and touched it.

REYNA

REYNA GAPED AT THE SMOOTH FLESH OF HER HANDS. HER sternum rose and fell with a sensation she never expected again. Breath. A heartbeat.

Someone wailed in the distance.

Reyna followed a line of fluorescents pointing her along the hallway like arrows toward the sound. She passed by quiet, dark rooms, save for soft whirs and beeps from within.

Another guttural moan echoed.

Reyna sprinted along the hospital hallway and burst through its end double doors. A surgical team stood around a steel table but didn't acknowledge her intrusion.

"Excuse me?" Reyna grabbed her throat, surprised at her true voice. "What hospital am I at?"

The surgeon continued their operation.

"Where am I?" Reyna shuffled closer. "I need to get back to San Diego. I have to—"

A patient writhed and bellowed on the table.

"I told you to give her another dose!" the surgeon barked.

"I did," an anesthesiologist replied.

"Her muscles are still seizing," the surgeon ground. "It's not enough."

"Sir, if I give her more, she could …" The anesthesiologist side-eyed a man with his head hung over the patient, clutching her hand. The anesthesiologist lowered their voice. "We've already administered more epidural than typical. It's impossible she isn't responding."

"This doesn't make sense!" the surgeon snapped.

Reyna stepped closer. A blue curtain hung across the female patient's chest and her arms extended as though she lay atop a steel cross. Incoherent prayers mumbled from the man hunched vigil over her. He glowered at the surgical team.

"Do something!" Papá's bite snapped through space and time. Reyna curled inward, a child again. "Why aren't you doing anything?"

The surgeon shook their head. "I've never seen this. Her vitals are normal, but the baby— it's like she's taking your wife's … life."

Papá launched from his chair and stomped toward him. He thrust a finger at the patient's belly. "Get that thing out of her!"

The doctor rounded. "Someone remove this man. Immediately!"

"No!" Reyna's father twisted in a male nurse's grip. "*Mi amor!*" They wrestled him out the doors and Papá's protests muffled.

Reyna edged toward the patient.

Their same slender nose. The familiar curve of Reyna's lips.

She imagined warmth along the woman's smile, now set in a pallid line. A tear kissed Reyna's cheek. This woman was more than a picture. Beyond a make-believe memory. She'd been Reyna's mother. If only a moment.

The monitors beeped into an erratic choir.

"Blood pressure is dropping," the surgeon said. "We're losing her."

Her mother's lashes fluttered against the veil separating worlds.

"I did this." Reyna clasped her mother's hand, but it drifted through. "Please, don't go."

A tiny, high-pitched scream cried out.

The nurse crouched beside Reyna's mother with a blotchy, sobbing baby cradled in her arms. Reyna shuffled behind the nurse as her mother's head lolled toward her child.

"She's beautiful." Sadness shattered the nurse's voice. "What's her name?"

Beeps slowed on the heart monitor.

The room's shuffle muted. Her mother's gaze shifted past the nurse, though she bore into Reyna's presence with her final breath.

"Reyna."

The surgical room flicked into darkness and the world fell silent.

Reyna's internal flame reignited. Whispered over whatever force threatened to blow it out again. The flame became two, searing brighter and brighter. Reyna stared past the lights before her and met Brax's twin-flamed irises.

He smiled. "Welcome back."

"The soul crystal. How'd you—"

"I was looking for my brother's crystal on Nidus and found this one instead. When I touched it, I felt it was somehow connected to your soul. Maybe because ours are bonded."

"This can't be my mother's crystal." Reyna tried making sense of such sorrowful revelations. "A person's soul crystal is their Heaven. Why would her soul choose the day she died as her eternal paradise?"

"To relive the first moment she saw you, for all eternity?" Brax's smile could've detonated the sun. "It'd be mine."

Reyna's starry armor shattered from her face. Tears floated into orbs through space.

"I've loved you since the day we were created." Brax slipped a hand through Reyna's hair and pressed their foreheads together. "And I'll love you at the end, same as her."

A fiery blast sent Brax spiraling through space.

"If you won't use your power, I will!" Levant soared at her.

Reyna thrust an air gust at Levant, but nothing happened. She stared at her hands, dismay furrowing her features.

"I'm afraid air magic is useless up here," Levant taunted through a chuckle.

Reyna shot flames at Levant, and he met hers with his own. The colliding elements pushed her through space. She looked over her shoulder at the black hole's gaining size.

"I thought my magic inconsequential?" Levant dialed up his fire and jolted Reyna back farther. She grunted against his stream of flames, slowly diminishing the gap between them. "You may be the Dark Star, but I've wielded starfire long before you."

"So have I, asshole!" Brax careened into the God of Darkness like a fiery comet.

Levant sailed into space. Ice exploded from him in the direction he traveled and stopped his trajectory.

"Nothing is working," Reyna said to Brax. "The anti-gravitational push shoots me in the opposite direction every time."

"I've got your back." Brax swam through space's weightlessness until his spine met hers. "Give 'em all you got," he instructed over his shoulder. "I'll do the rest!"

The god charged and Reyna blasted a stream of constant fire, ice, and rock at him. Levant matched her ferocity, his own mixed magic pushing her closer toward the black hole. Brax ignited angrier flames from his position behind Reyna, like a personal jetpack propelling her against Levant's momentum.

"Lev!" Reyna shouted over the roaring elemental chaos. "We can find another way!"

"I'm a god!" His expression blazed with fury. "I cannot be destroyed!"

Reyna squinted at a shimmering object fast approaching behind Levant. Her eyes flared with recognition.

"Brax!" Reyna shouted over her shoulder. "When I tell you, blast us from Levant's path!"

"Got it!" he replied.

Reyna continued firing elemental magic. Her reflection enlarged within mirrored panels of the satellite hurdling toward them.

"I'm sorry." Cancer's immortal heart wept from deep within. "Now!"

Brax thrust his fire upward. They shot from the satellite's path and the truck-sized contraption of blinking lights and steel panels slammed into Levant.

Levant snatched Reyna's wrist.

"No!" Brax's yell muffled across their increased distance.

Levant remained pinned against the satellite, holding Reyna tight as they soared toward the black hole. Stars whizzed by. Reyna's head spun. Her other arm flailed for purchase. Metal met Reyna's fingertips, and she pulled herself onto the satellite beside Levant.

"Let me go!" Reyna tugged against his hold.

"You must fulfill the prophecy!" Levant's fingers crunched into her crystal armor.

"If you ever loved me, even for a second, let me go!"

Hesitation clenched in his jaw. "I can't!"

The satellite jolted to a stop.

Levant's hold on Reyna broke. He slid a short distance along the space station and grabbed a steel extremity. Brax held on to the mirrored plate and his other hand jetted fire away the black hole's pull, but they remained stationary.

"Reyna!" Muscles strained in Brax's neck. "Crawl to me!"

She drifted along the equipment, searching for whatever she could grasp as her legs floated helplessly behind. She reached for Brax and wrapped a hand around his wrist.

"I'm gonna let go of the satellite now, okay?" Brax smiled through gritted teeth. "Ready?"

She squeezed tighter and nodded.

"Hold on!" Brax let the apparatus go and it soared toward the black vortex.

Fingers sank into Reyna's other arm.

She peered at Levant, his legs swaying in the black hole's pull. Brax blasted more firepower, but the linked trio inched closer to space's vacuum.

Exhaustion etched between Brax's brows. "I can't hold us much longer!"

Brax wasn't powerful enough to get them a safe distance, and

Reyna couldn't use her magic without knocking him, Levant, or both free. The parts of her that were Cancer couldn't forgive Levant's choices, though wicked as he was, it didn't erase what they had shared long ago. Reyna didn't know if it'd been real for Levant, in whatever warped reality he'd lived, but it'd been real for her.

Levant's hand slid from Reyna's elbow to wrist.

"Help Brax get us out of here," she shouted at the god. "I gave Neoma a second chance—I can give you one too!"

"You were my second chance!" Levant growled. "Why would you offer me anything?"

"Because Cancer loved you." Reyna closed her eyes, desperately trying to own her truths. "Because I loved you. Our time is over, but yours doesn't have to be!"

Levant's grip slipped from Reyna's wrist into her hand.

She instinctively jolted forward, and Brax roared against the momentum. Reyna's fingertips curled into Levant's knuckles.

"You're the only creature who treated me like a man. Made me feel things I never thought possible." Levant studied their fingers groaning at the joints. "You're the closest I've ever come to understanding a universe I helped create and I refuse to live in it without you." Levant peered at the fragmented stardust over his shoulder.

"Let me help you!" Reyna replied. "You don't have to be alone."

Emerald irises containing nebulas of a million unexplored galaxies beheld her. He smirked. "I haven't been yet."

The God of Darkness released her.

His repeated words from Cancer's memory echoed through Reyna as the event horizon stole him into its oblivion.

Brax rocketed himself and Reyna away from the black hole. They soared toward Earth's city lights webbing across its continents. Still, the planet slowly gained, caught in the hole's hold. With enough distance between the phenomenon's pull, Reyna jerked Brax to a stop.

"What're you doin'?" Brax demanded. "We've gotta get back to Earth."

"What happens once the planet is swallowed?"

Brax ran a hand over his mouth. "It's a long shot, but I'd rather take our chance on Earth."

"It'll absorb everything if I don't close it."

"How you gonna do that?"

Reyna stared at the black abyss of broken space and whispered goodbye to the future she and Brax might've shared. She faced him with so many unsaid regrets. His expression spiraled into rejection.

"No." Brax grabbed both her arms. "Hell no! You're not sacrificing yourself!"

"I need to try," she said.

"If a god getting sucked in isn't enough to close a black hole, what makes you think you'll be? I won't take that chance."

"It's not yours to take." Reyna smiled softly, honoring his moment to process the inevitable she always suspected might accompany her other magic. "The black hole is a dead star because I extracted its light. If I give the light back, including other magic within me, it might be enough."

"You can't know for sure," Brax insisted.

"My only certainty is how my life has been better with you in it." Reyna rested her hands on his chest. "Brax, you have such beautiful gifts to give instead of take. Go back to Nidus. Help our friends. Our people."

Brax studied the crystallized obsidian along Reyna's arm and took her hands into his. He rubbed small circles along the glassy jagged rock coating her wrists.

"Neoma said if a celestial wielded all four elements, they wouldn't be bound by the same rules of balance as her and Levant." Brax reasoned, "If an imbalance of power is what created the Dark Star, what allowed you to open the black hole, maybe balance could close it."

"How can I create balance?" Reyna asked.

"By sharing the burden with me."

"Brax," her resolve crumbled.

"No one person should carry all darkness or all light." Brax threaded his fingers through hers. "Let's close it together."

"What if your body can't handle it? What if you—"

"I can wield matter created by all four elements. I was made to do this with you."

For a moment Reyna and Brax floated in blaring silence. Suspended in time undiluted by circumstance, duty, or imminent ends. They existed between the world and nowhere, belonging only to the infinite ether of each other's arms.

"I love you so fucking much, Sunshine." Brax laced his fingers through her hair.

Reyna pressed his other hand against her bare cheek.

"Why?" she murmured.

"Why do I love you?"

"No." Reyna lost herself in the beacon of his eyes. "Why do you call me Sunshine?"

"The sun is the purest light, even when surrounded by total darkness." Brax flashed his crooked signature grin. "I may reign over the sun, but you've always ruled me."

Reyna captured Brax's lips between hers and begged the cosmos for one last breath.

One final exhale, so she might breathe common sense into his soul. A single sigh, so Brax would understand the desperation behind what he meant to her. Half of a heartbeat to show him though hers might've failed, it'd never fail him.

She wanted so many things, but as obsidian crystals cracked and crawled from Reyna's arms onto Brax's, something inside her sparked. Reveled in all she'd found by losing herself to this life.

To him.

Starlight emanated from their embrace.

Two stars. Forever bound on a collision course. Unable to avoid one another if they tried. Reyna and Brax never needed to remake the world.

They'd been remade in it. Together.

The universe exploded into light and Reyna smiled.

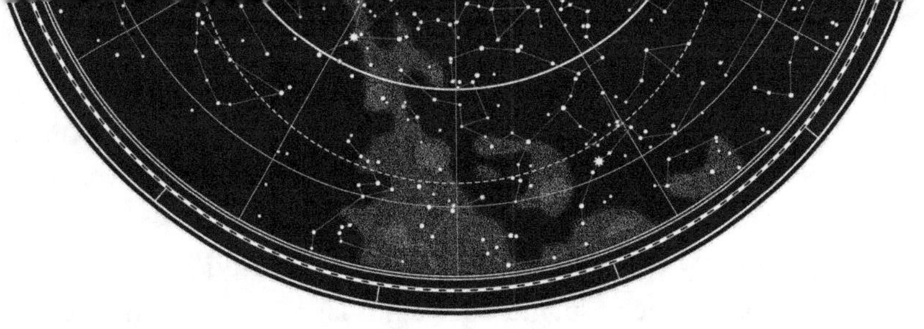

CHAPTER

FIFTY-SIX

S UNRISE YAWNED OVER THE BRINK OF TWILIGHT. REYNA lifted her chin from atop her knees where she sat in the sand. She welcomed the sea's soundless breeze through her hair. Waited for its salty tang along her tongue. Listened for whitecaps against the shore or screeching gulls, but none came. A string of lyrics, without a melody.

"I don't recognize this beach," Reyna said to the presence beside her. She peered along the pink sandy shoreline tapering into dense white mist both ways. "Shouldn't my eternal Heaven be someplace I remember?"

"A person cannot reach the Next until they've experienced their heart's true desire in life," replied the woman who resembled Anemone but also didn't. "The happiest day of your existence has not yet come to pass."

"So, I'm not dead?"

"No." Anemone's perfectly replicated coils wisped in the breeze. "You're not dead."

"And you're not Anemone," Reyna stated.

"I'm not," they replied. "I've borrowed her form to ease your mind, but I've always been a part of Anemone, as I am all others." Their eyes closed, basking in the morning sun. "I'm the nothing and everything."

"You're the Infinite All-Knowing," Reyna replied.

They nodded. "I'm everyone who's ever lived, hopes to, and does."

Reyna's brow raised. "Do you ever speak plainly?"

The faux Anemone giggled. "I've not laughed in an eon. I can see why the God of Darkness was drawn to you."

"Is Levant dead?" Reyna asked, unsure which answer was worse. Her time with the god had been such an unsolvable puzzle between loathing and loving, she didn't know where she fit anymore.

"He and Neoma are where they're meant to be."

Reyna wanted to press for a more direct answer, but another plagued Cancer for more than a century. "Why remove Levant's light when he did nothing wrong?"

The Infinite All-Knowing hummed with understanding. "Even the best intentions require a piece of one's self. It's what makes our choices so precious. Creating life capable of sustaining and birthing new life unto others, requires the utmost sacrifice."

"If Levant kept his light, this might've never happened."

"The Dark God believed he couldn't find love in absence of light yet did. The goddess possessed light and instead pursued a love of power. Both were unable to see beyond what they believed they lacked. Good and evil are not beholden to light or darkness. It's what we do with what we're given that shows us who we truly are. They lost one another to difference. You and Brax found each other in yours."

"Brax!" Reyna hoped utterance of his name might resurrect him from whatever grave she prayed he didn't occupy. "Is he …"

"The sun and moon do not cease to exist, even when they cannot be seen." The imposter Anemone grinned. "Brax is waiting."

"For what?" Each of Reyna's questions, heavier than the last.

"Remains to be seen. Neither of you are dead because you're both immortal." The Infinite All-Knowing stood and brushed sand off Anemone's purple sundress. "Though neither are alive because you are no longer human."

"Brax isn't immortal." Reyna stood. "He's half Zodiac. Half mortal."

"The moment Brax allowed Levant to carry him across the threshold of space, his human life ended, and he became his full Zodiac self once more. He sacrificed his mortal life and with sacrifice comes—"

"Balance," Reyna finished.

Anemone's look-alike nodded. "The Dark Star was created from a need to reset balance, but the prophecy never said the Dark Star would be a single being."

Reyna's mouth tumbled open. "We're *both* the Dark Star?"

"Indeed."

"Did we close the black hole?"

They nodded. "Your magic's equal distribution was powerful enough to counter the black hole's need to absorb. Earth's inhabitants live on."

Absorb.

The word that haunted Reyna's entire human life, vanquished, by sharing what she'd desperately tried to subdue. Prophecies certainly had an annoying sense of humor.

"I offer you two choices." The Infinite All-Knowing pointed along the ghosted coast. "I can return you to the aftermath of what's transpired. You and Brax would lead the Zodiacs into a new age on Nidus, as Goddess and God of the Twelve." They pointed to the beach's opposite direction. "Or, you'd be reborn into a new family. You'll possess no magic and hold no memory of this life."

"I gave away my soul in the Forgotten. How can I be remade mortal?"

The hazy mist thickened, closing in around them.

"One cannot surrender what no longer belongs to them. The night you bonded with Brax you accepted a piece of each other's soul. Yours will always live on in him, as does his within you."

Fog swirled at their ankles.

"What about Anemone?" Reyna persisted. "She bonded her soul and deserves a new life too!"

Mist flurried around their waists.

"Once Anemone's bonded meets Final Ascension, they'll find each other amongst earthly reincarnation."

"The prophecy said, *two shall remain and together they'll reign.*" Indecision crippled Reyna. "Am I meant to pick the first choice?"

"I believe a wise friend of yours once said it best." Anemone's doppelgänger grinned through the mist enveloping their face. "Prophecies are predictions. The only person who decides what happens next is you."

There were so many souls still counting on Reyna. Bridges to rebuild. Amends to make. Wounds to heal. But she was tired.

She tasted what normal life could be like, even if under the most abnormal circumstances. A family who reminded her she belonged. Friends who'd stand by her, even when she faltered. The freedom to smell, taste, touch, and see places most couldn't imagine if they tried. To experience a love she could memorize and relearn. Again, and again.

Reyna closed her eyes and welcomed her new life.

Consciousness flickered like a lens unable to keep focus. She curled her fingers through the sand at her sides and damp grains sank beneath her fingernails. Various muffled shouts approached. Their words foreign, but panic, distinct.

"Doctor!" a silhouette yelled in English as they hunched over her. Sunlight glinted between their dripping hair, and rough, sandy hands wiped at the wet hair clinging to her face. They whispered across her lips like a hot prayer. "Wakey, wakey."

Her eyes opened.

Sunlight winked through her apartment's large wooden blind slats.

"It's too early," she groaned at the city whirring outside their open window.

"It's only early if you fell asleep."

She smiled. "I did fall asleep."

"Whose fault was that, hmm?" His grogginess rumbled against her ear. "Where was your mercy for me last night?"

"Buried. In the same place as yours."

"Sunshine …" The unmistakable grin in his voice stretched. "Am I rubbing off on you?"

Reyna sighed at the liquid fire pooling under her skin. "That's the idea."

"Much as I'd love to oblige"—Brax groaned into the pillow beside her—"we should leave for Nidus soon."

Reyna's heat was replaced with shame.

How could she be lying in bed with her lover like this? Content. Cared for. Safe. Not remembering, the second she remet the waking world, what today meant for so many? Reyna stared at the ceiling amongst her untamed thoughts.

"Hey, come back to me." Brax pulled her into his bare chest. "I'm sorry. I didn't mean to upset you."

"You didn't," Reyna lied.

"I know what you're thinkin.'" Brax's large palm smoothed her rogue flyaways. "Anemone would want you to be happy."

"Doesn't make it less hard." Reyna wrapped an arm around his torso.

"Goodbye never is."

"Anemone dedicated her existence to making the lives of others better. I wasted mine hiding."

"I get it." Brax shrugged and rested his chin atop her head. "My life was spent runnin' from all the good shit I could've had. All 'cause I didn't have the balls to put in the work to deserve them. To deserve you."

"I never want to take our second chance for granted."

"Technically"—Brax's head bobbed side to side—"it's a third chance."

"They do say the third time is the charm."

Brax's lip curled good-naturedly. "I think that's something losers say."

Reyna lightly smacked his shoulder. "Are you calling me a loser?"

"Insult one of two most powerful and unbelievably sexy deities of the universe? Never." Brax bucked upward and rolled on top of her. "Besides. Second, third, fourth or fifth chance. Doesn't matter. I'd bet on all of them, as long as they're with you."

"Hopefully this'll be the last we need."

"Every day is another chance to do better. We can't undo what's done, but we can make things right. You showed me that."

Reyna smiled big. "I love you."

"I love you, loving me." Brax dragged a soft, vicious kiss along her mouth. "Now, get up. Fuck knows I am." He slid from bed, tucking his evidence into white pants. "At this rate, we'll never get outta here if you don't."

The end of Neoma's and Levant's reign had struck up discourse across Nidus. Some favorable. Some not. Mostly, a general unease amongst all the unknowns. Reyna couldn't relate more, but also recognized transparency over what happened, crucial at regaining the island's trust.

Balance was built from sacrifice.

Even if it meant sacrificing the way Nidians viewed Reyna forever.

Today would be Nidus's first and last memorial service.

Anemone wasn't dead, and though Reyna reminded herself daily, it did little to soothe the absence of her friend. Reyna would ensure Anemone's memory lived on throughout Nidus, forever.

Reyna tugged on a light blue A-line sundress with bell sleeves. She ran a brush through her hair and glanced at the newspaper clipping wedged into her full-length mirror's frame.

Unidentified Flying Object Crashes into Indian Ocean.

"Heard anymore news coverage lately?" Reyna wove her hair together.

"Things are settling." Brax sheathed his broad shoulders into a tangerine button-up, forearms flexing with the motion. He peeked through the blond hair in his face at Reyna watching him fasten the short sleeve shirt. She never imagined a person dressing could be more erotic than getting naked. Yet somehow, Brax always made whatever came after sex as desirable as the act itself. He adjusted his collar. "NASA is more interested than anyone. Our little light show made their year."

"How so?" Reyna braided another bundle of hair.

"Outside a vanishing black hole?" Brax smirked. "Or the whole you and me burning through the sky like a meteor into the ocean?"

"Won't Earth's shift cause problems?" Reyna secured two braids behind her head and flipped them into a loose crown, allowing the rest of her hair to flow along her back.

"Not enough to sound the alarm." Brax stepped behind Reyna, gaze raking over her in the mirror. "The tides have changed a little and the constellations have shifted slightly. Nothing catastrophic. Halley says it's been a little warmer, but I'm sure people will chalk it up to global warming. I'll keep an eye on things while I'm here. Meanwhile, your focus should be on Nidus."

"When are you leaving?" Longing cinched her chest.

"Tomorrow."

"Why so soon?"

"The faster I find him, quicker I'll return to you." Brax cocked his head. "Besides, this was *your* idea. Say the word and I'll stay."

"No, we need to find him." Reyna's shoulders deflated. "Nidus needs all its Zodiacs, and the Zodiacs need each other."

"Scorp has a lot of cash and contacts, which'll make it easier for him to stay hidden. He'll take a while to locate and maybe longer at convincing to come back."

"If anyone can bring him home"—Reyna's head rested against Brax's collarbone—"it's you."

"Ya know." Brax's laugh rumbled at her back. "Not many women would task their lover with recruiting his ex."

Reyna raised an eyebrow. "I'm not most women."

"Which makes me the luckiest bastard alive." Brax snatched Reyna's hand and spun her into standing at his chest. She rose onto her toes and pressed her mouth against his. Brax's tongue slid past her lips, in promise of a swift reunion. Reyna deepened his claim, with her vow to forge the way until he returned. A pact of working side by side, even when they couldn't be.

Brax slowly backed Reyna toward the full-length mirror, and they stepped through. Into a new era of Nidus.

FIFTY-SEVEN

REYNA PRIMPED AND POLISHED ANEMONE'S MEMORIAL INTO late afternoon, never once slowing. She'd been at rest her whole life. Watched. Waited. Wanted. Today, Reyna would work and withstand. Welcome the beautiful and hard moments. She buzzed with life. Overflowed with purpose. She was steadfast in her determination to achieve not perfection but pay homage to the perfection that was caring about someone.

Brax helped arrange the preparations, though Reyna insisted on a heavier hand. Unlike her papá's and abuela's funerals dressed in dark silhouettes, Reyna crafted a commemoration honoring Anemone's contributions. She instructed citizens to drape themselves in all nature's most beautiful colors. Not only in celebration of Anemone, but the sacrifices made by all factotums in lieu of the Zodiacs' hundred-year absence.

A Calidian steward flanked by several assistants held out their paper lanterns to Reyna. "Where should these go, my goddess?"

"Where guests are arriving, along the shore." Reyna pointed past white sandstone steps leading toward the beach. "Please be sure everyone receives one before the ceremony."

"Of course, my goddess." The stewards bowed and fluttered onward.

"Settling into your new role, I see." Orion's warm timbre announced his presence. His hands tucked into light green pockets, and he'd traded armor for a more relaxed white linen shirt, per Reyna's lax dress code. If she hadn't known Orion as the most brutally kind and selfless general of an army, she'd swear he was an old client readying himself for a long vacation. Stars knew, he'd earned more.

With no further need to weaponize obsidian, the Zodiacs agreed Neoma's battalion was better dispersed amongst the regions. They'd help maintain peace, order, and ground-level guidance amongst much uncertainty. The potential of Levant's survival within the black hole took residence in Reyna's mind, but she also wouldn't live in fear of what might happen. Neoma had and it cost her everything. Reyna needed to trust in what she, Brax, and the other Zodiacs built in the interim. And if ever presented with such a threat, they'd tackle it together.

"I've asked them repeatedly not to call me goddess." Reyna smiled at Orion with melancholy. "It doesn't feel right."

"Always hung up on titles, Lady Reyna." Orion matched her smile. "The Infinite All-Knowing has graced you and Leo with a gift. You should embrace it."

"I want to, but I also want to be more than a goddess." Reyna tucked a sea-whisked hair strand behind her ear. "I want to be someone Nidus can count on. Someone they can know."

"A title doesn't remove those," Orion replied. "The one wielding it does." He stepped between two columns and stared out at the sea. Reyna joined alongside him. Wind murmured through the swaying palms as magenta and orange painted the sea's sunset.

"Can I do anything for you?" Reyna asked.

Orion inhaled deep and slowly shook his head. "I need to work through this on my own. I'm not sure how to feel yet."

"Like a title, it's okay if you can't put a name on what you feel." Reyna slid her hand over his mountainous dark knuckles. "I can't replace what you lost but know I'm in your debt and I'll do whatever I can to help you move forward."

"Thank you, Reyna." His smile drifted from their hands to her face. "Not making Neoma's mistakes is a good place to start."

"My goddess," Halley said.

Reyna cringed and Orion offered a conspiratorial grin. Reyna faced her newly appointed advisor and her smile fell a fraction at who stood behind her.

"You asked that I make you aware the moment Anemone's kin arrived," Halley said.

"Thank you." Reyna addressed Orion and Halley, "Would you please give us a moment?"

They bowed their heads and descended the stairs.

"Thank you for hosting us, Goddess of the Twelve." Juniper bowed in succession with Anemone's family behind her. Reyna recognized them from a previous meeting upon first arriving back on Nidus. The visit to Anemone's family home hadn't been easy but had been met with more respect and kindness than Reyna felt worthy.

"Please." Reyna lifted a hand. "If anyone deserves to call me by my mortal name, it's you. I'm humbled by Anemone's contributions and the grace you've already shown me." Reyna summoned the day's purpose to the forefront for strength. "I was saddened hearing of Elder Thea's ascension. I wish she could be here."

"It's never easy when a loved one ascends." Jumper offered a sad smile. "But we believe Thea ascended so she might prepare a place for Anemone once she's reborn."

Reyna asked, "Do Nidian family members also reunite after reincarnation?"

"Not always," Juniper replied. "Though it's said they'll sometimes cross paths on Earth. With Nem and Thea bearing factotum magic, we believe they'll certainly be reunited."

Reyna's hope soared at the possibility.

"Nem sticks with people, whether they like it or not." Juniper grinned softly. "I doubt reincarnation will keep her from finding what she wants."

Tension eased from Reyna's shoulders slightly. "I wish you'd reconsider moving into the palace. With Brax and me in Omphalos now, there's too much space. Virgo has already given their blessing for your moving in."

"I appreciate the offer." Juniper bowed her head. "But I'm needed close to home in the city."

"If you ever change your mind, my room and possessions are yours. Whatever you need, as long as you need it."

"My goddess?" Halley poked her head from the stairs. "It's time."

Reyna led Anemone's family toward a driftwood altar overlooking the sea. Hibiscus, oleander, and marigold decorated its slender bowed posts, bleeding almost seamlessly against the sky's brilliant canvas. Reyna smiled at the bright orange flowers. A personal reminder of what waited beyond the fold, not only for Anemone, but for every soul.

A caress of fire brought Reyna back to the present.

Brax's fingers brushed along her arm as he led her onto their makeshift altar where the other Zodiacs waited. She peered over the beach now blanketed with brightly clad Nidians, illuminated by the lit paper lanterns they held. A bold, victorious, loud sea she'd gladly throw herself into.

"Thank you for coming," Reyna elevated her voice. "For centuries, the Zodiacs were a cornerstone of Nidus, but today for many, we're still strangers. Myths. Who despite our desire to remain upon Nidus, failed you. We left you to mend your communities and find a new way forward. A place we find ourselves once more. And yet, like the mortals you'll reincarnate into, you persevered. Made your own way. Neither by Neoma's hand, nor ours. You became more than the signs you were born under. Unique. Nuanced. Full of life, ideas, and aspirations outside of what's been designated to you. I know ..."

Tears tingled behind Reyna's eyes. Her smile tightened at Anemone's family stationed at the crowd's front. Brax squeezed Reyna's fingers, and she rediscovered her voice.

"I know Final Ascension is revered on Nidus, but Anemone didn't meet hers like she should. She was claimed within the Forgotten in service to me. She faced her final moments, as she embraced all else, with unparalleled bravery. And though she'll reincarnate someday, it's a sacrifice I can never repay and will never forget."

Reyna raised her hands, signaling the crowd to ready their lanterns.

"It's now known, the Forgotten feeds into Nidus's rivers and sea. And so too will Anemone's spirit. With these lanterns, we all become stars born of fire, swathed in earth, and carried by the wind. Let our light shine over her waters, now and forevermore known as the Anemone Sea."

The Zodiacs released their lanterns, and the crowd followed. Lanterns floated along the breeze like embers, gaining in ferocious beauty with each succeeding wave unleashed. One by one, bits of risen fire stole back the sunset. Ignited a sky unmatched by any other.

An island. Forever bonded.

"Talk about a half life," Aquarius soured as he sipped his wine from across the beach bonfire. "We need to introduce a few earthly delicacies to Nidus. Barley already grows between Parhelia and Flora. Lemme bring in some hops and we'll get this place on track."

"To what?" Prisha crossed her legs atop the rock she sat. "Getting shit-faced?"

"I'm on board." Brax swigged with a wink. "Could be a couple other notable plants we could cultivate too."

"Right there." Aquarius pointed his index finger and glass toward Brax. "God of the Twelve said it. It's law."

"Nidians are still souls in progress," Ethan's Irish baritone rolled. "We should keep Nidus clean."

Brax laughed. "Doesn't get any more organic, Beefaroni."

Jade shook her head. "You lot would have this island plastered by the time they were reborn human."

"There are worse ways to come into the world." Reyna raised her glass.

They toasted with agreeable laughter and drank deep.

Reyna nestled into the furnace of Brax's chest. He slung an arm around her shoulder and rubbed the goose bumps prickling along her arm. The memorial's bustle had settled with twilight and the Milky Way of lanterns long since drifted beyond whatever might exist over the horizon.

"It's a shame Gem didn't stay tonight," Prisha addressed Reyna beside her. "I wanted to know her better, as Tessa."

"She and Charlie are spending time together in Flora while Andre visits his family after being in hiding for so long," Reyna replied. "Even though everyone's memories have returned, reincarnation gave us whole new lives. Tessa and Charlie missed out on a lot as mortal siblings. Plus, I think he still doesn't feel right coming around."

"From what I understand, he betrayed you. More than once," Jade noted. "Maybe it's best he stays away."

"Charlie was put in a horrible position." Reyna stiffened a little. "There were many times I could've spoken up or confessed my run-ins with Levant but didn't. If I'm worthy enough to drink with you all now, so is Charlie. Ultimately, he helped us and that's enough for me."

"Scorpio didn't." Jade's brow quirked at Brax. "I still say you're daft going after him."

"He's one of us," Reyna insisted. "Nidians born under his season need him and the Zodiacs need to be united. Brax is leaving tomorrow, but once he returns, he'll oversee matters in Omphalos while I oversee the Forgotten. As Lord Regent of Death and Sexuality, Scorpio could be instrumental to my work in the underworld."

"Give Scorpio time," Aquarius chimed in. "He's a stubborn shit, but he'll come to his senses. Especially since the other Zodiacs are with us."

"How can you even contemplate going back to the Forgotten?" Prisha frowned at Reyna. "The Dark God is gone. Let the underworld die with him."

"When the Infinite All-Knowing revealed Anemone's soul wouldn't be trapped forever, I realized how much we don't know about the Forgotten," Reyna replied. "It's important to Nidus's ecosystem and has been neglected for too long. Neoma wanted nothing to do with it, Seph wasn't qualified to run it, and Levant's"—the god's name gave pause—"interests laid elsewhere. I won't stay indefinitely, but not all from Earth will pass over into the Next and it's important we understand why. What comes after life, deserves as much care as the before and during."

"Spoken like a true goddess." Brax stood and dusted his pant legs. Reyna shivered at the sea breeze's free reign along her exposed spine. His hand extended toward her. "Speakin' of which, the goddess and I have important business to attend."

"At this time?" Reyna's attention drifted around the fire and circled back. "What's so pressing?"

Prisha waggled her eyebrows and Reyna's cheeks heated.

"Take a walk with me?" Brax extended his hand farther.

Reyna uncrossed her legs from the blanket and smoothed out her dress.

Woos and immature innuendos drawled from the fire as the pair meandered toward the dark shoreline. Apparently, being gods of the universe didn't excuse them from the good-natured wrath of their friends.

Reyna never dreamed she'd be so lucky.

"This is all still new. Everyone will adjust." Brax tucked his hands into his pockets. "But ya can't forget to take your own advice too."

Reyna looped an arm through his. "Which is?"

"Cuttin' yourself a break, much as you do everyone else." Brax veered them toward the abandoned altar. Flower petals scattered the platform's base, fluttering across sand like autumn leaves. Driftwood creaked beneath Brax's feet as he led Reyna to the altar's center where a lone lantern waited. A few stones weighted the twig-woven base, and an unlit candle sat in its middle.

"What's this?" Reyna smiled. "I thought we released them all."

"Nope." Brax knocked the stones aside, snapped his fingers, and a flame sparked. Gold candlelight spilled over their skin. "I knew you'd be caught up with everyone else, so I saved this one for you."

Reyna gazed into eyes she'd lost and found herself in a million times. "How will I do any of this without you?"

"Sunshine, you've been doing incredible things long before you met Braxton Riggs and I can't wait to see all you'll do, long after." He handed Reyna the lantern and her bare hands smoothed over his.

"What *we* will do," she amended. They gently lifted the lantern, and it floated into the diamond velvet sky.

"I'll be home before you know it." Brax pulled Reyna flush against his chest and threaded fingers through her hair. The sun and moon stood tangled in each other's arms. Neither ready to rise or fall.

"Home." Reyna smiled against his lips. "I like the sound of that."

Acknowledgements

The easiest part of writing this book will be thanking those who made writing this book easier.

Six years is a long time to work on any project and I couldn't have reached this milestone without the integrity, time, and heart of all those who made writing this book a little less painful.

A college admissions advisor once commended my parents for supporting my interest in pursuing a creative field, on the grounds a lot of parents don't. I'll second that praise. Thanks Mom and Dad, for embracing my passion and recognizing the value of what my creativity could bring into the world. Thank you to my brother Doyal for putting up with all the theatrical performances I definitely didn't force him to participate in as kids. My creative outlets always thrived first and foremost at home amongst my family.

Thank you to my supportive husband, Patrick, who despite not being an avid reader, listened to my wacky story ideas and pretended to know what I was talking about. You are the Gemini to my Capricorn. To my daughter, Ella, who reminds me we're all pieces of a beautiful world undefined by social convention.

To my critique partners, Cass Maren, Emerie Rogers, and Whit McVey, who read my manuscript in its roughest form. They were the first readers to embrace Reyna and Brax's story and offer tangible feedback I could run with. Especially my Capricorn soul sister, Cass. Her countless hours of friendship, support, and devotion not only for the story I wanted to tell, but the integrity of my characters has been invaluable. When I started writing a novel, I never imagined I'd meet one of my best friends, states away. A certain *angry-against-a-tree* scene also thanks you for your contributions.

To my enthusiastic and dedicated beta readers: Lina C. Amarego, Blake Barrington, Shannon Burton, Ashley Drogs, Shay Fuentes, Jenny Gray, Madeeha Idrees, Sara McClafin, Lisa Nicholls, Jessica Powers, Erika Robles, Mandy Rodrigues, and Sarah L. Richhelm.

A very special thanks to Melissa Tully, for sharing her perspective as a Mexican American woman on Reyna's story. Any misrepresentations portrayed within this book are entirely my own.

Thank you to my editor, Anne-Marie Rutella, and proofreader, Sharon Strahand, for your enthusiasm and impeccable attention to detail.

To the incredibly talented artists who took my visions and breathed new life into them: My cover illustrator, Jenn Rubio, my cartographer, Andrés Aguirre Jurado, and my book formatter, Stacey Blake at Champagne Book Design.

Thank you to my Advance Reader Copy readers and social media street team who made the road to my debut an unforgettable experience. Your unwavering support and excitement reminds me why it's so important to do what we love.

I never anticipated the truly personal connections I would make when I joined the Instagram author community. Thank you to anyone who ever shared advice, words of encouragement, or general excitement around my story. Being seen, heard, and embraced by a community of peers has made me feel less solitary in my writing ventures.

Most importantly, a huge thanks to you, reader. No matter your experience with my novel, thanks for taking a chance on Reyna's journey beyond the stars and back.

ABOUT THE
AUTHOR

A.J. Lexa puts ideas to paper from the lake haven suburbs of Detroit, Michigan, where she lives with her husband and daughter. When not reading or writing, A.J. enjoys lake life, collecting fairy figurines and binge streaming her favorite shows. After 15+ years of advertising for national and regional brands, A.J. decided the stories in her mind could longer be condensed into sixty second commercials. They needed more magic. And kisses.

Website: www.ajlexa.com

Instagram: @aj.lexa

Email: ajlexa.author@gmail.com

Sign up for the Letters From Lexa newsletter

LEAVE A REVIEW

Thank you for reading!

Leaving a review for *Lines Between Stars* helps increase my visibility to new readers and lets them know if they might enjoy this story. If you could please take a moment to post a few sentences, or just select some stars, I'd be forever grateful.